AUTHOR'S NIGHTMARE

BOOK ONE

I0693866

AUTHOR'S NIGHTMARE

BOOK ONE

Ian B. Urns & A. C. Erinle

Podium

To Finn.
Our friend, our fan, our Secret Third Writer.
(We're still not giving you any of the royalties.)

All rights reserved. No part of this publication may be reproduced, stored in a retrieval system, or transmitted in any form or by any means electronic, mechanical, photocopying, recording, or otherwise without prior written permission from Podium Publishing.

This is a work of fiction. Names, characters, places, and incidents are either products of the author's imagination or used fictitiously. Any resemblance to actual events, locales, or persons, living, dead, or undead, is entirely coincidental.

Copyright © 2025 by Ian B. Urns and A. C. Erinle

Cover design by Mario Teodosio

ISBN: 979-8-8953-9352-9

Published in 2025 by Podium Publishing
www.podiumentertainment.com

Podium

AUTHOR'S NIGHTMARE

BOOK ONE

PROLOGUE

Kenny's POV: Day 0

We were all gathered together the day it happened. Cádo had some sparring match scheduled with a regional fencing champion, and he'd wanted us to make a day of it. We watched him trounce the guy during the afternoon, and went back to his place for drinks in the evening. That was the plan at least. But plans are fickle things, always more dynamic than you'd expect, always vulnerable. Always carrying that particular, nasty tendency to change depending on circumstance. Not least when that circumstance happens to drag you through some portal between worlds.

Bernard and I were sitting in the stands, talking during the match. There was hardly anything else to do, given how one-sided it was. Few people could make Cádo break a sweat, and his opponent was definitely not one of them that day.

So we chatted away. For a pair from walks of life as different as us, we had an odd amount in common. We all did, I suppose. People tend to when they decide to write a book together.

I was the rich boy of the group, and uniquely humble despite the fact, from older money than either of the others could trace their families back to. Incredibly humble, in fact. Bernard often said I was snooty, arrogant, and only about half as smart as I thought he was, which I reckoned made me three times smarter than most everyone else.

By contrast, Bernard's upbringing was slightly weird. Not weird in the funny way, though. More in the "raised by a paranoid schizophrenic in an apocalypse cult" sort of way. His family had been poor for generations, and working-class spirit ran through their veins, almost as thickly as chromium dust.

And he was a genius. Never forgot anything he put his mind to remembering, thought seemingly four times faster than most, ran through multi-line equations in his head, even while distracted. It probably wasn't the cause, but this intelligence definitely gave him a lot of excuses to mouth off and vent his massive ego everywhere. God himself could've descended to tell Bernard he wasn't important, and the only answer he'd have gotten would have been sneering laughter. Probably followed by an accusation of fascism.

"Has Cádo gotten faster?" Bernard asked, eyeing the match rather absently, thoughts a mile away. I was hardly focusing any more intently, but frowned at the question.

"Maybe," I said. "He's training all the time."

Cádo was. He'd been an Olympic champion by the age of sixteen, and five years later he kept on swinging away. It was as if he were worried about being ambushed someday. Whatever the exhaustive habit said about his obsession, it said much more about his actual abilities. As of a half minute ago, the man had switched to his left hand—his weaker one. If he noticed how much it pissed off his opponent, Cádo gave no indication.

"We'd be millionaires if he put that much focus into writing. Well, me and him would be. You've already got that covered," Bernard grumbled, leaning his head back, sighing. "God, he's taking ages. Can you give him a shout? Tell him to hurry it up? Maybe throw something at his opponent to distract them?"

I grinned at his irritation. Bernard never could sit still for long, always fidgeting, or switching tabs, or building something the government didn't want him to. If patience was a virtue, then he was about as saintly as Emperor Nero.

"Hey, Cádo, hurry it up, would you?"

Cádo glanced over at my call, parrying one swing without even looking and stepping back from the rest. He let his annoyance show, but turned back to the fight with a new vigor as he switched hands again. It wasn't long before the match was over. Two touches to him in barely twice as many seconds.

"You two never let me have my fun," he complained, marching over to the stands and unclasping his protective headgear. His curled hair spilled out, tousled by the exercise, but not sweat-coated. It hadn't taken as much effort as it appeared, apparently.

"We let you have plenty," I shot back. "You just never have enough fun to be satisfied." The headgear came down onto a bench, and Cádo was sprawled along it an instant later.

Bernard piped up, eyeing the discarded gear. "It's a lot more bearable when you're just doing martial arts. At least there's something to watch."

Cádo shrugged. "What can I say? I was cursed with skill."

"Oh, no, I was talking about watching you get hurt without all the pads and stuff. But yeah, sure, I suppose the struggle is something, too."

Bernard and Cádo shared a grin as the conversation stretched on. It was a while before we finally took our leave. Everything moved slower for us back then, lazy. We had as much time as there were waking hours in a day. More or less. Close to one of those hours passed before we all finally came back to Cádo's home.

All of us were fairly well off by that stage of our lives. Our book, *Chronicles of Destiny and Bone*, had sold better than expected, and we were all sitting on a sequel deal. Cádo's home was his home, not simply his family's, and he'd made sure to buy a fairly big one. Maybe it was just because he'd gotten used to that sort of living area, but also because he needed the room to hold all his damned trophies.

We were in the living room when conversation moved onto politics. Unfortunately, with Bernard there, politics quickly moved into a debate about whether or not the government was harvesting circumcised babies' foreskins to de-age their elderly elite.

Then the change happened.

It was subtle at first, hardly noticeable at all, really. One could only have expected to catch it if one had paid attention to the tiniest of details, such as the sudden taste of ozone in the air, or the building violently imploding in on us. Then we were falling.

What we fell through really can't be described. It could barely be felt. To force it into words, the entire experience was like sailing through an ocean made out of liquefied rainbows, only to be caught in a giant whirlpool and suddenly dragged to the depths, and then God himself telling you about half the universe's great secrets, while lying about the other. All while the magic mushrooms you dropped twenty minutes ago finally kicked in.

If that's a bit abstract, then unfortunately, there's no way you'll grasp what happened to us, because it's as grounded as I can make the explanation. What matters isn't the particulars of sensation or sight, though, only what happened next. We landed.

There was a fairly gradual deceleration before all three of us belly flopped onto the hilltop, which was lucky because whatever terminal velocity might be in the netherworld, it's probably not survivable.

A few moments passed with our ears ringing and brains shivering, bearings completely stripped away by the trip and senses trying—and failing—to adjust to our surroundings. It all dawned on us eventually.

We were outside. It was daytime, not evening, and the terrain was vaguely European. The air was frigid, the wind sharp, and the city we'd all been in just minutes ago was gone. In its place were rolling hills and bowing trees, from the base of our hilly perch to the horizon.

Similarities or no, we were all different people, and our disparate reactions probably conveyed that better than any words could.

Cádo was amazed, all awe and grinning astonishment as he let himself ponder the sight, staring at everything around us. I was pure, distilled nerves. My hand instantly moved for my phone, but I realized I'd left it on the kitchen counter. Half a second after that I was screaming, calling out for my father, for friends, for help. For anything at all that might drag me out of the nightmare.

Bernard was not a dazzled optimist, and he wasn't a panicker like me. He was something much worse.

The moment he realized what had happened, he began working the information over in his mind, making deductions, then drawing conclusions. All of them were wrong, and they led him to one rather particular response.

Thinking back to his mother's teachings, Bernard turned on his heel and took off at a sprint to locate something he could use as a weapon for when "they" inevitably made the second move of their nefarious scheme.

And so it was that the first few minutes spent in our first alternate world were dedicated to chasing down a screaming psychotic before he could harm himself or, much more likely, someone else.

I noticed Bernard's sprint first but was slow. Cádo, of course, was the fastest of us, but by the time he started running, we were already fifty feet ahead. It took a while before Bernard finally stopped, and we pulled in to approach just a few yards short.

He was hunched down beside a tree, muttering to himself as he picked out the pointiest of several nearby rocks to use as a makeshift shiv.

"Bernard, calm down," Cádo tried, saying the exact wrong thing to any paranoid who was calmed up. Bernard snarled at him, actually snarled, like some sort of animal.

I cut in before things could worsen. "We're with you," I said, voice low and soothing. "You know we are, but we don't know what's going on. What have you noticed?"

Bernard stared at me as if I were an idiot. "We were suddenly transported to God knows where!" he practically shrieked. "Why am I the only one behaving rationally about this?"

Apparently settling on a rock, Bernard tore it from the ground. It looked like the sort one might use to kill a man whose only weakness was meat tenderizers.

My real name wasn't Kenny. My friends just called me that. I'd been born Keyinde Johnathan Adebayo, in Nigeria, and I'd dealt with a lot of very irrational, stubborn old men in my time while shadowing my father and learning how to run his company. It meant I was absolutely lightning at defusing Bernard when the situation called for it, and few situations ever had as much as this one. I took a careful step forward.

"If we need protection, then you can offer it better by sharing what you know, yes?"

That, at last, got through to Bernard, who nodded and stood. Cádo let out a sigh of relief. Apparently he really hadn't been in the mood to choke out his friend today. I couldn't blame him; Bernard was a biter.

"Follow me," Bernard breathed, taking off at a jog once more. We followed him, reaching our destination a minute later. It was the exact spot we'd started. Bernard gestured out to the landscape before the inevitable questions could come, eying the rest of us.

"See what I mean?"

We didn't, and he sighed.

"God, apes, fine then. Look at that river, yes? And those trees? Now focus on . . ." He described the relevant features, one by one, and it was I who finally got his meaning. Cádo, bless him, needed it spelled out. He'd never been as good with the more concrete aspects of our work.

"That's impossible," I snapped, glaring at Bernard. I shouldn't have; it wasn't his fault. He didn't control the truth.

"We're probably all hallucinating in some facility," Bernard agreed.

Cádo ignored both of us, growling out his question. "Will someone explain it to me with small words, please?"

I gave him the answer, with about as much tact as I felt capable of. "This seem familiar, Cádo? Does it match any descriptions you've heard . . . anywhere?"

Of course it did. The landscape around us was exactly as it had been when we'd all first read it mentioned.

In a passage from *Chronicles of Destiny*. Our own fucking book.

CHAPTER ONE

Kenny's POV: Day 1

I'll skip the freakout. It went on for ages, and we didn't really get much done during that time. A lot of screaming, I suppose, a bit of flailing around and running about. Other than that, though, it was fairly uneventful. I certainly wouldn't describe the ordeal as particularly productive or useful and, frankly, it lasted an embarrassingly long time.

What came next was possibly more embarrassing, but it's also too important for me to just skirt over. *Yay.*

Around the ten, maybe fifteen, minute mark of our freakout, there was this big light. Now ordinarily, you understand, we were fairly normal guys, not prone to screaming over something as minor as a sudden glow. But, as of the last half hour, we'd all had a fairly particular experience with mysterious, incandescent energies and, as a result, we'd all developed a fairly unified response.

I screamed and turned around to run away, Cádo squatted in some martial arts stance, and Bernard chucked one of his several newly acquired self-defense rocks at the source. Not one of us actually achieved anything with these actions, but if nothing else, they gave us something to focus on besides panic.

Except for mine, seeing as my response *was* to just panic.

The source of the light turned out to be some tall, veiled lady standing just a few meters from us. We couldn't see her face, though her eyes were glowing in the shadow of the hood, and she seemed to be looking at all of us at once. She didn't need to ask for silence; it just sort of happened, and then she spoke through it.

"Welcome, dreamers. You are, I take it, confused as to the current situation."

Bernard opened his mouth to answer, and I hit him before he could pollute the conversation with his latest conspiracy theory.

"We are," I cut in. "Are you here to educate us?"

Bernard was at least my equal when it came to planning and strategy, and he had plenty of his own experience in negotiating, but for now he'd be no use to any of us. Given a few hours, his mind would calm down and he'd be lucid again. I'd seen enough *episodes* of his to be confident in that much, but until then it seemed I'd be in charge of the talking.

"In certain areas," the woman replied, paying no heed to our little scuffle. "In others, I am afraid, you will need to be your own mentors. Tell me, Emperor, have you yet discovered your innate gifts?"

So, she *spoke* like someone who'd gotten lost on her way to the renaissance fair, too, rather than only dressing as such. Brilliant.

Hold on, innate gifts? I frowned. "Well, I am aware that I have a remarkably big—"

"Gifts new to this world," she clarified, before I could go on to describe any of my several abnormally large organs. "They will have existed only upon your arrival, but will not abandon you now that you are here. Yours, I suspect, will be the only one accessible for the time being."

I frowned again. I didn't like being left in the dark, and this lady was dumping me into Challenger Deep. If she hadn't spoken like a chronically depressed computer, I'd have suspected she was getting off on it.

"How do I discover these gifts?"

She turned at that, starting down the hill. Every step she took, the woman grew more and more translucent, then transparent. Fading away like misty breath dissipating on a cold day.

"Look at your companions, the way you've learned to look at everyone. But more so."

With that, she was gone. A rock cut through the air where she'd just been standing, and I turned to glare at Bernard.

He shrugged. "Had to make sure she wasn't just invisible. She's not. Unless . . . she can simply phase through things *and* turn invisible at once . . ."

I ignored him, focusing instead on my vision, thinking back through my memories to try to discover what the hell that lady had meant.

"She called me emperor," I said, thinking aloud. "So what if she means I need to look at people . . . as if I'm weighing them up for some manipulation?"

It wasn't nice to give voice to this theory, but I couldn't doubt it held weight. Years shadowing my dad had taught me just this sort of thinking, and decades of practicing it had made him a billionaire.

Bernard, though, shook his head. "Can't be that," he said. "I'm at least as big a bastard as you are in that area. Though . . . she did say emperor. We don't really have those in our civilization anymore, right? So what's our equivalent."

I nodded, catching his train of thought then running alongside it. "Well, my dad and his class, obviously. But I already tried . . . Hm."

That was when it dawned on me. I didn't get taught to manipulate as much as I was taught to weigh, to . . . appraise. Everything has its value, as dear old dad used to say, and figuring it out will make you rich.

Hesitantly, I eyed Bernard.

Tall, wiry. Like some big, stretched-out rat. His hair was unkempt, eyes big and blue, face edgy and scruffed. The face was most notable, really. Looking used, in the same way that a bare-knuckle boxer's fists did. In the same way most everything about him did. I'd never known whether he did that on purpose, looking like he'd just crawled out of a fight and through a sewer by choice. It certainly seemed in line with him; he was actually proud of being born in a—

Everything flashed before my eyes at once, so rapidly, so deeply, that it almost floored me.

"Are you alright?" It was Cádo asking, concern warping his voice. I struggled to give him an answer besides just grunting acknowledgement.

"Yes," I hissed. "Yes, but shut up and let me focus."

I stared at Bernard, studied him. Studied him like I'd spent a lifetime studying people, but more so. I picked up his demeanor, his mood, his likely goals and all the classic hits, but so much else was joining it now.

[Appraisal]
Class: Revolutionary
Level: 1
Condition: Fine
Modifiers: None
Statistics: Strength 6, Speed 6, Dexterity 8, Stamina 5, Toughness 6, Alertness 8, Charisma 3, Intelligence 10
Inventory: Jeans, T-shirt, flick knife, rocks (x7)
Class Abilities: Detect Element I

Good God, it was like a game. I'd never played that many, but I knew a character sheet when I saw one. This wasn't pen and paper, though. More . . . Yes, RPG. RPG mechanics squeezed into a real world. We'd been shunted into a fucking LitRPG.

Bernard and Cádo were confused by my swearing, but they soon joined in once I explained the situation. It took us a while longer to gather our wits after that.

"Alright," Bernard said. "Well, whatever we end up doing, we need shelter soon. It'll be colder at night than it is now, and I'm already losing feeling in my toes. We can talk while we travel."

It was a good idea, so we followed his lead, heading downhill in a direction Bernard assured us held some small villages and a town. His memory rarely ever failed us, and unless God had decided to be even crueller than he already had been today, I saw no reason to assume an exception was coming.

"We're next to the River Grazgry, a few hundred miles south of Shadervhor," he explained confidently, breath visible in the cold air. "You added them in yourself when we were making the maps, remember?"

I didn't, but I took his word for it. Grazgry and Shadervhor were two of the most important places in our book's setting, featured more prominently in its earlier arcs. If Bernard said we were near them, he was probably right.

Cádo broke our contemplative silence first, always the hardest of us to faze. That particular trait would do a lot of life-saving in the coming months, but I didn't know that at the time.

"What are my stats?"

I eyed him.

"Seriously?"

"Yes, seriously, it's important we know."

"He just wants to get a dopamine hit from seeing his big number," Bernard said, snickering. I figured he was probably right, but all of us could use the distraction, and I in particular would benefit from practicing this weird power a bit more.

So I looked, tightening my eyes, concentrating as I did before. It still took a while, but if I wasn't imagining things, the display came quicker this time. I was more cognizant of it, too, able to examine how it appeared to my eyes. A stream of numbers and letters running through my mind. Not quite visual, and not quite entirely imaginary, it felt like remembering a sheet I'd read before with perfect clarity. Interesting.

[Appraisal]
Class: Dragonknight
Level: 1
Condition: Fine
Modifiers: None
Statistics: Strength 8, Speed 8, Dexterity 8, Stamina 9, Toughness 7, Alertness 8, Charisma 6, Intelligence 5
Inventory: Jeans, flannel shirt
Class Abilities: Beloved I

Cádo was a simple man. He heard that he belonged to a class called the fucking Dragonknights, and he squeed. It took a while for me to calm him down enough to convey the more particular points of his readout.

"Eight strength then." He grinned. "So I could body Bernard."

Bernard made a deliberately exaggerated show of shock. "What?" he cried. "No way! Y-you mean I'd lose to an Olympic athlete? Cádo, mate, that's just impossible to believe!"

He shared a bickering laugh with Cádo while I frowned to myself. Suddenly curious about something else now.

Holding a hand out, I stared at it—studying the creases of my skin, scrutinizing the dark flesh while I tried as hard as I could to examine myself as if I were just some random person—and mustered all the cold distance that let me bring up my friends' information. It was blessedly quick.

[Appraisal]
Class: Emperor
Level: 1
Condition: Fine
Modifiers: None
Statistics: Strength 5, Speed 5, Dexterity 6, Stamina 5, Toughness 5, Alertness 8, Charisma 9, Intelligence 9
Inventory: Jeans, shirt, jacket
Class Abilities: Appraisal I

I was a bit miffed after my second read of the information. Somehow "Appraisal" sounded rather mundane compared to whatever the fuck Cádo's "Beloved" did. Then again, we'd gotten more use out of my power than either of theirs so far. Names could be unassuming.

We were halfway down the hill by the time we started to make sense of the information, and the sky was darkening.

"So we know that bigger numbers are better," Bernard noted. "Unless we're just horribly wrong about how our respective strengths line up. It seems like a stat of five is about average?"

I could agree with that. I was tall but fairly wiry, so average strength seemed about right.

"Makes sense that I'm the only one with double-digit intelligence, considering how dumb both of you are," Bernard continued, doing a remarkably close impression of someone who was three words away from being shoved down a fucking hill. "Other than that . . . I don't think we can use the rest of this data until we have more information. There wasn't exactly a hint about how we might use *our* class abilities."

I nodded, having come to more or less the same conclusion. Although . . .

"We can level up, most likely," I pointed out. That was how these things tended to go, at least, and it seemed pointless to have a listed level if it couldn't increase.

Bernard nodded. "Probably, unless we're just stuck at whatever level we start with. That would be just typical. I wonder how we level, assuming we can."

Cádo gave us the answer to that, oddly enough. "I hope it isn't the traditional way we strengthen ourselves in real life." He grinned. "If I'm still level one after all these years, you two'll be stuck at it forever."

Bernard nodded, thoughtful. "Good point."

Cádo frowned. "It was?"

Ignoring him, Bernard continued. "If you of all people are still stuck at level one, then either we won't be growing at all, or the growth will come through means other than just . . . exercise. That, or it *is* exercise, but we couldn't benefit from it before coming here."

He studied us both, and it was I who caught on first.

"Are you thinking of killing one of us and seeing if you get experience points?" I asked, pointedly.

Bernard snorted. "God no, of course not. No, I'm just wondering what would happen if I did. Anyway, it's getting dark."

It was. And, it was dark enough to move conversation on from that particular ravine by force.

"I say we make camp for the night," Cádo declared, and neither of us were in a state to argue.

If we'd known what sort of evening was awaiting us, we'd probably have started preparing to sleep hours earlier.

CHAPTER TWO

Cádo's POV: Day 1

Bernard had been lying when he said it would get cold. It'd been cold before, when he first said that, but once the sun was fully down, things became nightmarish.

I'd spent my fair share of time in the woods, hunting, tracking, camping and hiking. I knew my way around a fire, and I'd spent the last decade building as much strength and endurance as I could without pissing blood in training. But I'd never tried to settle myself into a forest without tools before.

Building any sort of campfire was a harder prospect unequipped. I was strong, but cutting fallen logs with my bare hands was beyond even me, and Bernard's picked rocks weren't faring very well even in my hands. In the end we got maybe two sizable chunks of wood; the rest of our fuel would essentially just be kindling. So we gathered as much of it as we could manage.

Fortunately, the terrain around us was far more thick woodland than farther up in the hill. Within ten minutes, all three of us had an armful of twigs and sticks, and we didn't stop searching there. Spreading out, scrying farther and wider, all while Bernard picked a decent spot to make fire. He ended up settling on the base of a particularly big tree, probably figuring its yard-wide belly would make a serviceable windbreak. He was probably right.

I'd never been as involved in the writing process as either of my coworkers, to be clear. Bernard had quite literally written to live, and Kenny had spent all of his own rich-boy free time practicing the craft. Between training and contests, I'd been much more distant and hands-off.

Still, I knew enough about my own setting to be sure that getting caught in its woodlands after dark was . . . not ideal. I was hesitant to wander too far from the group, and as things got darker, that hesitation only deepened. The moment we had a pile as big as any of our torsos, all three of us huddled up with our eyes on one another's backs, barely even resisting the urge to try to stand all night for fear of an attack. We were already cold then, frozen almost to the bone through our thin shirts and kept functional only by the wasted heat of worked muscles. We wouldn't be going anywhere until morning.

The woods seemed to enjoy taunting us, rustling leaves overhead and snapping unseen twigs from every direction. The fact that Bernard didn't explode was one of the few mercies we enjoyed, but he sure got goddamn close.

"How did you get the fire started?" I asked, more to break the silence than because I actually had any investment in what the answer might be. Bernard must've been as desperate to hear our voices as I was, because he replied near instantly.

"Flint," he whispered. "I had a flick knife in my pocket already, and . . . Oh."

"What?" Kenny pressed, leaning in, eying him.

Bernard shook his head. "Nothing, I just figured something out. Anyway, I made sure to snatch a flint while I was arming myself. Flint, plus steel. Might fuck up the edge of my knife if we do it too much, but we can generate sparks at least, and carve wood into shavings so they have something to ignite."

I might've admired his foresight, had he not given both me and Kenny something more important to focus on. Bernard sighed before we even needed to ask. He always had a way of sniffing out what other people were thinking.

"Fine, I just realized that whatever interface Kenny sees telling him things bases the name of objects on what either he or its wielder identifies them as." He held up his knife, the blade grinning orange with firelight. "Both of you would call this a switchblade, yes?"

We both nodded, but from the corner of my eye I saw Kenny's face stiffen with understanding.

"I call it a flick knife," Bernard continued, "and so did Kenny's . . . ugh, *menu*. So, either he subconsciously thinks of it the way I would because of my owning it, or the menu assigns names based on the way an object's owner perceives it."

It really wasn't that useful at all, thinking about it, but Bernard had realized as much when he figured it out himself. It was why he'd not wanted to share it. He always hated wasting breath.

Still, the revelation did something more than illuminate us. It distracted us. For those few luxurious minutes, we all had something to focus on that wasn't the horrible ice clotting every gust of wind to roll across our camp.

The world got colder, and we started piling more kindling onto the fire, desperately hoping that the pile lasted longer. Then the world got colder again, and we were closing in around one another, guy-code forgotten as we pressed our shoulders in and shivered, conserving what warmth we could manage.

It was after maybe an hour that the snow started falling, and that was when we truly knew we were fucked.

A lot's happened to me since I first dropped into this world. People have kicked me, punched me, bitten, slashed, and shot me. I've been set on fire, half-drowned, almost eaten by a bear, and spent an afternoon picking bits of metal out of my ribs. None of it, not one scrap, has been half as bad as the cold was that night.

My fingers went first, all the sensation in them just halting dead in their tracks. My toes must have been a lot closer to the flame because they lasted a good few minutes longer. Then the chill was running up my limbs, reaching the ankles and wrists, and I found myself crying. The tears froze against my cheeks, and still things got colder.

I thought of home, trembling with the effort of not weeping outright. And things cooled ever more cruelly down into the sub-zero range. My thoughts of home became dreams of a damned blanket, or anything at all to put between myself and the sky.

At some point I know I fell asleep because I woke up to a slightly warmer world. Slightly.

Everything was white, and viciously cold. I groaned, moved, felt everything in my body scream at me and fell still. I lay there for a couple of moments more before a hand came down on me.

"Cádo," Kenny whispered. "You need to get up. Dude, come on, we're moving."

Part of me wanted to just lie there, and I might have, if Bernard hadn't spoken first.

"You need circulation; it's dangerous to lie there any longer."

That brought my mind to the thought of blackened, shriveling toes. Amputations, hobbling footfalls, and a lifetime of knowing I'd never compete with the best again. I got up.

Somehow standing made everything real again, and I shivered even before the cold bit through my clothes. My thin fucking clothes.

It's hard to remember things after you've almost died, and I'd definitely been flirting with death the night before, but enough of my pondering had stuck. The emotions of it all, at least. Suddenly my mouth tasted sour.

"We're never going to get home, are we?" I said, more to myself than anything. When I looked up, I met Kenny's eyes and realized in an instant that he'd been having the same thoughts.

He shook his head, though. "We have no way of knowing, and about a thousand things that demand our focus before that. Now let's go! Bernard's certain the town is just a few more days at most."

My vision was blurry, eyes almost held shut by the frozen fluid they'd been leaking during my sleep, but after a few moments of blinking and rubbing, I could just about make out Bernard packing up what was left of our stuff.

Well, packing up is a poor choice of words. He was just stuffing the best of our remaining kindling into his arms. There wasn't much unburned, maybe a quarter-hour's worth of scavenging, but if that meant a quarter hour less time in the cold, it was worth it as far as I was concerned. He paused before we continued, then picked a few sticks out from the pile.

"What are you doing?" Kenny asked, eyeing him. Bernard didn't answer with words, instead moving toward the dying remnants of our campfire and holding the sticks over it. Their ends ignited soon enough, and he drew them back with care.

"Hold them upside down every so often," he advised, handing us both a torch. "The flames will rise and eat the full length of the wood that way, should last a while. We need to stay warm even on the move."

We didn't stay warm, not even close, but we stayed alive at the very least.

There was no conversation on our way down the hill that day. Whatever words any of us had for each other had dried up in the night. I was thinking about home again, and thinking about how I'd never see it again. My family, my friends. My damned home.

I had a rug, a real nice one, I'd stumbled onto completely by surprise in some tiny little store near where I lived. I'd miss that, and for some bizarre reason that was the loss that stung deepest. Little things like that rug would be hard to come by in our new world.

You might have expected a walk like ours, trudging through ankle-deep snow and getting chewed on by the elements with every step, to feel sluggish, endless, slow. It didn't. I barely even noticed the stretch it took to finish because I was too busy dreading what would happen when it did.

Twelve hours passed, maybe. It was hard to tell. The air warmed a little, then cooled all the way back down to the vicious, frigid depths that had almost killed us the night before. By then we were more ready than we had been.

Bernard had been thinking during our march, and just a few minutes into it, he'd picked some big log up off the ground, half-buried in snow. I'd been too preoccupied with my misery to see what he was doing with it, but I'd seen him fiddling away with a rock from the corner of my eye. When we stopped for camp, I got it.

At one end of the log, he'd carved bark and wood away to leave an opening, sort of a half-crater clinging to its ass. It wasn't all that deep, or wide, but I could recognize the makeshift shovel in an instant, and Bernard was quick to hand it to me.

"Kenny and I will get the wood this time," he told me. "You're on plow duty. We want a big patch of snow cleared beside a tree, then piled up on each side of it as high as you can manage."

I frowned, thought about it, then everything clicked into place. Igloos. We didn't have the time or gear for great big bricks of ice, but this would surely work well enough, right?

Well, if it didn't, we'd never know. I didn't think any of us had the reserves of life to keep kicking through another night of frozen hell. I got to digging.

There was a certain technique to shoveling snow that I won't share here because it's about as mentally stimulating as being on the receiving end of a lobotomy. In any case, I was done fast enough. If anything, I was glad for the chance to actually use my arms.

But it brought my awareness to another issue, too. My body heated up, the cold dissipating somewhat, and in doing so, allowed room for another sensation to slip in. The fucking hunger.

How long since I'd eaten? Well over a day now, surely, and I was certainly feeling it. Everything inside my body was slowing down, blunting. I was getting stupid, tired. One day without food wouldn't kill someone, but it felt like it would. And I didn't want to imagine another twelve-hour walk if I woke up like this.

Kenny and Bernard came back for the final time with great bundles of wood, and we set up inside our shelter. It wasn't very good, not really. I'd hammered the interior to keep the snow hard and compact, hoping that it'd stop the fire from melting it but, other than that, it really was just a white blob. Still, a white blob was better than a white horizon as far as not killing us went.

We didn't chat at all this time. We just laid back, rested, and agonized over our empty stomachs and homesick minds. The sky grew darker, the air cooler, and the forest creepier. Sounds growing so common and spine-chilling that we hardly even noticed when the snapping of nearby twigs became a bit too regular.

"What was that?" Bernard whispered, a full minute before either of the sane people present became worried enough to echo him.

Kenny made the first suggestion.

"A wild boar?" he asked. "Or . . . something?"

Even he didn't sound convinced.

"One of us needs to check," Bernard said. "Our little shelter is open to the elements. If whatever's out there goes for us, we'll be cornered in here."

All eyes turned to me, of course, but I'd already steeled myself for that. Fear always shocked me in how it stunted other people. It had only ever made me sharper.

I stood, stretched, readied myself, and made for the exit on a stomach that suddenly felt much, much fuller.

Nerves of steel or no, even I was taken aback by the great, snarling bear waiting outside for us.

CHAPTER THREE

Cádo's POV: Day 2

It wasn't a big bear, maybe five hundred pounds at most, but it felt like one—a really, really big fucking bear. Brown furred, not black, and coming at me about as fast as something you'd compare a really fucking fast and pissed-off bear to. It had claws, teeth, probably rabies, and definitely a searing hatred for me and my entire bloodline. I, on the other hand, had a big stick I'd taken from the firewood pile. Two feet long, maybe three or four inches wide. My choices were clear.

I dived to one side and desperately tried to scramble away.

The move must've been well timed because the bear stumbled past me for a few feet while I clawed my way back to a standing position. It turned, and I moved on instinct at the sight, bringing the log down hard against the horrible thing's face. The skull wasn't where I'd guessed it'd be, though, and the angle was shoddy. It all but bounced off, then the bear was on me.

Back home, back on Earth, I'd seen a few documentaries and survival tips on how to handle a bear attack. What were they?

Ah, yes. Play dead, they said. Too late for that now, its jaws were closing in on my face. I had nothing to stab it with. Fuck, I didn't have the space to even hit it very hard with my stick, and half a second of pushing against it told me exactly what my odds of physically holding the thing back were. None. I had just enough time to get calm and realize, really realize, that I was about to die.

Then Bernard was slithering up behind it.

By now the bear's head was halfway to my neck, jaws wide to clamp down and end me. Bernard might have tried stabbing away with his little pocket knife if he'd been a normal person—might've even pissed it off enough to switch targets—but he wasn't and had never been normal. Instead Bernard, with utmost care, took one of the bear's ears in one hand, calmly moved the edge of his switchblade to just under its base, then leaned into it with all of his weight.

Edged, modern steel carved through skin and gristle like it wasn't even there, and the bear's ear dropped down to the ground so easily that the knife's trajectory wasn't even slowed, blood soaking into the cloud-white snow beneath.

The bear screamed, rounding on Bernard just as he took off at a sprint. As the creature tore off me to hammer after him, I took an instant to thank whatever God might be watching for making my friend so weird.

And then I was standing up, stick back in hand, muscles tightening with anticipation. I wasn't going to leave Bernard to the fate he'd saved me from.

Problem was, he was being chased by a bear, and it was closing in fast. I sprinted after them, Kenny falling into step alongside me, both of us calling out to the shrieking paranoid.

"Veer right!" Kenny yelled, already panting from the exertion. Bernard must have heard because he made a sharp turn when the animal was only feet behind him, just barely avoiding a mauling. The bear dug its heels in, slowing, turning, and rounding on him just in time to catch my stick hard across its snout.

This swing was better than the first, and I couldn't suppress a grin as I saw the animal stumbling back.

When you're lucky enough to land a good hit, land another one before the other bastard can get his senses back. I acted on Bernard's old brawling advice before it even registered, bringing the log down again with a sharp *thwack*. The bear snorted, groaning, and I hit again and again. Every blow sending blood flecking from its face, adding, in some tiny part, to the crimson streak that already ran down its head and neck, where Bernard had taken the ear.

Bernard and Kenny did their parts, too. The former with his knife, the latter with the largest rock he could manage.

Stabbing quickly and sharply, Bernard jabbed his steel in and out of the bear, holding the blade to protrude directly out ahead of his closed fist and punching it into the animal like a boxer working a bag. It barely seemed to do anything at all, but it was a good enough distraction.

Kenny's approach was clearly less practiced, but I was no less grateful for it. He brought a big rock the size of Andre the Giant's fist down into the thing's back while it focused on me, snarling with a mix of fear and fury all the while.

We kept it stun locked for a while, just wailing away, killing it one irritation at a time. The problem with death by a thousand cuts, though, is that there aren't many weapons that can survive being used a thousand times when their wielder is an Olympian and their target a bear. I brought the log down one last time on the snout, catching it right between the eyes, and this time a great *snap* rang out, sickening me to my stomach for all of a second before I realized what it was.

The log had broken, and the bear was stumbling back, recovering fast. I swung again, using the remaining foot of wood I still held, then swearing as it bounced off, with its length and torque suddenly halved.

I wasn't able to move before the bear did this time.

A paw the size of a coffee table caught me on the side, and the entire world toppled over. There was wind and snow breaking against my face, then I was upside down somehow. Around that time, the ground decided to punch me in the back. I'd flown easily half my body length before even hitting the snow, and I slid and rolled another half a Cádo before stopping.

Everything was a maze of confusion, fatigue drowning the world out. The bear might've started chewing off my hands and I wouldn't have noticed until a few more seconds of mewling let me regather my wits. I could only hope it wasn't.

Fortunately, I didn't wake up to find myself the starter in a three-course meal. I had Bernard and Kenny to thank for that.

They'd worked quickly while I was seeing stars, Kenny distracting the bear with Bernard's knife, and Bernard doing what God had made him to do. Improvising a weapon. The bear made a single, critical mistake in focusing on Kenny for one moment too long, then Bernard was on it.

He'd taken a pair of sticks from the fire, small ones. Kindling. Perfectly sized to be clutched in a snow-covered hand, to keep from burning him, and inserted up the poor animal's nostrils. The effect was instantaneous, and considerable.

I almost felt sorry for it, watching the bear snarl and scream and thrash around. Bernard was dislodged instantly, rolling away, scrambling back as the animal went mad. It almost convulsed, coiling and rolling about, scraping the snow away to reveal hard dirt beneath. Smoke drifted from its face all the while, burning wood still hot and searing despite the huge paws impotently smashing at its snout. It only took a few moments before the bear was up again, turning and sprinting off into the woods, bouncing off trees and fleeing in blind horror at a pain it likely wasn't even equipped to understand.

It was all we could do to convince Bernard he shouldn't sprint after the fucking thing and finish it.

For a few minutes, we grinned to each other, celebrating our victory as we stumbled back to the fire, Bernard spasming and twitching now that the fight was over. Then it happened.

A sudden weakness overcame me, and a sickness, too. My legs folded, my head spun, and before I knew it I was on the ground, convulsing as my ribs screamed in agony. Adrenaline subsiding to let all the pain I'd not noticed before come flooding in.

What happened next came in flitting, broken-up images and memories. I remember being dragged and carried along to our camp, placed down by the fire, resting in agony. I remember hearing Kenny and Bernard talking, worried. The words just barely settled in my mind. With me hurt, we'd be travelling slower and carrying less wood. I tried to stand, to tell them I was fine, but every move I tried to make—every breath I tried to take—just had my ribs aching all over again. Finally I lay still.

The night passed, and I barely remembered the morning. I was leaned against someone's shoulder, half-pulled down the hill as we continued our trek, groaning in pain with every step before we finally made camp again.

That night wasn't as cold as I'd feared. Kenny and Bernard had spent longer gathering firewood, which meant we'd spent less time travelling and sentenced ourselves to another day on the hillside. The hunger worsened as time stretched on.

We packed up, stood, and moved again. Cold, exhaustion, pain, hunger. And fear. We never knew when another bear might come, and it ended up being Bernard of all people who talked us down, explained how to process our fears, and calmed us.

God, was this how he felt all the time? My heart broke at the thought.

Night after night we grew weaker, more scared. Every shadow was hungry, every snapping twig was a moment's warning before some new monster lunged for us, and every step we took toward the town left us less certain it even existed.

I was lucky to have been drifting in and out of consciousness. If I'd been awake for the full trip, I think it might have . . . changed me. I'm not sure it didn't change Bernard and Kenny.

But one day it ended. A gasp, a careful shake to wake me up, and then a pointing finger for my bleary eyes to follow as it indicated a dot on the landscape ahead. I grinned at the sight. Buildings. Houses, halls, thatched roofs, and plowed roads. Human habitation, with smoke and civilization breathing out into the air.

We hurried, and suddenly everything nature threw at us was less substantial. Just having the town in sight made us braver, and our hope kept the cold back. The energy of desperation seemed almost completely balanced with our growing hunger and fatigue, and the next days of travel practically flitted by.

I tried to hide my worsening condition, to keep from ruining the second wind my friends had gained, but they'd always been smart. I don't think either of them failed to realize how much weaker I was getting. It seemed to only speed them up.

We closed in on the town, marching toward it, each of us smelling like shit and somehow looking shittier. The last thing I saw before sleep took me was the snowy ground giving way to trodden dirt paths.

And the last thought I had was a strange mixture of relief and fear.

CHAPTER FOUR

Bernard's POV: Day 5

We'd all been fucking idiots to think anything would actually come of reaching the town. We weren't on Earth anymore.

Our world was called Redacle, and it was one of those "grimdark fantasy" settings for edgy assholes who thought they were clever. Like us. All dark people doing dark things for dark reasons—rape and murder, starving orphans, and big, horrible monsters pulling people's arms off. You know, the classics.

All well and good to write. Except settings like those are known for their egalitarianism in the same way that Adolf Hitler was known for his racial tolerance and compassion. So, pretty much the moment we were within town bounds, a pair of bastards in big gambesons with big sticks marched over and started barking demands.

Vagrants. We were vagrants now. That was fine by me. I'd been a vagrant before, but Kenny looked like he might well be sick.

"Names and intentions?" one of the men asked. My brain was slowing down with the cold, and slowing more with my hunger, but I got there in the end. Eyeing his uniform, remembering where we were. A town guard. A Redacle town guard, which meant there was a very particular set of non-disastrous responses possible here.

"Solitaire and Shango," I answered, resisting the urge to spit on him and forcibly defying my natural instincts to clamp up and demand a lawyer in the presence of cops. "Our friend here is hurt; we need a healer for him."

The guard eyed Cádo flatly, apparently unmoved by such trivialities as a man fucking dying right in front of him. I wondered whether he'd be equally unmoved if he took Cádo's place.

"You'll be here for Magus Corvan then. Big hut on the far end of town, one road down from this one. He takes payment up front."

I caught his implication just fine, and eyed Kenny, waiting for him to reply. He'd be better in this situation. Kenny always got along with humans better than me.

"Much obliged, sir," Kenny said, forcing a friendly smile that went unreturned. We were past the guard a moment later, and he shot a look at me. "Solitaire?" he asked, incredulous.

We'd agreed beforehand on using false names while we were here, for one major reason. We didn't know for sure we were the only ones who'd been isekai'd into this fucking place, and if someone else here recognized the setting, they'd likely recognize its writers, too.

Neither of us wanted to get jumped by a bunch of idiots who decided that it must have been the authors' faults when they ran into them in some mysterious fantasy land.

All discussed, all agreed on, all concluded. But only he had shared his choice of name before then, I'd made mine up just before speaking to the guard. Apparently, it had surprised him.

"What's wrong with Solitaire?" I frowned, and Kenny—Shango—only snorted.

"What *isn't* wrong with it? It's like something out of a young adult novel."

I couldn't fight my chuckle. Having your testicles turned into icicles tended to squeeze the humor out of a man, but finding the town and, more importantly, hearing it had a healer had reinstalled a bit of my old boyish whimsy.

"At least I didn't name myself after one of my people's gods," I shot back. "Isn't Shango a damned dictator?"

Kenny—Shango, now—always while we were here, shrugged.

"Ancient king. It tends to happen."

Any other time I might've thrown in a few choice words about *modern* kings, too, and modern governments for that matter, but we had more important things to worry about.

Perhaps surprisingly, the guard's directions proved reliable. We were soon standing outside a squat, oddly well-maintained house distanced quite a bit farther from its neighbors than the rest of the homes.

We'd gotten a good look at the place on our walk over, though we hardly needed to. Redacle, as a whole—and in particular, our current location on the continent of Vorhazh—was a vaguely late-medieval setting. The buildings showed that that much hadn't changed. All wood for the most part, with the occasional stretch of cobbled walls. They were small and numerous, and even with however many hundred dotted around the town, there were probably no more than one or two thousand people living here.

Magi were rare, and magical healers were rarer still. The former was just a blanket term for people properly trained in the most common form of magic, and the latter, magically speaking, was almost always a magus who specialized in repairing the body. It was lucky to find even one of either in a town like this; usually they stuck to cities. Cities had more people, and wealthier people. Cities had more things that called for a person capable of blasting down trees and cutting through plate armor.

One foot inside the hut and everything already smelled like smoke and salt. It was almost nostalgic. My mother's homes always had that same scent whenever she was making explosives.

It was a dingy interior, lit by candles dotting the various walls, and every surface seemed covered with shelving units holding twice their weight in containers. Jars, vials, pots, and bowls. Herbs hung in big racks, and an open flame crackled in a far corner of the room. There was a cauldron dangling over it. A fucking cauldron. Christ.

We were able to get maybe two paces in before the place's owner appeared, stepping out in front of us and staring at me and Shango as if we'd just kicked his mother and fucked his dog.

"I don't do charity," he said. "You'll be looking for the temple." He had a modern accent, one I'd expect from Yorkshire, maybe. Made sense. I usually wrote with modern accents in mind.

Shango answered, as we'd agreed, speaking with a calm I wasn't sure I could've mustered myself with our friend leaning unconscious against me.

"Our friend is dying," he explained. "He needs treatment."

The healer glanced at Cádo, unmoved.

"Ten silvers for conventional treatment, three gold for arcane healing."

It was an absurd price, even for Redacle, and he was asking it to make us go away. Shango must have known because he changed tactics instantly.

"We can work the price off," he began. "Look at our friend. He's strong, really strong, and he can fight."

"And so are we," I cut in to reinforce his point. "How often does the chance come along to get three workers of our size? We could guard your shop as well as any five normal men, hunt for you, even . . . enforce."

The more I spoke, the harder it seemed to find ways in which we could leverage our stature to actually benefit a healer of all people, but I was desperate not to let the advantage go unused. We'd noticed almost immediately how significant it was.

Childhood and adolescence on Earth, in modern nations and wealthy families, had seen all of us fed a protein-rich diet filled with vital nutrients, which the people in this world were denied, just as our own ancestors had been hundreds of years ago on Earth. At six foot two, I was pretty tall back in England. In Redacle, though, I was a giant.

That had to mean something; it just had to.

"I don't need assistants, definitely not a pair of meat-headed thugs."

The man didn't sound like he could be moved, but Shango was never one to give up on something he wanted.

"There must be something you need," he tried, desperate now. "Anything. What do you lose by naming a price and keeping him alive until we fail to pay it?"

The healer paused, thought about it, and then spoke slowly. Carefully. "There . . . might be something," he began. "Jungua sap. You've heard of it?"

Neither of us had. Shango's confusion was genuine, and mine was, too. Mine, though, was eerie. I remembered everything, which meant this wasn't something we'd added to the world. Were we not in Redacle after all?

"We haven't," Shango replied, hurriedly. "What is it?"

The healer's scoff almost earned him a headbutt before I remembered our circumstance, and his magic. Fortunately, he was quick to answer.

"It's a remedy for infection, and a damned good one. Cleans wounds out like nothing else, but I'm out of it, and the idiot merchant from Wolney didn't bring my last shipment. If you can fetch some more for me, I'll take the price out of your friend's healing fee. That'd leave him alive, and the three of you in a mere two gold and fifteen silvers' debt."

Wolney. I committed the name to memory. Most likely it was a city, but there was no time to be checking that now. I turned to Shango.

"Deal," he declared. "Where do we find it nearby?"

The healer gave us our directions, speaking about three times slower than I would've needed to carve them all into my mind. By the time he was finished, I'd started to feel the familiar twitches of adrenaline oozing back into my muscles. He was hiding something, I could tell, and whatever it was, I knew enough about this shithole of a world to be certain it might get us killed.

No surprise there. I was working class. Getting me killed was what people did.

We left Cádo with the bastard, not having much of a choice in the matter. Moments after setting foot outside, the exhaustion hit us both.

It'd been days since we'd rested. Properly rested. Since we got here, it had all been marches, starvation, and ice. And it looked like we had more of the same ahead of us. I felt worn thin, enough that it was almost tempting to just leave my friend for dead.

Almost. Shango would have kept that from being an option, if it even had been in the first place.

"Right," he said, speaking with a breathy voice that told everything I needed to know about his exhaustion. "Three things we need, yeah?"

I thought about it, and agreed. Food was the first. I was already weaker than I'd ever felt before, struggling just to move around. Cádo was a big guy, maybe a hundred and ninety pounds of lean muscle and springy fencer, but hauling his weight shouldn't have been half as hard when split between me and Shango at once.

If something half as dangerous as that bear attacked us now, we'd die. Which meant a meal was highest on our list of priorities. I poked my ribs and felt them poking back from beneath the skin.

Maybe two meals. After that I could waste all the time I wanted wondering what the fuck a bear was doing awake and attacking me during winter anyway.

Second came weaponry, of course, and the third priority was one that defied instinct to consider. But there was no doubting its use.

The last few days had been too hectic for us to spare any time for introspection or experimentation, but we had room to breathe now, and we'd fought off a bear less than one week ago.

It was time to have Shango take a peek at our stats and see whether we really could level up in this world.

CHAPTER FIVE

Shango's POV: Day 5

[Appraisal]
Class: Revolutionary
Level: 1
Condition: Haggard
Modifiers: None
Statistics: Strength 6 (4), Speed 6 (4), Dexterity 8 (5), Stamina 5 (2), Toughness 6, Alertness 8 (6), Charisma 3 (2), Intelligence 10 (9)
Inventory: Jeans, T-shirt, flick knife, rocks (x5)
Class Abilities: Detect Element I

I swore. Bernard's statline hadn't improved at all. His level was the same, his abilities were no different. In fact, assuming the numbers in parentheses showed figures after modifiers, his statistics had actually fucking *dropped*. I guessed the hunger was responsible for that. This wasn't good at all.

"That bad?" Bernard—no, Solitaire—asked me. He'd always been good with faces. If anything, it was relieving. This meant his edge wasn't entirely worn away by the emptiness in his stomach and the ruin his body had become.

"That bad," I concurred, swearing as I turned my focus inward. My own statline came up soon enough, and it was just as disheartening as Solitaire's.

[Appraisal]
Class: Emperor
Level: 1
Condition: Haggard
Modifiers: None

Statistics: Strength 5 (3), Speed 5 (3), Dexterity 6 (3), Stamina 5 (2), Toughness 5, Alertness 8 (6), Charisma 9 (8), Intelligence 9 (8)
Inventory: Jeans, shirt, jacket
Class Abilities: Appraisal I

My guts almost dropped out, seeing my intelligence. Cleverness had never been a resource I was short of, having one ninth of it drained away somehow scared me more than the starvation. I swore again.

"We need a baseline," Solitaire began, "to see how we compare here. Try eyeing the other people across this street."

I nodded, turning the ability outward, scrutinizing passersby's numbers.

Fours, largely. Almost exclusively in fact. Maybe one in three people had even a single stat above or below it, and the vast majority who did were off by only a single number. One particularly big man with an easily six foot frame and arms that showed it was sitting at a strength and toughness of six, and I saw some utterly gorgeous woman walking along with a charisma of seven. It was all I could do not to march over and try my luck with her.

But no, there was a time and a place for distracting myself with luxury. Food first, then a weapon. Rolling in the hay could be my nice little reward if I somehow managed the rest. Assuming the primitive women here didn't panic at the sight of probably the first black person they'd ever seen or even heard about.

"Threes, fours, and fives," I told Solitaire, forcing my mind from the idle fancying. "Overwhelmingly more common is the fours, though. Occasionally there's some higher figures. That giant who went by a few minutes ago was at a six in strength. Oh, but most of the women are sitting at two for strength and such."

He nodded, as if some suspicion had been confirmed.

"Sounds like we're dealing vaguely with a bell-curve distribution, though I'd need more data to be sure. Fours . . . So at the moment we're about as strong as the average man here." He eyed some of the pedestrians, clearly taking in just how tiny their bodies really were. Not just short, withered, and scrawny—almost like children. Modern lifestyles on Earth tended toward a fairly flabby physique with how sedentary they were, but this was something else.

I felt a stab of worry, too. I was *weaker* than most of these men? Fuck, I needed a sandwich.

"Food," Solitaire declared. "That's our first priority then. Weapon or no, we won't be surviving anything in some shitting fantasy land with our current conditions what they are. You get food, I'll see if I can scrounge us up something pointy or heavy."

Though I nodded, the words felt oddly distant to me. As if the prospect of searching the town for some meal were removed. It was hard to process all this, hard to keep treating everything as real.

Hard to believe, even, that Solitaire hadn't just been right when he said we were all hallucinating somewhere. But those uncertainties were useless. They'd change nothing if they were right, and kill us all if they were wrong. So, I dismissed them, shoving them to one side of my mind to make room for more productive thoughts.

"That healer said something about a church," I pointed out. Solitaire nodded.

"Yeah, he did, about charity, right? That sounds like a good place to start for filling us up. You see if you can find it, and I'll go and arm us." He was marching off before I could say anything, forcing me into an agonizing half-jog to catch up.

"Shouldn't we stay together?" I asked. Solitaire thought about it, then eyed me.

"We're half a foot taller than most of the men here and look desperate. Anyone who gives either of us trouble deserves a Darwin award. At least for a while."

His confidence was infectious, and we went our separate ways. Infectious, but not virulent. I brought one of our rocks with me, a nice jagged one, and kept it tight and palmed in my pocket while walking. It occurred to me that this was the first time in days I'd actually been on my own, and the extra space gave my mind plenty of time to work and process things.

Mostly, I just stared at the people bustling around me, but I got some thinking done, too. In particular I eyeballed my rock.

RPGs gave weapons stats, too, right? It felt weird that this one wouldn't . . . unless I just needed to examine it closer in my inventory. Curiously, I eyed the rock in my hand, bringing the menu up within a single second now, then staring harder, more intently. I scrolled through my inventory until I reached the object, turning my full focus onto it.

After a full minute without results, I was forced to give up. But something still snagged at my wits. My class ability was called Appraisal I, not simply Appraisal. So . . . there were stronger versions. If I could unlock one of them, would they give me more in-depth information?

It was hard to imagine any other way a fucking Appraisal ability might power up, but at the same time it wasn't exactly reassuring. We still had no idea whether levelling up was even on the horizon. Whether it was or it wasn't meant entirely different things for our future prospects in this world.

More information. We always needed more information. More importantly, though, we needed to pay that healer and have him reassemble the gory jigsaw puzzle Cádo's ribcage had turned into.

My worries kept me company while I explored the town of Jhigral, taking in the sights and committing them to memory. I wasn't Bernard—Solitaire, dammit—so I couldn't just make maps in my brain at a whim, but I reckoned a few repetitions would help me keep track of the whole place. In the meantime, it gave me a nice distraction while I tried to find the church.

It wasn't that hard, in the end. Churches tended to be pretty recognizable. England had been sure to plant plenty in my own country, and we'd based most of our setting's lore on generic pop-culture medieval Europe. The big, rectangular box surrounded by six-pointed holy symbols and windowed with stained glass would've been easily noticed even if I was drunk.

I didn't waste any time marching to it, guts squirming and chest tightening. Redacle charity. I was here for Redacle charity. It wasn't much, just some bread, maybe a bowl of stew, but knowing what I knew about this world . . .

Fuck, that much might mean draining all the charity they had.

Inside, the place was just as grandiose, but I was used to much bigger buildings on Earth. And the priest wasn't half as hostile as anyone else had been. There was a place inside for me to sit, and it was warmer than anywhere I'd yet set foot. Within Redacle, at least. There were a few other people there for me to share the charity with, and all looked like they damned well needed it. That I hadn't been turned away at the door, that I'd been ushered through to join these wretches without even a moment's pause, was, if anything, a telltale sign of how ragged I probably looked.

And my spending no more than two seconds dwelling on that fact was an indicator of how much my hunger had grown to eat everything else in my head.

I left with a full belly, having been fed broth and some dried-out wafers. The stuff tasted like nothing at all, except a slight reduction in my hunger, and right now that was the best thing I could hope for.

Solitaire and I met up soon enough, and he presented me with weapons. I decided not to ask where he'd gotten the big fucking lump hammer. We had more pressing matters.

In the end, the two of us spent another day and a half in Jhigral. We ate, we recovered, and we rested by bunking in the crook between two buildings and huddling. By the end of it, our bodies were still achy and pained, but the weariness felt much more like a mere sensation than an ailment. I checked Solitaire's stats, just to be sure.

[Appraisal]
Class: Revolutionary
Level: 1
Condition: Worn
Modifiers: None
Statistics: Strength 6 (5), Speed 6, Dexterity 8 (7), Stamina 5 (3), Toughness 6, Alertness 8, Charisma 3 (2), Intelligence 10
Inventory: Jeans, T-shirt, flick knife, rocks (x5), lump hammer
Class Abilities: Detect Element I

Yep. Back to normal, more or less, which was a damned relief. The stamina and dexterity drops were concerning, though, but if nothing else, I'd expected a lot worse.

Five days hadn't been long as far as hunger spells went, but it'd been enough for Solitaire to visibly thin down. His face looked like it was pulled taut, cheekbones pressing into the skin, and his eyes had almost sunken into the sockets. I couldn't have looked much better. It was lucky, I decided, that we'd been careful to hurry our way down that mountain. What would another day of this have done? Another two?

A shiver ran down my spine as we stood up.

"So," I croaked, "jungua sap. Know the name?"

Solitaire shook his head, frowning.

"It sounds like something I'd come up with, though. I . . . Hm, I think maybe this world is filling in the blanks for our own setting, basically using our book as a template and then adding in things that we *might* have included had we decided to focus on a particular region."

I nodded. It made sense to me, and it was absolutely fucking horrifying to hear. Our world-building was definitely not very friendly to the poor idiots who happened to be living inside said world.

Still, nothing we could do about it now. I buried the stab of weird guilt that reared its head up at the thought of how many people were starving on our account, and we set off.

CHAPTER SIX

Solitaire's POV: Day 7

Shango had insisted twice now that we really were back to full strength, and I still wasn't convinced. He'd always been better at the biological side of science—studied it, practiced it, even enjoyed it. But he was still a human, and humans lied, constantly, for a thousand different reasons or for no reason at all. It was just what they did, that and plan to kill me and vehemently lie about it.

And I couldn't see the stats that he told me about.

It could be that we were still weak, and Shango just wanted me to think otherwise. To use the placebo effect to artificially push me up into better functionality. It was fair enough, really. I'd probably have tried the same thing myself. The problem with clever clogs like me, though, was that too much thinking left convenient little tricks like that a lot less reliable.

I felt worn still, no matter what. And I knew that something was deeply wrong with my body. Shango had lost about five pounds already, and it'd be naive to assume I'd somehow escaped in better condition. Even if we were back up to full strength, one meal a day wouldn't keep us there for long.

At best, we were feeling a second wind. At worst, we weren't even gifted with that. This mission had to succeed. Which brought me to the next point of concern. I'd done some thinking, once my head was a bit clearer, and had come to some very obvious conclusions. One was more dangerous than the others.

"We shouldn't be getting this much preferential treatment for an errand like this," I noted to Shango. "We're heading, what, a half day away and back again? Any idiot could do this. Why wouldn't he just pay us a few coppers and get it over with."

We'd used a classic *Dungeons and Dragons*-style coinage for Redacle, fifty coppers to a silver, fifty silvers to a gold. That this man was offering us to keep our friend alive for one day's work was . . . suspect to say the least. Treatment like that was worth easily five times what our work would get.

So we were being played, but how?

"Maybe he's desperate," Shango suggested, not sounding hopeful even to me. "Maybe he's a prick, even around here, and can't find anyone to help him."

No. No, for two reasons. For one thing, that bastard was very much *normal* here, and I'd thought bloody modern humans were bad. But for another, there was no reason he'd make the pay jump for us . . . Unless he really did desperately need the sap, to the point of wanting to have us running after it before we could hear about the situation fully.

I swore. We should've been gathering information during our stay, not lounging around watching ourselves recover. The hunger had made me worse than weak. I'd been stupid, and soon I might be dead.

This time, at least, our journey was a lot easier. We'd planned to make it down the mountain in three days last time, and we would have if Cádo hadn't decided to go into a coma. We didn't have dipshit to carry now, though, so we made much better progress.

Both of us had eaten right before setting off, figuring we'd time our daily charity meal to have another one waiting for us once we returned, so we weren't in too much trouble camping out again with our typical snowdrift strategy. We didn't make a fire, though. Whatever was waiting ahead, fire might attract it. We just spent extra long setting up our little shelter, watching the darkening woods from a peeking hole, and waiting. Fortunately, I'd nicked a few strips of cloth to wrap ourselves in and to keep anything from dropping off this time.

We weren't waiting that long. Dark was still new when we caught the smoke rising high. It was barely visible, only registering because it caught a few beams of the setting sun's light, but it was there for sure. Humans, right where we needed to be going, right in the middle of a danger zone. Camping.

It was bandits. I knew it was bandits, Shango fucking knew it was bandits, but it was still a challenge actually convincing my friend of the fact. I never quite understood why, but for some reason most people had a much harder time killing Homo sapiens than they did animals.

What was more annoying was the fact that it was usually the ones who needed killing that *didn't* hesitate. Life was full of those little inconveniences, I supposed.

Despite the shocking revelation, it occurred to us that nothing had really changed in our plan. Mainly because we didn't really have the luxury of changing anything. We'd still have to go over, get the sap, and get past anything trying to stop us. All that had happened now was we'd gotten a glimpse of what might try.

So we left our shelter and hurried over to the smoke.

Whoever was guarding the sap, they were probably watching for people coming for it. No doubt their entire scheme was just jumping enterprising merchants, healers, or alchemists who wanted to gather it, and who tried to close in past them. In which case, if we were lucky, they'd not be nearly as prepared for people moving over *toward* their camp rather than away from it.

If we weren't lucky, we'd die, but there wasn't anything we could do about that, so we didn't think about it.

Shango took the lead for one very important reason—it was his power we were banking on. Slowly, step by step, we closed in on our targets, and soon enough we caught physical sight of them.

They were standing around a bonfire, numbering only three, one seated a bit farther away from the others with his eyes away from the fire rather than toward it.

Lucky then. If they'd thought of our snow-sheltering strategy, then they might've been able to have a sentry farther from their camp, and we might've stumbled into their sight without knowing. Good thing pre-industrial humanity was so fucking dumb.

From his vantage point, Shango was able to study the bastards good and proper. He whispered the findings to me. All were armed, obviously, but not well. Two had knives, one had a spear, and their clothes were just the ragged scraps they looked like. Their physical stats were about average for the world, though one was sitting at an impressive intelligence stat of six. He might sense something was up.

It was fairly easy to come up with a suitable strategy, rudimentary as it was. Shango backed off into the woods, moving as silently as could be expected with all the snow crunching underfoot. I went in another direction, circling the bandits, keeping a tight grip on my hammer.

I'd stolen it, obviously, but it was well worth the risk. The thing was some big stone-smasher, with about a yard of handle ending in a head bigger than my fist and made from solid iron. At a guess, it probably weighed about six, maybe seven, pounds. At a calculation, it weighed six point eight. A bit on the heavy side for fighting humans, but I hadn't been sure we wouldn't get attacked by another fucking bear.

Soon I was around the bonfire, perched behind a tree in the snowy shadows, waiting for Shango to give me my opportunity. It came fast.

The first rock went wide, sailing past the sentry's head. He stepped back, surprised at the sudden movement, shifting his footing and turning his head to gaze out across the darkness. Then Shango's second throw came, casting a larger stone this time.

I didn't see exactly how or where it hit, but the bandit was stumbling back as the rock bounced from his body, crying out and clutching his face. The two others were on their feet in an instant, scrambling for their weapons and hurrying to his side. I already had mine, though, and I was moving before they'd even gotten up.

The hammer came down just as one of them turned to face me, catching him hard in the shoulder. I heard bones break like twigs, and he went down screaming. His friend was quick, turning and lunging with their knife in a swing I barely leapt back from in time. I tried to bring my own weapon to bear, but he closed in faster than I could out-wrestle its unwieldy weight. He'd be on me before my swing was on him, so I abandoned the bludgeon and reached out to catch his knife-arm by the wrist.

He had all the momentum, sending me lurching back, struggling in the snow just to keep my footing. Right before I could bring my size to bear, a foot slipped out beneath me and I went down, knife lunging closer for me and missing my neck by an inch where it hit the ground. The bastard fell down on top of me.

I leaned in, switched my grip to wrap it around the bandit's torso, then roared with exertion as I hauled him up and over, slamming his back down into the snow to my left, then finishing the motion to roll on top. I had the mount now, and I didn't hesitate to use it. Swinging an elbow down for his head, aiming to catch a temple and knock my enemy's thoughts from his skull.

He blocked it, the fucker, folding up and covering himself with his forearms. I switched tactics quickly, leaned over him, pushed his head down with one hand to keep him stunned in place, and reached for the knife.

Apparently, I'd gotten the smart one, because he clearly realized what was happening and chose the perfect moment to shift his weight under me and send me toppling off of him. I rolled to my feet quick enough, missed my grab for the knife, and then stumbled back as a punch barely slipped by my head. When my vision came into focus, there were two bandits circling me.

Shango hadn't managed to distract the sentry for as long as we'd planned.

The smart one closed in first, and I backed off just as his friend moved to one side, trying to get behind me. I switched tactics again, lunging forward and slamming my shoulder against the first, sending the bastard down. I turned in time to catch a punch across my head, staggering from the shock of it, then grunting as more blows started peppering my ribs. I folded over, coughed, grabbing the tiny little cunt hammering away at me and dragged his face into my forehead.

The headbutt smashed his nose to bits, painting my scalp in foamy blood and knocking him flat, letting me stomp down on his neck to finish things, just as the smart one was back on his feet. I heard scraping as I turned, wondered why he wasn't already on me, and figured out he'd gone for the knife just in time to throw myself back from his slash and fall flat in the snow.

He was over me in an instant, blade held high, coming down for my guts too fast and too centered to dodge. So I didn't. Instead, I brought a leg in and lashed out a kick for his groin in the moment before the drop. I grinned at the sight of him doubling over and the wheezing sound that escaped his lips, then moved out from under him and threw an uppercut into his face on my way back to my feet.

This time, I was on the fucker before he could rise. Grabbing his knife-hand and bending it back, teeth gritted, snarling with my face inches from his as the metal came closer to his neck. He strained against me with every ounce of strength in his body, but there was no contest between us.

He was some fucking cave-dweller, somehow less civilized than King fucking Henry the Eighth and with a body to prove it. The wrestling match was over in moments, and ended with gurgles and blood fountaining from around the new metal ornament jutting out of his jugular.

It takes ages for someone to die properly; we humans are just built like that. Other animals? No problem at all. They have a heart attack if you fart on them too hard, but our adrenal system is insane. People have lived for hours after being cut in half, gotten holes poked in them without even noticing until well after the fact.

The bandit was no different. He kept on twitching, wheezing, and trying to move long after Shango sprinted back up to my side and started retching at the sight. Both of us eyed him in silence while he finally went still, and I glanced at my friend.

Disgust was written on his face. Horror, regret, guilt. I didn't feel any of that. Odd.

Well, maybe the stupid bastard shouldn't have planned to ambush me. Shame it was so cold. If it were warmer, I could've whipped my cock out to piss on his corpse.

A noise drew both our attention back to the side, where we found the first bandit—the one I'd sledgehammered—lying down and trying to crawl away. Shango began muttering at the sight, weighing what we ought to do, how to handle him. I didn't feel the need to consider my own options out loud.

He was a killer. That much I was fairly sure of, either directly or indirectly by camping a life-saving medicine. More importantly, we needed money, and I knew a good way he could get me some. It'd be a lot easier if he were dead, too.

Shango might disagree, or else take an age deciding that he didn't. If he decided to spare the guy, then I'd be forced to either argue or disregard his thoughts entirely by acting on my own. That wasn't ideal.

So I moved fast, lurching toward the crawling man, plucking the hammer back off the ground, and swinging it down all within a few seconds. It landed on his head with a meaty crunch that even I felt a little bit queasy hearing.

His legs kept kicking for a few more seconds, weirdly enough. Eyes drifting to face in different directions, sickly gurgles escaping his throat as the convulsions spread. Brain injuries tended to be funny like that.

He died faster than his friend, though.

CHAPTER SEVEN

Shango's POV: Day 7

My focus lapsed. Not for long—a moment at most, an instant at least. Just the span of a few thoughts. Hardly any time at all, really. It was, if anything, impressive that the tiny stretch of time was long enough for Solitaire to waltz over and fucking kill a man right in front of me.

I spent a while staring at the ruined mess he'd made of the man's head, then a while longer staring at him. Solitaire finally snapped me out of my stupor. He didn't say anything, didn't even flash an expression at the killing. He just knelt down beside the dead man, pulled out the other bandit's knife, and started pressing the blade into the corpse's mouth.

That, at last, was too much.

"You fucking killed him," I snapped, earning a glance from Solitaire. He looked *irritated*.

"Yeah," he said, turning back to whatever the fuck he was doing. That gave me something else to focus on, distracting me even while my thoughts were already churning around like some damned whirlpool.

"You executed him!"

He didn't even look up this time, only shrugged.

"I needed him dead. Do you know how much human teeth sell for in time periods like this? I don't actually, but I know for a fact there was a market for them. No prosthetics, you know?"

It was sickening, how casual he was about everything. Literally sickening. I dropped down to my knees, hurling up a streak of acrid vomit as my throat convulsed and nostrils burned. There wasn't much left in my guts, after the hunger and last spew, but it was enough to twist them. The snow's frigid touch barely even registered to me. I just kept kneeling there as steam from my own spilled insides wafted upward.

When I looked up, Solitaire was still poking away with his knife, still focused entirely on the work.

"You should get over this quickly," he sighed. "I need help. We're looking at close to a hundred teeth between these three, and so far I'm averaging less than one per minute. I want to be here for as few hours as possible."

"YOU FUCKING EXECUTED SOMEONE!" I couldn't keep myself from screaming any longer. Everything about this was wrong. You'd think I whispered for all Solitaire reacted.

"I did," he replied, calm as ever. "And I'd execute another if it improved our chances of survival. These bastards were camping out and killing people who tried to gather medicine in a world with barely any at all. You want to mourn them? Do it quietly. Now stop distracting me; this molar's really deep."

I stared at him as he worked, and Solitaire didn't even glance back. In the end, there was nothing more I could think to say. So I just watched and waited, not able to bring myself to start hacking away at the men's mouths, but not willing to stop him either.

We *did* need the money. With the debt we'd accrue by having Cádo healed, we'd need all the money we could get. And there were certainly worse people to get it from.

Worse corpses, really. I couldn't argue at all with taking the teeth, but the way he'd brought that hammer down . . . The way he'd looked at me afterward. I cursed, grabbed a knife, and knelt down beside one of the corpses, getting to work.

It was a relief when we finally finished, pockets filled with bloody, gummy teeth and hands covered in red crusts. An hour had passed. Not as long as it could've been. Not as long as it *would* have been without me. Luckily, we'd had the fire nearby while we worked.

"Let's get the sap," I grunted, feeling drained already. More than that. Hollowed out. Somehow tearing the teeth out had been harder than fighting, or what little fighting I'd done. The kills had been quick, near-instant even, just one action and then a display to feel bad about. This had been an age of prolonged, sustained decision-making.

And my reward was a bloody, sticky, revolting cluster of dubiously valued enamel tucked away into my clothing.

We moved on for our prize, trudging along through the snow, and while we walked, it occurred to me that we'd just won a damned three on two. Something about that had to have progressed us, surely.

[Appraisal]
Class: Emperor
Level: 1
Condition: Fine
Modifiers: None
Statistics: Strength 5 (3), Speed 5 (3), Dexterity 6 (3), Stamina 5 (2),
Toughness 5, Alertness 8 (6), Charisma 9 (8), Intelligence 9 (8)
Inventory: Jeans, shirt, jacket
Class Abilities: Appraisal I

What the fuck.

Nothing. No mention of experience, no skillpoints, no stat changes, no level increase. We'd gotten fuck all from that. The bottom dropped out of my chest as I walked, suddenly overcome with the urge to find whoever dropped us into this hellhole and show them all the neat tooth-extracting techniques I'd spent an hour mastering.

We'd never seen jungua sap before, never even built it into our world, but both of us recognized it when we finally found the right spot.

I'd imagined the stuff as runny and sort of amber-colored, almost like olive oil. Solitaire, apparently, had envisioned it as purple and gluey. When we found it, it was a green, frictionless sludge.

There was something to be inferred there. I could understand one of our two conflicting mental images taking precedence—we were the writers after all—but neither one was correct in this case. Why was that?

Hold on, back up. How did we tend to settle disagreements in the writing room? Well, we'd argue our points, try to convince the other. Often there was a fair bit of shouting involved. Then . . . someone would compromise, or more frequently everyone would, and we'd end up with something completely different than any of us originally suggested.

A synthesis.

So that was what we could expect from all the blank spots in our worldbuilding—some new congealment of our different ideas that we could only predict by having some big argument in the exact right headspace and coinciding with the same conclusion.

In other words, we couldn't bloody predict it. Splendid.

Solitaire wasn't exactly happy when I mentioned my observation, and worse, he could find no fault in its logic. We began our journey back to Jhigral, sap in hand.

We must've been getting used to the cold because the next twelve hours passed by like a breeze. A hundred-mile-per-hour breeze, mind you, carrying gravel in its winds, but we'd still take that over the journeys from before. Before we knew it, we were back in town, marching in past the wall and looking at everyone with a bit less . . . fear.

Seeing the place again, it felt transformed. It took me a moment to realize that the change was all us. We'd killed men, Solitaire directly, me by helping as best I could. After something like that, it was hard to be scared of the dark alleys and mean looks from before.

Hard to be scared, and so much easier to focus on the other details. I felt my heart throb as I saw people lying about without homes, trying in vain to find some shelter from the snow between buildings or under debris. Just like we had.

The homeless had never been an uncommon sight where I was from, of course, but seeing this many . . . Seeing them this withered and starved, I was nearly tempted to march over to the nearest guard and stick one of the knives we'd taken from the bandits in him.

I decided against it. Something told me that would lead to an undesirable outcome.

Mercifully, we got to Corvan's shop before I could see much more of the eternal class struggle, and entered the place's warmth with no small amount of relief. It took a minute more before the old bastard came out to see us again, but when he did it was almost worth the trip just seeing his face.

We might've walked over and started pissing on him to less surprise than that, and when Solitaire pulled out the sap, that surprise quickly turned into a deeper, more considering look. He snatched the stuff up, nodding crisply.

"Alright then," he snapped, as if affronted to have been shocked at all. "I don't know how you did it, but a deal's a deal. I'll put the worth of this toward healing your friend, and you can all work off the rest."

Both of us nodded. I could physically feel Solitaire fighting the instinct of every cell in his body to behead and eat the magus while screaming about socialized healthcare but, mercifully, my friend kept himself restrained. This time.

A tremble rippled through me as I remembered what he'd done to the bandit, and then the magus was turning back to Cádo, eyes locked on him, mumbling words to himself, as if we weren't there at all. Neither of us could resist watching.

Magic, at least this world's magic, was nothing new to us. We'd designed it for fuck's sake. We knew how sorcerers could instinctively command something they saw as an element, we knew how wizards could learn the "nouns" and "verbs" that made up reality to twist it in particular directions. We'd never *seen* it, though.

This wasn't some exposition-dump on paper. It was tangible, real, authentic magic. The arcane happening right before our eyes. There wasn't a thing in the world that could've prepared us for it, so yeah, you can be damned sure we stayed and watched while Corvan's hands started to glow and the air around him smelled of ozone.

Healing incantations we recognized—reknitting flesh back together, purging bacteria from places it didn't belong. Even the magus probably didn't understand half of what he was actually doing. The room trembled slightly while it all happened, the power at work enough to bleed out into other, more tangible, forms of energy. And Cádo convulsed.

Now, in hindsight, had we known that we'd be accidentally creating or influencing a world filled with actual people, we probably wouldn't have made magical healing so agonizingly painful.

But we hadn't *known*. How could we?! Do you ever catch your idle imaginings and stop yourself from accidentally manifesting an asteroid in some world you don't even know exists? No, of course not, because that would be stupid. So, we maintain that what happened next was completely not our fault, and just a horrible accident.

It still screwed us to watch, though.

Cádo was the strongest man either of us knew, and here he was thrashing around, moaning like some tortured rat. Corvan snarled at the sight, glancing at the two of us irritably.

"He's freakishly strong," the magus snapped. "Hold him down."

We hesitated, almost argued, then did what he said. It was for Cádo's own good.

Mind you, holding down an Olympic athlete is actually quite difficult. Solitaire did it easily enough, big bastard that he was. He'd also inherited some wiry, rat-like musculature from his family that made him bizarrely strong for his build. I'd inherited wiry muscles, but no uncommon pound-for-pound strength. Even one-armed, even with his ribs broken, Cádo nearly sent me flying more than once.

As the healing dragged on, we tired, and Cádo seemed inexhaustible. The strain was getting worse, his adrenaline-fueled convulsions building stronger, before at last, they started to die down. The magus sighed.

"Not reforming bone anymore," he breathed. "Now I'm just repairing the flesh around it. We're almost done."

Sure enough, it was all over a minute later. We were panting, gasping, aching across half our bodies, and standing with hair plastered to our scalps in sweat. But Cádo had a new color to his cheeks—apparently an indicator that white people were no longer dying—and his inhalations were finally coming strong and unbroken.

We'd expected that. What took us by surprise, though, was when this glorious bull of a bastard actually opened his eyes, looked around, and sat up not ten seconds later. Even the magus was stunned.

"So," Cádo began, throat croaking and scraping from days of disuse. "Did I miss anything important?"

CHAPTER EIGHT

Cádo's POV: Day 8

We were poor, in debt, and I think that wizard had missed a spot in my spine, because it hurt every time I tried to sit down. All in all, it could be worse. In fact, it had been, several days earlier.

Kenny and Bernard—Shango and Solitaire, as I'd spent several hours practicing—were both looking more than a little ragged, but at least they'd eaten recently. I only had that luxury when they took me to the church for our charity meal. It was there that we discussed what had happened, and what we'd do next.

I'd known, dimly, that something was wrong with me; even delirious and suffering from an IKEA home-assembly ribcage it had been obvious. The moment I'd woken up with a fresh brain, I'd figured out I was unconscious before. That and the memory of fighting a bear with no more than rocks and a can-do attitude meant that it wasn't hard to figure out what had happened.

Solitaire and Shango's story, though, was new to me. I hadn't even been there for it, of course. I had to keep myself from crying when they shared it.

We were friends, best friends even. We'd been there for each other during some of the worst times of our old world, but clearly the worst of Earth was a different test altogether than what this new land had thrown at us so far. Hearing what they'd done, hearing how they'd killed . . . It was the steel my spine needed.

"So, we're hobos now," Bernard—Solitaire—concluded.

I nodded, grunted, and continued eating my stale bread and soup.

He and Shango stared at me.

"You . . . seem to be taking this fairly well," Shango noted, and it occurred to me that perhaps I should've been more expressive.

I shrugged. "I just had my rib cage turned into a jigsaw puzzle by a bear, then reassembled by a wizard. And I think a piece is still lodged in my asshole. Give me some time, and I'll see if I can muster a nice, big scream of horror for you. For now . . . I don't know, man, work in the morning isn't even the second worst piece of news I've had this week."

That earned a considering look from Shango and a grin from Solitaire, who slapped me on the shoulder.

"Right you are!" the Scouser laughed. "That's just the kind of spirit that'll keep us from starving to death!" He seemed oddly pleased. Not just about me either. As if he were growing happier, rather than more fearful, as our situation worsened. There was something deeply *consistent* about his reaction, but I was too hungry and miserable to bother articulating it.

Shango didn't join his laughter, frown lines deepening into trenches across his face. "That's not a small ask, though," he noted. "How do we even do that? We were almost killed by some random wildlife."

I cut in, then, sensing that my friends were about to start another of their classic bickering sessions. "You guys do have a spear, yeah?"

They eyed me, nodded, and I smiled.

"Well then, we'll be fine. I can kill a bear with a spear."

Now, being truthful, I actually wasn't sure I could at all. But, I figured we needed confidence right now, and from what I'd been told, Solitaire and Shango had just watched me nearly out-wrestle them both at once while unconscious. True to my guess, they seemed a bit lifted up by the knowledge.

"Alright," Solitaire continued, "let's see if we can't find some work."

Redacle had been a gaming setting before a novel one, made for tabletop RPGs we used to play together, and as an inheritance of that beginning, it was absurdly, ridiculously filled with things that needed killing. Most towns had a missive board, and Jhigral was no exception, and most missive boards were packed with potential work. Bandits, like the ones my friends had run into, but also magical creatures.

Goblins multiplying in the shadows and stealing crops, magical contaminants driving animals mad—which, thinking about it, might have been what caused that bear attack—and however many other potential sources of danger. Or, if you were in need of it, sources of money.

One needed only to look and read.

We couldn't read. Fuck.

It took us a few moments of staring to find that much out, but there was no denying it. Whatever force translated every word we heard, it wasn't doing it for the written passages. In this world, we were illiterate. Most adventurers hired a clerk to follow them around and resolve that issue, but we couldn't afford to hire shit. Nobody would give the weird, foreign giants the time of day, and we had no money to provide any real incentive for them to change their minds.

And we were getting hungrier by the hour, which meant a delay wasn't on the table. Swallowing our annoyance, we set off to go into the issue blind.

Well, not quite yet. Solitaire and Shango insisted on making a stop at a weird little shop—a dentist from what I could tell. They spent a while inside, and when they came out, they had a few coins to their name. Six silver and twenty-one coppers, enough for another spear. Or a bow and some arrows.

It was a no-brainer—we picked the range weapon. Apparently, that had been the one thing the others hadn't looted from the bandits, having accidentally broken it in the fighting.

With me no longer dying horribly from bear combat, we were able to take our time scanning the land as we left. Jhigral seemed to be a northern town, surrounded in snow as far as the eye could see—apparently, we'd arrived just in time for winter.

The majority of its neighboring landscape was woodland, but it was also a coastal town, quite close to the ocean on the interior of a great bay. Cave systems were known to run through the ground beneath it, but that was no surprise. Cave systems ran underground everywhere in Redacle. Tabletop game setting, remember? Can't go dungeon crawling without crawlable dungeons. Particularly not dark ones, which magnetically attract suitably horrible creatures to dwell within.

Now here was our dilemma: Roleplaying games had a particular logic to them. You kill something big, you get an expensive, valuable reward. Cool. But we weren't sure how much of this version of Redacle had been "randomly generated" around us. Our world-building was fairly in-depth, but it was most likely that any given creature we encountered was something none of us had coined. Solitaire and Shango had already filled me in about their theory regarding that fact. If true, it meant we'd be dealing with unknowns, and they might not necessarily give us much reward.

Even if they did, they might be as tough as that bear, or as tough as ten of that bear. There were creatures in our original world-building capable of smashing houses to splinters and throwing men hard enough for them to burst on impact, and durable enough to have entire squads of modern soldiers unloading into them and barely even notice. We had no guarantee that any given fight we picked would end in our favor.

So, it was a tough decision, picking where to head next, and we made it slowly and agonizingly. We'd asked around for the more dangerous spots to avoid, of course, and while we were already thinking, we figured we'd keep on asking. Around twenty minutes of this led to us getting the information that finally settled us into a particular course. For better or for worse.

Trolls were horrible, evil bastard things. They were about eight feet tall on the lower end, but hunched enough to appear closer to six, and muscled like a chimpanzee on bull testosterone. Their fingers ended in talons, not nails, and they were omnivorous in the same way bears were. Except, unlike bears, their favorite food was fucking bear. If we'd encountered a troll on our second night, I had no doubt that we'd all be dead men, and probably without doing much to even bother it first.

And they were a semi-common sight in the region, with one in particular causing trouble for some local traders by attacking the road to Wolney.

We could've ignored it. If I'm being honest, we even *should* have ignored it, but we didn't because we were still two full gold in debt, and troll bone marrow sold to apothecaries for about double its weight in silver. Which made the matter just tempting enough that we were actually considering fighting the thing.

It was the worst kind of decision, our hands pressed into a fight we were sorely outclassed and underprepared for, with no choice at all due to our current circumstance. And we might've suffered a disaster for it if Shango hadn't thought to bring up his menu again.

"We've levelled up!" he yelled—practically screamed, really. It made me jump, and Solitaire almost put a knife through him as we stared at our friend. Then his words clicked, and we were drilling him for details.

CHAPTER NINE

Shango's POV: Day 8

[Appraisal]
Class: Revolutionary
Level: 2
Condition: Worn
Modifiers: None
**Statistics: Strength 6 (5), Speed 6, Dexterity 8 (7), Stamina 5 (3),
Toughness 6, Alertness 8, Charisma 3 (2), Intelligence 10**
Inventory: Jeans, T-shirt, flick knife, rocks (x5), lump hammer
Class Abilities: Detect Element I

Solitaire's stat spread was a familiar sight by now. I'd begun using him as my go-to for comparison almost on instinct. What caught my eye this time, though, was the latest addition near the top of the screen in my mind's eye. A single line, small enough that I nearly missed it. And vital enough that it changed everything.

Level two.

My heart raced, and I started scrutinizing the screen more, looking for any other differences. I found one quickly.

Current Experience Points: 83/110
Unspent Skillpoints: 1

I steadied myself before the excitement could grow too much, turning to Solitaire and barking the information out at him so quickly that I wasn't sure anyone but he could have followed. He nodded, eyes hard, grinning in anticipation.

"So we can level," he said, giving voice to the fact left him laughing almost as hard as I was, and soon Cádo was joining in.

I was a bit more focused than either of them. Looking inward now, I brought up my own stats.

[Appraisal]
Class: Emperor
Level: 2
Condition: Worn
Modifiers: None
Statistics: Strength 5 (4), Speed 5, Dexterity 6 (5), Stamina 5 (4), Toughness 5, Alertness 8, Charisma 9 (8), Intelligence 9
Inventory: Jeans, shirt, jacket, dagger
Class Abilities: Appraisal I

I squinted, looking longer, and sure enough;

Current Experience Points: 83/110
Unspent Skillpoints: 1

The same unspent experience as Solitaire. Interesting. I was fairly sure I hadn't contributed as much as he did to our bandit killing, so did that mean we were levelling through some other means? Well, yeah, we must've been. I checked right after that, and we'd achieved no experience at all. But what?

Getting the sap and having Cádo healed was the only other thing that struck me as a possible source. I decided to check Cádo to verify.

[Appraisal]
Class: Dragonknight
Level: 1
Condition: Fine
Modifiers: None
Statistics: Strength 8, Speed 8, Dexterity 8, Stamina 9, Toughness 7, Alertness 8, Charisma 6, Intelligence 5
Inventory: Jeans, flannel shirt, spear
Class Abilities: Beloved I

That more or less confirmed it. We received experience by completing . . . Fuck, I suppose they'd be called *quests*. Cádo had been too busy bleeding to death to help with the first one, so he hadn't gotten any experience from it.

It was annoying. He was, by far, the deadliest among us. Seeing him level up and become even more so would've given us a lot of reassurance. But we still had something to show for it.

"Unspent skillpoints," I called out. "Any idea what that might be?"

We didn't take long to draw the obvious conclusion, but what could I spend them on? More particularly, how exactly could they be spent?

I decided to try mine first. My appraisal would just make it easier to see the effects. It took a lot of fucking around before I finally stumbled onto the solution.

There was something in me, a weight of experience and knowledge, a big bundle of . . . change. The result of our trek for the sap.

Every decision alters a person. Every event leaves them a tiny bit different from before, and I meditated on that difference right now, comparing who I was to how I'd been before venturing out to save Cádo. It was like doing cocaine, if the cocaine was on cocaine.

There's no way to put what I felt next into words. I'm sorry, there just isn't. You'd need to feel it. To try, at least, it was like . . . like being aware of the tissues in your bones, the fibers in your muscles. Can you imagine that? Feeling all of them at once, on the *cellular level*. And being able to control them, choosing which ones to . . . to multiply, to grow.

My own body was mine to command, more or less. Flooded with an ethereal power I couldn't even name, all I had to do was decide where I wanted to put it.

Admittedly, the process might have been just a shade less intuitive, were it not for the fact that the words **[Skillpoint Expenditure in progress. Select Stat to increase.]** kept flashing in front of my mind's eye. Still, I'm sure my humongous, nine intelligence brain would've figured it all out regardless.

The only question now was what to actually spend it on. That question lasted about half a second before I chose intelligence.

And found no result. Weird. I tried again. Nothing. So I experimented, thought of what my next choice would be.

Toughness. I didn't want to die, I didn't want to end up like Cádo had, and I didn't want to find myself crippled for life. So toughness, for survivability. For fortune.

The thought was only idle in my head for an instant before I felt the energy coalescing, infusing me . . . changing me. Then it was gone. No, not gone, used up. *Spent.*

I moved a bit, testing my body, and finding no difference. Pulling up my character sheet again, I examined it.

[Appraisal]
Class: Emperor
Level: 2

Condition: Worn
Modifiers: +1 Toughness
Statistics: Strength 5 (4), Speed 5, Dexterity 6 (5), Stamina 5 (4),
Toughness 6, Alertness 8, Charisma 9 (8), Intelligence 9
Inventory: Jeans, shirt, jacket, dagger
Class Abilities: Appraisal I

So, my toughness had increased. Just to be sure, I checked the secondary section, and sure enough my unspent skillpoints were at zero.

But I didn't feel any different. I winced. This demanded experimentation.

"Solitaire, can you punch me—"

He did, instantly, flooring me and making me see stars as blood ran down my nearly flattened nose. I got up, swearing, seeing his stupid face grinning through a curtain of tears.

"I didn't break it," he informed me, as if that fact would disarm my criticism. I spat blood out and stood.

Then the humor died. Solitaire had always done stuff like this, had always been . . . an asshole. And all of that felt different, now that I'd seen what he'd done to save Cádo. Impishness came across differently, in a man from hell.

Nose still bleeding, I felt it for damage. It wasn't broken, at least. Solitaire had been right about that, but I still glared up at him.

"Put a point into toughness?" he asked.

Fuck him for punching me, and fuck him for being this quick even dealing with concepts only I could see.

"I did, but I didn't really notice much difference there, did you?"

Solitaire shrugged. "Your nose didn't feel particularly hard, but I didn't hit it that hard either, so . . ."

Stupid fucking idea. He should've hit me just for thinking of it. I considered the change. If I'd wasted a skillpoint, I'd be very annoyed, and quite possibly dead, but I didn't know for sure it *had* been wasted. What was my strength stat? Five, normally. What was Cádo's? Eight. A three point difference, and Cádo couldn't exactly toss people around, however strong he was. So, individual skillpoints probably wouldn't be pushing us up entire rungs on the combative ladder.

I cursed. Shame I couldn't have spent it on some decent armor instead.

The three of us discussed matters a while longer, bouncing ideas around before we finally found ourselves satisfied that we probably weren't wrong about what we *thought* we knew. Probably. That meant it was Solitaire's turn to spend his skillpoint.

Oddly enough, he chose toughness as well, despite what he saw happen to me. I suppose it was understandable. If two more meant the difference between my strength and Cádo's, it'd leave us a lot hardier. Eventually at least.

And then we were done. No more errands, no more delays. No more excuses. There wasn't a thing holding us back except our own cowardice, and none of us could find justification to indulge in that any longer. Reluctantly, just about shitting ourselves all the while, we began our march out into the great beyond.

We must've been adjusting because the frost barely even registered anymore. Might be that having Cádo back was spoiling us, with all the extra timber and torches. Our target—Ghrizun Wood—was just a few miles from town, not even an hour's walk. That still left a lengthy journey for us, though. We were *modern*, used to luxuries like cars and planes, and we didn't cross countries often enough to be content just tolerating a stretch of boredom like that. So, of course, we chatted.

Truth be told, there was surprisingly little to actually chat *about*. None of us were very well caught up with any of the shows we'd been watching, nor did we have any funny highlights from gaming sessions. Really, the Wi-Fi in Redacle would've made such hobbies untenable, let alone the giant hairy monsters trying to chew our heads off.

One thing did demand conversation, though. Cádo's name. He'd been unconscious when Solitaire and I picked our new ones. Thinking about it, we were lucky he hadn't called either of us by them and given the game away before he knew. It was bad enough we'd gone this long without bringing it up to him; uncharacteristically sloppy really. We were sure to catch him up quickly once the topic occurred to us, but he took his time in finally choosing one.

"Beam," he decided. It was absolutely perfect—Solitaire and I both had stupid ones as well.

Something was changing about us now. We'd picked new names, set a goal, had a direction and an aim, and we'd actually gotten our feet beneath us. An idiot could've told us how weak we still were, and yet for the first time in a long time, I felt like we had some sort of chance. Perhaps no more than five hobos, instead of three, but that was still up from where we'd started.

I eyed Solitaire as I thought about it. New names, new goals, and things I'd never seen in my friends rearing their ugly heads. Maybe we would survive what was awaiting for us further on in the woods, but something told me this world would leave its mark one way or another.

I could only hope it wasn't as deep a brand as I feared. There'd already been enough drawn out of my friends, and I wasn't sure what it'd do to me seeing more.

CHAPTER TEN

Solitaire's POV: Day 9

Shango was mad at me. No, no he wasn't. He'd been mad at me when I hit him. What he was now had evolved from mere rage and crystallized into something far more permanent. Disgust.

The smug bastard probably thought he was hiding it, as if I couldn't *smell* the revulsion on him. All those furtive little glances, the long, silent ponderings. The guilt and flashed glances at my weapon—glancing for what, exactly? Did he think I'd hurt *him*? He was a fucking idiot if he did, however often we gave each other licks, but what other reason could he have?

Well, obviously he was scared I'd hurt someone else. Which I would, if they threatened me or my friends. Action is no less inherently forgivable than inaction. Intention is nothing compared to results. Killing people by sticking up the road to life-saving medicine left them just as dead as smashing their head in with a hammer. So what I did to that bandit was fine; it was moral. It was the diffusing of a land-mine. I'd done a humanitarian act and was owed thanks, not derision, for the results.

But Shango had never seen things that way. Nobody had, except me, apparently. And I'd known that when I did the guy in. I probably would've kept him alive, if I hadn't needed those teeth. Ifs, woulds, coulds.

He was dead now, and my pocket held a nice chunk of silver we'd gotten for selling all his and his friends' pearly whites—or cheesy yellows, as it were—and if the bow slung over my shoulder gave us odds even one percent better, it was worth killing fifty of that bastard.

But Shango had never seen things that way. I resisted the urge to swear as I glanced at him. This wasn't a rift that would close soon.

But Cádo's wound hadn't been one that would heal ever. The choice was clear, and I didn't regret it.

Which was, of course, why I had to tell myself as much a dozen times. Thank you, brain. Cunt.

The trees were properly white now, snow having thickened even more in the week or so since winter started. If we'd put our minds to it, igloo construction would've been either a lot easier or a lot harder. I supposed we'd find out which the next time we had cause to stray from town for a night or more.

It meant something else, too. Tracks were visible as anything in the world, but brief as well. It took maybe half a day for snowfall to cover even a deep footprint, and less for something small and light like a rabbit. Fortunately, we were after a *troll*, which gave us a bit more wiggle room.

What we did not have, though, was a tangible idea of what we were looking for. Oh, we all had a vivid picture of trolls themselves. Our publishers even had official art drawn up of the things. We hadn't spent long describing their feet, though, and even I couldn't recall any art depicting them. So we couldn't guess what their tracks might look like. It'd be just our luck to follow what we thought was a sure trail, only to wander into some dragon's den.

We trudged on all the same, determined—or, rather, opposed to getting our legs broken by a wizard—enough that the bite of the air didn't do much at all to slow our progress through the woods. With six eyes peeled, it didn't take as long as it might have for us to stumble onto something worth following. Big, dinnerplate-wide gouges in the snow left by what looked like big hands.

I'd always pictured and written giant chimps, when it came to troll body types, which made that a fairly promising sign. A giant chimp knuckling the ground as it moved might leave gouges like that, in snow at least. We went after it.

Hm, a very promising sign. More evidence that the blanks in our worldbuilding would be filled in by the agreements we'd reach if we *had* discussed the missing elements. I had to keep myself from entertaining the thought any longer. Speculation was a luxury enjoyed by people who weren't about to fight Prince Kong with less weaponry than the average biker gang.

Another half hour came and went before much of anything at all happened. We almost missed the noise at first—that's how loud the wind was. A low, snarling grunt cutting over the sound of air bouncing off tree trunks. Instantly, we were on edge, ducking low, readying weapons, talking in careful, whispered tones.

Something big was ahead, possibly hungry, and definitely not the sort of enemy we'd enjoy fighting.

But we'd heard it, and it very likely hadn't heard us, which meant a fight was optional.

That was good. That was very fucking good.

Our preparation was quickly decided and quickly executed. I took the bow, a big long thing almost as tall as this world's men, and climbed a tree. We had five arrows, each close to a yard from ass to nose, and I could only hope they'd be enough. Because my friends were still on the ground twenty feet below me.

Beam took the front, spear ready, trembling either from the shivers or the fear of fighting a monster. Shango was in back, knives out and stomach about one "boo" away from emptying itself down his leg, and now all that was left for us to let everything kick off.

It did, with a great big howl.

Olympians are insane, really. Beam had the lung capacity of a whale, and he used all of it in shouting over the wind, screaming hoarse and jagged like a bull being fisted.

A few moments of silence followed, then the sound of something big and angry charging our way. The only warning we'd get.

The troll wasn't that big, really. It was only a head taller than a world-class powerlifter; it was *only* as muscular as a chimpanzee, and it was only coming at us at a leisurely pace of thirty fucking miles per hour. Beam was ready, but I was in range before him, letting an arrow go and resisting the urge to shout a swear after it.

Mum always did like archery and bow making. In her words, it was safer than guns—in that the government would have less grounds to label her a terrorist if she was proven to have created them. I wasn't gonna win any awards, but I was a decent shot. And the one advantage of big enemies was big targets.

The arrow hit its chest, just above the nipple, and went bouncing off. I swore, carefully fished out another, fired by the time the troll had managed another forty feet. Closer now, much closer, which meant a sharper angle and a faster arrow. This one stuck in, earning a roar of pain and slowing the monster somewhat. It was within a few paces of Beam when the third arrow caught its shoulder.

My friend might've died if not for that, the enemy smashing into him like a battering ram, finishing what the bear started. Instead the troll's sprint turned into a stagger, and Beam's spear found a nice new home in its ribcage. We all laughed at the sight, grinning while eight inches of steel disappeared into the fucker. Then it backhanded the Olympian clean off his feet, and we started swearing again.

I can't imagine what Shango was thinking. A big, grey-skinned animal hunched over on two legs, with mangy flesh covered in scars, four eyes and a jaw shaped halfway between an ape and a dog, slapping an Olympian several feet back right in front of him, leaving him the only enemy within killing range. Most people would've freaked out, but not him. He just went calm and rational.

The troll came in like a blur, and Shango shifted his grip on one knife, holding blade-first, cocking an arm back and throwing. His technique was dogshit, luck was absurd, and the tip caught his target right in the stomach. The troll screamed, turning away in shock, giving Shango just enough time to dive out of the way while the troll cleared the last ten feet.

That was around the time arrow number four caught its back, and I was dropping down while I readied the last of my ammunition.

Falling twenty feet without injury isn't easy, but it's doable, depending on the circumstances. It helps if you're athletic and helps more if you're used to it. It helps a *lot* more if you're tall and lithe because big people have thick bones, and thin ones have less mass.

What really helps is falling through eighteen inches of soft snow before you hit the ground, though. That was what let me keep my balance and shrug the drop off with nothing more than bent knees, and that's why the final arrow found its mark only seconds after the one before it. The troll was spinning at me, shrieking, and Shango did the exact right thing as he closed in to slash his remaining blade along its arm.

Again, the troll was turning, too fucking stupid to realize that every time it did, it just gave us another opening by slowing its killing momentum. I started sprinting, closed in, flick knife drawn, teeth gritted, and panic high as I realized I'd be too slow. Then Beam smashed into it from the side.

It came as a surprise, even to me.

To clarify, I do know I'm mental. I'd have to be catatonic not to, but there are different grades of crazy. Mine is good for self-preservation, for caution, for contingencies. The blend of insanity I experience, however you want to describe it, is most fucking certainly not the kind that would have me charging dick-first at something ten times stronger than a human.

Well, it was probably only five times stronger than Beam, and he was lucky enough to have been born with that exact mania. He hit it like a cavalry charge, shoulder first and with all his momentum braced perfectly into a last-second jump. It succeeded in sending the troll stumbling, at the cost of knocking my friend flat again, but this time he was ready. Rolling as he landed, jumping back up to his feet, and turning into a fucking roundhouse kick before any of us could even realize what he was doing.

Shinbone met skull with a fairly satisfying crunch, and the troll looked rather confused as it dropped to one knee. More confused than hurt, sadly, but that was where I came in.

I circled it instead of charging head on, despite the sight of it rising to tear my friend apart. I'm not the charging-into-danger sort, like I said. I always prefer to think things through, take my time, prepare, consider, then act.

Being honest, it didn't actually take much considering to decide what I'd do next. I closed in, then jumped just as Beam had, timing my leap to bring my heels against the troll's back, knees bending to fall *into* it with the last of my forward momentum, taking the instant between stopping and falling to grab both the arrows still jutting into its back, then kicking off like a springboard.

Arrow removal is difficult, done properly. Lots of careful cutting around the barb, slow easing, gently guiding it out to avoid it ripping anything free upon exit. I didn't do that as I launched myself away, one shaft gripped in each hand. Between the two barbed points on each end, I probably took about a pound of meat with them, and a giggle escaped me at the sound coming from Mister Troll when my back hit the snow.

This was the part of my plan I hated most—faith. I wasn't Beam. I couldn't dance to my feet and run before the thing was on me, which left me hanging out to dry, making a really big wish that he would do something stupid in time to save me.

And he did.

I heard snarling, screaming, then gagging. I hurried to my feet just in time to witness Beam dragging the troll back into a fucking choke hold. I took one look at its talons and figured out all on my own how many seconds that maneuver would keep working, and then I sprinted forward. Shango was beside me, suddenly, and we split up again to approach the troll from different angles.

It was bleeding, crimson drizzling from the stomach, oozing from its other three arrow wounds and *gushing* from the new spots on its back where I'd yanked a pair of meatballs out. The snow around it was sticky and red with what looked like two, even three liters of blood. But the flow was slowing down now, and a creature this size probably had a dozen still left in it.

What was a category two hemorrhage again? Twenty percent blood loss, if I recalled correctly—if; God, I'm so humble—which meant that it would be slowing and weakening. But not as much as I'd like.

So, best to dry it out a bit more then. I went for the neck.

Beam lunged back from a swipe, and I leapt in under it. Shango distracted the fucker by hacking at its elbow from one side, and the moment he took its attention was enough for me to close in and go to skewer its carotid.

Except this was a *troll*, not a human. Its skin was centimeter-thick armor, its flesh made tougher by the same magic that was partially responsible for its inhuman strength. I would've opened all the big veins up nice and proper if I'd poked a human, but against this thing they held.

Which turned my killing blow into a pissing-it-off blow. I tried to get out of arm's reach an instant later, but I was too slow.

The talons came around, and this time they tore deep into my arm, and I was launched.

CHAPTER ELEVEN

Beam's POV: Day 9

Solitaire was lying still, blood fountaining from his arm, body twitching with pain, strength leaving him. He was hurt, and it was my fault.

It was my fault because I'd gotten myself hurt in the first place, and left us trapped in debt. It was my fault because I'd been too slow, too weak, and too fragile to fight a stupid animal on my own. It was my fault because, for all my years of training, I'd never learned how to kill something, only to win matches.

The animal was recovering, and everything seemed to be moving in slow motion now. Snowflakes descending as if they were falling through syrup, the wind's howls long and drawn out like a wolf's cry, pain blossoming across every inch of me like arctic fire.

I stood there, staring, regretting, silently apologizing. And then the troll took its first step toward my friend. There was no thought left to be had after that, only action.

Sprinting took me to it in moments. My eyes caught it swinging around, trying to slash at my chest long before the motion was complete. I dug my heels in, using the thick snow to halt myself, the jagged talons coming just short of me. The troll was off-balance now. All its weight had been behind that swing, and it hadn't a human's motor skills or knowledge of momentum to mitigate torque. I'd judged the spacing and time perfectly. This was my chance.

My last kick had worked nicely, so I threw another one, this time aiming low. Aiming perfectly. My shin caught the creature right in its belly, crashing into the back of Shango's still-jutting knife, driving it inches deeper inside. A roar of pain and a stream of crimson told me it was a success.

I struck before the fucker could recover, jumping and landing a dropkick into its chest while it was already stumbling away. I'd never have tried the move against a human, for one very vital reason. I didn't want to kill a person, and punting someone backward wasn't the sort of move that let you avoid such risks. Redacle had educated me on what a mistake that mindset had been.

The troll fell, on its back now, and Shango was right beside me while we stomped and kicked at its skull. Blood poured from it, slowing its moves by the moment, but it managed to climb in spite of us. Like an adult being wailed on by little kids. Solitaire was fond of saying that even kids could kill an adult; they just needed a bit of guts and something pointy.

"The knife!" I screamed at Shango. "Snatch the knife up."

Bless him, he was smarter than me. I might've been left confused about which one, panicking, adrenaline shattering my thoughts. He realized instantly that Solitaire had landed a stab before going down and dropping his weapon. Without a word, Shango lunged for the fallen blade while I kept kicking away at the thing. And then it was up and pouncing at me, but slowed by its weakness and easily sidestepped. My elbow came down on that magic spot in the back of its neck, the one everyone's taught never to go for in sparring, the one that'll get you kicked out of an MMA circuit. I felt the connection with a satisfied snarl, and watched the troll fall again.

Then Shango hit it.

He wasn't a strong man, nor a heavy one, but he was moving at a full sprint, and he did the smart thing—he braced the knife with the handle against his own body. All of his momentum was behind that knife, and the full length of the blade was stuck into the troll before Shango bounced off upon impact.

Another roar, another distraction as it thrashed in the snow, trying to stand and stave off this unseen attacker at the same time. I was about to hit it again when I saw how much more blood was bubbling out, and then thought better of it.

The troll took a long time to die, but it managed to do so eventually. Veins emptying themselves out into the ground, body weakening, slowing, then stop- ping. Shango and I took a moment longer to examine its corpse before we were confident about not being jumped again.

Then our focus turned immediately to Solitaire.

He wasn't as hurt as I'd been a few days ago, at least judging by his continued consciousness. One of his arms had been shredded, talons carving deep into him like meat cleavers, but the wounds, although viciously severe, had already been bound by some scraps of cloth he'd pocketed from the bandits. That might've been the only reason he was able to even look clearly at us while we approached.

"How are you holding up?" I asked, kneeling down beside him. Solitaire answered by swearing, slurring, and spitting into the snow. We took that as an indicator of urgency.

Initially, the plan had been to head back to Jhigral with the troll's corpse behind us, me dragging it all the while, the other two taking turns to pull alongside me so they could rest between sessions. We estimated it would've perhaps tripled our travel time to do so.

With Solitaire out of commission, though, he was more than just unable to help. This added extra weight that we needed to move. We'd left early enough in the day, but it was already closer to evening than noon by the time we caught sight of the first houses again.

That time left room for a lot to happen, and Solitaire didn't handle it well. His condition worsened, restlessness increasing, strength fading. Early on he'd been walking alongside us, then behind. Around the halfway mark we'd forced him to lie on the troll and let us drag him. It slowed us less to pull him as weight than it did to match his shambling pace with just a troll pulled at our backs. That's how weak he'd gotten, and things hadn't improved by the time we arrived.

He was conscious, and that's about all that could be said of him. Every few dozen steps I tortured myself with another glance back at him, and the trail of flecked blood clinging to the snow behind us.

Arrival to town couldn't come soon enough, and we made a beeline for the magus. Corvan received us reluctantly, but his eyes nearly bulged at the sight of the creature we had with us, face pale and awed.

"A . . . troll," he noted, dully. "You . . . killed it? The three of you?"

Shango and I had agreed to let him do the talking, and yet even Shango had a note of smugness in his voice when he replied. "It caught us by surprise," he lied. "Took some quick thinking on our part to take it down, but we managed in the end. How much are they worth exactly?"

Corvan eyed the creature, then turned back with a sorry smile.

"Alas, despite their ferocity, troll corpses are not worth much as a rule. I could take it off your hands for . . . perhaps a few silver off your debt. They are of some alchemical value."

"This corpse is worth fifty silver, easily," Shango countered evenly. It was only then I realized that he'd known the entire time, but the reason for his lie still escaped me. Corvan's face was beet red at having been called out.

"Forty," he snapped. "I'm the only magus who'll have use for it in this town, and we both know it."

Shango took a moment to weigh that, and in the end nodded in agreement.

"Forty it is," he sighed, gesturing to the corpse, then stiffening and carrying on. "We need treatment for Solitaire, too."

The magus snorted at that, smugness suddenly returning to his face with a vengeance.

"I can heal him," he said. "Of course arcane healing is difficult, and expensive. It'll be another . . . seventy silver for a wound like that."

Shango seemed like he was about to accept, face contorted in bitterness, then Solitaire spoke up. He'd been awake the entire time, not nearly as hurt as I had been only days ago. Limply lying against the troll, too wounded to move around or even spare enough energy for speech. He spoke now, though, his biting tongue cutting out with all the vigor it usually did. His carved-up arm might as well have been a paper cut.

"We don't need magical healing," he declared, wincing at the strain it took him to do that much. Both me and Shango eyed our friend as if he were insane, because he fucking was, but Solitaire only eyed us back defiantly.

"Your arm—" Shango tried, then halted as Solitaire's voice bludgeoned his own to one side and crushed it underfoot.

"My arm is badly hurt, but most of the issue is blood loss, which has already been stemmed. I'm not getting much worse, now anyway. All we need is disinfectant, proper stitching to make sure my condition doesn't plummet further, and I'll be fine in a few weeks."

Shango shot back quickly, affronted by our friend's stupidity, "A few weeks with you out of commission might get us killed."

Solitaire had a thoughtful look in his eye, glancing at the magus. "Can you give us a moment to speak?"

Corvan grinned, apparently already sure we'd be forking over the money for a magical healing session. "Be quick about it," the magus ordered, moving into the back room. The moment he was gone, Solitaire turned back to Shango.

"Quickly, pull that menu of yours up again. I have a sneaking suspicion there's been another change."

CHAPTER TWELVE

Shango's POV: Day 9
Current Wealth: 5 silver
Current Debt: 6 gold, 15 silver

[Appraisal]
Class: Emperor
Level: 3
Condition: Worn
Modifiers: +1 Toughness
Statistics: Strength 5 (4), Speed 5 (4), Dexterity 6 (5), Stamina 5 (4), Toughness 6, Alertness 8, Charisma 9, Intelligence 9
Inventory: Jeans, shirt, jacket, dagger
Class Abilities: Appraisal I
Current Experience Points: 73/120
Unspent Skillpoints: 1

It strained my eyes and my mind, but apparently I could look at unspent skillpoints and experience at the same time. That was useful.

Well, probably not actually, but it was just convenient enough to be worth the headache. And it confirmed that we'd benefitted from the troll-slaying. Probably? I shared my findings with the others.

Solitaire was the first to answer, battered though he still was.

"Do me," he demanded, eager enough that it drew a pained snarl from him. I hurried up, if only to keep the idiot from *oozing* everywhere in his excitement.

[Appraisal]
Class: Revolutionary

Level: 3
Condition: Critical
Modifiers: None
Statistics: Strength 6 (2), Speed 6 (2), Dexterity 8 (3), Stamina 5 (0), Toughness 6, Alertness 8 (5), Charisma 3 (2), Intelligence 10
Inventory: Jeans, T-shirt, flick knife, rocks (x5), dagger, bow
Class Abilities: Detect Element I
Current Experience Points: 73/120
Unspent Skillpoints: 1

"You've gained experience too." I grinned, then eyed Beam.

[Appraisal]
Class: Dragonknight
Level: 2
Condition: Fine
Modifiers: None
Statistics: Strength 8, Speed 8, Dexterity 8, Stamina 9, Toughness 7, Alertness 8, Charisma 6, Intelligence 5
Inventory: Jeans, flannel shirt, spear
Class Abilities: Beloved I
Current Experience Points: 0/110
Unspent Skillpoints: 1

"And so have you."

So we'd all gotten stronger, but why? The troll was worth a hundred points. Were the bandits just worth none? Did humans specifically not give us experience points? What was going on?

Solitaire, annoyingly, was the one to pose the most likely theory.

"It's *Vampire: the Masquerade*-style experience," he explained, awfully smug for a man oozing enough blood to fingerpaint.

I, not being a nerd, and even having had sex with women on occasion, was a bit confused.

"Explain," I demanded.

He did.

"We get experience for accomplishing our tasks, not for killing enemies. Surviving, saving Beam, dragging that troll back, etc. So we can only expect to receive power-ups as a reward for actually getting things done." He grinned. "It seems that what constitutes a task is a bit arbitrary, since we didn't get anything for making it to town, but this is still very good news."

I didn't need him to explain why. If we had a system like that, it could be damned flexible. For all we knew, we could gain experience and grow stronger by just making money and becoming landlords or something. We might not even need to risk our necks at all.

Then again, if we weren't marching out into the wild, we wouldn't get much benefit from becoming arrow-proof in the first place. Either way, it was a matter for later. At the moment we were still very, very killable, and sitting on unused skillpoints.

I focused, drawing on my experiences during the last mission—fuck, of course, it really was based on accomplished goals—and feeling it congeal in my mind. For the second time I tried to move it into intelligence, focusing more intently on *how* this time.

Neurons, I decided. They were the best predictor of intelligence in animals. Humans had sixteen billion in our cerebral cortex, chimpanzees around six. Dogs, a mere five hundred million. How many extras could I manage by leveling up?

Apparently none. The power simply refused to move in that direction, and I was left growling out my annoyance again.

"I can't make myself smarter," I spat, glancing at my friends. "Anybody have any ideas why?"

Solitaire had a look that told me he'd tried exactly the same thing, and met the same result.

"Maybe it just doesn't work for anyone?" he suggested, thinking now. "It makes sense. If one level-up is noticeable, what would we do with a dozen? A hundred?"

I considered that. How big was the difference between eight strength and five? Very. So what about eight intelligence vs. eighteen?

It was hard to imagine, considering the annoyingly noticeable gap already separating me and Solitaire, that a man with intelligence even approaching twenty would have much difficulty achieving anything. I wasn't sure whether we were talking steam or nuclear, but he'd definitely be changing this world's technology in less than a single lifespan, even with no more starting knowledge than everyone else. Doing all the things that a human would with sticks, stones, and twine when dropped into a society of apes. Perhaps a society of dogs.

Reluctantly, I turned my focus back to the other stats. Alright, so I couldn't figure out how to travel through time, talk people into suicide with a two-minute conversation, and deduce people's life stories at a glance. There were other means of survival, ones that might actually be more immediately helpful than just having a bigger brain. I put my skillpoint into toughness again.

The familiar sensation returned, skin tightening, muscles grinding, bones quivering as energy suffused every inch of me. By the time it was done, I'd been so overwhelmed that the sensation of change barely even registered. But I did notice it. I felt sturdier, more solid. And I checked my screen eagerly.

[Appraisal]
Class: Emperor
Level: 3
Condition: Worn
Modifiers: +2 Toughness
Statistics: Strength 5 (4), Speed 5 (4), Dexterity 6 (5), Stamina 5 (4), Toughness 7, Alertness 8, Charisma 9, Intelligence 9
Inventory: Jeans, shirt, jacket, dagger
Class Abilities: Appraisal I
Current Experience Points: 73/120
Unspent Skillpoints: 0

I snatched a glance at my friends, suddenly curious what they'd gone for.

[Appraisal]
Class: Revolutionary
Level: 3
Condition: Critical
Modifiers: +1 Speed, +1 Toughness
Statistics: Strength 6 (2), Speed 7 (3), Dexterity 8 (3), Stamina 5 (0), Toughness 7, Alertness 8 (5), Charisma 3 (2), Intelligence 10
Inventory: Jeans, T-shirt, flick knife, rocks (x5), dagger, bow
Class Abilities: Detect Element I
Current Experience Points: 73/120
Unspent Skillpoints: 0

Solitaire had chosen speed? Well, I could hardly blame him, actually. The option of sprinting away from that troll—or a few extra feet per second to our side steps—might've saved a certain someone half his arm.

Beam was next, though, and if anything I was more curious about his menu than Solitaire's. He'd not even spent a point before now.

[Appraisal]
Class: Dragonknight
Level: 2
Condition: Fine
Modifiers: +1 Strength
Statistics: Strength 9, Speed 8, Dexterity 8, Stamina 9, Toughness 7, Alertness 8, Charisma 6, Intelligence 5
Inventory: Jeans, flannel shirt, spear
Class Abilities: Beloved I

Current Experience points: 0/110
Unspent Skillpoints: 0

Strength? Well, actually, perhaps it made sense. It might not be possible to increase toughness high enough to make much difference in troll hunts for a while, and our ability to stab through their tough hides and musculature had been horribly ineffective.

I nearly caught myself regretting my own choice for a moment. Then I noticed something very interesting.

"Cá— Beam," I began, "We have the same toughness stat."

He eyed me, skeptical.

"You . . . sure?" was his answer. He was trying to be polite, obviously, but he might've saved himself the bother. I've been reliably informed that I have the build of a ten-year-old girl, while he, as he has established with exhaustive detail, is a literal Olympian.

And yet, the numbers didn't lie. Apparently, my sixty-kilogram ass—well, probably more like fifty-five now—had just as much damage-soaking ability as his eighty-kilo length of muscle and sinew.

Solitaire let out a laugh.

"Good!" he declared. "That's a helluva difference to be seeing already. I look forward to not dying when something farts on us one day."

We shared a grin, which lasted about a second, then evaporated as a certain fucker stepped back into the front of the shop.

"Time's up," Magus Corvan snapped, affixing all three of us with a sneering glare. "What'll it be, you getting healed or not?"

All eyes turned to me, and I resisted the sudden urge to start hitting my friends for leaving this decision squarely in *my* lap. I weighed the matter.

If we healed Solitaire magically, we'd only worsen our debt with this trip. On the other hand, it would leave us where we'd started—except with spent experience, slightly better stats, and more knowledge of troll hunting for our next outing.

Withholding our money, though, would leave us with an alleviated debt. Forty silver, out of six gold. Which would leave five gold and ten silver still unpaid. It wasn't a huge chunk, no matter how you sliced it. Barely even a chip in the great financial wall looming before us.

So, did I value a head start in reducing that, or did I value a chance for a do-over with better odds than before? Either one could screw us in both the short and long run.

For all I thought about it, the matter really didn't take that long to be decided. Solitaire's bowmanship had been a big part of what let us take the last troll down. We needed that, as well as whatever other skills he might save us with. In the end, we'd have to take another step into debt before we had enough space for a running start on our jump to freedom.

Yeah, that sounded logical. Hopefully it'd only take a few dozen repetitions before I had myself actually believing it.

"We'll take the healing." I said at last, hating every word that came out of my mouth. Solitaire eyed me, but he didn't glare. That was something at least.

The healing process was amazing, obviously. It was fucking magic. But the wonderful nature of the arcane was a bit less impressive when it was just serving to add another weight around your ankle. I found myself looking away halfway through, partially from bitterness, partially from apathy.

Solitaire was healthy and fine by the end of it. That was all that mattered. We said our goodbyes to Corvan, which consisted largely of a set of fuck yous, and took our leave from his shop, stepping outside just in time for the dark. And the cold.

A few more silver jingled away in our bag, and we spent them on a night in one of the town's cheaper, shittier inns. The walls were thin, and the windows were made of wood and open to the air. Every time a breeze hit the building's exterior, at least a tenth of it rolled in to torture us inside, and we spent the entire night shivering, coughing, and groaning in a corner, wrapped in our wafer-thin blankets and cursing the world.

People knew we were in pain. They knew we were suffering, that we needed help—help they had full power to give. And yet nobody lifted a damned finger, they all just . . . ignored us.

More than once, I glanced at Solitaire and found him staring out into nothing at all. Thinking, always thinking.

I did some thinking of my own, back to when he'd caved that bandit's head in and the hammer we'd long since abandoned. It would be far too risky carrying stolen goods through town, but I could still picture it vividly. Almost as vividly as the look on his face when he swung it. Not cold, like the ice around us. Hot. Molten, like the blood and brains he was spilling out into the snow.

Why had Solitaire killed him? For his teeth, and pragmatism, and our friend? I wasn't so sure. He'd always been angry, always been *furious*, even, at the world itself. At the humans—always humans, never people, in his words—who ignored all the evils he saw around us at every hour of the day.

Redacle was worse than our world had been in centuries, and its people were no less than you'd expect. If he got the chance, if he had the power, would he kill more of them?

I genuinely had no clue at all, and somehow I felt cold as we pressed our shoulders together for warmth, even despite the heat his body radiated.

We were what we experienced. I knew that better than anyone. And for the rest of that night, I was left wondering what the fuck this new world was doing to my friend.

CHAPTER THIRTEEN

Beam's POV: Day 10
Current Wealth: 4 silver, 20 copper
Current Debt: 6 gold, 44 silver

A full thirty copper pieces for one room for one night felt like a rip-off to me, but apparently we didn't have many options. Had I known the sort of night we would have, I might've been more insistent on sleeping elsewhere.

The room was better than our little snow mounds and fires, but only just. We emerged from it like butterflies from a cocoon, if the butterflies in question had mistakenly cocooned themselves inside one of those CIA sensory deprivation tanks Solitaire kept insisting Osama Bin Laden was being stored in. Stiff, achy, still cold and fatigued.

We had enough leftover coins for a meal at least. A dozen copper bought us some bread, soup, etc. The church turned us away, though. Apparently they'd received word that we could afford to be sleeping at inns and didn't take kindly to freeloaders. Which was fair enough, honestly.

We'd been full-on poverty stricken already, and it felt wrong to ask for charity reserved for people still trapped there. But it still screwed us a bit. Looked like keeping ourselves decently fed would be costing more than we'd been expecting.

I looked down, feeling my body and frowning at the withering that'd begun to take hold. I'd kept up my exercises ever since waking up, or at least as close as I could manage, but there was a lot more to being a modern-day Olympian than just putting in the hours of training. I needed protein, and a dozen other things I couldn't even remember the names of. We were barely even getting meat, let alone modern supplements.

My muscles were fading away, fast. I hadn't lost a point of strength yet, but I had a feeling that that was still coming. If I'd been conscious and exerting myself for the five days of starvation, maybe I'd already be dropping down the stat scale.

"What's our next move?" I asked the other two, speaking through a mouthful of stew. It had been expensive to get a bowl with actual meat in it, but I'd insisted. I needed to maintain as much of the head start modernity had given me as was possible.

Solitaire answered with certainty, Shango with doubt.

"Another troll," the former declared.

"I don't know," sighed the latter.

They eyed one another, with Solitaire making his case first.

"We're better equipped to take one on now, stronger, more experienced. Our one disadvantage is we have three arrows instead of five, but that's easily fixed."

I saw him wince at the mention of our arrows; he's the one who'd broken two, yanking them out of the creature's back. Probably saved our lives in the process, but still not great long term.

"We could buy more arrows," I suggested, and Solitaire chewed on it.

"What do you think, Shango?" he asked at last.

Shango hesitated. He'd been doing that a lot today, ever since we'd finally kicked back in our room. I could imagine why. The frantic scramble for food, warmth, and water of the last few days had kept me from really registering anything that'd happened to us, but settling down in our shitty inn had brought a few hours with nothing to do. So, I'd finally had the luxury of thought.

My experience in Redacle so far had been fairly limited. I missed home, missed my family and friends, but all of that was somehow dull and distant, even with long stretches of downtime. I'd still not asked about any particulars from when Solitaire and Shango had headed out to save me, but even I'd figured out they'd done something that Shango at least regretted in the process.

Maybe I'm just a coward, because I was too scared to ask what it was. All I did was watch and wait for him to swallow it all again before giving his answer.

"We go troll hunting," he sighed, throat tight with worry. We all shared a solemn nod, taking a moment to let the shock of finally deciding on a target wear off. Then we were walking.

Our first destination was a fletcher because we needed arrows. Ideally, we'd have just stocked up on fifty of the things and pelted all the trolls we encountered from afar until they were pincushions, but there were limits to strategies like that.

The first was that, apparently, medieval longbow arrows are actually surprisingly heavy. Each one was close to two ounces—sixty grams in non-freedom units—so even just the ten we ended up with weighed over a pound put together.

It wouldn't have been an unmanageable weight if he hadn't also been carrying them. All of us had pockets, but we didn't have *bags*, and those cost extra. A decent sack of burlap would've set us back the better part of a silver coin, and even that would only let us transport them *to* the fighting. A quiver, fitted for our freakishly tall frames? Well those were going for more than we had.

The woods greeted us as they usually did—by trying to kill us. We were used to it by now, though, and wrapped up nice and snug. One thing we'd decided *had* been worth our dwindling coins were some thick furs to cover ourselves with, and they were magic for keeping the heat in. Made me wonder why our modern clothes had been so shit.

Made me glad that we hadn't indulged in a bath, even as the reek of my friends slowly progressed along the spectrum of chemical warfare.

As it turned out, troll hunting was actually quite easy. Well, troll *finding* was at least. Bloody big noses, trolls, capable of finding you first from miles away. But brains smaller than a person's fist, so they made quite a bit of noise while they charged their way on over.

Just like last time, we had as much time to prepare as we could've hoped for. Except this time we'd rearranged our strategy a bit, and received a few advantages we hadn't before.

Shango went up the tree. We'd spent the better part of our journey practicing his marksmanship. Tossing logs into the air for him to shoot, trying to hit particular branches, that sort of thing. It probably tripled, even quadrupled, the length of our walk, but we'd set off just after dawn anyway, which gave us plenty of daylight to burn. And the result was that, after hours of practice, his marksmanship was almost not shit.

Well, okay, that's unfair. Sure he didn't have *my* coordination, but he had a particular way of judging things that I wasn't sure I'd have ever matched without my exhaustive training. It felt much more like the way Solitaire gauged things, almost mathematical. He wasn't going to be shooting any apples out of people's mouths, but he was absolute lightning when it came to hitting a moving target. Actually out-performed me when Solitaire was tossing the bigger logs up.

More importantly, his accuracy improved a lot faster than his general combat ability could have. And even though his frame was fairly unimpressive by Earth standards, he easily had the strength required to draw this world's standard longbows on account of not having sixteen ounces of lead dust in his blood where the protein should've been. So long as he didn't have to fire for more than a few minutes straight, he'd do fine.

Solitaire and I had a much less safe and cozy position. I was right where I'd been before, bringing up the front and tasked with not dying for as long as I could manage. Solitaire was helping me, and the hope was that between his bigger frame and natural meanness, he'd do a much better job of leaking the troll's strength away while I kept it distracted.

In truth, there were about a hundred things we'd rather have accounted for that none of us had, but the closest we came to actually doing anything about that was spending an extra few minutes hauling a thirty pound rock up into the tree with Shango.

According to Solitaire, we were looking at around five to eight hundred joules of kinetic energy if it was dropped on our enemy from that height. Neither of us knew what that meant, and we didn't need to figure out that having a brick the size of a toddler smacking the top of your skull would hurt. We called him a nerd and prepared for the fight.

The roar of a troll, the sound of something heavy smashing through thickets, snow being scraped and barged aside, then a big, gray streak closed in on us from far ahead. I readied myself for it to attack, spear high, feet planted, breathing steadied. It came at us just like the last one had, a hairy ball of screaming, vicious asshole zeroing in on me like a meteor.

Much like the last one, it started getting pelted with arrows before it closed in. The first missed, the second caught its chest, the third its shoulder. Then it was within spearing range. Shango wasn't the only one who'd received tips from Solitaire on our way here, and I put mine to use with earnest. Aiming low now, letting the spearpoint bite deep into the inner thigh of the troll and lunging to one side, I dropped my weapon instantly and rolled to avoid a collision.

It slowed to a stop, rounding on me just in time to leave its back exposed for Solitaire's attack. Both knives came down hard into the rear of one knee. Another arrow hit its side almost simultaneously.

With one flexed arm, Solitaire was sent flying away, and it was my turn to engage again. I closed in, knife out, teeth gritted and thrusting with a stab that broke the skin, but not much else. It flailed at me, the way I was learning trolls tended to do, and I ducked again. Solitaire was still getting to his feet, absolutely fucked by the impact he'd taken, even without the sharp bits to worsen it, which meant I was on my own for a few moments. Excellent. No chance of anyone else getting hurt again.

A claw swiped high, and I went low. The troll's giant body closed in, only for me to do likewise, pinning my knife outstretched between us and letting our combined momentum drive six inches of metal deep between a pair of ribs. I was knocked clean off my feet, thrown back and landed badly and rolled awkwardly. I came up quick enough. The troll was still reeling—the only thing that saved me, I guessed—with the knife stuck clean in its chest. I turned and sprinted in the other direction, opening enough distance for Shango's shot to be clean.

It was. Another arrow landed deep in the troll's leg. It roared in a way that had me cringing, like nails on a chalkboard, and I looked back to assess the damage.

Blood fountained from its thigh, arterial in volume and steaming in the cold air. I'd seen the other troll bleed more before it went down, but not by a lot. We were close to finishing this one. This was no time to retreat.

I stopped just in time for it to start, squared my feet and waited for its approach. Another arrow caught it in the chest meters from me, and I was jumping an instant before impact. Drop kicks are never a good idea. There's precious few exceptions to this general rule, and all are situational.

For one thing, you need to be close to Olympian in your physique to do them properly. I *was* an Olympian, normally, and I could only hope that I hadn't lost that much through starvation. The second requirement is that you need an enemy who you know for a fact is slower, dumber, and clumsier than you. One ape man, check. The final requirement is more just the sort of situation where, if the above two conditions are met, it might actually be worth doing. You need an enemy too tough to realistically hurt with any of your much-fucking-easier and safer kicks. Check.

The troll probably wouldn't have blinked at a haymaker from Mike Tyson, but my drop-kick was hard enough that it actually springboarded my body about a yard backward off the creature's sternum. Even that monster stumbled, as might a smaller tree, and it was given just enough pause for two things to happen.

Shango shot it again, and Solitaire knifed it clean in the neck from a dead sprint.

The arrow left a nice big opening, and the blade hit cleanly. Driven through skin, muscle, and fat by all the force of a grown man crossing twenty feet every second.

Truth be told, I'd never actually seen an artery get cut open before then. Solitaire had, going by his reaction, or lack thereof. It took about a second for any blood at all to be visible, and less than three for it to be soaking the troll's entire neck and shoulder. Within another ten, the creature seemed half painted, legs weakening beneath it as it dropped to lie face-down, slackening, weakening.

Maybe the last one had died to a nicked artery, actually. This one looked almost identical in how it moved before passing on. I felt just as queasy at the sight.

Shango came down from his tree with a lot more grace than Solitaire apparently had last time, climbing slow and steady, not simply jumping and hoping the snow let him live. We all circled the creature's body, but only after he'd put the rest of his arrows into it.

Dead, alright. Dead as a doornail. According to Solitaire it was small, as had the last one been, but as far as I was concerned, the thing couldn't have been small enough. Better an easier fight than a bigger reward. We'd get plenty of silver either way.

Just moments after we took its arms and started pulling, though, everything went wrong. The sound reached us, snapping undergrowth, pounding feet, and the flit of movement far ahead reached our eyes. But it was faster than before.

Another troll, hurtling toward us far more quickly than the last two. Too quickly for us to take our familiar positions before it burst out through the needle trees, revealing a body three feet higher and probably a ton heavier than the one lying dead at our feet.

"Fuck," Solitaire breathed, just an instant before it charged.

CHAPTER FOURTEEN

Shango's POV: Day 10
Current Wealth: 2 silver, 11 copper
Current Debt: 6 gold, 44 silver, 20 copper

In my admittedly limited experience fighting trolls, I had to say that, so far, I certainly preferred to do it from quite high up in a tree. Unfortunately, I was faced with a pair of issues in my current situation. The first, of course, was that there wasn't really much time to get into one. And the second was that even if I did . . . I wasn't entirely sure that the giant fucking animal staring me down at the moment couldn't have just jumped up and snatched me off the branch.

My mind raced, and I had a million thoughts in a split second. They led me to perhaps the only conclusion they could have, and I raised the bow to start putting arrows in the thing.

The troll was here, it had seen us, it was going to kill us. With a bit of luck, I'd hurt it enough that the stupid fucking animal bled or rotted to death after the fact.

I tightened my eyes as I tightened the bowstring, staring at the creature, seeing what I could glean about it. The menu came up quickly enough.

[Appraisal]
Species: Troll
Level: 15
Condition: Fine
Modifiers: None
Statistics: Strength 30, Speed 7, Dexterity 1, Stamina 5, Toughness 30, Alertness 3, Charisma —, Intelligence -5

That marked the first time I'd managed to bring my menu up in the heat of battle. Shame I was too busy worrying about having my head chewed off to feel any pride about the fact.

Thirty strength, thirty toughness. So we're fucked then?

I loosed an arrow anyway, almost as much out of curiosity as to what it'd do rather than any actual hope of hurting the thing. True to expectations, the barb—hastily torn from the dead troll's flesh—simply bounced off the larger one and went spinning out through the air with barely a drop of blood drawn.

That got its attention. Beady eyes turned on me, and the creature hunched low to sprint forward. I gave myself two, maybe three, seconds before impact. Nothing I could do about it except hope I died quicker instead of slower.

The sound of a heavy, metallic thud caught my ear perhaps a tenth of a second before the gray streak flitted by in my vision. Not troll sized, nor troll speed. This moved more like my arrows.

And it hit the creature about as hard as those arrows might have, if they'd been fired from a cannon instead of a bow.

It stuck in deep, displacing a jet of blood and sending the creature sidelong with a confused, dazed backstep. My eyes were already on the shooter, finding two newcomers on the scene. One was tall, the other short and broad, and both wore armor made of full steel plates. Given the cold, that was nearly a superhuman feat in and of itself. Only one had the crossbow. The other was coming in with some big, meaty blade made of a metal too light in coloration to be iron or steel. Both had visors down, and their faces were hidden completely, but I recognized them in an instant.

I had, after all, worked with the man who'd first written them into the world of Redacle.

Witchfinder Elites, the holy soldiers in our setting's ongoing war against the forces of evil. They were assholes, most of them, but in this particular situation, against this particular enemy, I couldn't think of a group I'd rather be seeing make a sudden appearance than them.

The two of them moved without any sort of communication passing between them, or at least any that I could see, and yet despite the fact, both of them seemed perfectly in unison. The one with the crossbow reloaded, forcibly turning some huge wheel geared up to the weapon and dragging its string back along limbs of thick steel. His ally was already sprinting ahead to cover him while he did, broadsword held ready and thirsting for blood.

I'd like to proudly say that I charged in right behind him, gripping my bow by one end to heroically bludgeon the troll with it in place of a better weapon. I'd like to say that, but I didn't, of course, because I actually have a functioning cerebral cortex. Instead, I stood where I was and watched the steelshod lunatic rush in and start hacking at the creature's leg.

Almost before I could even react, it reached down and swiped for him, body moving far more quickly than anything of half its mass should've been able to manage. The Witchfinder rolled out of the way like he was a *Dark Souls* character, rising faster than I could blink and slashing again at the still-outstretched fingers. Steel hit flesh and came out the victor. Two taloned digits fell into the snow, blood raining down around them.

The troll didn't like that one bit, and *definitely* didn't like the arrow that whistled neatly into its eye an instant later. More blood, this time joined by sticky, syrupy jelly dribbling down one swollen cheek, and now there was a sharp cry running out through the forest while the monster flailed and thrashed, stamping around, kicking several times my own bodyweight of snow into the air as it spasmed.

Obviously, the man fighting it was an expert. He did a perfect job of weaving around its frantic stomps and slashing again and again, opening up long, deep gashes in the creature's leathery body, any one of which would've been a mortal wound if he'd been chopping at something human-sized. They did enough to enfeeble the monster, in any case, causing pain and weakness as it slowly lost speed, legs becoming shaky.

Perhaps he noticed, too. Perhaps that was why he got cocky and went for a headshot. Maybe he was just stupid. I really couldn't say. But I do know the effort didn't work out. One moment his sword was carving some neat calligraphy into the monster's forehead, and the next its giant fist came out of nowhere and caught the side of the Witchfinder's head.

His feet left the ground, then his back found a tree some dozen feet back. He bounced off it, landing in the snow and sinking easily a foot under the weight of his armor. The Witchfinder was quicker to stand back up than any of us would've been, even with all the metal on him, but the troll was quicker still. Another impact smashed his body against the wood, then another, then another. Crossbow bolts thudded into the animal's giant back, but they seemed to merely annoy it, even as steam and smoke began coiling from the places they were stuck.

I considered helping; I really did. And that's not me being a stand-up guy either. I could hear metal plates grinding apart and bones breaking, even from where I was standing ten meters back. I don't think anyone could've just ignored the sound.

But I just stayed where I was. We all did, staring and watching until the Witchfinder fell down as a mangled, ruined smear of pulped meat and spilled ichor. Then the troll turned, sweeping across us, beady eyes falling on the remaining crossbowman.

Beam was insane, too. I'd forgotten that little tidbit, until he started moving and instantly attracted the thing's attention.

Well, alright, he probably wasn't just acting on impulse. In all likelihood, he'd realized the thing was about to attack the other Witchfinder, and that this time it wouldn't have to fight a melee specialist powerful enough to hold their own. He'd probably gauged how fast it'd catch up to any human, and accounted for that fact when he decided to buy our new ally some more time to stick it with arrows. I imagine his show of quick thinking and tactics was as praiseworthy as some of the best in history, and might even have won him some award in a righteous world.

Still, fuck him, because he was stood right next to me when he took off, and the troll made a direct beeline for *all* of us at once. I'd guess that hadn't been in his little calculations. Fortunately, I was already running before his lack of warning could cause any issues, my instincts for blatant cowardice proving just as fast as his instincts for battle.

Ten yards separated us from the monster, and we'd started running first. With that in mind, it was fucking incredible how little time it took for the thing to be breathing down our necks. We ran like our lives depended on it, because they did, Solitaire right beside us, death looming somewhere between our lower intestines and assholes. Not one of us even glanced at the pursuer, because not one of us had the speed to spare.

Our aim was instantly chosen and quickly approached, a row of close-growing trees some thirty feet ahead. It was as far from us as the troll was, which, as Solitaire would later tell me, meant that our success came down to one crucial factor.

Was the monster twice as fast as us?

It was, as it happened. Closing, closing, closing. By the time we were five meters from the trees, it was four from us. By the time we were just three strides short of freedom, we were within its reach.

And then the crossbow bolt hit it in the face.

We didn't see the impact, but this close, and with that much sheer power, we actually *heard* the sound of flesh giving way and teeth getting torn from gums by the metal point's path into the monster's mouth. It bought us a precious second by sending it rearing up and snarling, then we were all between the trees, feeling their branches snag our clothes and taking solace in knowing they were close enough together that the monster couldn't have even fit between them.

Granted, our newfound joy died a bit as we saw it rip one of the fucking things out of the ground.

They weren't big trees, barely twenty feet high each. Maybe they were even saplings. Still, however much strength it took to do that, it wasn't a force we'd be fighting. We couldn't leave the outcropping. This fifteen-foot stretch of huddling wood was our only safety, which meant we'd be stuck waiting for the troll to tear its way in and start killing.

Another crossbow bolt hit it, and it ripped out another tree. One more tree came free just as the third bolt caught an elbow, and the troll seemed to get a bit distracted. Two bolts both managed to hit an ear and a kidney one after the other, finally drawing its attention to the shooter.

That was when Beam stabbed it in the balls.

I, for one, have never received a spear to the testicles, but going by the reaction it got, the experience probably isn't great. Granted, Beam didn't manage to get much penetration, and the troll wasn't exactly losing a lot of blood, but the thirty or so seconds it spent thrashing and screaming made all the difference in the world.

Solitaire, being the massive nerd he is, counted the wounds while it died. Later on he told me there'd been twenty-nine. Each one lost a liter or more of blood, on average, and that seemed to be the magic amount. Just like the two weaker ones before it, the *giga-troll* collapsed into the snow. Body twitching one final time, the way dead bodies apparently did, wounds still smoldering where the crossbow bolts jutted out of them. My nostrils burned with the smell of charcoal as I stared at it, silver reacting with the creature's magical flesh. I spent a few minutes soaking the sight up.

Then Solitaire snapped me out of it, elbowing me sharply.

"Stats, now," he breathed. "Before Sir Wanksalot comes over."

I glanced up, saw the Witchfinder was going to check on what was left of his comrade, and recognized the small window we had to examine ourselves. Hastily, I pulled up my menu.

[Appraisal]
Class: Emperor
Level: 6
Condition: Worn
Modifiers: +2 Toughness
Statistics: Strength 5 (4), Speed 5 (4), Dexterity 6 (5), Stamina 5 (4), Toughness 7, Alertness 8, Charisma 9, Intelligence 9
Inventory: Jeans, shirt, jacket, dagger
Class Abilities: Appraisal II
Current Experience Points: 73/150
Unspent Skillpoints: 3

It was a Herculean feat of will that I didn't audibly squee on the spot.

CHAPTER FIFTEEN

Shango's POV: Day 10
Current Wealth: 2 silver, 11 copper
Current Debt: 6 gold, 44 silver, 20 copper

Three skillpoints, *three*. That was more than I'd have dared hope for from this trip.

But of course it was. We'd killed one troll, and that had been the plan. The second was utterly spontaneous, and given the sheer size of it, I was half convinced we'd been cheated with even this reward.

But no, there was no time for thoughts like that, I had some fucking powers to improve. I turned to my friends while the Witchfinder did whatever to his new partner-shaped smear, bringing up their menus just like I had my own and fighting back the urge to literally vibrate with glee as I almost dared to imagine myself one day winning a fight *easily*.

[Appraisal]
Class: Revolutionary
Level: 6
Condition: Worn
Modifiers: +1 Speed, +1 Toughness
Statistics: Strength 6 (5), Speed 7 (6), Dexterity 8, Stamina 5 (4), Toughness 7, Alertness 8, Charisma 3, Intelligence 10
Inventory: Jeans, T-shirt, flick knife, rocks (x6), dagger, bow
Class Abilities: Detect Element II
Current Experience Points: 73/150
Unspent Skillpoints: 3

[Appraisal]
Class: Dragonknight
Level: 5
Condition: Fine
Modifiers: +1 Strength
Statistics: Strength 9, Speed 8, Dexterity 8, Stamina 9, Toughness 7, Alertness 8, Charisma 6, Intelligence 5
Inventory: Jeans, flannel shirt, spear
Class Abilities: Beloved II
Current Experience Points: 120/140
Unspent Skillpoints: 3

I grinned, telling both Solitaire and Beam about their new powers even as I saw the two of them figuring it all out on their own. None of us said much after that, all having something far more important to focus on. The only exchange between us was some idle questioning about the big troll's stats, and some widening eyes upon hearing them.

Toughness again. I saw no other choice. It hadn't saved me this time, but it could have. There was a nugget of doubt in my mind at the selection now, after seeing what that troll could do one-armed. I was dubious I'd ever be resilient enough to withstand this world's biggest threats but, if nothing else, I could widen my odds against the smaller beasts. Or humans. I funneled all of my skillpoints with a practice that was deepening every time I gained a new one, letting the glorious sensation wash over me.

[Appraisal]
Class: Emperor
Level: 6
Condition: Worn
Modifiers: +5 Toughness
Statistics: Strength 5 (4), Speed 5 (4), Dexterity 6 (5), Stamina 5 (4), Toughness 10, Alertness 8, Charisma 9, Intelligence 9
Inventory: Jeans, shirt, jacket, dagger
Class Abilities: Appraisal II
Current Experience Points: 73/150
Unspent Skillpoints: 0

I did feel different now. Warmer. It was like the winds had died down around me, the snow half-thawed midair. All the heat the woodland had been drawing from my flesh was resisting eviction, now clinging to me far more fiercely than before, and it slowly bled back into the tips of my fingers and toes.

There's a lot I've experienced since coming to Redacle, things that continued for years after these first few weeks, but even to this day, not many measured up to the experience of seeing, *feeling*, that I was gaining tangible progress from my rising numbers. Growing stronger, safer, more secure in my place.

I caught the growing feeling of invincibility and throttled it to nothing. I was level fucking six, and I had no delusions that a solid hit from that giant troll would've been the end of me, even now. The very beginning was no time to be getting cocky at all. Not in a world where the levels went to fifty or higher.

[Appraisal]
Class: Revolutionary
Level: 6
Condition: Worn
Modifiers: +4 Speed, +1 Toughness
Statistics: Strength 6 (5), Speed 11 (10), Dexterity 8, Stamina 5 (4), Toughness 7, Alertness 8, Charisma 3, Intelligence 10
Inventory: Jeans, T-shirt, flick knife, rocks (x6), dagger, bow
Class Abilities: Detect Element II
Current Experience Points: 73/150
Unspent Skillpoints: 0

Solitaire had chosen speed again. I was almost tempted to question him, but it would have been an instinctive, gut reaction and unproductive. I'd specialized just as much myself and was hardly in a position to argue. Besides, if anything, our most recent altercation was proof that running ability would be saving our skins a lot more reliably than mere durability or killing power.

[Appraisal]
Class: Dragonknight
Level: 5
Condition: Fine
Modifiers: +1 Strength, +1 Speed, +2 Toughness
Statistics: Strength 9, Speed 9, Dexterity 8, Stamina 9, Toughness 9, Alertness 8, Charisma 6, Intelligence 5
Inventory: Jeans, flannel shirt, spear
Class Abilities: Beloved II
Current Experience Points: 120/140
Unspent Skillpoints: 0

Odd that Beam was the only one among us dispersing his skillpoints, but then, he was the one among us who already excelled in areas of physicality at all. Even good looks, lucky bastard. He probably figured he was best off just widening the gap that already separated his individual abilities from other people. Probably, he was right.

"Does . . . anyone feel any different?" I asked, eagerly.

Beam shrugged. "Lighter maybe?" He seemed to question his own answer, which didn't inspire a lot of confidence.

Solitaire didn't say anything at all, to begin with. Just sidestepped. Sidestepped faster than Beam could have, and grinned. "Apparently I do." His laughter was the same sort I'd heard a thousand times before, but tinged with a relief, and a desperation, that . . . warped it. It was the laugh of a starving man who'd finally found himself a meal, strained and wild and just a little bit touched by madness.

"He's coming," Beam hissed, and Solitaire reacted whip-fast, instantly snapping himself still and becoming as rigid as a damned cage bar, just in time for the Witchfinder to trudge on over.

Would he have noticed any difference, if he'd seen him suddenly moving around as if he'd spent ten years training between minutes? Probably not, given the circumstances, but better to be overly cautious than under. We were fairly sure our rapid levelling up wasn't a feature of this world, as it hadn't been in our books. Which meant that keeping it to ourselves was probably the best move, if only to unbalance the people who thought they'd already gotten our measure.

Forward thinking, and useless at the moment, because if the bastard in shining armor marching over right now put his mind to it, I suspected he could have killed us all at once either way.

[Appraisal]
Class: Witchfinder
Level: 25
Condition: Fine
Modifiers: +9 Strength, +7 Speed, +4 Dexterity, +3 Stamina, +9 Toughness, +7 Alertness
Statistics: Strength 16, Speed 13, Dexterity 10, Stamina 10, Toughness 15, Alertness 13, Charisma 3, Intelligence 3
Inventory: Plate armor, arbalest, sacred razor, dagger

Interesting, it seemed stronger people gave more comprehensive information when I appraised them. And it seemed that, as suspected, we were more than a little bit fucked if this guy came flying at us. It was interesting how high his stat increases were, given his level, but not enough to bear thinking about right now.

Part of me wanted Solitaire to try and speak first, but I knew that I was the best suited for the job. I always kept my cool better, and what we probably needed here was a negotiation in any case. If it came down to intimidation, we were fucked.

"Thank you for your help," I called out to the man, speaking with about ten times as much confidence as I felt. In fact, I even sounded slightly fucking confident. If he noticed, it had no effect on him, save to turn his visored face toward me and leave me seizing up beneath a glare that felt oddly similar to that of a sniper.

"I wasn't here to help you." The Witchfinder's voice was completely beyond my expectations. Not some brutish, hulking grunt, not the velvety drawl of some refined man of thought and nobility. He just sounded like a guy. An echoey guy, speaking from behind a few millimeters of steel, and a royally pissed off guy, but still nobody I couldn't have run into at a bar.

It was a miracle, all considered, that he managed to send such a palpable chill dancing down my spine. My heart skipped a beat before I answered, and I barely burped out its normal rhythm while I did.

"Well," I forced a smile, "You still did—"

I didn't see the punch, and I barely even felt it. One moment Sir Droolsalot was standing a few feet from me, the next he was a big silvery streak in the air, disappearing from one place then replacing himself with a wall of black and a storm of dancing stars in my vision. My feet left the ground, my thoughts left the stratosphere, and when I finally came to, I was lying on my back at least six feet from where I'd been when the blow came.

The Witchfinder was standing over me a moment later, visored face turned down, body blocking the sun that was only just creeping past noon.

"My partner and I had been tracking that troll for weeks," he snarled, so savage in his anger that a few flecks of spit actually cleared the coverage of his helmet and fell down around me. "We had our hunt all lined up and ready to finish. Then you and your idiot friends started hunting its children for *money*, and drew it out of its hiding place."

My idiot friends were already moving in around him, Beam marching up front, Solitaire circling from behind. Both had knives, and in an instant the Witchfinder's hand was filled by a short sword I hadn't seen scabbarded before. All of us froze, except for him. His voice suddenly more calm, not less, for the blades drawn.

"I'm not going to kill any of you," he said. "Even though each one of you deserves it, that is not the Witchfinder's way. I serve God, and do His bidding in cleansing this world of monsters, daemons, and practitioners of dark sorcery. You are . . . not among them. But see to it that you never cross my path again, for I will never forgive any of you for killing my friend with your stupidity."

Not one of us moved. We didn't twitch, we didn't speak, we barely even breathed. It was only when the Witchfinder had turned himself around and stalked off into the woods that any of us broke the silence.

And, of course, it was Solitaire who did, voice edged and hushed.

"Let's hurry up and grab the trolls," he said. "I want to be out of here before that crazy bastard can come back with his mates."

I spent a moment staring at him, completely stunned by the lunatic's suggestion. It was so absurd, so reckless, that it took me the better part of ten seconds to actually formulate a coherent answer, and even then it was riddled with gasps.

"Are you insane?!" I demanded, feeling my temper flare up and body burn with adrenaline—compounding my newfound resistance to the cold, it almost left me sweating.

"Are you?" Solitaire snapped back, never one to enjoy being questioned on matters he took seriously. "How much did we get for the last one? Forty silver? That big fucker's got to weigh two, even three times as much! I wouldn't even give up the little one, let alone that."

I glanced at the corpse, and even I had to admit it was a tempting prospect. If not for one tiny little issue.

"It weighs two or three times as much," I noted, trusting Solitaire's estimate almost as much as I would the result of dropping it down onto some scales. "How exactly do we drag that back? Let alone with the smaller one, too."

His smile didn't waver.

"I can help now," Solitaire said, flatly. "And we have about twice as long to do it. Plus, Beam is about twenty-five percent stronger. I'm around twenty-five percent stronger than you, too, and you're around two fifths as strong as he was before. So, in total we can apply around fifty percent more pulling power."

That earned a frown from me. Was he just pulling numbers from his ass?

No, he wasn't. But he knew that I'd be confused, too. The bastard always grinned like he was grinning now, especially when he knew someone would be baffled by him.

"I kept a very careful power scale when writing stories set in Redacle," he explained, smugly. "Magical creatures overcome the square-cube law by gaining extra pound for pound strength that lets them lift their own weight, no matter how big they get. It's why size is such a pure advantage for our monsters, and it's how I know that each one-point increase to a stat is around a twenty to thirty percent buff from the previous level. It's consistent with basically all the numerical differences we've seen, and we can test this hypothesis more if you want."

If you want, implying the only reason we'd have to test it was to satisfy me. As if his guess were as good as law.

It might well have been, too. I grinned even as I swore at him. Sometimes it was rather useful to know someone with more brains than sense.

Then I was frowning again. I couldn't work numbers like Solitaire could, but I wasn't a *moron* either.

"One and a half times the pulling power, but three or four times the weight?"

He shrugged. "It definitely is going to be harder," Solitaire conceded. "But much more lucrative, too, and as I said, we have more time. At worst, we can leave one of them to finish our trip with the other if it's harder than expected."

I considered his words, turning them over in my head, trying to find a fault. Then swore when I couldn't.

Solitaire grinned away while the three of us started moving, grunting with the effort as we all started dragging our prizes to stack onto the other. It'd make them easier to move at once.

CHAPTER SIXTEEN

Solitaire's POV: Day 10
Current Wealth: 2 silver, 11 copper
Current Debt: 6 gold, 44 silver, 20 copper

One day I was going to get tired of being right, and a few hours of hauling a fuck-ton of feral assholes behind me was almost enough to make it *that* day.

It wasn't, of course, my ego being an eldritch thing, more than a match for any weight the universe could possibly assemble, but holy shit did my back hurt after that particular exercise. It hurt an hour into it; it hurt two hours into it, and by the halfway mark to Jhigral—ten thousand or so seconds if my counting was right—it hurt even more.

There were, I was learning, many more factors to hauling a fucking troll carcass than I had been made aware of. The first was grip.

Skin is hard to grab, particularly when you're sweating. The skin of an eleven-foot death blender made of hatred and hunger was, apparently, harder still. The hairs along its fingers and hands were too short to grip, and just long enough to reduce traction. The thing's arm was big enough that it had noticeable mass on its own, and just holding it over my shoulder was physically tiring. I'd found that closing my fingers around its own was the easiest way, so long as I curled the taloned digits and was careful not to nick myself on the damned nails.

Finally, there was the smell.

God, the smell. I've cleaned public toilets. I've even made explosives out of my own shit, and the sheer reek of that creature still wakes me up in a cold sweat even years later. Presumably, the Witchfinders had meant "giant, gaping asshole in the ground" when they said it'd been cornered in a cave, because Jesus Christ this thing was trying to kill me from the nostrils out.

It was a nice distraction from the pain at least. But an inherently temporary one. Humans adjust, it's just how we're wired. A lottery winner and recent amputee will, obviously, be on opposite ends of the happiness spectrum, but overwhelmingly converge to roughly within the norm when interviewed again after a year. And I was apparently no different, because with every step my senses became less acute, and my mind less clouded. Smell and touch both faded into the background, and everything became the walk, and the destination.

And something else. Something so minor I barely even caught it, and almost combat-rolled away from the fucking troll in a reflexive panic even when I did.

Hydrogen, Oxygen.

"Fucking fuck!"

The exclamation left me before sense could enter me, and by the time my synapses had stopped disemboweling each other, I could already feel the adrenaline rush I'd spent three hours walking off rearing its ugly head up all over again. Brilliant, now I'd be knifing shadows for the rest of the day.

I had more pressing concerns than something as minor as long-term, untreated psychosis, though, because the moment I relaxed even a shade, I saw the words jump out at me again.

No, not out at me, not into me either. Just . . . there, exactly like picturing sentences even as I said them. Abstract and non-physical, some sort of representative entity existing only within my understanding of the concept it referred to.

Hydrogen, Oxygen.

Well, that was fucking useful, wasn't it? Two words, two words with an obvious connection. I considered what they might mean.

I was an idiot, obviously, to need to consider it at all. I was standing surrounded by snow. The ground was snow, the sky was snow, and even the air immediately next to me was clotted with more bits of snow. Frozen water. Hydrogen two, Oxygen one. Moron.

The more interesting detail, though, was that I was being shown the water's chemical components at all. Why was that, exactly? I thought back to what Shango had told me of my sheet, and drew the obvious conclusion.

"What's wrong?" he asked, then scowled when I gestured for him to shut up. I'd apologize later; there was thinking to be done at the moment.

The first of it came as I eyed Shango himself, staring, glaring even with my concentration. He was always quick, it was what I liked most about him. I saw that quickness in how immediately Shango's face lit up with understanding.

"What are you looking for?" he asked, eager.

Detect Element.

I'd not given the name of my own power much thought, we'd been told outright by the veiled lady that it, and Beam's, wouldn't come into play as quickly as Shango's had, and we'd always been faced with more pressing issues. But now I saw a hint that it might just be the latest tool on our belt.

Oxygen, Hydrogen, Nitrogen, Carbon, Calcium, Phosphorus.

I almost jumped again, despite being half-ready this time, but I just about kept my shit packed together while I watched the words jumping out into my consciousness. They were half in my head, half in my gut, and I knew each one more instantaneously and cleanly than I could ever have hoped to understand a written word at all. It was like having thoughts emptied into the broth of my mind. Horrifying, on a principal level, but plenty useful for now at least. I compartmentalized my worries and piped up.

"Detect Element," I breathed, still half in awe. "It lets me . . . Well, it meant actual elements, as we understood them."

Shango's gaze was intense, and immediate.

"By we, you mean—"

"Our homeland." I nodded.

It was Beam's turn to stare now, but his reaction gave way to excitement far more quickly than Shango's.

"So what can you do with this?"

By the tone of his voice, I knew he was expecting something spectacular. My only answer was a shrug.

"Find chemicals in trace amounts, maybe?" I answered, unsure.

Shango's body had, according to my ability, been made up of around six elements. But that was wrong. I probably didn't know everything that was found in a person, but I knew for a fact our bodies had traces of potassium, magnesium, and even copper, if I remembered correctly. None of that had showed up.

Which made sense, because if everything that was in everything got displayed for me, my vision would perpetually be filled with long, winding lists of several dozen substances lurking in the quantities of nanograms within whatever I happened to be staring at. There was *probably* more than zero uranium in either of my friends, but if I picked up on something that scarce, there'd be no point in picking up on anything else.

So could I not get any idea of how much of something there was in a sample? What was the minimum threshold to detect an element? Would it tell me about distribution? I would have to experiment with this.

The worst thing about answers was that nothing in all the world is half as good at creating questions. And I didn't have the means of experimenting myself into resolving them. Not in this moment, and certainly not in this shitting woodland.

I looked up, seeing that both my friends were practically vibrating with impatience now, and sighed. Their disappointment was palpable, even halfway through the explanation, but the energy of having discovered a new power didn't quite evaporate completely. If nothing else, the time spent resting was appreciated when we got back to hauling the fucking troll behind us.

Beam did most of the work, as always, but that didn't mean there was any time for resting on my or Shango's part. Combined, the two trolls were just barely too heavy for any pair of us to budge, and just light enough that we could all manage together. Maybe if we had a better source of food and better rested bodies, the issue would be simpler. Maybe.

Jhigral loomed far ahead, and I had to actively stop myself from crying in relief. For two reasons. The first was that my mother didn't raise a bitch, but the more pressing one was that it had gotten colder since we set off, the darkening sky turning to a sharper climate. I didn't want to find out whether my tears would freeze against my fucking face.

I must say, it was bloody satisfying to see the looks on people's faces as we dragged our haul through the town's outskirts. We'd just barely gotten it between a pair of buildings, eager for the windbreak to give us a nice resting spot, when Shango nudged me and spoke in a carefully lowered voice.

"We need to talk."

I knew what it would be about instantly. Of course I did. The gravity of his tone didn't leave much room for doubt, and I, having a working memory at least slightly more advanced than your average chimpanzee, could still vividly recall how upset he'd been when I turned that guy's brains into an improvised layer of shoe dye.

Steeling myself, I nodded.

"Go ahead."

Shango didn't pretend to hesitate, didn't try to make me think he hadn't planned everything he was going to say already. I appreciated that. He was smart enough to know better than to insult me with obvious bullshit, and he was smart enough that this wouldn't take long. Hopefully.

"You killed someone who couldn't fight back," he said. I eyed him, waited to see if there'd be more. There wasn't, so I replied.

"He killed others first."

"You don't know that," Shango answered, hotly.

"He was blockading an antiseptic on a pre-industrial continent," I replied, forcing myself to keep calm, cursing how much better he'd always been at doing so.

"Even if he never personally killed a single person, he murdered God knows how many by denying them vital medicine."

I could tell that Shango was uncomfortable with the train of thought. He'd never liked where I drew ethical lines in the past, or how little I cared about the fine moral gradations between action and inaction, deliberation and indirection. To me, a killing was a killing. If the dead cared about how many layers of separation there were between them and their murderers, they were in no state to tell us.

It had always been a philosophical disagreement, but as of a few days ago it'd become practical. We weren't going to be able to just keep sitting on this or agreeing to disagree.

"Then I disagree with you just deciding to be judge, jury, and executioner." He was done thinking it through, and his voice was confident again.

I sighed. "We needed the—"

"I know we needed the teeth," Shango snapped. "I'm saying that if we need more, we . . . discuss it first, at least, right?"

That surprised me, and I eyed him. He was unyielding as he stared back, brown eyes hardened, not softened, by the doubt I saw in them. This wasn't just a matter of principle to Shango, I realized. It was about trust. He needed to know he could rely on me.

And that was . . . fair enough.

I nodded. "Deal," I agreed, turning now to Beam.

"You hear all that?"

He didn't hide the fact that he'd been staring, watching the whole thing unfold. Beam's nod wasn't nearly as hesitant as either of ours.

"Far as I'm concerned, our first priority is living. Anything after that is a luxury."

Shango blanched at the declaration, and I just filed it away. It was surprising to hear Beam be so brutally practical, and more than a little reassuring. We might just survive yet. Shango was speaking again before I could suggest we move on, though.

"That Witchfinder died because of us," he said, abruptly.

I studied him sidelong. "He died because of an unfortunate accident" was all I could say. What else was there? We had no way of knowing he was in the area, no way of knowing that killing more trolls would somehow threaten him, and no choice to do anything else even if we had. We needed experience, power, and money. Now we had it.

Something tugged at my gut, but I pushed the feeling aside and forced my face into a facsimile of certainty. "We can have the luxury of ethics when we're wealthy enough to live," I pressed. "Until then, it's us or them."

Shango agreed on that much, at least, and he nodded.

The three of us got back to hauling our load from the alley just in time to see several men crowd the far end ahead.

CHAPTER SEVENTEEN

Solitaire had a tendency to overreact; it was impossible to be friends with the guy and not realize as much. I'd watched plenty of freak-outs on his part, from the time I found him wiring explosives into Shango's walls in case someone tried to sneak in through them, to that unfortunate occasion where some idiot had woken him up from a nap and almost been perforated with an illegal firearm.

Still, the fearful spasm he gave off at first sight of the newcomers struck me as unusually rational. I couldn't think of many good, innocuous reasons they might've had to be pulling up in front of our alley's exit.

Shango spoke first, of course, always quick and eager to smooth over a situation when he smelled danger coiling around it. His voice rang out across the walls of our passage like oil on the surface of water.

"Can we help you?" His smile was forced, his friendliness more so, and he was loud enough that I almost missed the sharp sound of hard-heeled boots tapping the cobbled street behind us.

I turned and cursed. There were more men coming up through the alley behind us, all short and wiry, the way Redaclans were, but numbering roughly a dozen in total. They wore dark fabrics, baggy and padded, and moved the way I was used to seeing in men who were approaching a fight. It was Solitaire who'd grown up being taught how to spot people that wanted to kill him, but I had enough sense to read the writing on the wall here.

"Good evening, gentlemen," one of the men said with some accent I'd never heard, and pronouncing every word with about as much zest as a water cutter filled with orange juice. "I can't help but notice that rather impressive carcass you're dragging behind you. I don't suppose you'd mind giving us a look at it, would you?"

All of us were on edge instantly. We'd fought for it, almost died for it, and spent hours suffering in the snow for it. We did, in fact, fucking mind. Shango gave our answer without any need at all for communication, even while Solitaire and I tensed up beside and behind him.

"I appreciate your interest," he replied, "but I'm afraid we'll have to . . . decline." The men continued closing in, four ahead, seven or more behind. We all started moving in, covering one another. I was staring down the bigger number at the back of the alley, while Solitaire and Shango turned their focus to the ones blocking our destination. Could we fight them, if it came down to it?

"All stats of threes, fours, and fives," Shango whispered to us. "They're not particularly special."

Not special, but they still outnumbered us. I wasn't sure what difference our newfound level ups would make against that.

The alley was tight, maybe five feet wide, but two men could still come at us at once if they moved right. I could hold two off, given my new stats, but I wasn't sure at all how long that would last.

One knife might change that, or a lucky hit with any other weapon hidden in those baggy clothes.

The men closed in, and my heart raced as I raised my spear, fists tightening around its handle so strongly that I worried it might break.

"Come on, gentlemen," the man called out again, sounding almost sympathetic. "Be reasonable. What do you expect to gain here—a pathetic death in some dirty alley? Look, I'll even hand the three of you a few silvers for your trouble." His words trailed into silence, voice hardening like fired clay. "Take them, and give us the fucking trolls before we give these walls a new coat of red paint."

Several things happened, all practically at once. The first was that Shango actually considered his offer. I heard about this later on. Apparently, he'd been more worried by the sight of the men than I had, because he was already halfway into his first response when Solitaire reacted.

His was quite a bit more . . . explosive. And messy.

Solitaire often said that he who hit first would generally hit last, particularly when they also hit second, third, and fourth. Particularly when they hit with something big and heavy. He still had the rocks on him, and he put one to good use with a sudden, overhanded throw that had about as much speed and motion behind it as a haymaker.

It was a good one, too, and at as close to point-blank range as he probably dared risk. A pound of rock left Solitaire's hand, then joined the closest thug's face less than the blink of an eye later. Shango insists he could *hear* the nose popping, even to this day, and I definitely heard the thud of someone's body dropping down an instant later.

My own movement came before the sound even registered. I lunged, just before the man closest to me did and put my spear through his shoulder. It was too dark to see the full color of his blood, but it foamed out thickly enough that I was sure he'd be out of the fight. His friends, though, were closing in fast to replace him.

There was no time to drag the weapon free and bring it back around, so I didn't. Letting the spear go and darting back from a slash, I saw a dirty knife slice the air inches ahead of my face as the first bastard missed me. He kept on coming, momentum dragging him forward even as he tried to bring the blade back around, and I closed in with an elbow aimed clean for his face.

It caught him between the eyes, and he dropped like a sack of bricks. The second guy was on me by then, though, pouncing and snarling as his fist flew out, brass knuckles glinting where they clung to his skin. He scored a lucky hit, my foot catching on one of the trolls while I sidestepped, the metal thudding dully into my own skull.

My legs were weak, head numb, thoughts scattered. By the time I realized what was happening, another punch caught my face. Teeth came loose, blood spattered a wall, and I was falling.

Wake up, fool. Wake up and kill them. They're here for our treasure! Show them how steep the blood price is.

The words fuzzed deliriously around in my head, alien enough that I barely even believed I'd thought them, but enough to galvanize my senses just in time. I focused as the man raised one foot to bring down on me.

Drawing my own leg back, I lashed out a faster kick than his, and winced as it connected with his knee. The joint didn't crumple, but it certainly gave, and he limped rather than walked back from me.

Again, though, more were coming. Two at once now. Fuck.

I might've been a sitting duck, if I hadn't sped myself up a bit. I might've been drooling out the last moments of my life with a fractured skull if I hadn't become tougher. And if I hadn't put those skillpoints into strength, the haymaker I threw after surprising them both with my rise might've only knocked my victim down.

But I'd changed since arriving here, and so had my body. I felt a sickening shift beneath the gangster's skin where my knuckles split open his jaw, and then he was continuing past me to roll and spasm with pain in the dirt. An elbow folded the next, then I whipped my head away as a knife stabbed over his shoulder for me. Two more, again, always two more, and two more behind them. An alley wide enough for just that many, two at a time.

I punched another, felt a knee in my ribs and resisted the urge to fold. Elbowed, I cried out as something sharp bit into my back, then turned with another strike that launched one of the tiny bastards into a wall. It was almost like fighting children, but they were too numerous for it to bring me any solace, and even a child could kill, given a knife.

One of those knives clipped me, drawing a dash of blood just before I smashed its wielder's face in. Another struck more deeply, burying inches of itself beneath my ribs, and my body just stopped.

That was the first time I've ever been stabbed, and it was a pain I'd not felt since the cold on that first night. A pain to drag all the air from my lungs, all the sense from my mind, all the joy from my heart.

Panic took me instantly, then terror, as I felt myself weakening, and by the time I'd even realized my limbs weren't obeying me anymore, another pair of brass-coated knuckles cracked against my head.

Like fighting children, and it was a lucky thing, too. I lost consciousness from that punch, but I lived. Just about. And I kept my cognizance long enough to see Solitaire and Shango wrestled to the ground, pinned against the hard dirt road by a flurry of stomping feet and lashing fists.

Then the dark came.

CHAPTER EIGHTEEN

Shango's POV: Day 11
Current Wealth: 0 silver 0 copper
Current Debt: 6 gold 44 silver 20 copper

We woke up hours later, and frankly, we were lucky enough to be waking up at all. I'd been conscious still when they started beating us. When the fight stopped being a fight and descended into mindless cruelty. I'd heard the kicks and punches bouncing off my own body, felt the sting of my own innards sloshing around inside. I'd known the visceral, indescribable fear of being certain that I would've died already without my choice of skillpoints, and the horror of lying there, immobile, wondering whether what fate had befallen my friends.

None of my bones were broken. That was the first saving grace I noticed, testing it with utmost care as I gently pressed down on them to check. Ribs first, some pain but nothing sharp, then knees, elbows, collar, and jaw. It took me more than a few minutes to be certain, and only after I'd triple checked did I finally allow the relief to permeate me.

Broken bones now might have killed me anyway. I could feel the coin pouch absent from my side, and I'd already noticed the trolls were gone. If we were left with weeks of healing to do, we'd be dead before then.

We. Not me, we. My friends hadn't been checked yet, and even if their beatings had been less extensive, they hadn't put half as many points into toughness.

Solitaire was closest, having been beaten down right beside me, and I barely even needed to move to reach him. I still moved, though, and my body protested harshly in response. Aches, dull, deep, and burning like hot coals from an hours-dead fire. They'd be with me for a long time, I knew. I could only hope they didn't affect movement as much as they were gnawing at my mood.

With a careful hand I felt first for Solitaire's neck, and almost wept when I felt the familiar pressure of blood circulating beneath. He was breathing, his heart beating, and that meant he was living. Or his body was at least. Until he woke up I couldn't be sure what might be wrong with him beneath the surface, couldn't know whether those vicious fucking thugs had turned the smartest man I'd ever met into some drooling vegetable, but for the time being I'd found a beating heart and pumping lungs.

A rush of rage went through me, displacing the relief and driving my fist down hard on his chest. It did exactly what I might have hoped, dragging Solitaire awake with a gasp and a slurred curse, eyes wide, face tight with pain. His thoughts were visible in his expression and filling me with a delight I'd never known I could feel. He sat bolt upright, then moaned in pain, convulsing back halfway to the ground as he felt all the same agonies I had.

No broken ribs, at least, or else he'd still be thrashing around. It'd been stupid to hit him like that without checking first, but I had no time to dwell on that. Beam was still asleep.

I examined him more gently, and was joined in doing so by Solitaire after a few moments. Again, it seemed we'd been lucky. No massive, crippling injuries. Beam's bones, at least, seemed intact. His body wasn't swelling enough to be suffering from internally pooling blood, and his breathing was stable, if strained. The one point of concern was a stab wound beneath the ribs, which Solitaire assured me would be more painful than dangerous. Sitting back, I considered the merits of waking him up.

God knows how we'd survived the night, with all the freezing cold, but we had. I could feel the chill now, though. Were we all fit to move? If not, waking Beam up would only be torment, exposing him to cruel weather that he couldn't escape. And that was assuming he wasn't in some recovery coma.

Hang on. I was an idiot. I didn't need to trust my own judgement on this at all. I looked at Solitaire.

[Appraisal]
Class: Revolutionary
Level: 6
Condition: Haggard
Modifiers: +4 Speed, +1 Toughness
Statistics: Strength 6 (4), Speed 11 (8), Dexterity 8 (6), Stamina 5 (2), Toughness 7, Alertness 8 (7), Charisma 3, Intelligence 10
Inventory: Jeans, T-shirt, flick knife, rocks (x6), dagger, bow
Class Abilities: Detect Element II
Current Experience Points: 83/150
Unspent Skillpoints: 0

Well, that didn't tell me much. "Haggard." What the fuck did that mean?

No, hold on, it did. I'd seen that condition before; it was how we'd been shortly after our arrival. Worse than the day before, and better than near-comatose. So . . . not a disaster, hopefully. I turned my gaze to Beam now.

Condition: Haggard.

Not as awful as it could've been, though the fact that our stats were all low again didn't do much to inspire my confidence. We could move. We had to move. And we would move, or else we'd freeze to nothing where we lay. Reluctantly, I leaned over to shake my friend awake.

With no money, our next direction was a bit . . . uncertain, for all of a few minutes, then the familiar pangs of hunger took us, and we made a beeline for the church. I worried at first that they might reject us again, but instead they took one look at our faces and bodies and brought out steaming bowls of porridge. We all sat down together, eating and talking, and only when we'd finished our meals did we start asking some questions.

"Excuse me?" I asked one of the nuns, a middle-aged woman with kind features that seemed to have been worn just a little bit toward apathy in her hard years. She turned warm eyes on me, regardless.

"Yes, my boy?" she replied.

I steeled myself and explained what had happened to us—the ambush, the number of men, the result. She didn't seem remotely surprised and only nodded in understanding.

"Hengrard," she said darkly once I was finished, spitting at her feet. "He's the ringleader for most of the local toughs. As dark a man as I've ever met. If there's anything unlawful going down in Jhigral, you can bet he'll be responsible."

I swallowed, having known, of course, that we'd been mugged by a genuine gang, but nothing about the extent of their influence.

"Aren't there proctors to help?" I frowned. "From the king?"

Proctors were one of the few saving graces we'd given Vorhazh—elites who, in the tabletop, had averaged levels comparable to a Witchfinder and wielded the power to butcher normal men by the dozen. They were authoritarian, and harsh, but never corrupt. The means required to ensure that last fact were grim enough in and of themselves.

She laughed at their mention, just a shade too scornful for my liking.

"Proctors? Out here? My boy, we get maybe one in the entire region of Jelric every year or so, and they're almost always headed straight for Wolney. There's less than five thousand people living in this town, as far as the censures can count. Why in the world would anyone bother sending a proctor here?"

My face burned with fury, even as I nodded in understanding. Of course. It made sense that rulers in worlds like this didn't bother with the little people. That was just how we'd written Redacle.

The nun moved on shortly, leaving us with a solemn warning that we'd need to clear out after a few minutes, whatever the weather. We barely even registered her words, all of us back to intense thought and vicious fury.

"Animals," Solitaire said, flatly. "We've landed in a world of animals."

I eyed him and realized I wasn't quite able to tell how serious he was.

Solitaire saying things like that about people—generally people as a concept—had been common enough back home, but I'd never seen him execute one of them in cold blood there. And I'd never found myself feeling so close to convinced that a person might have done something good in the process.

"Well our first priority now is food," I cut in, deciding I'd rather not deal with whatever he was getting at. "If we only eat what the church gives us, we'll starve. We've all seen that much already. The weaker we get, the less we can do."

"We're already weak," Beam cut in, wincing. "You said we all had massive stat penalties, right? What more can we do?"

I swore.

"Fight something big and risk dying to it, I suppose," Solitaire sighed. He seemed worn thin suddenly. "We got experience for that giant troll, so I think we can safely conclude that magical creatures still level us up, initial goal or no. Now's the strongest we're likely to be until we can afford more food, and since bastards three through twelve nicked all our money, that means we need to go out and get some more to replace it. The longer we wait, the harder that will be. There's no choice at all."

I nodded, and swore again. They were both right, damn it; we just didn't have any choice. I missed my home, I missed my bed, home-cooked meals, and the internet. I missed my family. I just wanted to leave.

There was no time for me to deal with thoughts like that. I had to live first, then I could mope around as much as I wanted.

"What's our first move?" I asked. "Another troll?"

Beam was nodding instantly, but Solitaire's answer came slower, more thoughtfully.

"I think we should spend a few hours on . . . experimentation," he said at last. "You remember what happened with my, uh, element-spotting power?"

I nodded.

"Well, you told us that our class abilities had a two behind them instead of a one, right? Maybe that's why it just suddenly emerged like that . . . And maybe, that means there's more for the rest of us to get. Maybe your Appraisal has more tricks available." He turned to Beam. "And maybe we can find out what your Beloved does."

"Alright," came a new voice. We all turned toward the sight of another nun, this one rather less warm than the last. "You've had your five minutes; clear off now."

We did so without much complaint, all knowing better than to piss off the literal hands that fed us. Once we were outside, the cold was as present as ever, but somehow was a bit more ephemeral than it had been an hour earlier.

Now we had a goal, a priority. Now we had, if we were incredibly lucky, just a pinch of hope.

CHAPTER NINETEEN

Solitaire's POV: Day 18
Current Wealth: 0 silver, 0 copper
Current Debt: 6 gold, 44 silver, 20 copper

We'd been hungry for a week, dying one day at a time, withering and shutting down. It was the straw that broke the camel's back when Corvan called on us, ordering another payment of the debt.

As it turned out, there hadn't been more than three trolls in the forest. We found that out by spending days of our lives nearly freezing in the search, finally giving in only when we realized it was taking longer and longer for feeling to rush back into our fingers.

Town was warmer, but still colder during the day, and we couldn't even afford a shitting room anymore. We killed most of our daylight hours experimenting, trying to find the boundaries of our class abilities. The rest was used on hopelessness and the desperate, pointless search for some opportunity to avoid starving.

My Detect Element, apparently, had been with me from level one. We'd known that already, of course, but it was only after a few days that I discovered it worked via taste and deduced that the second level was when it had allowed me to just look at things for information.

Taste still gave me more, though. It was how I'd gain insight into chemical percentages in a material, and without that there'd be all sorts of issues with trying to reliably create anything at all.

Of course we didn't actually have the *facilities* to make something new yet, which meant it was still fucking useless. Just our luck. What was worse, however, was that Beam still hadn't managed to find out what his class ability did by the week's end.

Well, we didn't give up easily on eating. We tried to find work, and there wasn't any. Tried to hunt animals, and almost got arrested for poaching. Tried to simply beg in the streets and got spat on.

I'd never liked people, always found them cruel, simple, irrational. Had I gone back to Earth after my time here, it might actually have softened me up for them. Because modern humans were nothing compared to the savages I was living around now.

Yeah, savages. There's no other word for them. Immoral, stupid animal-men. Their brains were shriveled and undernourished, their ideology about as complex and ethical as that of a rabid dog, and they still had the audacity to look at *me* with scorn for dying in front of them. Oh, it wasn't anything new, not really. I was used to people trying to murder me via starvation already. But these ones were taking long leaps in doing it hard enough to demand separate categorization.

The rage in me grew with every day, so intense that it almost kept me warm against the snow and wind. Almost. But I didn't have any real defense against the elements, and no defense against the hunger. All I could do was sit around and watch myself shrivel.

We had to move every night, because the guards would beat any vagrant sleeping in the same place too often. After a while we were recognized—all of us over six feet, so it wasn't unexpected—and had to start sheltering out of sight altogether. There were gathering spots for such things, and some even had fires burning, so we took a measure of solace in the company of other people in similarly fucked situations.

When we'd left for our troll hunts, the sight of the beaten-down impoverished had elicited sympathy. Now we were among them. It had been a steep fall, but nowhere near as steep as our drop from Earth to this stinking shithole in the first place. That thought kept me company even more than my friends did. I didn't belong here. It wasn't my place.

My place was at the top of this world. I was better than its people, and I would make them better by ruling it. Such a shame that justice wasn't a universal force alongside gravity or friction. Such a shame that cruelty, apparently, was.

It was the eighteenth day, and I woke up stiff, achy, and groaning. Beam and Shango were already up beside me, looking about as bad as I felt, and the three of us took our customary few minutes of miserable silence before standing to do anything.

Not that there was much to do. Go to the temple for food and try again to find work. Kill the day until we were back somewhere warm and unknown enough to sleep safely without being killed by either the cold or the guards. Another day, another torment.

Beam spoke first, stretching, popping his joints, and wincing. We'd all found that trying to move any fraction of our bodies only made the hunger more noticeable.

"I'm scared."

I heard him, but I didn't understand him, not at first. I just refused to. Beam had fought trolls without blinking, and had not even hesitated before charging a bear. He'd roundhoused something four times his weight. And he was scared.

The knowledge made me scared, but I hid it. Because I knew that my own fear would have very much the same effect on the others.

"We'll find something to do," I lied. "There must be work somewhere, and if not, it'll emerge eventually."

Beam didn't answer me, and neither did Shango. They both just looked ahead. Apparently, even I could only tell the same lie so many times before they saw through it.

"Any ideas, either of you?" I was actually more annoyed that they didn't believe me than I was uncomfortable at the lack of hope. I gave silent thanks to dear old mother for that particular neurosis, and then pressed my friends when no answer came. But Shango interrupted me.

"I want to kill myself."

I froze, Beam stared, and Shango only continued staring ahead, as if he were completely oblivious to the effect his words had had on us.

"Don't be stupid," I snarled, and he carried on his aimless stare right up until I grabbed his shoulder. "Shango!"

The look in his eyes stopped me. Complete calm, complete lucidity.

"I'm miserable, dying anyway, and hopeless," he told me, as if each fact was just an item on a shopping list. "If I'm going to end up some rotting corpse here, I'd rather die quickly than slowly."

Finally his lip curled, the only expression of note he'd made today. "I haven't found a tall enough building yet."

Since I was old enough to think about thinking, I've prided myself on how quickly I did it. A lot of emotions flitted through my mind, but the one I ended up settling on was resignation.

Everything Shango had said made sense, every part of it rational. It made me angry—no, furious—and miserable, too, but none of that was his fault. The root issue here was where we'd ended up, and it'd be pathetically childish of me to forget that just because he'd decided not to lie about his intentions.

However mature and cerebral I might have reacted, my heart still broke all the same. I hid the fact with practiced care.

We didn't stay there much longer. Come daylight, the town warmed quicker than you might expect, and we'd learned its guards were practically cold-blooded in how their activity grew with the temperature. They'd leave the hideouts unchecked by night, but the moment puddles stopped freezing, their patrols would continue as normal.

Within the hour, we were walking our usual circuit around the place, asking around for jobs, mechanical and routine. Do the same thing enough times and it becomes a reflex, something your bodies are occupied by while our minds wander. That wasn't a good thing anymore. It hadn't been ever since Shango's mind started wandering to his grave.

The lumberjacks had as many hands as they needed, as did the basic laborers. Nobody believed that we could even assist the chemists—or as these morons called them, alchemists—and apparently signing on as a guard took a surprising amount of training. Presumably in learning how to get a sufficiently hard erection while bludgeoning poor people.

One failure, then another. Each one now feeling like another nail in our coffins. Each one making my blood warm a degree closer to boiling. Interesting, that was new. I was close to actually losing it. My plan to poach anyway started forming, thoughts flitting around to calculate what our odds were of being caught, how best to hide or explain the meat, what route the woods' patrols were most likely to take. It was important to get everything right, because if I were stopped outright one last time . . . it'd push me over the edge.

I wondered what I'd do when that finally happened.

As it turned out, fate had plans other than my finding out. Our trek around the town was interrupted by several very familiar, unwanted faces, encircling the three of us while we moved down an alley.

We all had a very particular memory associated with situations like this, and I specifically have a very particular reaction to encirclement period. The rock was already bursting one of the men's lips when another spoke up.

"GOD! Fuck! Stop, wait! We're here to talk!"

I was halfway through tossing another chunk of stone when Beam caught my hand, his strength still clear in the grip, even after another week of hunger and cold. Even after the beating these bastards had given us last time.

"What do you want?" Shango demanded, his voice harsh and eyes combative. Was he intending to turn this into a fight? To die that way? Bloody selfish prick if he was. I had no intention of getting stabbed in an alley.

The speaker answered him quickly, apparently fearful of another rock, by the way his eyes flitted to and from me every moment.

"We're here with a request for a meeting. I'll guess you already know who it's from."

Shango paused, frowning in confusion.

"Hengrard?" he asked, then continued after receiving a nod. "What, does he want to beat us again?"

"Will you be accepting?"

I caught the flash of sunlight on brass knuckles, and heard the sound of a frozen puddle cracking behind us. From what I remembered, it had been a fairly deep one, and frozen almost fully through. A big bastard then, to have enough weight to do that. We wouldn't be winning this fight any more than the last.

Shango glanced at me questioningly, and I conveyed the fact as well as I could manage with nothing but a few spasming facial expressions. He seemed to get the gist somehow.

"We accept," he managed tightly, eyes still understandably untrusting. "Lead the way."

CHAPTER TWENTY

Shango's POV: Day 18
Current Wealth: 0 silver, 0 copper
Current Debt: 6 gold, 44 silver, 20 copper

There'd been a few factors at play when I agreed to attend the meeting, and only one had been the fear of being beaten into another coma.

Most pressing was the desire, the need, for something to do with my time. I wouldn't continue living the way I had been, and had yet to figure out a suitably painless way of dying. Until that happened, a break in the monotony was much needed. Besides, I actually had no idea why Hengrard even wanted to speak with us anyway. If it was to offer work . . . No, it couldn't be. Could it?

Yeah, it could. Of course it could. But was it? I didn't want to accept the possibility, to even weigh the odds, because of one simple fact—I'd almost reached some semblance of peace. There was a reassurance in rock bottom, a certainty in knowing there was nothing worse coming your way than what you already had. Hope would destroy that reassurance, shatter my certainty, and leave me falling again. I could feel it happening already and was desperate to cling to my illusion of relief.

The second factor was that I quite liked the idea of either blinding, crippling, or killing the man who'd stolen our fortune before I died. That was a very Solitaire thing to think, I knew, but in my defense a lot of his worldview and habits were a lot less insane when you lived in Redacle as opposed to Earth. I'd just have to make sure I kept telling myself that.

We were led into some old building that had clearly been important once, but had long since been left to decay and die. It was at least three stories tall, a rare example of all-stone architecture, and had windows boarded up with wooden shutters on every side. A fortress then, or as close as the king of some regional town's criminal underclass could get. If anything, it was impressive that the place was as big as it was. I started moving through the figures in my head, then gave up. Math was never my forte; instead, I whispered the question to Solitaire.

His estimates came back frustratingly fast. Three, maybe four thousand people in Jhigral. Call that three or four hundred starving and unemployed, and a quarter of them turned to consistent, violent crime. So we were looking at maybe a hundred men under Hengrard's control. Seventy five on the lower end.

Well, sixty seven to ninety five, actually. I felt a rare smile spread across my face. Beam had put at least four in the hospital, or would have if this world had anything worth comparing to one. I'd hit one in the chest hard enough that I felt bones break, and Solitaire had bitten another's throat out and squeezed one more's groin so hard there'd been blood washing his fingers right up until he went down. All things considered, I was quite happy to have made a dent in the bastard's operation, however small.

Hengrard himself was located in the center of the building, probably for reasons of safety. We were led through more than a couple of winding corridors on our way to him, and a single glance at Solitaire told me he was memorizing every turn we made on our way in. There were more than a few.

We soon came to the man's office and found him sitting behind some big wooden desk, parchment and quills scattered across it like something out of . . . well, a fantasy novel. He didn't look pleased to see us. Good, the feeling was mutual.

"Gentlemen," he called out, not even bothering to force a smile to contradict his tone. "I will be frank—I was hoping we would never meet again."

"Didn't know you were that sensible," Beam cut in with his usual tact. Solitaire just eyed a metal letter-opener on the desk, staring at it as if it were some big, juicy steak. I could practically see him counting guards, considering the likelihood of managing to put it through the leader's neck in time.

I decided to speak before he could get any of us riddled with shanks or cudgeled to death. "We weren't expecting to see you either," I replied, "after you tried to kill us and all."

He scoffed, as if I'd just said snow was blue.

"Oh, you call *that* trying to kill you? No, we left you alive and uncrippled on purpose. Your debt to Corvan is well known, and I'd rather not draw the ire of a magus."

So he might be too hesitant to fight back properly if another battle started? Interesting. Not that one *could* start, as we were now. If all three of us jumped our past selves from that alley, I doubted we'd even bring down a single one before getting left unconscious in a gutter.

Starvation was a bastard of a thing.

"After you beat us into unconsciousness and robbed us then," I snapped back, glaring openly at him, well past the point of caring enough about diplomacy.

He smiled thinly and shrugged. "You resisted my offer, and I have mouths to feed as well, you know. A lot more. Regardless, I'm not interested in hurting you again. If I was, you'd have come here with arrows through your knees first. I would like to make you an offer."

I frowned, eying my friends with a silent question. Beam looked just as confused as I was, but Solitaire had a thoughtful expression. I decided to see where this might go.

"What sort of offer?" I asked, watching his face carefully as it shifted and moved.

"The sort that gets you food, warm beds to sleep in and, if you're very useful, perhaps enough coin to pay off most, maybe all, of your debt to old Corvan." He said it all so simply that I almost didn't register the magnitude of his offer.

Of course, to him it was all small stuff. Matters of no import. Food? Not a problem. Warmth? Who cares? Only the coin will have registered.

But to us, he was bargaining with life itself. I had to stifle my knee jerk reaction to start begging and scraping.

"You're in trouble," Solitaire observed, eying the man like he were some hyena. "Someone's moving in on your territory, right? Someone you're not certain you can outfight. Maybe a Witchfinder, but I'd bet it's just another gang boss— someone from Wolney perhaps? You're scrambling to get as many fighting men as you can before it all kicks off, in the hopes that you'll still be in charge when the dust settles."

I must say, it was bloody satisfying to see someone else glare at Solitaire when he did that. Diplomacy was my area, but you should never underestimate a paranoid's ability to unravel ulterior motives. Even, on occasion, ones that actually existed.

By the expression on Hengrard's face, Solitaire had hit the nail on the head. The gang leader didn't look pleased. In fact, he looked like he just had shit smeared across his face.

I spoke to consolidate his victory before the enemy could adjust. "And you remember how well we performed against your boys," I cut in, "even half-starved, already beaten, and chilled to the bone from miles of walking through snow. Even while we were exhausted from dragging the weight of two war horses behind us. Which makes us dangerous to fuck with, and useful now, right?"

Hengrard glared, clearly taking his time before speaking again. I was quick, and I made a point of surrounding myself with quick people, but I knew better than to take his slow response time as a mark of unintelligence. If anything, taking the time to think every sentence through was a point in his favor, and against mine.

"You have the broad strokes right," he conceded at last, with all the eagerness of a dehydrated man giving up water. "Eliza Wodal is the name of the woman who runs the gang threatening to move in. See, a while ago they had a few men posted in an ambush point in the woods, guarding the road from Jhigral to some fancy tree with medicinal sap. Those men went missing, and now she's using it as an excuse to declare war, blaming it on us. I don't know if she killed them herself just for the excuse, honestly, or if she's just a moron, but either way the result is the same. She has a hundred men to my seventy, which means the fight isn't gonna be in our favor. Unless you join in."

I almost shat my entire fucking self, and to this day I have no idea how all of us kept straight faces. Solitaire, I suppose, just had a naturally evil face that always looked like he was sneering, Beam might not have even been paying attention, and I was just about tearing every muscle in my head trying to keep the surprise from showing. It almost kept me from thinking through everything else Hengrard said.

One hundred on seventy—that was bad. Terrible actually—unfavorable fucking odds that I really didn't want to be on the wrong side of. On the other hand, this meant high pay. I'd seen the desperation in this guy's face; it was palpable. He didn't want to lose whatever he'd built here, and he didn't want to lose his life, which meant that he could be wrangled for a damn sight more than an affordable fee.

Was it worth it? I didn't know. We were hardly in fighting condition now. I could feel my stomach aching still, even feel my own body's weight just pressing down on my legs from above. As of the last check, even Beam was sitting at strength seven now, new skillpoint expenditure included. If Hengrard thought he'd be getting the wrecking crew equal to double its number from before, he had another thing coming.

No, but he wouldn't be expecting that, surely. I could see the sunken cheeks and weakness in my friends even now; he must've been just as aware. Which meant he had other help available, or some other reason to think we could make up the difference.

So which was it? I thought it through long and hard, like Hengrard himself. And then gave the only answer I could. "You have a deal." I'd forced myself to say it, burying the bitterness that came with working for the bastard who'd mugged me. "Now what in the hell makes you think we have a chance?"

CHAPTER TWENTY-ONE

Beam's POV: Day 41
Current Wealth: 0 silver, 0 copper
Current Debt: 6 gold, 44 silver, 20 copper

I wasn't sure exactly how Shango managed to wrangle us a few weeks of free food and housing, but he did. I wasn't sure how he managed to convince that deal to hold after Hengrard saw that we were each eating about double the usual amount, but he did. The situation was dire—a fight against three for every two usually was—but it was a hell of a lot better than starving had been, and it was something we could actually influence. None of us were planning on simply idling while it approached.

The road from Jhigral to Wolney was long, winding and, according to Hengrard's report, predicted by Elementalists—magi specialized in influencing and weighing the weather—to be impassable due to snow for at least a fortnight. So we'd had a bit of wiggle room to prepare, recover, and steady ourselves.

We used it well.

Bread and porridge was easily acquired, but I insisted on bargaining for a ration of meat, too. Some mutton and goat flesh from Hengrard's stores, just a few ounces each per day, but it had enough protein to make at least some difference when combined with our other measures.

As we saw it, our main priority was physical power. We were haggard and worn thinner than ever before, so getting to a fighting condition would be difficult. But I'd trained harder in the past. Compared to the pain of seeing my body wither away in this world, the effort of pushing it back up to "merely" exceptional barely even registered.

Push-ups, squats, sit-ups, and lots of running. I did them by the hundreds, by the mile. Jumping and sidestepping, improvising support beams for pull-up bars, and calisthenics until the cows came home. It was oddly comforting. Even as I felt aghast at how difficult the simplest exercises had become, I realized I was essentially back to my roots, working just as hard and just as slow as I had when I'd first begun seriously trying out for the Olympics all those years ago.

That, and it was amazingly fun to watch Solitaire and Shango fail alongside me.

My friends swore, begged, bargained, and bitched, and I didn't let them get out of a single exercise. Pushing them right alongside me, taking motivation from the knowledge that they'd use my stopping as an excuse to quit themselves. All the while we prepared. We were practically inhaling eggs and meat, porridge and bread, guzzling water to hydrate our tortured bodies, and resting only as a reluctant concession to the logistics of muscle-building.

By the end of the second week, we'd gained most of our mass back. Not all as muscle, though. Our bodies had, apparently, adjusted to starvation and started piling on a bit more fat. That was fine—if anything, fat would help; Solitaire politely let us know that it was better than any other soft tissue for stopping a blade—but it was disheartening.

So we worked even harder the third week.

It ended quickly, time compressing amid our focus, and soon enough we heard word that a large number of men had been sighted moving to Jhigral from the numerous roads connecting it to Wolney. Time was up, and the fight was on us. All we had left was to see how well we'd prepared.

For his part, Hengrard was more than competent at outfitting us. We all got thick woolen clothes, warm, but more importantly coiled and tough enough that they *might* stop a knife. Our own weapons were ones we'd already practiced with, and of comparable quality to what most of Hengrard's boys would be using anyway, but we had the chance for a few choice surprises, too.

Solitaire, back on the very first day after our deal, had asked for a giant pile of horse shit. Literally. I hadn't known why, hadn't asked, and he'd just giggled when Shango had. I figured we'd find out soon enough. Sooner than I'd liked, actually, because it was on the afternoon of the twenty-third day since our deal, and the forty-first day since our arrival, that we were called on to ready ourselves for it.

As modern humans, it was nothing new for us to see the assembly of people. They were countable—in the dozens on our side, and that was nothing at all back home. Solitaire would've seen two, even three, times as many in high school—Shango probably saw even more just occupying individual market streets in Nigeria. Me? Fuck, I'm fairly sure your average football or baseball game in the U.S. filled its stadium with easily a thousand times as many.

It was a different thing entirely, though, to know that they were all on our side, all armed, and all ready for a fight. And that was what let it all sink in. This wasn't some bar brawl. It was a fucking war. And we were on the outnumbered side.

Among the three of us Solitaire spoke first. He wasn't as good with people as Shango, definitely wasn't half the businessman, but he was king when it came to matters of killing or being killed.

"They'll be attacking, right?" he asked, then continued before anyone could answer. "That's our advantage for being able to defend a prepared position, if you had enough spies to hear what Wolney's Elementalists were saying, then I'll guess they have enough to know what's happening here and where we're hiding out. So they'll be cutting in through the Ratpass to reach us as quickly as possible with all their forces concentrated."

Hengrard hesitated, thought, then nodded.

"Makes sense."

It did. The Ratpass was a long stretch of trench about fifteen feet wide that cut right through the city's center. Apparently, it had once held a redirected river, but long since fallen out of use. Dried out and left to a neglected state of disrepair. These days it was just a good shortcut. And a relatively tight one.

Solitaire grinned. "Then let's go and meet them there," he declared, setting off at a brisk pace. "Their numbers won't be as good in there, they won't have as easy a time surrounding us, and I have a little surprise stashed away just in case."

That got him a lot of skeptical looks.

"The base is . . . fortified?" one man asked.

Solitaire shrugged. "It can't hold all of us. Who's waiting outside?"

Hengrard was quick to respond. I realized that Solitaire had been pretty damned sneaky in engineering a way of forcing him to. "Reserves," he snapped. "Ready to ambush them when they try to break in."

Solitaire grinned. "Then lend 'em to us, and we'll ambush them when they're trying to approach instead."

It took some convincing, but apparently Hengrard wasn't particularly attached to his men in the first place. He probably didn't think any of the ones not inside could do much good, probably hoped that the lack of encirclement would do a lot of heavy lifting. Maybe he was just stupid. I really wasn't sure how Solitaire and Shango managed it, but we were soon moving in to fight a hundred men with barely twelve on our own side. We hurried, moving almost at a jog, and shortly we were on the Ratpass.

Then, we saw the enemy moving down it further ahead.

There were a lot, and they were moving with purpose. Whether it was a hundred or not, I really couldn't say, but the crowd seemed at least a bit bigger than ours had been in full, and a lot bigger than the group we had now. It was like comparing an elephant to a person, almost, and every bit as demoralizing as you'd expect. They were almost to the end of the Ratpass now, just fifty yards from scaling the big slope at its head. When they reached it, they'd be on us.

Solitaire stepped forward as if those half hundred paces were a hundred miles, moving to a large pile of planks and rubbish, shifting it aside to pull something out. A barrel. He grinned.

"What . . . is that?" Shango asked him, concern palpable in the question. Concern palpable in me, too, as it would have been in anyone who knew Solitaire and had seen him pull something out from a hiding place.

Our friend didn't answer, just pulled out a tinderbox—probably loaned from the gangsters—and lit a big fuse protruding from the top.

It was that, at last, that made me realize the obvious.

"You didn't!" I gasped, and he looked over his shoulder, laughing.

"Why do you think I needed the SHIT?!" he said, sneering. "God, do you know how long I've waited to do something like this?" He turned to the group at large and shouted, "Alright boys and girls, everybody step back, this is gonna be a splash zone."

Our enemies must've seen us because they were running faster now. Barely fifty feet away, and closing in fast. Solitaire tipped the big barrel down the ramp into the Ratpass, watching as the wooden keg—maybe half his height and two feet wide—rolled and bounced and thudded hard onto the stone floor below. The fuse kept burning, flame now an inch from the base. By the time it disappeared into the wood, the enemy was already upon it.

Explosions were common on modern Earth, but, oddly enough, being near them—let alone near them regularly—was not. The first thing that hit me was the sheer dirtiness of it, smoke and soot blowing out in all directions at once, like a mushroom cloud. The second thing was the pressure.

My teeth rattled, ears ached, eyes watered as heat and force battered me at once, sending me back a step and looking away while the screams rang out below. I heard Solitaire laughing, barely, over the din. Then the air was clearing, and I risked a look back to see the result of his work.

Limbs, everywhere. Most were within twenty feet of the epicenter, some scattered far enough that they'd landed past the scorch marks. The atmosphere was full of churning smog, all white and gray, a smokescreen I could barely even look past. Behind it bodies were strewn about, ten, a dozen, twenty. I could only estimate it as a significant portion of the enemy. More were wounded, lying there screaming, clutching ruined faces and gushing wounds.

There was a terrified tremble running through our team, and then Solitaire was roaring out another cackle. "Come on, while they're reeling, or are you boys too scared to fight even with a wizard on your side?!"

There was something different about him, and it was infectious. A sudden animalism to his voice, a savagery to his eyes, an eagerness in the way he began running down the slope, knife clutched tightly in one hand, length of wood tighter still in the other. Solitaire barely took two paces before I was after him, and not even three before the rest of the men were charging down, roaring and laughing.

Our enemies were still reeling when we reached them, else we'd probably have been cut to pieces, and I felt all the old reflexes start taking over as we closed in. My spear went through one of their necks before he even knew I was there, and this time I had the chance to rip it free before stabbing another, gutting this one with a twist of the shaft and letting entrails spill out like worms from a corpse as he fell.

An instant later, the rest of our men crashed into theirs, and everything became chaos.

CHAPTER TWENTY-TWO

Solitaire's POV: Day 41
Current Wealth: 0 silver, 0 copper
Current Debt: 6 gold, 44 silver, 20 copper

I had a man's cock in my mouth, and not in the fun way. He screamed while I chewed away at it, biting through fabric, skin, then veins and gristle, tearing what was left of the mangled organ free with a sharp wrench of my neck. The man spasmed beneath me, and I was an instant away from smashing his brains out with my rock when I caught movement out of the corner of my eye.

A quick roll took me from the axe swing's path and left the blade stuck in the first man's belly, worsening his already sub-average day. In the time its wielder took to free it, I was already up and throwing. My rock bounced off his cheek, sending him a stunned step back and leaving a chance for me to bowl him over in a tackle. He struggled, I strangled.

A fist caught my face, and I answered with a headbutt that knocked the fight out of him. Before it could come back, I was turning the limp gangster over and gripping his skull and jaw as tightly as I could. One swift wrench was enough to snap the spine, then I was standing again, moving onto the next one.

He was ready for me, and wielding a big, horrible meat cleaver already stained with someone's blood. I glanced around, saw that half our boys were dead, and the enemy had begun to galvanize, so I decided that not getting gutted was the better part of valor. There were always better ways to fight a nasty, dangerous man than face-to-face, even if you couldn't wait for him to take a nap.

I turned and sprinted for the slope, asshole in hot pursuit. He was almost on me, my pace deliberately slow, and then I dropped to the ground and lashed out a kick to his knee. It struck, with all of my force meeting all of his momentum, challenged by bones left shriveled and thin by a lifetime of pre-industrial nutrition. The joint broke, the gangster fell, and my boot was coming down on his neck before he could even scream. I felt the snap run through my leg, and it was oddly satisfying.

It didn't take long to spot my friends in the melee after that—even though it had long since shifted to resemble a remarkably pointy mosh pit. Beam was running around and kicking the fuck out of everybody, using his spear half like an actual spear and half like a bloody club, and seemingly equally deadly with either. Shango was a bit more restrained, circling the fights, staying defensive and clinging close to the Olympian. Both, however, were dangerously near to being encircled. Bollocks, I'd been hoping to save my last surprise for later.

I wasn't actually a wizard, by the way. That was what we in the gaming community refer to as 'a lie.' What I *was*, was very, very clever and well supplied with horseshit, charcoal, and elemental sulphur—all the ingredients for black powder. I'd used most of it in the big bomb which, by my count, had either killed or de-limbed seventeen of the enemy. The rest had been split between two things—one, a surprise waiting back near the "fort," and the other . . .

Well, the other was in my pocket.

I withdrew the pipe bomb—fashioned from a chair leg, makeshift fuse, and the rest of my explosives—and knelt down with the tinder, keeping an eye out for attackers while I lit it. I was a safe distance away from the actual fighting, though, and got it done soon enough. Standing, I steadied my aim and chucked it at the greatest concentration of the enemy.

Now, I'm aware you probably think it was extremely dangerous and unwise to throw a deadly bomb into a fight my friends were actively engaged in. To answer your inevitable criticism, however, let me just say that you're a massive pussy, probably boring to be around at parties, and likely will be useless when the government tries to kill everybody.

My aim was perfect. The bomb arced just as I'd hoped, and it went off at around chest-height. I didn't quite see how many it killed, but it had everybody nice and panicked again. Beam and Shango were given time for pause, and I was on them an instant later.

"We're leaving," I told them, and they both nodded and turned to sprint along with me as we tore away from the fight.

It wasn't as smooth as I'd have hoped. The other gangsters, apparently, saw the way the wind was blowing and started running, too, scattering in all directions and leaving the enemy free to pursue. We had a head start, and we were plenty faster, but the difference wasn't as big as I'd have hoped. We tore down one alley, making a really big wish that we lost our pursuers.

We didn't. Footsteps raced after us from behind, echoing along the cobblestones, bouncing off the walls. It was one of the scariest sounds I've ever heard. Scary enough to risk a glance over my shoulder and confirm the numbers.

Three. Well, it could be worse. One was a bit big, massive really, but besides that it seemed we were ahead of the curve. I heard Shango swear beside me and glanced over to see he was looking, too.

"The big guy's fucking level thirteen." He swore again. I joined in this time, and started running faster.

We were faster than two of them, but the big one tore ahead of his comrades, closing in with a terrible certainty. I realized then that he'd catch Shango and Beam without a doubt.

But not me. I'd put all my skillpoints into speed, and I had been a decent sprinter even before that. By now I was the fastest, and I had the feeling I could pull ahead of this one even in the worst circumstances. Now, though, when he'd be catching two others first?

As the saying went, I didn't even need to be faster than him. Just faster than the slowest one in our group. Faster than Shango. I felt a chill run down my spine, as I realized what needed to be done.

I turned, rock already in my hand, wrist flicking at the end of my throw to send it hurtling at the bastard as fast as I could manage.

"Fight them here!" I roared, just an instant after the stone hit a chest. A useless throw, really, such a light projectile would never do anything unless I caught the face, but it stunned the bastard and galvanized my friends. All of us halted at once, then charged the big fucker.

I reached him first, much to my regret. He surprised me by lashing out with an open palm, stopping me instantly from my sprint and punting me onto my back. All the air left my lungs at once, and I lay there gasping while he closed in, and then he was driven back when Beam smashed into him. Shango seized my shoulder, dragging me to my feet with a concerned stare, and I forced a grin to calm him. Both of us moved to help Beam at once when we realized the big one's friends were arriving.

"One each," I barked, picking a gangster at random and lunging for him. It was a mistake. I was still winded, and the sudden stab of pain in my torso slowed me to a stumble, letting him crack a haymaker against my jaw that drove me back again. I caught Shango fighting the other from the corner of my eye, then I found my footing and closed up to block another punch.

The enemy seemed unarmed, which was likely the only reason I hadn't died already, but he was damned good at using those fists, even with nothing in them. By the time I'd recovered enough to move quickly, he'd already landed a dozen more hits. Bruising forearms and biceps, catching my head once. He was fast, skilled, and clearly experienced. He'd probably been in more fights than me, and he definitely seemed better trained. All that, and I'd lost my knife in the melee before.

It was a shame he was half a foot shorter than me, or he'd probably have won.

Another haymaker came, and I lowered my guard for it, ducking down into the punch to catch fist with forehead. I felt the knuckles breaking against me, heard his cry of pain confirm it, and then I was lunging to grab him. He backed away, desperately scrambling to break my hold as I snagged clothes with my curling fingers. Something tripped him and he went down, almost dragging me with him before I solidified my footing, corrected my hold and hauled.

One hundred and ten pounds of gangster lifted high into the air, flailing and yelping in surprise, not stopping until he was already raised fully over my head. I held him there for a moment, even looking into his eyes as our heads rested conveniently facing one another. Then I reversed the motion, and all the muscles that had been fighting gravity now gave it a hand.

He hit the ground shoulder-first, and probably broke every bone within inches of the impact point. He actually bounced a few centimeters into the air before coming to a rest, and lay there gasping while I cocked my leg back and threw a kick into his ribs. They broke, he rolled, then stopped at a wall. Blood was leaking from his lips, and his eyes were dazed and cloudy. Not a problem, for now. Probably not a problem ever again.

I turned to see Shango's opponent was just as fast, and winning. Landing punches everywhere my friend's guard wasn't, kicking at legs to trip him, sticking his fists in all the nasty spots dear old mum had taught me to aim for. The gangster didn't notice me closing in until I was already on him, the poor bastard. He'd turned just in time for his face to catch the headbutt I'd thrown with all my velocity at him.

His skull cracked beneath mine, and he started falling instantly. I caught him, hoisted him up, then headbutted him again in the same spot. Then again, and the cracks became fractures. Another two, and the fractures widened. By the time I finished—by the time my skull was pounding with the pain of being used as a bludgeon—the gangster's head didn't really resemble a head anymore.

That was just about dead enough for my taste, and I let him fall. Turning, I flashed a grin at Shango only to see him staring ahead in horror. I slowly followed his gaze.

Beam hit the ground, rolled four yards to a stop at our feet, and coughed where he lay.

The big fucker stalked after him. He was taller than any of us, muscled like a boar and pale as a Klansman's uniform. He looked like Kratos, and even more pissed, eyes flicking between his dead and dying friends, and all I could was manage to do was raise my hands before he was on me.

CHAPTER TWENTY-THREE

Shango's POV: Day 41
Current Wealth: 0 silver, 0 copper
Current Debt: 6 gold, 44 silver, 20 copper

Solitaire was already lunging for the big guy while Beam groaned at our feet, and I was following after him, only hesitating for an instant. A giant fist came around for my friend's head, and he caught it with his brow. I expected to see the knuckles break, like so many others had meeting his favorite trick. They didn't. Solitaire stumbled back, shocked and dazed, while another blow came in for his guts. This one was barely blocked, tossing him flat against the ground. It wasn't like watching a brawl. It was more like watching a man with hammers fight one without.

For a moment the enemy's focus was entirely on Solitaire, and I took that opportunity to throw a punch of my own. Swinging my whole body around, using it to lever my arm, keeping the thumb out of my fist. Everything I'd been taught. It bounced off the man's cheek like he was some giant boulder, actually making my wrist sting, and the sight of his eyes coming to rest on me had me just about shitting myself.

Then a heel shot up from the ground to catch him between the legs, and he folded over, stumbling back amid a string of curses as Solitaire rolled and stood, staggering back into the fight like a drunkard and chasing the enemy further back with a haymaker. For one wonderful, precious moment, the man just kept out of arms' reach and carried on reeling. Then his pain subsided, and he was back at us with all the speed of a pouncing lion.

Solitaire seemed to be his focus, backstepping while the big man chased, and I followed. My punches thudded into his back one after the other, but it felt more like a wall of stone than flesh, and I suspected my knuckles were hurting more than his body. Solitaire was faring little better, covered up to weather the bombardment of punches smashing into his guard from every side there was, balance shaking by the step, face twisted up in effort and pain. His back was soon at the wall, retreat forcibly halted, and I felt a stab of panic as I saw the giant rear up for his widest strike yet.

It never landed, because Beam was on him first, slamming into his ribs shoulder-first with all the speed of a sprinter, driving the man back with all the pneumatic force of a wrestler, circling around the moment his momentum ceased and lancing the man's lower back with elbows that wouldn't have been entirely out of place in some professional MMA ring. Solitaire was big, broadened now by Beam's training, and he'd hit the guy hard before, but Beam actually smashed the man down onto his knees.

He wasn't that low for even a second before Solitaire moved in, swinging a hip-height kick around that cracked perfectly against the giant's vulnerable temple. He dropped like a sack of rocks.

I realized then that I was just staring while my friends fought and bled. The anger that filled me had me by their side a single instant later, all three of us stomping away at the bastard while he tried to rise.

We were stronger than we'd been on arrival now, including Beam, thanks to his skillpoint. And there were three of us to his one, all of our focus on the beating, all of our minds locked in, calling on our months of training together, hunting together and surviving together. So, it was incredible how little it did.

My heel clipped the giant's chin, and he barely flinched. Solitaire's knee found an eye socket, and the man only growled. Beam landed some bloody overhead kick right into the back of his neck, and all it did was send him forward a step. A step, I saw, that he now took with both feet flat on the ground, having managed to fully stand up.

A fist came, Solitaire dodged, and I went low for the guy's groin. He must've seen it coming because a knee hit my chest, and next thing I knew, the sky was looking down at me, laughing. Eyes watery, vision fuzzy, head ringing like someone was smashing away at a bell inside it.

Why was it gray? Snow was white, wasn't it? So why was it gray instead of white?

I pondered the matter for about as long as it took my brain to finish getting the high score in cranial pinball, then my consciousness stabilized, my thoughts stopped being runny around the edges, and I remembered that my friends were still fighting Kratos. I sat bolt upright, cursing as I saw the display ahead.

Beam was down again, and rising back up slowly, and Solitaire was clinging to the giant's back like some feral beast, snarling and spitting, fingers digging into all the painful spots. His face was pressed against the side of the man's head, and a scream was cutting the air. I took a moment to realize it was coming from the giant, and then I saw why.

Solitaire yanked his face back, and a spray of blood jumped after it. Clinging to his hair, cheeks, scalp, raining down to stain the dirt. In the side of the man's head, where Solitaire had just been pressing his mouth, I saw a mess of mangled flesh and oozing veins. It looked like fucking hamburger meat, not least of all the ear, which seemed to have been fully chewed off.

Just before I could wonder where it was, Solitaire spat the mangled thing out at the giant's feet, then shifted his place on the man's back to start biting at the other. Fucking hell.

Almost fortunately, he never managed to complete the task. The giant slammed himself back-first into an alley wall, with Solitaire pinned between the bricks and his shoulder blades. Coughing something fierce, my friend dropped from him just in time to catch another punch across the face, which just about flattened him. I was on the giant now, kicking at a knee this time and actually connecting quite well. The man cursed, turned with a slight limp, and swore after me as I turned to sprint away before he even rounded. He was pursuing fast when Beam came flying at him.

He ducked, wove, punched, and elbowed, lasting all of a few seconds, then falling back down. I came in with another kick, this time to the ribs, and almost fell over with the force of it. The giant, though, barely took a step back. Then he was coming back for me.

This wasn't like fighting the troll. This was an opponent that could think, and there was something fiercely terrifying about that.

I punched him in the nose, and to my surprise he actually blinked. After that, he punched me.

When I woke up, Solitaire was being strangled, suspended fully off the ground in a two-handed grip, legs kicking out feebly beneath him. Beam was groaning, lying face-down and not moving nearly enough for my liking, and everyone else was still gone.

I groaned, stood, shuddered, and charged, punching back, belly, ribs. All to no avail. Panic started building when Solitaire turned red, and I jumped up to start chewing at the giant's other ear.

Either my friend had the bite force of a pit bull, or there was some technique to dismemberment via jaw that I'd not learned, because I found the remaining side of the man's head putting up a lot more resistance than I'd expected. I abandoned the effort after Solitaire went from red to purple, and cursed.

Time for my last Hail Mary.

I dug a thumb into what was left of his missing ear, pressing the digit into yielding flesh, watching with disgust as more blood welled from the mess. A scream told me the giant was feeling it, his head turning to deny me access, arms folding on instinct to make his body more compact.

Arms folding, with Solitaire still held in them, bringing him closer to the bastard's face. It didn't even take an instant before two more thumbs were stuck in the giant, this time each one pressing down on an eye. He screamed, let go instantly, and reached up to pry Solitaire off. Solitaire didn't let him, letting go before he could, dropping down and swinging an uppercut up directly into the giant's groin.

The kick that followed sent Solitaire almost as far back as the troll had, and he wasn't moving much when he landed. I actually blocked the backhand the giant threw next, but I might as well have blocked a sledgehammer swing. I still ended up groaning in a heap.

And that was it. I was fucked. I tried to move, but my body had other plans. It was all I could do to crane my neck and see the giant approaching me, face tattooed, bald head scarred, neck and shoulder completely red where the unending ear blood had soaked through. It looked like I was going to die.

That was . . . fine. A curious thought, but I could hardly deny it. I'd already been planning to off myself a few weeks ago. At least now I'd go out having fought with a bit of hope first. I closed my eyes, waiting for the stomp that would surely snap something important enough to kill me.

And it never came. I looked up, surprised to find a dense light spewing across the alley, my eyes watering at its intensity. Skin itching with the touch of something else, something I recognized only from Corvan's healing magics.

We hadn't asked why Beam picked his name, but he'd told us later. Beam, like a streak of light. Beam, like a sunray. Beam, because that's what he always got told his smile was like. Beam, to remind him not to let that smile slip while we were here.

Yeah, a bit of a drama queen, our friend, but one tends to be when one competes on a global scale. Anyway, he was getting the last laugh now, because fuck me, was that light bright. Bright, gray somehow, and coming from between his hands.

I could just barely make out a shape—long, sort of cylindrical, humming, and ephemeral in its form. It looked almost like some energy sword from *Halo*, like light given mass, and I had about a half second to admire the fact before he lunged with it. The air screamed as he moved, as if even *it* was scared of his new weapon.

And I could feel the magic coming off it from across the alley.

CHAPTER TWENTY-FOUR

Beam's POV: Day 41
Current Wealth: 0 silver, 0 copper
Current Debt: 6 gold, 44 silver, 20 copper

I was fairly certain that, generally speaking, corpses didn't *actually* have visible stink lines coming off of them, let alone dully glowing flies mere minutes after death. The one I was looking at did, though.

At first I thought maybe I'd just been hit harder than I initially suspected, but they got clearer, not more faded, as my vision focused and my headache subsided. They were all tinged gray and just barely luminous, like some deepwater animal dragged up to the surface and allowed to glow in the air. And yet they jumped out in my vision. Something about them demanded my attention, registering as clear to me as my own heartbeat.

Groaning, I rolled onto my side and glanced up. Kratos was making his way to Shango. At best I had about five seconds before my friend was dead. I moved faster, shuffling toward the corpse, ignoring my body, which was swearing at me with every inch cleared. I was beside it soon, forcing a foot underneath me and then standing with a roar.

Something brushed against my hand, and I didn't need to look to know what it was. The gray . . . mystery. Whatever was emanating out of that corpse. I ran my fingers through it, then closed them into a fist, binding it into my grip and feeling it solidify.

It felt like death, decay. Like the corpse was resting in my hand, touching my mind, whispering at my thoughts. My fatigue started to bleed away, and in its place I felt something new. An emotion that wasn't mine, an instinct that wasn't human, an urge that wasn't natural.

Yes, yes! Now tear him apart! Sunder him!

That voice, echoing around in my head, was definitely not my own. It wasn't that of anyone I knew and was far more coherent than any of the fuzzy hallucinations that sometimes accompanied a blow to the noggin. I knew all that, but I didn't have the time or luxury of giving it any more serious thought. I tightened my fist, finally glancing at what it held.

Gray, swirling energies. I might have guessed as much, but now they'd congealed into something solid. A long bar, cylindrical and thick, heavy like a chunk of wrought iron. I could feel the strength in it, and something more. An icy sensation leaking out of the material and up through my arm.

It made me want to move, to kill. I obliged it.

A roar escaped me, running out of my mouth on instinct alone, and it snapped the pale giant's head around just in time for him to see me come flying across the alley at a sprint. He raised his guard, and I swung my new weapon for his head, missed, then twisted around to bring it back for his ribs. It was a motion I'd practiced a thousand times—ten thousand—and it was all the easier with how light this weapon was compared to the swords I'd trained with.

Light, and viciously deadly. As if it weighed ten times more on the moment of impact. I felt ribs crack as it bounced off the bald man's side, and the weapon fizzled out of existence before I could repeat the motion. My enemy was still stunned, hunched down and clutching his wounded torso, precious seconds bought for me to adjust to being without a weapon once more.

So I lashed out a kick for his head. That same technique had staggered a troll within our earliest days in Redacle. I was stronger now, and this fucker was definitely no troll. He went down instantly, and I followed him, taking the mount position on sheer muscle memory as hours of grappling came back to me. I was slamming elbows and hammer fists down onto his head for what felt like a minute before he finally made his move.

It was a simple one, but effective. He just grabbed me, then hauled me off him like I was a little kid, sent me rolling and scraping along the jagged alley ground while he stumbled to his feet. I managed to stand just in time to leap back from a haymaker, which might've cracked my skull open otherwise. Then my back hit the wall.

He didn't hesitate even an instant, another punch flying for me, this time forcing me to block. Easier to guard against a fucking baseball bat, the sheer size of his arm almost bowled me over, and an instant later his giant hands were closing around my throat, squeezing. I tried to pry the fingers off, to no avail. Tried to break his grip with all the techniques I'd learned, and none worked. It was like getting throttled by a fucking powerlifter, by a bear. Raw strength being applied in enough volume that skill and experience went entirely out the window.

And then I remembered his ribs.

I kicked them, hard, right in the injured spot, and he released me. I took a step back, even while I darted to one side, resisting the urge to let myself recover and forcing my body to throw another strike. This one was far better in form, and the power it injected into his side was enough that I could feel the bones shifting place where my knuckles touched them. Kratos was kneeling again, this time coughing up blood, and I allowed myself a single instant to ready the finishing blow.

It was another kick, carefully aimed and perfectly executed, heel catching his neck right at the base. That magic spot where the spine transitioned from torso to skull. Something cracked, and the man started spasming. I watched while he kicked and gibbered beneath me.

Solitaire was right. It really does take fucking ages for someone to die properly. But he did. I let a few stomps come down on his neck and skull, once he was finally still. Just to be sure. And then I was turning to my friends.

Shango was absolutely fucked, but still conscious. He eyed me with a mix of confusion and awe as I helped him stand, turning sharply to where Solitaire had fallen. Even that motion made him wince—he was in bad, bad shape. We all were, I supposed. Whatever had come over me to let my body move the way it had, it was wearing off. I could feel all the aches and pains return. Worse now, and probably agitated by my adrenaline rush. I could only hope I had enough left in the tank to make it back to our hideout.

Solitaire was groaning but conscious when we got to him. He'd gotten the worst of it, apparently, having fought the giant about as much as me, without years of Olympic training to help out. He mumbled something about the one percent and lizards while we slung him over our shoulders. He sounded like himself, at least.

That left the two of us confident enough in his recovery to spend a few minutes searching the alley for discarded weapons, retrieving a few knives, pocketing them posthaste, and making our way out.

Shango didn't wait long to speak once we'd begun our trek back to homebase. His questions came rapidly and pointedly.

"What the shit was that light you conjured?" he demanded, eying me like I was some specimen in front of a microscope.

It was disconcerting, but I wasn't in any mood to be particularly bothered by such things. I answered him.

"I have no idea," I said, honestly. "I just . . . I wanted a weapon, and then I saw this weird gray stuff floating around the corpse . . . So I grabbed it, and it became a club."

Shango didn't look mollified by the information. I pressed on.

"There was this voice egging me on as I used it, too, telling me to kill the guy." He blanched, and I winced, sighing. "You think I've snapped."

Shango snorted.

"Of course not. Hearing voices alone? Yeah, sure, odds are you're crazy. Going nuts exactly as you start using some weird magic, though, is one coincidence more than I care to count. I'd guess there's more to this than either of us know."

And that was all we said on the topic. It wasn't a long conversation, and I was grateful for that. More grateful, though, to have had it at all. It hadn't registered to me how worried I was about the idea that I'd cracked until I said it aloud. And Shango dismissing the notion was exactly what I needed.

A bit convenient, that. Was he just saying it to keep me functional while weapons were still drawn? Maybe. I didn't imagine I had any way of knowing if he was. When someone like Shango wanted to trick you, you'd be tricked. And yet, he was my friend.

I'm not Solitaire, not even remotely. Trust always came easy to me. I took comfort in it while we shuffled our way back. As my body became heavier, more pained, and slower with seemingly every step, that comfort grew ever more important.

But not as important as it was when we got back.

The big, robust building the rest of our side was camped out in still held strong, but the enemy had clearly gotten to it before us. They were crowded around it, surrounding the place in some big ring, all however many dozen were left. They held cudgels, knives, all the same weapons as the bastards in the alleys. Swapping arrows with defenders propped behind windows. All of them seemed either lightly injured or in perfect health, and the panic Solitaire's bomb had spread through their numbers was nowhere to be seen.

We were cut off, outnumbered twenty or more to one. And we were a lot more beaten up now than before.

Solitaire's POV: Day 41
Current Wealth: 0 silver, 0 copper
Current Debt: 6 gold, 44 silver, 20 copper

So, we were fucked.

Not the nicest realization to be greeting me upon waking up, but I had always been a practical fellow. Better to accept reality for what it is than whine and bitch about what it *ought* to be. Even if there's a lot to whine about.

Fifty feral, malnourished ape man bastards between us and salvation. Some among them, according to Shango, packing levels nearly comparable to Kratos. We'd been operating on the assumption that there wouldn't be many humans over level one in this conflict, and that had been false. Tragically so.

We sat around planning while the enemy readied themselves for their attack on the building. It was annoyingly far from any other structures, so jumping onto its roof was out of the question. The ground was paved, too, which ruled out digging— though, I reckon we'd have needed wooden beams and a few weeks for that to be practical either way. If calling the guards would have done anything, they'd have already been swarming the place, too, so it appeared we'd be on our own.

Fighting through them was technically an option, but then, so was stabbing ourselves in the balls, and I didn't fancy our chances with that either.

Now, all of us are fairly clever guys. Even Beam, weirdly enough, when he's not busy swinging a sword like his dopamine receptors are activated by kinetic energy. It took us some time to think up a workable plan, but we did. Eventually.

Mind you, that plan was not exactly perfect. Or complex. It might actually have been a matter of debate whether it even constituted a plan at all, come to think of it, but it was the best we had. Better to accept reality for what it is than whine and bitch about what it *ought* to be.

We waited until night fell, checking our bodies for wounds—which were more painful than damaging—while killing time as Beam practiced trying to replicate the fucking magic sword powers he apparently had, and Shango and I tried to figure out if we had anything similar. No luck on either account. We finally found the skies dark enough for us to make our move, which was honestly more worrisome than relieving. Our move was a crude, risky, terrifying thing. And now we'd used up our last excuse to delay it.

I came out first, despite my wounds. Movements sluggish, body aching, but alert enough for what needed doing. I had a knife held tight in one hand and was wrapped in the darkest fabrics we could scrounge up, now or never.

The enemy was still encircling the building, and I approached one of them from behind. He was a few yards from either of his friends at best, but light was expensive in primitive worlds like this, and so were decent nutrients. His vision wouldn't be nearly as good at picking up shapes in darkness as ours—modern humans. Was that right? I swore I'd remembered it correctly, from some article about pre-industrial society and sleep patterns.

Well, time to bet my life on remembering correctly. I closed in behind him.

Dear old mother had been a careful teacher. Clever, focused, and with a genuine passion for ensuring her lessons stuck. The jagged old bitch had made nice and sure to keep me quiet when I moved, picking me up on every creaking floorboard and hard footstep, teaching me how to glide through obstacles. I couldn't fight like Beam, probably never would, but that was fine by me. The best way to start a fight was by instantly killing the fucker you were fighting, before he knew there was a fight coming.

My knife found the neck easily enough, always a good place to cut if you want something dead quickly. I pressed it hard against the skin, then rolled it along the outside, cleaving through the carotid, moving to nick the jugular in one motion. Nick, not sever completely. That was annoying, I let the pressure ebb too early, probably bought the bastard a few extra seconds of life. I'd have to correct for that next time.

Next time, but not now. Now I focused on leaning in, grabbing him, wrapping an arm tight around his chest and squeezing down on the man's voice box. Keeping him from making any noise. I held him still, hoisted him back so he couldn't kick the ground and alert his friends, and felt his heartbeat slowing against me as his struggles weakened. Then he was still. I held him a few moments more, to be sure his veins were nice and empty.

Looking around, I could just dimly make out the two men closest to us. Both had their eyes ahead, watching the building, both were upward of twelve feet away. They would've probably still seen me if the moon was out, or if the world was lit by a modern city's artificial glow, but for once the world was doing me a favor.

Everything was dark enough that even a lifetime of easy-carrot access didn't let my baby blues catch them clearly in the gloom.

I smiled in relief, let out a breath I'd been holding a bit too long, and advanced on the second. He died quicker.

By the time the night was too light to continue, I'd killed eight people and counted how many were left. Forty-six. Not a bad haul at all. But we wouldn't get another chance at this. I knew that much the moment the first alarmed cry made its way out across the town of Jhigral.

Ugh, people were always so whiny when they got scared. Did it cost so much to shut up? To bite your tongue? To just accept reality for what it was, rather than whine and bitch about what it *ought* to be? I wish I could kill more of the simpering, spineless animals.

"Fucking lethal, man!" Beam grinned, slapping me on the back about as hard as a normal person might have, if their fist were a sledgehammer head. It was good to receive the accolades, in any case, not least because it meant I was back within arms' reach of my allies.

We kept an eye on the enemy, even while grinning about our victory, and it was Shango who first noticed the change when it came.

"They're moving," he whispered, urgently. "Reorganizing."

They were. Their circle became tighter, men moving closer together. Structured like that, they covered much less ground, and yet they were all tighter packed by a good few meters. I wouldn't be trying another killing with them sitting like that anymore.

Well, that was fine. We had all day to think of something new anyway. After having Shango check to ensure we didn't have more skillpoints at our disposal—apparently we'd not yet done something constituting a completed quest—we had nothing else to do but wait. It was fortunate that dear old mum had always been so careful about teaching me how to stash yourself among city streets to keep from being disturbed while you rested. The sky continued to lighten as sleep took us, and Beam volunteered for the first watch while we got some shut-eye.

He shook Shango and me awake not an hour later. We rose to follow his gaze and saw the enemy were moving again, standing and readying weapons. It was fully light out—or as light as it ever got in this shithole—and we could see the weapons clutched tightly in their arms as they marched on the fortress.

"Fuck," I said. It was about the most accurate assessment I could've made. Things were about to kick off.

There wasn't a lot we could do. Our sole advantage was that the enemy likely wouldn't expect three people to attack them without backup. Because those three people would be slaughtered. Not wanting to bank on achieving a sixteen-to-one kill/death ratio with that edge alone, we sat and waited for them to finish storming the fort.

Shutters, obviously, were the first priority. Great big lump hammers were drawn out from the crowd to smash them in, cracking the wooden panels nailed across them, then splintering them. The frames broke next, and soon enough men were scrambling inside, walking over tarps thrown down over the jagged openings. We heard fighting and screaming ring out, and still we just watched and waited. An idea was forming now.

The enemy was hurrying inside, storming corridors and fighting. They outnumbered our side, but not by much. Maybe four on three at best, after the losses took both during the skirmish and at the Ratpass. So, if something delayed a portion of their forces from attacking the interior . . .

Fuck, it was worth a try, probably. They didn't seem to have many ranged weapons—perhaps bows were too expensive to trust hired toughs with—so it'd be melee only. We could try to cut and run if things got bad.

It was the closest thing we had to a guarantee of winning. I swore, and shared the plan with my friends.

They swore too.

More and more men poured into the building, and though the walls were too thick for us to actually hear anything, we could easily imagine the viciousness panning out inside. We'd been wrapped up in quite a similar fight just yesterday. The enemy grew less densely packed around it as they emptied their ranks through smashed windows, and our moment came closer with every heartbeat.

Then it arrived. The three of us took a second to curse our bad luck—the Veiled Lady, the universe itself, and possibly the Roman Empire, too, and then we were rushing ahead, knives in hand and veins clogged with adrenaline.

I took the lead, of course, getting my money's worth for those skillpoints spent on speed. Beam was behind me and Shango right on his tail.

We aimed for the center and the back of the enemy's ranks. Smashing into the spine of the crowd, intending to wrench it in half with sheer killing momentum. Well, we had that in spades.

A man turned toward me when I was within a few feet of him, but all he got for it was a dagger blade whipping across his neck. I smashed into the one closest to him and bowled the tiny bastard over, swearing I felt fragile ribs break under the impact as I plowed into the ranks, then I was slashing and punching in every direction around me. Beam and Shango reached the melee only seconds later, helping me beat back an opening. By the time we turned to retreat, we'd already killed two men and wounded God knows how many more.

By now, the enemy had figured out we were there. That was unfortunate, as I'm far better at stabbing backs than I am faces, but apparently they weren't eager to rush us. Our size probably helped with that, and doubtless our kill count was leaving them nice and intimidated, too. I reckon it probably bought us a few more moments of backing off before another big bastard pulled up from the crowd.

He wasn't *as* large as Kratos, but he was still about Beam's height, and slabbed in muscle. He had a big lump hammer held tight and a look in his eyes that reminded me both of a praying mantis and someone with late-stage rabies.

I drew a lot of conclusions very quickly after that and landed on a fairly obvious one. If we got swarmed, we'd die. If we ran, they might not chase us, and our employer could still get finished off. We had to keep them tied up. We had to play for time.

I forced myself to take a step forward, held my knife outstretched, and snarled with as much courage as I could muster. The savagery? That just came naturally.

"Come on then, just you and me, you big fucker. Let's settle this like men!"

CHAPTER TWENTY-SIX

Solitaire's POV: Day 42
Current Wealth: 0 silver, 0 copper
Current Debt: 6 gold, 14 silver, 20 copper

Beam couldn't have fought this one, and I couldn't have explained why in the time we had. The giant was stronger, tougher, and angrier than me, without a doubt, but that hammer looked nasty enough to cleave right through whatever resilience my friends had gotten by spending skillpoints.

Well, in fairness, given the throb of my fucking ribs, I'd need to spend some of my own. But for now, I was still the fastest guy, which made me the best choice for this fight. There were just different things to consider when weapons were involved. Strength mattered less when it was pitted behind an edge.

And neither of my friends knew their way around a knife fight like I did.

Around me, men were jeering. They didn't like my odds against Gonads the Barbarian, and a quick glance showed that neither Beam nor Shango disagreed. That was fine. It'd just surprise them all the more when I gutted him. Or I'd be killed instantly, and get to die all smug and knowing without ever knowing I was proven wrong.

"I accept," he growled, speaking with a voice that sounded like his lungs were cast in iron. He came on so quickly that the crowd barely had time to start roaring in excitement, hammer whipping around for my head.

I didn't duck, and I didn't jump back. I lunged in, anticipating the swing and letting the handle catch my shoulder a full foot below the metal head. The fucker was so strong that I still felt the impact, but it wasn't damaging, and it left me nice and close. My knife was better at close range, biting deep into one giant pec the instant he took to stagger back from the stab.

Fast reflexes then. Very fast. Annoying. If I'd known about those, I'd have left him to Beam. Well, too late to pussy out now. As my mother always used to say, *when the shit hits the fan, you either start running or get splattered.*

I started running. It probably surprised him, the sprint was near-superhuman and ended with a flying knee to the chest that sent him down flat on his back . . . but didn't kill him. Odd. Did my force not increase alongside my stat-enhanced velocity? A thought for later.

I interrupted it by bringing the knife down hard into his face, but he turned his head just in time to take it through the cheek instead of an eye. Teeth came free where the blade smashed deep into gums, and his agony was loud enough to nearly burst my eardrums.

Then he grabbed me.

Bollocks, I thought, just an instant before he pivoted, turning as much of his strength and weight as was possible into the motion, despite the awkward angle. It sent me rolling away. He came up, and I came up faster, kneed his face again and rolled away as the hammer came back around.

I realized then that I'd dropped my knife, and could only swear as the giant closed in. He came at me like I was some big fucking tree he wanted to chop down, swinging left, right, always carefully ready to backstep, eyes watching me like a hawk.

He didn't look as confident anymore. There was blood running down his cheek, staining his collar, and he still winced here and there. I caught glimpses of the inside of his mouth, now that the knife was removed, flashes of white teeth covered in red, and I didn't think he'd ever be eating steak again.

Progress then.

Now I just had to stop him from eating anything else. Easier said than done, because apparently those bulging muscles could swing quite quickly. My foot slipped, the hammer clipped me, and I stumbled. Halted, I saw it coming up to fall down on me and realized there was nothing left but the Hail Mary.

So I tackled him again.

He didn't go down, obviously, but his balance was broken and his swing was halted. We grappled for an instant while he tried to figure out what to do, which gave me all the time in the world to reach down.

My fist closed tight around his balls.

There's a technique for crushing testicles. They're surprisingly tough, and if you want it done right, you can't just grab on and squeeze away. You need to take a second to measure your grip, add a twist, and try to press them against one another. Like cracking walnuts in your hand. I hadn't done it in quite a while.

Fortunately, I wasn't that out of practice. I felt the soft organs give with a sickening squelch, and heard their owner scream as he spasmed, hammer falling to the ground with a clatter. I was on it almost before it had finished rattling, snatching it up by the handle and taking a step back, putting some distance between us, rather than shrinking it.

I needed the extra room for my swing.

The hammer found its home in the man's torso, catching the lowest ribs on his left side just over his belly. They caved in like twigs under a combat boot, and he folded over, falling to his knees and convulsing. His body was experiencing more pain than it knew what to do with, his mind pulled in too many directions to respond properly. He was still reeling by the time I adjusted my grip and brought the hammer down again.

Right onto the top of his skull.

Bone was hardly an obstacle at all, even in a volume as big as this bastard's body. It shattered, caved in, gave way and let the metal sink deep into squishy brains beneath. He began spasming, properly spasming now, some bizarre seizure taking his whole body. He rolled around, gurgling, eyes aimless and limbs kicking. I hit him again. The second blow left him still as a statue.

Still as a corpse, really, because that's what he was. I eyed his ruined pulp of a head one last time to make sure, then let the weapon fall by my side.

All eyes were on me, and all mouths were agape, but silent. Weird, I hadn't even noticed when the cheering stopped. Its absence hit me like the hammer almost had, left me stunned, slow. It might've gotten me killed if the adrenaline hadn't kept my thoughts nimble and slick.

Right now, there were about thirty very confused, disbelieving enemies staring at me and my friends. I'd just won an impossible duel. And there wouldn't be another.

I turned to Beam and Shango, who were already sprinting as I called out my warning for them to do so. They answered quickly enough that we probably had a full two or three seconds' head start on the crowd at our backs.

Around my third stride, I felt something shift in my torso. Pain blossomed, slowing me, and I had to fight back the urge to stop running entirely. From my perspective, I was barely even jogging. Still, that was enough to keep me neck-and-neck with Shango at least. Any other time, that might've been a nice, satisfying reminder of how far I'd come. Now it was an irrelevance, and I ignored it.

Something hit the ground beside me, rolling and bouncing ahead. A brick? Fuck, of course, I wasn't the only one who could throw rocks. If I remembered correctly, even my idiot species had figured that out about a million years ago. Something thudded against my shoulder, another chunk of rock, and I snarled at the impact. But I didn't fall.

It hadn't been thrown very hard, things rarely were by the malnourished manlets inhabiting this world. The subsequent impacts that followed, though, were threatening to compensate for their weakness with volume.

There was an alleyway up ahead, and a nice, sharp corner. Turning there might buy us some distance, if we reached it. Distance might—probably would—make our pursuers lose interest. I risked a glance over my shoulder and saw their numbers had already dwindled to a mere nine. That was more than I'd like to fight, new Skills and muscles or no, but it was a decent chunk out of the battle going on. We might actually win.

A rock hit my nose, and I swore, turning back around and forcing my sprint to hasten even as my side burned in protest. We reached the alley a few moments later, footsteps and thudding stone ringing along the walls, echoing like an orchestra.

We hit the far wall without slowing down, bouncing off it to keep our momentum and hurtling on ahead. A few moments later, the sounds of stumbling and swearing reached us. I glanced back again, saw seven men now, and kept running. Another corner, then another, and now the enemy was down to five. That gave me an idea. My legs were burning, my side was splitting, and I was close to collapsing from the fatigue. My injuries had caught up to me while I moved, and I needed to rest. We'd put easily hundreds of meters between us and our pursuers. Enough to get clever.

So I roared out a challenge, turning on my heel and moving for them. Shango and Beam were right behind me.

And the bastards ran. Of course they did. Even if they hadn't seen the result of my challenge, they were five shrimps facing down three bastards, who each probably outweighed them all combined. The alley, soon enough, only held us.

Then, and only then, did I finally let myself collapse against a wall, close my eyes, and let out a nice, long string of swears.

CHAPTER TWENTY-SEVEN

Shango's POV: Day 42
Current Wealth: 0 silver, 0 copper
Current Debt: 6 gold, 44 silver, 20 copper

We sat around for quite some time, pondering the best time to stalk our way back to the site of combat and check which side had won, before either claiming our reward or disappearing into the wilderness. I know, I know, we're so heroic I can hardly even believe it myself sometimes.

Fortunately, it didn't take us long to stumble onto the obvious. We had a perfectly effective way of checking whether we'd secured a victory for our allies or not, and it was built into my head.

[Appraisal]
Class: Revolutionary
Level: 8
Condition: Haggard
Modifiers: +4 Speed, +1 Toughness
Statistics: Strength 7 (5), Speed 11 (8), Dexterity 8 (6), Stamina 6 (3), Toughness 7, Alertness 8 (7), Charisma 3, Intelligence 10
Inventory: Jeans, T-shirt, flick knife, rocks (x3), dagger
Class Abilities: Detect Element II
Current Experience Points: 33/170
Unspent Skillpoints: 2

My heart lurched in excitement at the sight of Solitaire's level progression, and I quickly turned my gaze on Beam to verify.

[Appraisal]
Class: Dragonknight
Level: 7
Condition: Haggard
Modifiers: +1 Strength, +1 Speed, +2 Toughness
Statistics: Strength 9 (7), Speed 9 (7), Dexterity 8 (6), Stamina 9 (7), Toughness 9, Alertness 8 (7), Charisma 6, Intelligence 5
Inventory: Jeans, flannel shirt, spear
Class Abilities: Beloved II
Current Experience Points: 120/160
Unspent Skillpoints: 2

I told my friends about their results, and after some quick mental math from Solitaire, we'd established a few more facts. Namely, each level required ten more experience points to progress than the one before, and we'd managed to secure ourselves a haul of fucking hundreds from this fiasco. It almost made the days spent shitting ourselves worth it.

And it wasn't all we'd be getting.

"So, money," Solitaire began, reading my mind as usual. "What are the odds we're going to have some big, horrible man come up behind us and cut our throats when we go to collect it?"

It was a rhetorical question, of course. Solitaire always thought people were trying to kill him, but this time he had a fair point. We'd tipped the scales a lot in our side's favor, used the enemy's disorganization against them, fought hard and, of course, the giant fucking bomb hadn't hurt either. But that would be working against us now.

The more men Hengrard had left, the more emboldened he'd feel to just kill us. After all, he had a lot of rebuilding to do, and we intended to demand quite a lot of money. That was also to say nothing of the beating we still owed him. So how to play it?

"I could sneak up on him," Beam suggested. "Negotiate at knife point."

So help me, I actually considered his suggestion. But no. The last thing we needed was to make this a more volatile situation than it already was. Oddly enough, Solitaire was the one who came up with the ideal solution. I had to say, it was quite in character. And it was a good one.

It was good enough that we all agreed on it quickly and moved to encircle the base. Outside it was a . . . well, a warzone. Bodies piled around, blood spattered everywhere, discarded weapons being collected by those who remained on Hengrard's staff. We waited, watching from afar, picking out a suitable mark. Then Beam came up behind the poor sod, clobbered him, and dragged him into an alley with us.

Beam was the strongest, but Solitaire was by far scarier, so we had him speak to the poor guy. He was about our age, bless him, and trembling like he was in a blizzard as the world's angriest paranoid stared into his eyes.

"Make a sound and I'll cut your balls off and stitch them onto your chin," Solitaire said, snarling. "You'll spend the rest of your life looking like Peter Griffin, not that you even know who that is, lucky bastard." The man seemed to believe him, not to mention think him mad, and we waited a few moments to take a hand off his mouth.

"You know who we are?" I asked. He nodded without speaking, apparently taking the threat to heart. Good. "That'll make this faster then. We have a message for you to deliver to Hengrard."

It didn't take long to convey. The bastard was terrified enough that I could see him committing every word to memory even as I said them. He scurried away quickly after that, leaving us to our own devices. I took the time to activate my Appraisal again.

[Appraisal]
Class: Emperor
Level: 8
Condition: Worn
Modifiers: +5 Toughness
Statistics: Strength 5 (4), Speed 5 (4), Dexterity 6 (5), Stamina 5 (4), Toughness 10, Alertness 8, Charisma 9, Intelligence 9
Inventory: Jeans, shirt, jacket, dagger
Class Abilities: Appraisal II
Current Experience Points: 23/170
Unspent Skillpoints: 2

It was almost surprising to see my own figures raised as a match for Solitaire and Beam, but I was far from complaining. We needed the power. I needed it even more than they did.

I could see the familiar looks of concentration on my friends' faces, and no doubt the same one plastered itself across mine as I started pouring the skillpoints into myself. It was easy now, barely even a conscious effort. Within moments, I had my choices allocated.

Strength, this time. I could still remember the sight of that bald giant barely blinking at my punches and kicks. I didn't want to see that again, not when whatever I struck was killing my friend.

[Strength increased to 7]

I blinked. That was new, and convenient. Was it my Appraisal's improvement? I'd be pretty disappointed if all my upgrade got me was a few skipped lines of text. I made a mental note to experiment later, eying Beam and Solitaire, in that order.

[Strength increased to 10, Toughness increased to 10]
[Alertness increased to 10]

"Alertness?" I asked Solitaire.

He shrugged. "I wasn't faster, reaction-wise, even with all the extra speed. There must be *some* stat that improves it. There are plenty of people with inhuman reflexes in Redacle, so I'm betting on alertness."

My thoughts about spending two entire skillpoints on some experiment were . . . mixed, but before I could even say anything, I felt a sudden lurch of surprise as text flashed once more before my vision.

[Alertness, primary characteristic. Governs reaction time, nerve conduction, speed, and awareness]

It took a second for the knowledge to sink in, and I grinned when it did. Experimentation was important, compiling information was vital, using what you knew to build even more knowledge was life-saving. But damn, did it feel good to just be handed free intel sometimes.

"What are you smiling at?" Solitaire asked, with his characteristic uncertainty. Beam looked curious, too, and both of their faces lit up at my explanation.

"What did I do?" Beam demanded. "With the weird, glowy sword thing. Can you tell me that?"

I frowned, eyed him, and got nothing. Fuck.

"Apparently not."

He deflated, but didn't look too surprised. Solitaire still had enough enthusiasm for all of us. "Whatever that was, and I'm pretty sure it wasn't in Redacle originally, it was *definitely* magical."

We both stared at him, waiting to see where he was going with the observation, and he sighed.

"God, apes. Both of you. Beam can use fucking magic, geniuses. Maybe we can *all* use *more* magic, eh?"

That gave me pause. I was familiar with all the kinds of magic our world had to offer—well, except for a certain Olympian's brand—but I'd never even given it any thought until now. Always assumed that it was beyond us. We weren't born here, were we?

But we'd gained other abilities in transit. My Appraisal, Solitaire's Detect Element, and whatever it was Beam had done—I'd bet it was called Beloved. If we could get abilities like that, why not the native magic of this world?

It was a dangerous thought because it flirted with the most terrible emotion a person could feel in times like these. Hope. But damn, if it wasn't tempting to just indulge for a moment.

"We'll need to test it," I said at last, and Solitaire nodded. "It will cost money," I added, and he nodded again.

"We're about to get money," he noted, "or die, at which point I imagine we'll be past caring."

Horrible sense of humor, as always. I wouldn't have laughed at all if it weren't for the adrenaline still churning away in my veins. We stood there together, killing more minutes with conversation and planning, until we caught movement from the building. It was Hengrard, walking carefully, and with only a single man following him.

He seemed nervous. Good, that meant he was taking us seriously.

I moved out to meet him, marching on alone, and bidding my friends goodbye. For now. It was a damned scary thing to be doing, but there was no helping it. This negotiation wouldn't work if we all showed up together.

We'd arranged a meeting spot some miles from the base, and both Hengrard and I reached it around the same time. Standing in an alleyway, face-to-face, shivering from the cold and panting from the brisk walks.

It was the very same place his men had beaten us nearly to death. Perhaps a bit overdramatic, as far as meeting spots went, but I reckoned I'd earned a bit of melodrama.

"You saved my skin," Hengrard noted, eying me impassively. I eyed him back and said nothing. "You and your brothers are dangerous men," he continued. "Powerful, and getting more powerful, hm? If you wrangled five gold from me in a few weeks, I've no doubt you'll be sitting on a lot more before long. And you all seem to have a knack for killing."

That, at last, was blatantly untrue. I was known for my fighting ability in the same way fire was for its water resistance. I let him talk, though, already fairly sure where this was going.

"Unfortunately, you're too dangerous to leave alive. I can't pay you, not with my operation the way it is. And, I can't afford to leave a group like you with no less than two grudges against me. Where are your friends?"

His man came up beside him then, moving with the telltale grace I'd come to expect from those with levels in excess of one and skillpoints spent on raising physical characteristics. I appraised him silently.

[Level 6, Strength 8, Speed 7, Toughness 8, Alertness 7]

There was a meat cleaver in his hand, a big one. If we fought, he'd probably kill me, and if I ran, in my condition, he might well chase me. So, I did the only thing I could do.

"They're behind you."

He didn't believe me at first, but his man did, glancing back to see that Solitaire and Beam really were walking up at the pair's back. Solitaire had one man slung over his shoulder, blood dripping from an opened-up neck. Beam held two.

They'd been the men Hengrard had sent to follow him from a few hundred paces back, and close in to ambush us after he lured us in for the deal. Predictable, as far as betrayals went.

Hengrard's gangster didn't get a single word out before Solitaire spoke with all the niceties of a drill sergeant.

"Fuck off, or you'll die with your moron boss."

He didn't take long to respond, turning and sprinting away without another word. Hengrard eyed us all, thought for an instant, then turned to run.

Something flashed in the air, a knife. Solitaire's. He wasn't a bad shot, landing it neatly beneath the man's rib cage and sending him to his knees. We were all on him before he could rise, kicking, punching, stomping. Something happened to the three of us that I can't quite explain. I guess it's similar to the feeling that overcomes gangs when they egg each other on into lynching someone. A sort of group fury, fueled by our memory of what he'd done to us—our discovery of what he'd *tried* to do again—grabbed all our collective savagery and dragged it up to ever higher levels.

By the time we were finished, his corpse wasn't recognizable as having ever been his. Head smashed open, brains splattered out, bits of bone jutting from the wreck. We all took a seat by the mess we'd made, and chatted.

We talked about our new home, because somewhere between arrival and stomping people to death, it had actually sunk in that we wouldn't be leaving for a while. We talked about our financial position, everything we'd lost, gained, and might still steal back from Hengrard's gang while they were disorganized without him. We talked about shelter and how we were all sick of living exposed, rubbing elbows with the savage morons who made this land their home.

And in the process, we decided on our next move. Something the smarmy bastard had said before we killed him had stuck with me. We *had* gained a lot in these last few weeks. And our biggest payoff by far had come by killing humans, not monsters, which more or less made our decision for us.

After all, Redacle was a very mercenary world.

Might as well be mercenaries ourselves.

CHAPTER TWENTY-EIGHT

Beam's POV: Day 44
Current Wealth: 10 silver, 0 copper
Current Debt: 6 gold, 44 silver, 20 copper

It hadn't been that long ago that we stomped Hengrard's skull into a puree, but things already felt different. It was like we'd stepped into a new age. We'd gotten a good haul, rifling through his fortress in the chaos, and left with well over three gold. Things had been looking up.

They hadn't *stayed* that way, of course. You couldn't have a silver lining without a cloud, and ours was a dark, gray one indeed. Not an hour after putting our affairs in order, while we were all sitting and enjoying a rare, hot and filling meal in a tavern that didn't smell like piss, a certain someone approached us. Tall, robed, thin, and old, by this world's standards. Corvan, miserable as ever.

"I've been looking for you three," he said, snarling, flitting his eyes between me, Shango, and Solitaire as if he'd just scraped us off the bottom of his shoe. I remained neutral, not particularly caring what the old prick thought of me. Shango forced his usual, friendly smile, and Solitaire hissed and stabbed a knife into the table in front of him, tongue running along his exposed teeth and legs twitching under him as he readied himself to lunge. This did not seem to leave the magus any more annoyed than usual.

"How can we help you?" Shango asked, moving into his diplomatic role.

The robed elder scoffed. "Please, like you don't know. It's been weeks since you fools have paid me back a single coin, and your time's run out. Fork over whatever you have."

Shango remained straight-faced, even while my blood boiled and Solitaire's hands disappeared under the table to wrap around something horribly deadly.

"We don't have much—" Shango began, then shut up as the magus spoke over him.

"You looted Hengrard's base without anyone to stop you and spent close to half an hour doing it. I don't think any of you are stupid enough to not have gotten more than a few coins from that, so hand them over now."

"We didn't," Shango pressed, keeping to the story, meeting the man's eye unblinking. Corvan sighed, and a dark look overcame his face.

"Perhaps you need to be motivated," he began, quieter now, and somehow more dangerous. "You've seen me work magic, but not the killing kind, eh? Hand over half the debt you owe this instant, or you'll see firsthand what a magus can do when someone is stupid enough to draw his ire."

Magi were overrated, in an objective sense. They were all taught—and taught their apprentices—to retain an illusion of power that was greater than reality. It was the best way for them to wring more money out of a primitive, uneducated people, after all. Less powerful than believed, though, was not the same thing as lacking in power.

I didn't see much choice but to do as he said, and after a few moments it became clear that Shango didn't either. We spent a second dividing up the coins and realized that paying half the debt would cost nearly everything we had. Corvan's eyes gleamed as he accepted the gold and silver, practically drooling over the handful of currency.

"Is that all?" Solitaire demanded. His voice was hard with the same hatred that always flared up in him whenever someone crossed him. Corvan eyed my friend, as if he were some babbling child.

"For now," the magus told him, coolly. "From now on, you all pay me back a minimum of ten silvers each week."

It was a big sum to be demanded, and Shango was quick to argue. Quick, and fruitless. Apparently we'd burned our grace period with the few weeks taken to secure even this much of a foothold, and the man couldn't be swayed.

"I don't care how you get it," the magus snapped, readying to turn. He was done arguing. "Just get it, or suffer the consequences."

He soon disappeared from sight, leaving us all to contemplate and talk amongst ourselves. I was the first to speak up. There was an idea bouncing around in my head, and I wanted to see what my friends made of it.

"What if we learn magic from him?"

I was sure to keep my voice low, not particularly eager to give away any plans to the room. Shango was thoughtful, and I received a knee-jerk contradiction from Solitaire.

"The bastard would bleed our wallets dry," he countered. "Plus, letting him know we have magical abilities—if we have them at all—would only incentivize him to keep a tighter hold on us before letting us out of debt."

Shango thought about that, then sighed and nodded. "He's probably right," he conceded. "It's not worth the risk, not yet at least."

There was a unique frustration in knowing that my friends were making sense, and knowing that the sense only served to remove a potential lifeline. Without magic, I hadn't the foggiest idea how we'd keep ourselves afloat. Work had been scarce before the gang war, and that wasn't looking like it'd change. We were only halfway through winter.

Obviously they were thinking very much the same thing because Shango sighed, running a hand along his forehead in consternation.

"We might . . . We might be fucked. Unless anyone can think of something . . . we could steal?"

Solitaire spoke next, and his voice was even lower than mine had been. And harsher than Corvan's. "I think I have an idea."

We listened, and swallowed, and felt the frigid chill of danger run down our spines. But in the end, we agreed. Like so many of Solitaire's plans, this one was dangerous, dark, and twisted.

And it was our best hope.

That night, we headed to Corvan's shop. It wasn't a big building, by modern standards, but it was large for Jhigral. That was good; it'd make the noise less likely to travel all the way through it. The howling winds were another factor in our favor.

Even still, I was nervous watching Solitaire pick the lock on the door, carefully step inside, and gesture the rest of us in. We moved carefully, on account of the slumbering wizard upstairs, and started rifling around.

Of course, we found nothing of immediate value. No pure coinage, rather. We'd suspected as much—someone as untrusting as Corvan would've kept such wealth close to his own bedroom for security. Solitaire headed up for it alone. He was the stealthiest.

Minutes passed downstairs, the sounds from outside casting eerie musical ambience for the theft. Every creak made us jump, every second slipped by was another chance for the magus to wake up and obliterate our friend. Eventually, though, Solitaire came downstairs. Empty handed.

"A lockbox," he said, sighing. "Big, thick iron. Couldn't get in without waking the bastard, and it's bolted to the wall. Looks like we aren't getting our money back."

That was a blow, but one we could recover from.

Tentatively, Shango said, "Should we—"

"Yes," Solitaire replied. "You two go on, I'll do it."

Shango and I left the shop. I glanced over my shoulder as Solitaire took the big barrel we had propped outside and rolled it in, lighting the fuse.

In the end, the second bomb hadn't seen use in the gang war. That was lucky for us, because it meant we still had the few dozen pounds of black powder it held. And there was hardly anything better for faking a magus' death than some giant, mysterious explosion.

The blast before had, after all, been quite an easy thing to convince everyone was done with wizardry.

Solitaire came out sprinting, and he reached us—some fifty yards from the building—just in time for it to go up. A big fireball, a big wave of pressure, then wood crumbled inward and the whole thing collapsed.

A magus wasn't tougher than a normal human, not unless they were already defending themselves with magic, and there wasn't much chance that a normal human could've survived what we'd just done. Corvan would probably have survived if he'd shielded himself. Black powder wasn't exactly an anti-armor weapon, and even in large volumes its maximum pressure wouldn't be blowing apart any concrete bunkers. But Solitaire had been fairly sure he was asleep, and it'd take a real paranoid freak to protect himself under these circumstances.

The three of us watched the fires lick what was left of the building anyway, keeping our eyes on it until the guards swarmed around and started panicking. Their bodies made tiny little silhouettes by the bonfire.

"What now?" I asked.

Shango shrugged.

"We can't stay here," he noted.

"Questions will be asked," Solitaire said, agreeing.

Our debt was gone, but we'd exhausted our opportunities in Jhigral. On the bright side, there was no mad old wizard to chase us down if we tried to leave either. And we had enough spare coins to weather at least one day-long trip to another city.

"That mercenary idea," I began. "How exactly would you both suggest we get started?"

That was the question that seemed to stump them, but it was Solitaire who answered first.

"People always want each other dead," he noted. "So long as there's enough of them. And Wolney, as I hear it, has recently had one of their larger gangs crippled in some war. Seems like a good place to start looking for men, at least. And it's a decently sized city, rather than a tiny town. There'll be nobles to get jobs from, jobs more lucrative than bloody gutter fighting, and proper armorers to get decent gear from . . . And we'll even be able to learn magic, if we have the coin and ability. Magi aren't that rare, and they tend to prefer cities."

The more he spoke, the more Shango and I found ourselves nodding along. It made sense, it was logical and, for once, it gave us more hope, not less.

I turned back to the fire, soaking in the sight one last time before I climbed to my feet.

"To Wolney then."

The fire burned for quite some time, and Corvan weathered it patiently. He was a strong magus. Not the most powerful, but certainly a step above nine out of every ten others he met, rare as they already were.

Even still, he'd come close to death.

Had the sound of thudding and rolling not caught his half-asleep ears, he would have remained unconscious through the blast. Had his magic not come with a haste uncommon even to him, he would have remained unshielded as it tore him apart, and had his breath not stayed calm, cool, and controlled, his yards-wide protective field would have been a death trap. Its interior being choked of air as his lungs turned the stuff to poison, its user suffocated by his own breaths.

But Corvan had been lucky, skilled and powerful that night. And so the fool's weapon—for surely no magus strong enough to replicate it could have hidden their power from Corvan's eye—had failed in its task. Failed, and told him who his enemy was.

One did not live as a magus with so many enemies as Corvan and fail to develop the reflexive shielding that had kept him defended mere moments after he woke. And one did not keep from drowning in enemies without the knowledge of how to identify and kill them for their hidden attacks and subtle slights. It had, he had to admit, surprised him that vagrants had such skills, but it was often the man one did not expect who landed a killing blow.

He waited, for quite some time, until the fire had finally died to the cold. And then he waited a while longer. Finally, Corvan forced himself from the debris, crawling out from under the ruin that had once been his home and laboratory, and snarling at the wreckage of it all. Corvan was forced to use his mere physical strength alone, like some common laborer, his magic already depleted by the extended use.

He had not laid claim to large or impressive accommodations, he knew, but they had been his. His place of work, of rest. His home. His domain. To trespass within it was a crime that demanded punishment, to destroy them in such a way . . . well, that demanded death. He watched the licking flames and coiling smoke, thinking.

The fire had died, eventually. But even at its wildest, it was ice compared to the flames of his rage. They burned hotter with every step he took from the ruin.

And every step closer to finding the three imbeciles who'd dared to cross a magus.

CHAPTER TWENTY-NINE

Beam's POV: Day 44
Current Wealth: 10 silver, 0 copper

It would cost money to hire a carriage—a full silver for the trip. We weighed the prospect. A carriage could get us there in one day rather than two. It would get us there warmer, drier, and healthier. And that was to say nothing of the pure luxury that travelling on a vehicle would afford us.

On the flip side, of course, we only had ten silvers to our name—all that Corvan had let us keep at the tavern. It was no small thing to hand over a tenth of our total funds. Particularly when they'd already been depleted by another dozen copper on food, rest, and drink the morning prior.

In the end, it was the fear of the cold that made our decision for us. We were halfway through winter, which apparently meant that we were also at its coldest point, and at the longest nights of the year. That was no small thing to be moving through for days on end. This one piece of silver might well save our lives, and it would definitely save our health. We knew that we'd need all the strength we could spare in Wolney.

That, and there was also the remote, distant, barely considerable possibility that we'd be attacked by another bear, or possibly even the same bear. In objective terms, this was barely worth considering as a chance, but among our number was a paranoid, a coward, and a fighter who, surprisingly, even to himself, had apparently developed arkoudaphobia from the last one.

For five more coppers, we bought two thin blankets of woolen weave to share between us. They kept us warm enough on the ride.

It was funny, really. Two months ago I'd have been shivering in agony at the temperatures we faced beneath that fabric, even with Solitaire and Shango contributing their body heat to combating them. But we'd acclimated well since our arrival a month and a half ago.

Walking through this snow was a regular occurrence for us now, and we'd never had blankets or spots to warm up while we did. Compared to our days of trekking in the past, our journey was a damned vacation. That we'd all become more supernaturally durable against *all* kinds of harm—cold included—was surely of no consequence. Clearly, we had just become proper manly men with thick chest hair and bulging muscles.

Enjoying the ease of travel was fun while it lasted, in any case.

Of course, we didn't let ourselves relax. A day wasted was a day closer to the grave, and all of us had things to keep us busy.

Shango kept scanning things with his Appraisal, looking to glean any information he could, testing the limits of his eyesight and seeing if he could extend it. I did something different.

When I'd used my power, Beloved, I'd done so by feeling a weird sort of pull to a corpse. There weren't any corpses nearby, not animal, and definitely not human. Which meant my ability to experiment was limited. What there was, though, was my head. And so I thought, directing my focus inward and seeing if I could catch the attention of whatever it was that had spoken to me.

I'd heard a voice when I used Beloved; I knew that for sure, and I was starting to suspect that some of the thoughts in my head during our mugging in the alley hadn't been my own either. Whatever the presence I'd felt was, it was connected to my power.

So, I needed to see whether that connection went both ways, and if it would let me use my magic at will.

Hours of sitting around and thinking wasn't my forte, I have to admit. Give me hours of boxing, squats, torturous weight lifting—hours of anything else at all, really, over that. I persevered, though. If I could forcibly rewire every strand of muscle in my body before the age of sixteen, I could sit still and focus. Probably.

Despite my time investment, there weren't any returns, which frustrated me. And there kept being no returns well into the day. The sun was already setting when I began considering giving up, my annoyance burning hot enough that I barely even felt the cold anymore, sweat actually beading on my skin.

Fucking hell, another waste of time, after all. Well I'd gotten used to that, at least. It was no more difficult to deal with than the cold.

Rare to find a human willing to focus on something with no reward for so long.

The voice came just as I was an instant away from stopping entirely, and it froze me like a puddle in the night's chill. I had to resist the urge to answer it aloud, figuring that our driver might not understand—or worse, would—and took a moment to consider how best I could think out a response.

Unfortunately, it seemed that the very thoughts about what to think were conveyed without my even meaning them to be. The voice rang out again, knowing now.

Your mind becomes scattered so easily. I suppose a human is still a human—fickle, fleeting.

The immediate reaction I felt to that, of course, was irritation. And the voice was ringing out before I could even congeal that into an actual answer.

Don't be petulant. You wanted an audience with me, and now you have it. You ought to be grateful for this much.

It was fascinatingly tedious to speak with something in these circumstances. Having the voice react to my thoughts, with no distinction made between conscious ones and unconscious. It was like I was trying to shout over my own id just to be heard—and apparently, I was losing the contest of volume.

But I could adjust. I would adjust. I had to because there was no way I'd be getting useful information like this. And there was no option at all not to learn from this . . . thing, whatever it was. Not with what was at stake.

What are you? I asked, repeating the thought in my head until it drowned everything else out.

Apparently, that was the way to communicate because I got an answer quite quickly.

That question is irrelevant. Ask me a more intelligent one.

A prick, then, was what it was. Well, that was fine. I was friends with Solitaire of all people. I could deal with pricks.

Are you the one responsible for that power I used? I tried again, almost feeling stupid as the question echoed in my head. It was still the only way I had of asking directly, though. No helping that, so I didn't.

There came a fairly long pause before I received another answer, and this one somehow left me feeling on edge. Like some great guillotine was hanging over my head.

I am, and I am not. Your power is more than even myself.

Well, that was about the sort of answer I'd expect to get from some mysterious, ethereal presence. Which is to say, fucking useless. Frustrated, I buried my irritation and pressed on.

Does that mean you can teach me how to use it at will?

A pause, a long one, and then the answer came.

No, but I can . . . help you. Quicken your progress in learning yourself. You must understand that yours is not a power over death, but a power over nature. The winds become your scythe, the snow your shield, the wood your arms. Know this, truly know it, and you will never be without a weapon.

I tried to figure out whether that was useful or not. It was certainly *poetic*, and I'd be annoyed if a description like that was all I had to go on for figuring out a power in an actual RPG. But . . . no, it was pretty clear, too. I'd made a sort of phantom weapon from that corpse, and now I was being told that I could always have a weapon, wherever I was.

So, my power was creating clubs? I could work with that. The one I'd used in the alley had hit as hard as a sledgehammer and weighed next to nothing. If nothing else it'd give me a safeguard for when I was disarmed.

Thank you, I thought, and this time no answer came.

I took a moment to compile everything I'd learned, and then I turned to my friends with the information. They seemed delighted to have finally gotten a hint regarding our magic, and the emotion infected me.

Not least because it was *my* magic. I'd not imagined, two months earlier, that I'd be as miserable, cold, or scared as I'd been the last few weeks. But, I'd never have guessed I'd have actual magic to use, either. Knowing that I did was . . .

Magical.

We still had a good quarter of our journey left, but that would happen the next day. It was already growing dark, so we made camp by the side of the road. We began grabbing great logs from the carriage and creating what would best be described as a smaller bonfire. The driver wasn't very talkative, so we mostly kept to ourselves. Except to ask him about the occasional vital piece of intel regarding our destination.

It was a learning experience, and not a particularly reassuring one. Wolney was an old city, run by an aging governor who refused to pass his leadership to his heir. It was rumored he was going mad with age. Each year seemed to increase the hostility of the place, crime running rampant in its streets, and some even thought the guards were preparing to unilaterally dispose of undesirables from the gutter rats to the mercenaries.

That wouldn't be good for us, in any case. But it was also a damned big city. Easily half a million people lived there, almost as many as in a smaller modern city on Earth. That was good; it meant plenty of people to recruit for our company.

One benefit to travelling by carriage was not running out of wood. We kept our fire nice and big, blasting ourselves with heat all through the night. Come day, we continued our travels with a newfound tension.

Awaiting us ahead was the next step of our journey. Or its end.

CHAPTER THIRTY

Shango's POV: Day 45
Current Wealth: 8 silver, 28 copper

Wolney wasn't ever really a dot on our horizon, mainly because we couldn't see the horizon behind the big curtain of snow blocking it off. By the time it was within sight, we'd already come to within maybe half a mile of it. The city was small by modern standards, as I might've expected, but not nearly as much of a dwarf as was standard for medieval construction.

Jhigral had rarely contained buildings over three stories, while Wolney held multiple that towered as high as ten or more. It was surrounded by a big wall that looked easily thirty feet from bottom to top, and built to resist cannons rather than trebuchets. The closest thing to a vulnerability I could see was a portcullis that looked thick and heavy enough to decapitate an elephant.

All of that was functional, not aesthetic. Redacle wasn't as powerful as some settings out there—an army of dipshits with pointy sticks was still the major military construction after all—but there were enough magic users and weapons that certain innovations had been required past the real-world, late medieval era's status quo. If you were content with a wall that would hold against catapults, you'd have quite the nasty shock when you met one of those rare, one-in-a-thousand magi who could blast multi-liter chunks out of a stone target with every spell. And, if you had wizards who could hasten crop growth and help move refuse, then there really wasn't much reason not to expand your population a bit beyond the typical scope of your technology.

Fortunately for us, the gate was raised and kept up as our carriage rattled on past. A pair of lazy guards watched us enter the city, apparently not caring enough to even record our names. We moved through the streets, seeing what we could glean from our perch on the cart. We'd not have this vantage point for more than a few minutes longer, so there was hardly a better time than now.

Wolney's roads were cobbled, not dirt, but still clearly ill-maintained and dirty. The buildings we passed were mostly no bigger than in Jhigral, but far more numerous. Impressive in numbers, but not in nature, despite the handful of giants peeking into the sky. That was medieval wealth inequality for you. The people were just as numerous, seeming to crowd every stretch of city we laid our eyes on, all dirty and bedraggled, the way it appeared everyone in this world was.

Solitaire muttered something, and I turned to see his eyes had grown dark as he took it all in.

"Feudalism," he spat. "It's like if capitalism said the quiet parts out loud. Everybody's just a cog, and everything is built around keeping the great machine running. No point in having *workers* if they don't *work*."

There weren't many times that his social theories were anything but grating to hear, but it was hard not to find myself agreeing with him, looking at the display around us. The withered, tiny bodies of the locals hit something primal inside me. Urging me to help . . . and to tear down whatever was responsible. I'd always had some vague empathy for the impoverished, but this was far too close to heart for things to remain as removed as that. These people deserved kindness. This world deserved fixing.

But there'd be none of that for us. Not for a while, at least. First we'd have to figure out how to keep ourselves alive.

Still, the thought of actually changing this world for the better stuck with me. I'd not considered it yet, but now that it'd occurred to me, it seemed obvious. We were modern humans, with modern knowledge and a levelling rate that most of this place's inhabitants could only dream of. Maybe we could help people.

Perhaps we'd even been sent here to make the world better.

My considerations were interrupted as a lurch struck the carriage, and I turned my gaze back outward to see we were rolling into a new part of town. This one far better maintained. Its streets were paved, rather than cobbled, and cleaner by far. Filled with ten times less people, all of whom were dressed noticeably better.

Dressed better, and taller. It didn't take a genius to work out we'd come to a richer area; the nasty looks we got was enough to give it away. The carriage began to slow, pulling to stop at one side of the road as the driver turned back to us.

"There you are," he grunted. "Journey's done."

We nodded and gave our thanks, stepping down onto the road, feeling our legs quiver weakly beneath us from the long hours of disuse. The air didn't reek in this part of the city. That was something.

"Where to first?" Solitaire asked.

I eyed him, then eyed the street. We still couldn't read, so all of the signs were indecipherable to us. That was annoying. I swore.

"Let's ask around, see if we can find a mercenary pub, or at least one big enough to get work."

Well, we gave it our best go. Turns out people on the continent of Vorhazh, let alone the Eregar Kingdom, were rather unwilling to help kindly strangers with information. Most of them told us to fuck off, some threatened to call the guards, and none gave us so much as the time of day.

Solitaire seemed unsurprised.

"They're rich," he said, shrugging, "and our clothes don't look expensive. They've probably decided we're vagrants."

It needled me, sent bubbles of anger running through my veins, but I just gritted my teeth and bit the rage back. I was plenty rich myself, but this wasn't a foreign idea. Born with black skin, people the world over are quick to assume you're violent and stupid. Born with black skin and an African nationality, though, and they'll see a tribal savage to boot. Classism was new, but not novel.

"We could try the lower class areas," Beam suggested.

I nodded. Had to try them because we'd just run out of more affluent options.

There was less open hostility there, at least, and it didn't take long before a suitable dwelling was recommended to us. The Fucked Pig. A charming name for an inn, it had to be said. We hurried our way to it, eager for whatever help we could get.

It was about as nice a place as the title would suggest. Dark, weathered wood; reinforced, glassless windows; lengths of what appeared to be iron running through the walls; and a warmth emanating from the hearth that would've been pleasant, were it not tainted by the scent of cheap booze and odorous bodies. We stepped inside the establishment hesitantly and froze as we beheld the several dozen men and women drinking and chatting within.

All were grimy, toughened, and hard-faced. They were armed, of course, and most sat in groups. I appraised them quickly, tightening my eyes almost without thought.

Level eight, Level three, Level nineteen, Level ten, Level five, Level six . . .

There was a lot of variation, but none were as high as level twenty. And all were above one. Apparently, this was a place for people with a fair amount of experience under their belts. Well, that suited us just fine. We'd defeated two trolls and a score of people ourselves, even without counting Solitaire's pyrotechnics. We weren't green by any measure.

Still, we froze. Several of the people were staring at us, and all were still terrifying enough despite our trial by fire in this world. Part of me was certain they'd come flying at us with weapons drawn, and another part of me feared that moving forward would just make a fool of us all and ruin any chances we had of actually recruiting.

Beam saved us. He took one step forward, casual, as if he were strolling down a beach, and that broke Solitaire and I out of our stupor. We followed him eagerly, making our way to the bar. After that, my old instincts took over, and I leaned in to speak with the man behind the bar.

"Afternoon," I greeted him, forcing a smile that conveyed confidence I wasn't feeling. "I understand this is a mercenary spot. Are you the one who hands out contracts?"

Our time spent questioning the citizens of Wolney had confirmed this as the system at play. Contracts were put out and picked up by individuals specialized in such things. Mercenaries would find their way to bars like this, where the owners would take a small commission to hand them out to the overwhelmingly illiterate crowds that usually handled such things. The thing about the fighters of Redacle was that, given the superhumanity needed to be a good one, money and influence tended to hold a bit less sway in the grand scheme of things.

The systems of commerce and favor—hoarding, which left guilds to work in their neat little pyramids—fell apart when one tried to cage men capable of tearing off limbs. Mostly, this was a bad thing. It meant the most powerful in such circles tended to be combatively deadly and readily violent.

"I am," the man grunted, confirming his place in the hierarchy. That was relieving at least. I'd been half afraid he'd laugh at some misunderstanding the people outside had imparted on us.

"Excellent," I said. "Well, my—" I hesitated, thought about it, then continued "—my brothers and I are looking for work. Can you point us to some? We're skilled enough fighters, though not excellently equipped. We've managed to take down trolls before, and can easily bring down a group of over five men by ourselves."

Being honest, I'd been hoping to see some surprised respect flit across the bartender's face at that. All I got, though, was acknowledgement. I suppose it made sense. Trolls were big and horrible, but humans could kill animals just as strong as them even back in our world. The mild superhumans of Redacle? I wasn't shocked to see that it wasn't as big of a deal as I'd hoped.

"We have undead to deal with," the barkeep suggested. "Always a problem around Wolney. Rotters and such. You'll get yourself five copper for every rotter head you can bring back. Standing orders from the governor."

I hesitated, glancing at Solitaire and Beam. Well, only Solitaire really. Beam was as unfazed at the thought of fighting undead as he was everything else.

"Anything with a more . . . immediate payout we can try?" I wasn't sure how common undead might be in the forests. Maybe we'd be swimming in them, which brought its own set of problems to bear, but maybe we'd waste most of our time just looking for the things. I didn't want to spend longer out in the snow than was necessary.

The barkeep shrugged. "Nothing I can hand to a group as untested as yours."

My jaw tightened, but I nodded. "Alright then, thanks," I replied through gritted teeth. We were all heading back for the exit a few moments later, discussing the matter once we were outside.

"We're doing it then?" Solitaire asked. I hesitated. We needed the money, and this was just about the perfect job for us. Consistent, simple, relatively low risk. At worst we'd just received news that we could feed ourselves by venturing out into the local forests.

"We're doing it," I said sighing, still far from happy. "But not tonight, I feel . . . What's the carriage equivalent of jet lag? Carriage lag?"

"Being a pussy," Solitaire suggested.

We moved through the city, searching for a suitable tavern. None of us wanted one of the wafer-thin sort we'd last slept in, that'd leave us shivering in a huddle at one wall. A warmer place would cost extra, but in light of our good news, I figured we could afford to spend a bit more.

Still, we weren't exactly looking for a palace, and it didn't take us long to find a suitable place. Small, compact, but warm-looking enough and almost entirely cockroach free. We set up in the common room, intending to spend a peaceful evening basking in the atmosphere and unwinding with a hot meal.

We'd not been there for more than ten minutes when the red-headed giant stormed over to our table.

CHAPTER THIRTY-ONE

Shango's POV: Day 45
Current Wealth: 8 silver, 28 copper

We'd seen big men since coming to Redacle. The one whose balls Solitaire had burst was big, even by modern standards. Kratos had been given his nickname for a good reason, too, taller even than Solitaire and muscled like a fucking ox.

The man who approached us now was big as well. And yet, lumping him in with them seemed ridiculous. He was taller than any of us by well over a head, and if we'd all happened to be NBA players, I didn't doubt that he'd still have a good few inches on us. The bastard must've been seven feet, give or take an inch, and though he was no bodybuilder, the jagged muscle pressing out at his shoulders was clear even through the wool shirt that covered them.

Behind him stood maybe a half dozen other men of varying sizes, and upon the giant's face there was a broad grin that seemed very similar to the arch of some great doorway. His eyes caught lamplight as his face shifted, making them dance disconcertingly.

"Haven't seen you three around here before." He grinned, moving his gaze between us. "Don't take it you've heard of the tradition we have in these parts?"

"We haven't," Beam replied before I could cut in. "And I don't think we'll be staying long, passing through, you see—"

"This block is mine," the giant pressed, his voice crushing Beam's like some tiny little ship pulverized to splinters by a great wave. "If you want to drink here, you need to—"

Glass was a rare thing in most parts of Redacle, but not so rare that there wasn't the occasional bottle made from it, or that those bottles were more costly. That was a good thing in our case.

Solitaire hit him before he finished speaking, the bottle held tightly in his hand by its neck. It broke against the giant's face, shattered into bits as if it'd been shot, throwing glass and beer in all directions and sending the man a full step back.

But only a step back. He didn't fall, didn't even waver. A man the height of Terry Crews had just smashed him without warning, and he barely even seemed fazed. His eyes landed on our group again, and this time his grin was wider. Wide enough that I saw the blood running down his lips from where the jagged shards had cut his face.

"So, it's gonna be like that, eh?" he grunted, rolling his neck, as if we'd politely asked for a brawl rather than sucker-punched him.

I tightened my eyes and studied the man. I nearly shit myself.

[Appraisal]
Class: Warrior
Level: 11
Condition: Fine
Modifiers: Strength +4, Speed +1, Toughness +4, Alertness +2
Statistics: Strength 13, Speed 6, Dexterity 4, Stamina 5, Toughness 14, Alertness 9, Charisma 3, Intelligence 6

Seeing his stats, I had just about enough time to realize that they probably out-weighed the bear we'd been attacked by on our first night. Then he was lunging for Solitaire.

We'd all done this song and dance before, though, and Solitaire in particular had his response lined up and ready. He didn't try to meet the giant head on, didn't try to weave aside and counter, didn't even try to beat him to the punch and abort his attack with one of his own. He just turned and ran.

It was almost comical. The sight of my friend spinning on his heel and breaking out into a sprint across the tavern, the giant's moment of stunned surprise, then the fury that spread across his face as he hurried to give chase. Watching it all, I almost missed the opportunity that came when the seven-foot redhead was rushing right past me to get to the Scouser.

Fortunately, I had enough sense to hold out a foot and trip him.

The impact felt like it might rip my leg off at the knee, but I was just strong enough to keep my balance while taking the other man's. His leg was caught beneath him, so his body lurched forward, and four hundred pounds of fat-ass smashed face-first into the wooden floor. His head was just a few inches raised back up when Solitaire's feet came down on it, his jump having taken him a full meter into the air before landing on the poor sod.

I turned then, to see that the man's friends were moving in. Five of them, at least. One was busy picking up teeth that Beam had smashed out. I paused, thought, then decided that the five-on-one was slightly more demanding of my attention. I lunged in to help the Olympian.

Even now, I wasn't much of a fighter, but I had size, and I'd seen enough to know how useful that was. I shoulder-slammed one of the men, catching him in the chest and sending him bouncing off me as I gifted him all my sprinting momentum. He bounced again upon landing, rolling half-over and groaning, and then another was coming. Beam tossed one of the man's friends into him, sending them both down, and I turned my focus to helping my friend with the remaining two.

One of them punched him hard across the jaw, stunning him, and I caught the next one's arm before they could follow up. A brief wrestling match ensued, which ended when he kneed me in the balls. I groaned, folded, and looked up just in time to see the offending thug get knocked fully off his feet by a haymaker that would've given Satan himself a nosebleed. Beam's haymaker. The other guy, apparently, was already down.

My friend moved in next to me, putting himself between my body and the three men who were now getting back to their feet.

"Can you move?" he asked. I opened my mouth to speak, then felt a sudden, terrible hollowness in my groin. I vomited, and he sighed. "Tell me when you can." Beam threw himself at them without further ado.

While he fought, I heard a great crashing sound across the room and turned to see Solitaire grappling the giant. Well, grappling was the wrong word. My friend was on his back, climbing his enormous frame, fingers digging in to use ears, nostrils, and flabs of meat for grip. His face was just beside the enemy's, jaws closed tight around the man's cheek, chin, and brow. It was like watching a human being mauled by some feral chimpanzee.

A big human, mind you. And one with leather for skin, because he wasn't actually being hurt all that much, and every moment Solitaire came closer to being caught. I turned back to Beam, saw him snatching one man into a headlock while hammering away at another one's guard, and tested myself. The third was coming up behind him.

I could move, albeit at the cost of another wave of discomfort. It would have to do.

The man closing on Beam was bigger than the others, and I wasn't sure I'd be overpowering him as easily. So I didn't risk it. I snatched a wooden stool up from a nearby table, brought it around as I closed in, and turned my approach into a swing. Beam saw it arcing for him, doubtless realized what was happening, and sidestepped from the path. His timing was perfect, and barely an eyeblink passed between his movement and the wooden edge finding purchase in the enemy's face. The man went down instantly, and I stumbled back with the stool.

By the time I'd hefted it again, Beam had choked one man into unconsciousness and kicked the last so hard that I actually worried he might've died. We both moved our focus to Solitaire and the giant. Just in time to see our friend hauled from the man's back, hoisted fully over his head like some strong man's barbell, and physically thrown to soar a full ten feet and land viciously hard on his head. He bounced, rolled, then remained where he lay. Groaning and coughing.

In an ideal world, we'd have tended to him, but the big man was closing in too fast to allow that. Beam acted first, snatching the stool from my grip and handling its twenty-pound weight as if it were made of foam. He tossed it like a shot put, aim landing the edge perfectly against our enemy's face and . . . barely making him flinch. He was on the Olympian an instant later.

Honestly, I'd like to tell you that we proceeded to trounce the man. That we used makeshift weapons, skill, savagery and—most important of all—the power of friendship to finally put him down. Truth be told? We didn't. In fact I think we barely even hurt the fucker. By the time our brawl was over, there wasn't really a winner. Just the absence of a loser.

The big man had thrown us all around like dog toys for the better part of a quarter hour before finally steaming out, taking a seat on one of the remaining unbroken stools and his weight threatening to snap it. We did much the same, panting and glaring at the stupid fucker, while he returned our looks in kind.

In the time since our fight had started, the tavern had filled with extra faces, mostly there to watch the local tough actually get a run for his money. That was fine by me, but I could see Solitaire getting more agitated by the second. He had always hated crowds.

"You're . . . alright," the giant called out from where he was sitting some dozen feet away. "Didn't . . . expect that hard of a fight."

Solitaire muttered something, possibly about setting him on fire, and I tried to think of a suitable response. Surprisingly, it was Beam who gave one.

"Not bad yourself," he gasped, still out of breath, though recovering faster than us. "Didn't expect I'd meet someone who'd still be standing after me and my brothers fought him three on one."

That cracked a broad smile across the man's face, and his eyes danced.

"Didn't expect to meet three someones who could fight me, even together," he replied, apparently rather pleased.

Of course he was pleased. I shouldn't have bothered thinking of anything to say at all. We already knew Beam could speak meathead.

Whatever budding conversation might have continued between them, it was interrupted by a rather angry-looking man, who was storming over to us. I quickly recognized him as the barkeep and knew where the conversation was going before he opened his mouth.

"You fucking wrecked the place!" he snapped, glaring, surprisingly, at the giant instead of us. "This is the third time, Argar."

The giant, apparently named Argar, shrugged. He seemed apologetic in the same way someone returning a year-overdue library book might be right before borrowing another.

"Sorry, didn't expect them to be that hard."

It appeared to be the exact wrong thing to say. The barkeep's temper only shortened from there. What followed was a barrage of screamed accusations, of which I could only make out around half, and by the end the giant actually looked somewhat chastened.

"How do you expect to pay for this?" the barkeep snarled, apparently holding only Argar responsible, despite my friends and me having done our fair share of breaking, too. And that was when the idea struck me.

"We can put some money up for the damage," I cut in, studying the barkeep and the giant, as their eyes turned to me in surprise. "We were involved, after all, and we have a fair amount of cash on hand."

The barkeep seemed mollified, but Argar cut in somewhat suspiciously. "Why would you do that?" he demanded, glaring at me now.

I resisted the urge to smile as I replied, "Because you're going to work it off."

CHAPTER THIRTY-TWO

Solitaire's POV: Day 45
Current Wealth: 2 silver, 12 copper

All in all, it didn't take Shango long to smooth things over, and once he was finished we were down a few—well, many—silver. And up one giant, glass-proof gorilla. I was leaning against the wall in our room, nursing my ribs after they played up again in the fight, desperately trying to decide whether it'd been a good idea.

"You should see a physician," Beam said, sitting opposite me and wearing his concern openly as he eyed me.

I sighed, then resisted the urge to swear as the exhalation sent a painful stab into my side. "I don't need a physician. None of them are broken. I can feel broken bones, and I'll heal on my own eventually. I'd be healing already if Grognard the Barbarian hadn't decided to equip me as a weapon and attack a fucking table."

I coughed, and the coughing made me hurt more, which almost led to more coughing. Shango laughed from across the room, watching with a grin on his face. Prick.

"How well do you think you can fight?" Beam asked, and I felt a flicker of irritation.

"I'll be better in the morning," I told him. "I just need to avoid getting punched in the ribs. I'll have to hit the next fucker with something heavier. Just leave me in the back as a support role and I'll recover slowly. We'll be fighting shitty undead for a while anyway, right?"

They both nodded, and I sighed, leaning back and closing my eyes. Waiting for Shango to voice whatever thought I'd seen rattling around unspoken in his head.

"What if we leave you behind in the city tomorrow? Just for the day," he added quickly. "Let you go and try to find a teacher to learn magic from. Then you can get back to helping us, or even sit and pick up a few extra tricks while you heal, then come back better."

I weighed his words. It would've been convenient—game changing, even—if they'd been true. But we didn't have the money for serious magic tutelage just yet. I told him as much, and he shrugged.

"So spend the day working your way through the city's magi until you've got one willing to test you; bargain hunt. You working class men do love that don't you?"

"Eat a cock," I replied succinctly.

He did have a point, though, and I reluctantly swallowed it, nodding.

"Fine, I'll spend the day asking around for deals. I suppose . . . I guess you're not going after anything that tough anyway, and as I am right now . . ."

As I was right then, I'd not help that much. At worst I might even slow them down, have my ribs play up unexpectedly, get a friend killed. I didn't want to say any of that out loud, didn't even want to think it, but I couldn't exactly ignore the fact either. Bollocks.

"We have Argar now anyway," Beam noted, clearly trying to cheer me up. "He's tough enough to keep us safe at least for a day, and we're going after zombies of all things."

"And you'll be essentially protecting us anyway by saving the money," Shango added. "Every five copper we don't spend is one fight we don't need to pick with a rotter, eh?"

Somehow them trying to mollify me just made things worse. Like I was being babied, comforted as one might a screaming child. But I didn't lash out. That would just be cruel, and even I wasn't a big enough prick to make that my answer to kindness from friends. I forced a deceptive smile and nodded.

"Fine. And if I come back with the ability to blow up cities with my mind, all the better, right?"

We shared a chuckle that each and every one of us was feigning for the others' sake, then got settled and ready for sleep.

Morning came, and it was actually surprising to not wake up sticking to my makeshift bed on the floor or shivering like an addict being waterboarded in Antarctica. There were benefits to higher class dwellings, apparently.

Still, I was quickly reminded of my fight the previous night when my ribs started trying to free themselves from the rest of me, protesting their position with thick waves of agony. That lasted a while, and it was difficult even for me to keep the pain to myself.

Fortunately, Shango and Beam were up soon enough, groaning and yawning, both of them wincing a bit, too. We'd all gotten our share of scrapes and bruises over the last week, apparently.

"When are we setting off?" Beam asked, eager as always to be doing something.

Shango thought about it. "Rotters are undead, and in this world they're slowed by daylight. The more intense, the worse they move. So ideally, we'd be setting off later, catching them at high noon for the easiest fight possible."

"But that leaves us less time to hunt them," Beam countered. I was barely listening to the pair, focused instead on climbing to my feet without violently shitting down my leg from the pain. I grunted with relief, both for having successfully conquered my gravitational difficulties, and because my friends were finally approaching something resembling a conclusion to their argument.

"Early then," Shango sighed. "Hopefully the new guy makes up the difference."

My side throbbed again. Somehow I got the feeling he would, but that was none of my concern for the time being. My side throbbed again. Now I had my own task to attend.

I said my goodbyes, stepping from the tavern and making my way through the street. It felt odd to be moving through it alone. Really odd, disconcerting and all sort of itchy at the back of my spine, like being watched. I figured out why by the time I'd crossed my second road.

This was the first time since coming to Redacle that I'd been genuinely alone—no friends to watch over me, no allies to fight alongside me. If I was attacked right now by the sort of group I'd come to regard as a nothing-threat, it would end badly.

With no small amount of effort, I buried my concern. The one benefit of being a paranoid, of course, is that you get used to doing such things. Realistically, I wasn't exactly in any great danger of attack in such light hours. The knowledge did little to keep my edges blunt while I marched through the city, but it helped at least.

The first magus I reached wouldn't even see me, the prick. The second, thankfully, was not that far. About half a mile away. I'd expected as much; the magically gifted tended to congregate in larger cities with wealthier patrons available. Except that this fucker kicked me out the moment I asked to be tested.

Apparently, Corvan's personality was very much trade standard. Well, that didn't exactly surprise me. The book my friends and I had written hadn't given much information in the way of depictions for average magi, but in my head and Shango's they'd always been double-decker twats. Middle management, in a sense. Moderately influential and all the more obsessed with influence for it, made more petty, not less, for the small measures of magical power they had over others. Nothing to do but persevere.

I made progress on the third attempt, finding a man who offered me a test for the low, low price of three silver. More than I had on me, of course, but easier to work around than being ordered out of the place on threat of incineration. I put a pin in that appointment and moved on to others.

Another kicked me out, one more asked for four silver, then a third actually let me negotiate her down to two. That was still a bit high for my liking, but I kept her position in mind and moved on.

I had to do a lot of walking, and a lot of talking. God, I hate people. I hate *these* people more than anything, but just in the general sense, I hate people. Slow, plodding ape things, dragging me down with them. Dancing on the edge of a knife. You know that experiment where they gave rats access to water on one side of their cages and a button that makes them feel good on the other? Well, the rats invariably died of thirst because they just kept pressing the button. That's humans.

Still, there's always a time to cut cards with the devil, and I'm not stupid enough that I can't grin and bear a bit of displeasure for the greater good. If we were going to impart any sort of change at all in this world we'd need strength to do it, and that would likely come with magic. I kept trying.

It was well past noon, and the sun was coming precipitously close to painting the horizon orange. I'd ended up back with the woman who charged two silver and managed to negotiate her down to one silver and forty copper. It was still bloody highway robbery, but I'd come to expect things like that. Beam's health-care system had required more adjustment in any case.

"One silver and thirty," I tried, patience wearing thin. Beam and Shango would be back soon, and if Shango found out I'd not managed to find any price below a full silver he'd never let me hear the end of it.

The magus I was dealing with was younger than the others, and that might've been why her asking price was so low. Nonetheless, she wasn't stupid. A tall woman, brown haired and eyed, with slight features and a mean look to her eye, she'd surprised me with how fiercely she'd caught onto every word I tried to blindside her with.

At the risk of sounding slightly misogynistic, she wasn't nearly as air-headed as I'd expected an attractive woman to be. Inconvenient.

"What you're asking is ridiculous," she told me, her own impatience growing to match mine. "It costs nearly one silver just to administer the test. The materials involved are expensive and finite."

I took her words in, considered them with all due care, then nodded. And completely ignored them.

"And, on the other hand, if you can't go that low, you'll not make a profit at all because you won't be selling your services to me. One silver thirty is still getting you more than you had before."

She glared, but I could see she was considering it. That was the first step to changing a mind. Leave a crack in their convictions, then drive the chisel in.

"Besides, what if the test comes back positive?" I noted. "We both know I can't afford to get tutelage from any magus other than you in this city. That's why I came back here, and that's why I'm still haggling. If I am magic, that's money in the bank for you. You've got a new apprentice to draw coin from as payment."

The suggestion worked wonders, and I saw her face creasing with thought, doubt. Then, finally, reluctant acquiescence.

"One silver thirty-five," she said at last. I forced myself to pause a moment before nodding, extending a hand for her to shake.

"Ah . . . you're not from around here?" she asked, eying the hand like it was a big, flaccid cock left dangling from the end of my wrist. I withdrew it.

"No, sorry about that," I managed.

Men didn't shake women's hands in this part of Redacle. Stupid of me to forget, however excited I'd been. The magus was quick in breezing past it, in any case.

"Alright then," she sighed. "I'll administer the test. Wait here; I need to get the mana crystals."

I waited, and she was back quickly, bringing a pair of cyan-colored gemstones that looked as if they were a mix between glass and plastic in texture. She held them out, opened her mouth to speak, then paused as I gripped each one without needing to be told.

I grinned.

"I'm aware of how the test is done. I just needed a magus to do it."

She nodded, quickly moving on and reaching into another drawer, withdrawing a length of copper wire now and wrapping it around both the crystals. She placed her hands on top of them, careful not to touch mine, and focused.

After a few moments, it happened. A hum of light running into one crystal, then fading from it just as it looped into the other. Then a buzzing assailed my body. Not quite a sensation, more an . . . urge. To run, to hide. The very sort you might feel upon suddenly hearing hornets buzzing around you.

I resisted it, of course, and waited for the test to proceed. The lights returned, stronger, then moved from one crystal to another and sent another buzz through me. Then again, then again. Soon I was sweating with the irritation of it, but I held still for minutes more until the test was finally complete.

The woman took the crystals from me, sighing as one of them split rather noticeably along its center, and placed everything to one side. Then she eyed me.

"Congratulations," she said. "You have the talent."

CHAPTER THIRTY-THREE

Beam's POV: Day 46
Current Wealth: 0 silver, 27 copper

Leaving Solitaire alone in the city left me feeling more than a little unnerved. I told myself it was for the best, though. He was hardly in any danger, and giving him an extra day to heal was the best way I could keep him safe. An eerily small number of our journeys had actually gone according to plan before now, and if we ended up getting a surprise half as nasty as the bear or giga-troll on this one, I doubted his condition would let him survive long enough for more treatment.

Still, it didn't sit right with me. And I knew why. We were in this predicament because he'd been hurt, and he'd been hurt because I'd failed to protect him. Again. It seemed failed protection was the only kind I could ever offer. The guilt hung onto my shoulders like an anvil, keeping me company for our entire march into the woodlands. I kept it to myself, not wanting to bother Shango with such a triviality, and not knowing Argar enough to even discuss it with him to begin with.

Argar, the giant. He'd stuck to his word and come along with us, surprising me quite a bit in doing so. Somehow the man felt even bigger to walk alongside than he had to fight, towering over me by almost an entire foot, giant legs eating the road with great strides. He didn't seem to even feel the cold, despite not having furs nearly as thick as mine or Shango's, and he didn't complain one iota as we made our way into the woods.

Perhaps we had something in common then. Or perhaps he just didn't see much to complain about. The man hardly felt unhappy to be waddling into the jaws of death.

"What's the plan?" Shango asked, once we were a fair distance from the city. "Rotters don't really bleed, so arrows won't do us much good this time. Nor will our daggers or the spear."

"I can use my hands." Argar shrugged, and the sheer size of each shoulder as it rolled upward had me half believing him. Fortunately, saner heads prevailed.

"Let's make like Solitaire and start picking rocks up on our way," I suggested, scoring a grin from Shango as I did. We both knew our friend would never shut up if he caught us mimicking his habits like that.

We kept talking while picking our way across the woodlands, eyes peeled for particularly deadly looking stones. I picked up two, both a bit bigger than my fists, nice and jagged, angled things that looked perfect to stave in a head. Shango only got one. When I turned to ask if Argar needed one of mine, I saw the big man had torn an entire branch off a tree and snapped it across his knee, fashioning himself a club that probably weighed as much as my leg. It would probably do just fine, I decided. Better than anything we'd picked up from the gang war.

The forest transformed as we went deeper, air taking on an unpleasant edge that had nothing to do with the cold, but still sent shivers running down my spine.

Everything became darker for seemingly no reason at all, and an unnaturally gray fog began to congeal along the ground around our feet. Shango was the first to recognize it.

"Necrotic mist," he breathed. The term rang a bell in my memory. Death gas, essentially, also known as miasma. It was generated by undead, and generated more of them in turn.

Seeing it now meant we were closing in on where the action would be.

I noticed a couple of things as our walk continued. One was the smell, like an old folk's home, but more important was the silence. Save for the wind, and our own footsteps, I couldn't hear anything in this part of the wood. No birds, no rodents, not a damn thing. Even the insects were silent. It was like the whole world was holding its breath and waiting, waiting for something big.

Well, I certainly was. I forced myself to exhale, performing the calming, rhythmic oscillation of lungs that I'd learned in order to steel my nerves before a match years before. We'd fought bears, we'd fought trolls. Whatever was ahead, it didn't have anything on us.

That's what I told myself, at least, but as we crept deeper in, the seeds of unease only grew. Undead had some particular essence about them that frightened the living on an instinctual level. Was that what I was feeling?

Or did I just have better instincts than I thought?

Solitaire, I knew, would make fun of me if he knew I was this concerned about a gut feeling. Shango wouldn't, but he'd not take it seriously either. So I bit my tongue. Right up until the forest's silence was disintegrated by the shrillest, gnarliest screech I think I've ever heard in my life.

We all looked ahead at once for the source, and it wasn't hard to find. Five-foot-six, skinny as a ragdoll, and lumbering toward us half at a sprint and half at a limp. It was maybe twenty yards away when we first caught sight of the fucking thing, and that gave us all the time in the world to get ready before it came.

A walking corpse, blood-stained, withered and snarling like a rabid dog. The sight of an enemy at last gave my fear some direction.

I moved in to answer first, putting myself in front of Shango with a reflexive grace. Then I blinked, as Argar put himself further in front of me. The rotter was barely within arms' reach of him when his giant log came swinging around like a battering ram, catching it fully in the chest and halting its sprint to a dead stop instantaneously.

The undead fell onto its back, jerking around, and I saw ribs jutting from a ruined chest.

Argar didn't give it a chance to shrug the wound off, closing in more than a meter in one great stride, then swinging his cudgel down a second time. It caught the lower torso, shattering hips and crushing the spine at its base.

And the undead's legs stopped moving. So they could still be paralyzed if nerves and bones were damaged enough? That was useful to know, though not for now. For now, our enemy was a bit too mangled to do anything anyway.

I watched as it writhed around, trying and failing to claw its way to us as Argar stepped back, his lip curled.

"Never actually seen one this close," he grunted. I'd never seen one period, but felt urged to keep silent about that fact. The man was big enough already. No need to further my inadequacies.

"Why didn't you kill it?" Shango asked him.

Argar shrugged. "Smash a ribcage in—usually, that does kill something. Didn't know the rumors about undead being . . . like this were true."

I saw a slight quiver to his lip as he said that, and it occurred to me that the big man actually was unnerved. Scared even, deeply so. It seemed odd, but the more I thought about it, the more it made sense. He hadn't grown up on anime and video games. To him, zombies weren't just fodder to kill a few hours decapitating with virtual shotguns. God knew what kinds of stories people as primitive as his told about them, but they probably talked them up more than a bit.

To be fair, even Shango and I were playing it safe with all our meta knowledge. There was a reason we weren't hunting during the night.

"You need to smash the head to put a rotter down," Shango explained. Then he took a step forward to do just that, and hesitated. I could guess why, he probably wasn't certain he had the strength, rock or no.

But I was. I closed in while the rotter hissed at him, brought the stone down and felt its skull change shape beneath the impact. Then I hit it a few more times to be safe. Brown blood was sticking to the rock like glue, by the end, and the reek was revolting, but the rotter died about the same as anything else would have. I straightened up.

"So, more hunting?" I asked the other two.

Shango was quick to reply. "More hunting."

The deeper we went, the more apparent it became that actually finding rotters wouldn't be *too* much of an issue. They weren't exactly commonplace, of course, but there were a lot more than just a few, and if you made a bit of noise you'd attract plenty to throw themselves at you. We ended up bagging about half a dozen within the hour. Twenty-three within four hours.

But the sun was growing dangerously close to the horizon by then, and it was that that finally put an end to our hunting trip. Reluctantly, we started trudging our way back to the city.

It made sense, thinking about it, that you wouldn't find any undead close to the main seat of human habitation for the region. Guard patrols and whatnot probably kept their populations down like nothing else, and at worst, all of the lazier, stronger mercenaries would be vacuuming them up by day.

Regardless, though, it was still an issue. We couldn't afford to waste seven hours a day on transit if we were going to make progress from this. Five coppers per pop meant that we'd earned ourselves just over two silver with the day's work. Which wasn't much better than what three men our size could've managed with basic laboring. We needed to adjust our strategy.

And we needed more fucking money.

CHAPTER THIRTY-FOUR

Shango's POV: Day 46
Current Wealth: 2 silver, 42 copper

[Appraisal]
Class: Emperor
Level: 8
Condition: Fine
Modifiers: +5 Toughness, +2 Strength
Statistics: Strength 7, Speed 5, Dexterity 6, Stamina 5, Toughness 10, Alertness 8, Charisma 9, Intelligence 9
Inventory: Jeans, shirt, jacket, dagger
Class Abilities: Appraisal II
Current Experience Points: 33/170
Unspent Skillpoints: 0

[Appraisal]
Class: Dragonknight
Level: 7
Condition: Fine
Modifiers: +1 Strength, +1 Speed, +2 Toughness
Statistics: Strength 10, Speed 9, Dexterity 8, Stamina 9, Toughness 10, Alertness 8, Charisma 6, Intelligence 5
Inventory: Jeans, flannel shirt, spear
Class Abilities: Beloved II
Current Experience Points: 130/160
Unspent Skillpoints: 0

Ten experience points, apparently, were our reward for trudging across miles of snow and killing ten times our number of undead. I'd certainly done more annoying and difficult things for poorer rewards, but for the life of me, I couldn't quite recall when. And it was no less disheartening for it.

Well, truth be told, I wasn't entirely surprised. We'd clocked a while ago that difficulty and risk significantly increased experience rewards for defeating enemies, especially magical ones. With that in mind, gang-initiating mindless zombies of roughly average human physicality was hardly going to benefit us much no matter what. Still, I'd checked. If we'd been levelling quickly from the hunts, it might've been worth sustaining them for a while, to see how strong we could get. Farming enemies did become a universal strategy among so many roleplaying games for a good reason; though, people weren't risking their lives for them.

In any case, it was irrelevant. We weren't levelling up at any appreciable speed by killing them, so we had no reason to continue doing it, except for the money. And the money was quite good, too.

We were sitting together in the same tavern where we'd met Argar, eating some roasted chickens with a few carrots and potatoes thrown in—and not drinking. Hot meals were still a luxury. It'd only been recently that we'd begun regularly indulging them, but this meal set us back further—twelve coppers in total.

So we were down to two silver and thirty copper.

It was still progress no matter what. But after our night's sleep in the inn, that progress would be reduced by an additional nine copper for rent.

Expensive to live, painful to die, miserable to go on. But we had no choice in the matter, and so I pushed the observation behind me like so many others.

Solitaire leaned back, groaning with the motion. "My ribs are on the mend," he noted. "I'll be fit as a fiddle tomorrow."

The lying bastard. I didn't have the energy to answer or argue, but he kept on talking regardless.

"Which brings us to our issue of funds. Seems to me, we need a way of overcoming two limiting factors on the undead hunts. Time required to get there, and actual weight of the . . ."—his lip curled slightly—". . . loot."

Evidence. We'd need evidence, otherwise any idiot could just claim to have killed a hundred rotters and walk out of the merc tavern with ten silver in his pocket. Apparently, that evidence had been required in the form of severed heads.

So we'd watched Argar haul back about two hundred pounds of stinking, decaying skull and brain matter for twenty miles. If nothing else, the *weight* didn't seem to bother him that much.

"We could get a cart," Beam suggested. "A hand-drawn one, at least."

Solitaire sighed and said, "Carts cost money. If I'm remembering our notes correctly, a decent one would set us back about ten or fifteen silver."

I considered another way, then gave up. "Either way, we still have the issue of travel time. I don't see that going away until we're rich enough to afford a horse. More than one, actually, to carry all of us."

Solitaire grinned that evil grin he had, the one that promised he was about to say something very clever, and would make me extremely upset.

"I've thought of a solution for that," he declared, and without realizing it, Beam and I leaned in to hear it.

Solitaire continued, apparently enjoying the attention. "We build a shelter next to the woods. A small one, densely made with nice thick walls and boarded windows. That marks our base of operations, and while we hunt through the night, we can do so knowing we have a defensible position to retreat to."

"No," I snapped. "Absolutely not. It's ridiculous! we'd be torn to shreds during construction."

"We'd only build during the day," Solitaire countered. "And, actually, I was thinking we could take out a loan to hire some workmen to do it."

It was incredible. Somehow my friend had taken a plan so awful it almost made my eyes water and, with just a few extra words, managed to make it even worse.

"You want to put us in debt again now?" I couldn't believe that he could be so stupid.

Solitaire only shrugged. "Either that or we risk a night attack without some defensive fortifications. Way I see it, we need to increase our power here—both politically and literally—as quickly as we can. I want security here. I want to know that I won't wake up hungry tomorrow. I want—" His voice became strangled for a moment by emotion, and I realized why.

I'd always known I'd be okay, that I wouldn't starve. So had Beam. But not Solitaire. In our old world, he'd spent his life crawling up to a position as stable as the one we'd occupied right before being dragged here.

And then *he'd* been dragged here. We'd all lost everything, but everything he'd lost, he'd worked for, too.

But even knowing how much he wanted it back, I couldn't just roll over for an idea like this.

"This could fuck us, permanently. If we keep going as we are . . . we'll get where we need to be eventually."

"Unless something unlucky happens in the meantime," Solitaire countered.

We argued a while longer, both of us digging our heels in and refusing to back down. Eventually, it was Beam we turned to as a tie-breaker.

And he refused to do so. "I'm sorry," he groaned. "I just don't know, you . . . you both have good points."

I scoffed, Solitaire snarled, and all of us were forced to agree we'd come to a more final decision tomorrow. Sleep came like a rag of chloroform, harshly felt but quickly succumbed to, and then it was a new day.

We were out of the inn within half an hour, having wolfed down a quick breakfast, and made our way down the streets quicker still. Our rendezvous point with Argar was the tavern where we'd met him. None of us had exactly decided that. It had just sort of happened around the second time we met him. On our way there, however, something very interesting caught our eye.

Well, it caught our ear. It was some old man on the road, shouting about ten or fifteen things seemingly at once, his words barely intelligible. We closed in slightly as we walked past so we could hear better.

"Please, anyone! Anyone?! There's a hundred children there, and women, too. We can offer coin if that's what you demand, but we need aid! Please!"

The panic in his voice would've made it clear enough that the man was talking of death, even if it hadn't been plainly obvious from his actual words. We listened a while longer, managing to unravel that he was talking about saving his village.

I turned to my friends, and was halfway through asking what they thought about the prospect when Solitaire cut me off.

"Ask him how much he can pay," he pressed, and I felt my skin crawl. Sometimes the bastard was too cold-hearted, even for my taste.

Regardless of that, though . . . we did need money. I cursed, and approached the man.

He was short, even for a native of Redacle. Normally, I looked down on short people, literally. But being tall made me a giant here, and my chin was almost touching my throat as I tilted my eyes down to meet his. The man was withered by age, hair white, skin wrinkled, body shaking and unsteady beneath its own weight. He looked like he'd just crawled out of a famine, then staved off a case of bubonic plague and had been locked in a sensory deprivation tank for half a century.

"Excuse me," I began, then ground my teeth as the idiot kept on shouting over me. I had to raise my voice and almost contest his own volume just so he could hear me.

"EXCUSE ME," I roared, then lowered my voice once he turned to me. "My brothers and I are mercenaries. What exactly is it that you need help with? We may be able to assist."

The man might have had a heart attack then and there with how shocked he looked. To his credit, though, he recovered quickly and spoke quicker still.

"I come from a small village to the west of here, Rinchester. It's perhaps ten leagues from the city."

My blood ran cold. If I was remembering how big a league was, that would put the place deep in undead country.

"It's being attacked by rotters?" I guessed.

He confirmed it with a nod.

"Bloody hundreds of them, every night. They come like rats, swarming the streets, climbing over each other's bodies to get at us. We had guards, but most are dead now, and those that are left have started barricading themselves indoors to protect their own families. We lose someone else every night. There are more every time. I . . ." His voice turned into a quiet croak, and he choked on it for a second while we all stared and listened. "I lost my daughter the week before, and I'm not sure if her children have survived the days since I left for Wolney."

That explained why the old man was having so much trouble finding someone willing to help. Mercenaries were a practical bunch. If they were told they'd be facing down hundreds of undead, let alone hundreds every night, they'd be more likely to run away with their tails between their legs than lift a finger to help.

And if professionals who killed things for a living were smelling a lost cause, who were we to try and make it anything different?

I turned to Solitaire and Beam, saw the looks on their faces, then braced myself and glanced at the old man. "Give us a minute please," I told him. "We need to make a decision."

CHAPTER THIRTY-FIVE

Solitaire's POV: Day 46
Current Wealth: 2 silver, 21 copper

We're not actually considering this, are we?" I asked, careful to keep from speaking loud enough for the old man to hear—that *would* be awkward—but letting the urgency of my question convey itself all the same. Shango didn't look nearly as reassuring as I'd hoped. In fact, he looked like he was about to argue.

And he did, the bastard. I couldn't even rely on a coward's cowardice anymore. What was the world coming to?

"He said they'd pay whatever they could manage," Shango pressed. "How much do you think that is, exactly? Gold, surely, and probably more than just a few pieces. This is an entire village's wealth—an *entire* village with many members who are recently deceased and thus no longer in possession of their own."

It was a valid point, really. We wanted money, they had a big pile of it and were willing to part ways with the stuff. Not to mention the other loot—or, more politely, salvage—that was likely lying around. I was hard pressed to counter him, but I did my best not to.

"Fuck you! You're trying to kill me."

As far as retorts went, it wasn't my finest, but in my defense I was under the effects of my amygdala, attempting to tunnel its way out through my cerebrum. Measured against other paranoids, I like to think I'd have gotten fairly high marks.

"The reason nobody else is coming to collect this pile of money is because everyone dumb enough to try is already part of a pile of corpses, and I'd very much not like to join that company." That was better, and it almost moved Shango for a moment, but his face was resolute as ever.

"We have an advantage over them," he noted. "We can . . . you know."

Level up, grow faster, increase in power so rapidly that none of the people in this world would even believe it. Yes, I did know, and that wasn't something I wanted to bank on as an escape rope. It hadn't saved us before, and it wouldn't save us now. If we were killed at level eight, it didn't matter how quickly we could reach fifty. Dead was dead.

I told Shango as much and saw my words bounce off him like rain against a roof.

"If we manage to last a single night, like the people still there have done dozens of times over, how many undead do you think we'll manage to kill? How much experience will that net us?"

That was the first thing he'd said that actually gave me pause, and I considered it. Don't misunderstand me. I'm a coward through and through. Thing is, I'm quite a conscientious coward, and my sense of self-preservation tends to pick up problems when they're still on the horizon. We'd not fought anything over level twenty so far, and we'd scuffled with few enough things that we couldn't kill by simply jumping it as a group. But that didn't mean things would remain that way forever. If we were unlucky enough, we could run into a dragon, a demon, some other creature strong enough to kill us and the entire city we were standing around arguing in. Hell, we'd already run into the giga-troll, and it'd been pure chance that saved us then.

Redacle was home to creatures, and people, who could turn that thing into a red smear in the dirt without using anything more than their wanking hand.

There'd be no defending against a scenario like that. One couldn't account for a natural disaster, after all. Some things were just bad luck. But odds could be improved. The faster we strengthened ourselves, the lower our chances of encountering something we couldn't handle. How would our alley fight have turned out if we we'd been as strong as we were now? Better, no doubt. And how might our fight with the giant troll have gone if we'd had a few hundred dead zombies under our belt?

I genuinely couldn't say. And that fact alone had me considering Shango's insane suggestion.

"There's the people to consider," Beam said quietly, drawing my attention despite the low volume of his speech. I could see he looked pained. Torn, the way people were when one side of their brain argued with the other. I'd have to figure out what had him so hesitant later, because I didn't think my friend was the sort to have a second thought about saving people, period. Or a first thought, for that matter.

"I'm considering the people," I said, regardless. "And I'm considering all the *other* people we could help if we avoid getting mauled to death by zombies."

"And how high are our chances of biting off more than we can chew tomorrow? Or next week? Or in a month?" Shango pressed. "It's going to happen eventually; there's no doubt about that. The only question is whether we'll be lucky enough to keep surviving when it does, and I don't think we will."

Part of me wanted to tell him that the giga-troll had been an isolated incident, but I knew I'd not have a leg to stand on. We'd not predicted or even suspected it would be there, and we'd blundered right into its lap. He had a point, damn him.

So I weighed the odds, considered the chances, and then, finally, decided based on my own preferences. If we didn't take this job, I'd be left to spend every day worrying that it'd be my last, and checking behind every tree for some fucking dragon. If we did take it, and lived, would I be strong enough to feel secure?

I didn't know. But suddenly I wanted to. The thought of actually having something to abate my paranoid worries was more enticing than a city full of coin. I sighed, swore, and nodded.

"Fine."

We returned to the man and presented a far more united front than our conversation would have betrayed, all stony faces and grim readiness. Honestly, we did quite a good impression of dark, brooding heroes. It was probably still spoiled by the first question out of Shango's mouth, though.

"How much can you pay, exactly?" he demanded. The old man didn't seem surprised by the certified Yoruba moment occurring right before his eyes, and was actually enthusiastic when he answered.

Presumably, the monetary cost was of no concern next to hitting his jackpot and actually discovering a group of morons willing to charge in and help his village.

"We can pay at least ten gold, plus whatever the dead residents have that isn't divided in their wills."

Ten gold was no small amount of money. Particularly now that we had the cost of magic tuition to front. I could see Shango practically drooling, and being frank, I was probably not much more restrained.

"Take us to your home then," Shango said. "We'll help you out the moment we've collected our companion."

Once the details were hammered out, we watched the old man scarper for the city gate, where he'd await our heroic appearance. I swallowed my nerves, swallowed my bitching, and joined Shango and Beam in moving to Argar's tavern. The walk didn't feel very long. Things rarely did when you had possible death awaiting you.

Argar was drinking in his corner, laughing with a few friends, and I could practically see the smile drop off his face as we approached. I almost felt bad for a second, ruining the man's fun with our very presence. Then I remembered he'd snapped a table in half against my ribs and started wishing we could ruin it even harder.

"We're setting off for Rinchester," Shango told him, abruptly. "Heard of it?"

The giant paled and nodded. I suppressed a grin.

"Well, off we go then," my friend continued. "No point in dilly-dallying."

The giant, to his credit, did actually accompany us. But he lost about fifty courage points for bitching the entire way. Talking about hordes of undead capable of filling an ocean; piles of them rising up to the clouds; and stronger, greater creatures like skeletal reavers or liches, capable of exploding buildings and stopping rivers. Honestly, it was infuriating. There's only so many little nitpicks I can take.

Fortunately, I was given a distraction soon enough. Shango leaned in beside me, whispering as we walked.

"Any chance you can make more gunpowder?"

I resisted the urge to convulse and tell him I'd specifically made *black* powder, instead channeling the energy to something more productive.

"No," I replied, honestly. "Even if we had enough shit, it'd take me nearly a full day to make it, and we don't have enough money to buy the sulphur and charcoal for more than . . . maybe a kilogram."

"A kilogram is a lot, right?" he pressed. I hesitated, then shook my head.

"Not for the time investment, and not against undead. If they had functioning organs that could get liquefied by the overpressure, then maybe it'd be worth it, but as things stand, we'll be facing enemies that would only really struggle against explosions that break bone and tear muscle. That's not deadly enough for my taste. Even adding shrapnel wouldn't have as high a kill ratio as against normal humans."

He sighed.

"Why couldn't I have gotten a useful terrorist?" Shango grumbled, and I ignored him.

Truth be told, I'd been thinking something fairly similar since coming here. Had I known we'd get Shanghaied into our own book, I'd have prepared a bit better. Like with a nice combat knife instead of that shitty pocket blade, a small mountain of engineering, chemistry, and physics references . . . and a shotgun—a really big one, one of those automatic types. I grinned imagining the giga-troll getting its guts opened up by a spray of supersonic lead.

My idle fancying was cut off, however, when Beam spoke on the other side of me. His voice wasn't as low or cautious as Shango's, just . . . soft. All certainty, steel, and promise.

"I'm not going to let you get hurt again," he told me, and something about the way he said it sent a chill running down my spine. I eyed him, studied his unflinching certainty and tried to deflect.

"Thanks, but it's not a problem—"

"We're doing this because I want to save people," he said, uncharacteristically cutting me off, "and I'm not going to let you or Shango get hurt. Definitely not on my account, understand?"

He really hadn't left much room for any rebuttal, so I nodded, and he nodded back. I swallowed, making a note to pursue the matter further when I had time to consider what the fuck might be going on with him.

And then we saw the old man up ahead waiting for us by the city gate.

The exit to our next fight, or perhaps our imminent demise.

CHAPTER THIRTY-SIX

Shango's POV: Day 46
Current Wealth: 1 silver, 47 copper

If I'd known the old man expected us to pay for our own meals on the road, I might've actually thought twice before following him. Not just out of basic thrift, but due to the simple fact that his not having the food already on him was a dangerous sign that he'd been lying about what his village could afford to pay.

Well, maybe not. My motives for helping had been a lot more tied to compassion than I'd made out to Solitaire. He probably knew as much, but still, it was important to keep up pretenses in polite conversation. So much of adult dialogue was built on convenient lies, after all.

At the very least, our new employer had been able to afford a wagon, and we sat in it for the duration of the journey, wrapping ourselves in the blankets we'd bought on the trip from Jhigral to Wolney, and we staved off the icy elements with conversation, and glaring enviously at the far thicker layers wrapped around the elder as he drove the vehicle on.

It would be about four days before we arrived, double the length we'd spent travelling last time, and yet somehow it did not feel that long at all. We were adjusting, it seemed, to the slow, tedious way this world did anything. And I wasn't entirely sure I liked it.

Our journey was kept busy, though, despite the volume of sitting and shivering. We were, after all, riding our way into a combat zone, and not one of us was stupid enough to do so blind. So, we asked the old man every question that flitted into our minds and prepared one another for every eventuality we could think of. Thanks to Solitaire, the latter was near inexhaustible.

Rotters were one thing. We were confident enough we could hold out against them even at night, provided we had a suitably defensive position. It was quite another, though, to face the other creatures that might be among them. I wasn't sure whether we'd be dealing with dullahan, fomori, or beladonnan puppeteers, but there'd very possibly be some heavier hitters there with hundreds of zombies present.

Oh, you don't know what any of those terms mean in Redacle? Haven't read our book? Well, putting aside that slight against me, they're bad, awful, and fucking atrocious to fight, respectively. The weakest of them might have been more than our entire group could handle together. The strongest could have slaughtered us times a hundred. And the old man was more than likely lying about there not being any higher undead at all. He didn't want to scare us off.

Smart.

"If one of the big ones attacks, we should use trenches," Solitaire suggested, confidently. "Square-cube law and all that."

"What the bloody hell is that?" Argar asked, frowning in confusion, looking at him as if he were half mad.

I knew what the term meant, even though everything I'd ever learned about engineering had been against my will as part of the world-building process, and I understood what Solitaire was getting at. Elephants died to a fall easier than mice, after all. I explained as much to Argar, then paused as a new thought struck me.

"What if it's one of the . . . uh, magical ones?" I asked, mind flitting to dark thoughts of liches, vampires, and everything in between.

Solitaire smiled. "It'll kill the shit out of us, and there's nothing short of an Abrams squad we could use to do anything about it."

Ah. Well, he was honest at least, the fucker. I nodded, and tried to bury my concerns.

Truth be told, for all our strategizing, there wasn't actually that much variation to any of the plans. The overwhelming majority of them would be dealing with more or less the same variables, and we'd already done enough work writing about rotters to have figured out the ideal way of combating them. It was something Argar very much seemed to approve of, despite his reservations about the whole ordeal.

Well, they were zombies. Pop culture had done most of the heavy lifting years before we even wrote a thing. Dumb, shambling morons with no more innate durability than humans. Set up traps, barricades, buy some time, and you can kill them almost at your leisure. But they were fast zombies, at least by night, and numbers could overwhelm. And unlike a lot of other pop culture, we tended to be realistic in our portrayal of how thick the human skull is and how hard getting at the brains beneath could be. Semi-realistic, at least. We wouldn't be exploding heads with every swing.

This wasn't going to be easy no matter what.

Days drifted by in a lazy, chilly haze, and we took to sleeping while the sun was up. By nightfall, as far as we were into the woods, we knew the rotters would be active and plentiful, swarming the carriage and burying us in rotting flesh. The only way to avoid that was to save the horses' stamina and strength to expend on outrunning them.

Even so, there were more than a few close calls, where the creatures got nearer than we'd have banked on. Fortunately, we were all diligent, and the night vision provided by lifetimes of nourishing, vitamin-rich diets in the modern world let us spot the creatures well before they were on our escort.

Frankly, it was a miracle the old man had made it to Wolney without us. A suspiciously big miracle, even, which he didn't explain, no matter how much we asked. That brought on a whole new problem, because the lack of explanation almost had Solitaire leaning forward to cut the man's throat from behind, and left me and Beam stuck focusing on talking him out of it about five times per day.

Now, as I said, we'd been getting used to the long, winding journeys that went hand-in-hand with this world. But, it wasn't all that was gnawing at us during this trip. Before, we'd been going to Wolney. A place with work, with food, with inns. A place, if anything, that would be better than the dogshit little town we'd been leaving.

Now? Now we were leaving Wolney, and rattling toward a death trap. Which has a fairly unique effect on a man's state of mind, let me tell you. If I had to describe it, I'd do so with the analogy of a spring. Imagine one getting slowly compressed, forced tighter by the second, coiling inward and building up energy until, just as it reaches its absolute limit, a ten megaton hydrogen bomb falls right on top of you.

In this scenario, the spring is our journey, we're the idiots squeezing it, and the bomb was what we were jittering and spasming in fear of, building up as an inevitable future in our minds and trembling over. Well, I say "we," but it was actually only the normal people. Which is to say, me, Argar, and the old man.

Solitaire's default state of mind, apparently, is "the entire human race wants to kill me," so this was nothing new for him. If anything, knowing for a fact that he was riding into trouble seemed to actually comfort the lunatic. And, as for Beam . . . well, nothing ever could shake him.

Plenty could shake me, though. Including my own muscles, because by the time we were on our last day, I was shivering with an adrenal overflow so strong that I actually heard my teeth chattering. Beam and Solitaire picked up on it, of course, and I was braced for the mockery long before it came. Largely because it never did.

"Deep breaths," Solitaire told me. "Just focus on the feeling of air moving in and out of you; force it to happen slowly. Remember, you're in control of those lungs. They work as fast as you tell them, and no faster. If they're too quick for your liking, seize them and drag them down to a better pace."

I tried his advice, and it actually worked. Gave me something to think about, for one thing, and the fact that it was something I had power over . . . Somehow that was more soothing than the distraction itself.

He wasn't done with his advice.

"This will pass," he pressed. "You'll feel better, calmer, in the future. For now, you're still here, and you have an age to think about what you'll do next. So use it. What's the plan?"

I gathered my wits and tried to come up with something. It was Beam, cutting in next, who helped me along.

"What if there is a strong undead there?" he suggested. "How do we deal with that?"

"It's the worst-case scenario," Solitaire replied, catching his train of thought and chasing it. "So imagine that's already happened, that it's the only case. This is as bad as it can get . . . so, if we knew it's what was awaiting us, what would we do?"

By the time there was a village within our sights again, just barely visible over the dawn-reddened horizon, they'd managed to calm me down enough that my blind panic was starting to give way for . . . embarrassment.

It wasn't like me to lose my shit like that. I was meant to be the calm one, the cool one. I smiled at my friends and thanked them for everything, but somehow their help had just left me more hollow.

Finally starting to slow as we neared the village's outer ring was a welcome distraction, and I was practically counting the wheel turns as I waited for our cart to finish its deceleration so we could crawl out from under the blankets and leap down.

Well, not exactly crawl out from under the blankets. We kept those on as we placed boots back down on the snow and came round the vehicle's side. It was just hard to give them up, after getting so used to the luxury. Whatever effect it had on our cool factor, however, the townsfolk didn't seem to notice. They were too busy staring with a mix of awe, apprehension and, if my eyes didn't deceive me, actual happiness.

The old man rushed ahead to them, more eager now than any of us had seen him since he first found out we'd be helping. Apparently, his failure had been anticipated, even by himself.

It was odd, seeing the few dozen citizens as they swarmed the area around us. They all looked thin, frail, and as undernourished as most of the homeless people we'd seen in this world; and yet, most of them had grins on their faces and light in their eyes. Hope, I realized. Hope because of us.

In that moment, any regrets I still had about riding over to save this town evaporated, and I felt a bizarre new resolve creeping in to cast my spine in steel.

I tightened my jaw, straightened my back, and took a few steps forward, preparing to address the people we were going to save.

CHAPTER THIRTY-SEVEN

Shango's POV: Day 50
Current Wealth: 1 silver, 47 copper

I wasn't actually entirely sure how to start a heroic speech. Truth be told, I wasn't exactly a hero. I'd seen plenty of movies, though, and read a few books, graphic novels, and played through video games. I was familiar with a vague set of behaviors that tended to strike people as impressive and larger than life. The major problem was that they also tended to kill the person who acted them out, unless he had superpowers. I pretty much didn't, so being the real deal was sadly out of the question.

My pause to think wasn't long, though. The mind works quickly under pressure, particularly the pressure of half a hundred eager faces aimed in its direction, and my mind in particular was plenty fast.

"My name is Shango," I declared, "Shango . . ." Fuck, a last name. What was our name? "Belahont. These are my brothers, Solitaire and Beam." I gestured at them as I named them, and eyes landed on each of them in turn. "We're here to help all of you with your undead problem." Faces seemed to relax slightly as they beheld us all.

One thing that definitely helped the illusion of heroism was that we did halfway actually *look* the part, at least for now. We'd gained a lot of muscle during our frantic weeks of training in Jhigral, and though our money was starting to run low, we'd still been eating well enough to maintain it for a while. That, and the fact that none of us were less than six inches above the average peasant's height. We might've resembled demigods to these people.

Maybe not. One of them was certainly not as daunted as the rest, stepping forward with sharp eyes as she stared me down. She was a tall woman, and remarkably dark skinned, for this part of the world. Her tone was still a great deal lighter than mine, but she wouldn't have been out of place in the middle east back home.

"And what are you charging for your help?" she demanded, voice all but confirming my observation. Her accent had that deeply resonating, scraping tone that I recognized as, in this world, belonging to Vittonia.

That was strange. Vittonia was a good thousand leagues southeast of where we were now. She was very far from home to be living in some dog-water Eregarn village like this, and very, very grumpy to be receiving help. Vittonians were a mixed bunch, but most were used to violence and warfare. Their civilization existed as a series of city-states, infinitely disparate and eternally warring with one another. If you met one, chances were they'd at least witnessed a serious skirmish or fight. The land of mercenaries, they were oftentimes called. If anyone were to see through us, it was a Vit.

Still, I'd won over hostile clients before. The trick was patience. And I'd won over clever clients—the trick there was being even cleverer.

"We're charging a sum of however much you can spare," I replied, calmly. "We need to eat, too, sadly, and we need funds to do more good. But for now that's of no concern, because we'll only be collecting our payment if we all band together and manage to keep ourselves from getting chewed to bits by undead, hm?"

She didn't seem convinced, but most of the people around her definitely were, muttering happily amongst themselves as she took a step back, still eying us balefully. The woman seemed . . . oddly frustrated.

"They're mercenaries," the old man who'd brought us there declared, "and they've managed to kill trolls before, so I think we can safely trust them to help us deal with some rotters!"

I ignored the hollow, worried feeling his blind faith had growing in my gut. The people were now grinning openly at the man's testament, some even going so far as to applaud our presence. I couldn't correct that. We needed an attitude like that if everyone was going to make it through this.

"So," the man continued, turning back to me, "what are you going to be doing first? Sunset should be in around twelve hours."

Which meant I could safely take about eleven of those hours to prepare. I considered his question, then turned to Solitaire and Beam.

"Any idea—"

"Do you have any animal shit?" Solitaire blurted, cutting me off, practically screaming his question.

I must say, I have seen people stare *harder* at my friend than the town did then, but not often. It took a few seconds for someone to reply.

"The barn floor should be . . . uh . . . crusty with it?"

Solitaire nodded sharply and started marching away. "Bring me someone clever," he ordered. "In the absence of that, bring me all the people who know what sulphur is, and I'll vet them for usefulness myself."

Eyes turned to me, questioning, and I had to resist sighing. Give Solitaire a time limit, I supposed, and he'd invariably decide that being polite doesn't make the cut on his list of priorities. I gestured the people after him with as gracious a nod as I could manage.

"I thought he said explosives wouldn't be very useful here," Beam whispered to me. I turned to him and tried to convey my own confusion as well as I could without tipping off our audience.

"They'd still be better than nothing, if he can make as much as last time," I noted. "We couldn't buy enough ingredients, but maybe we can find them."

"Uh, excuse me sirs," came a voice from behind us. I turned to see it was the old man we'd followed here. "Thank you again for, you know, volunteering to help us, but can I ask what you're planning to do exactly?"

It was a valid question, and fortunately, we'd all discussed it well in advance on the way here. Solitaire had, thanks to his antisocial personality disorder, been preparing to defend a position from hordes of shambling attackers for most of his lifespan. I didn't trust anyone else I'd ever met, spoken to, or seen evidence of existing more than him to get us out of this situation. Which meant that the optimal thing, as I saw it, was making sure everybody else did what he said, too.

And that was where I came in. These were people. I knew people, and all I had to do here was make those people think I knew what was best for them.

The only thing that made this different from the standard dealings I'd learned from my dad, of course, was that I actually *did* know what was best for them this time. But that isn't the sort of thing one says out loud.

"My brother, Beam, will be practicing combat drills with your people. Spear thrusts, that sort of thing."

Beam eyed me like I was a moron.

"You realize I was a sword fighter, right?" he snapped. "And sometimes a martial artist, but never a spearman. I don't know the first thing about spear fighting!"

Fortunately he had the prescience to keep his voice low as he said it, and I did the same.

"You can thrust, right?" I demanded. "And you know how to parry, how to control a weapon. There should be *some* overlap."

Beam hesitated, and I slapped him on the shoulder.

"Well there you go, then!"

Before he could argue further, I turned back to the group.

"Furthermore, my other brother, Solitaire, will help you with your defenses. Believe me when I say he's studied methods of siege warfare that haven't even been invented yet."

It might have been a bit much, because more than one of the people turned skeptical eyes on me—even those who'd been happy to see us. Still, I didn't expect to win them all over right away. Give them one night to see what we could do, and they'd trust us by the end of it.

Either that, or they'd all die, and us along with them. The silver lining of that eventuality was that nobody would really be in a place to care. I thought it best to avoid it in any case.

"Alright," I called out, clapping to recapture the attention I'd sensed slipping away during my pause. "Everyone get moving, quick march. Beam will be training you, and I need to catalogue the resources available so we know what we can use."

Best way to take power is to get everyone too busy to notice it happening, as my father used to say. Besides, having a comprehensive list of materials would make it easier for Solitaire to violate the Geneva Conventions.

Say what you will about terrified, starving pre-industrial peasants with PTSD, but they were remarkably quick about hopping to obey. For the most part. The tall Vittonian woman who'd given us shit was still just standing at the back and glaring, but a sizable enough fraction of the others were desperate enough to help out. I watched them diffuse through the village, darting into buildings and storerooms and clearing out the crowded streets with remarkable ease. Something about the sight was oddly . . . inspiring.

But I didn't wait to enjoy it for long before marching onto my own work. I'd have to be quick if we were going to survive this.

CHAPTER THIRTY-EIGHT

Solitaire's POV: Day 50
Current Wealth: 1 silver, 47 copper

I'm aware that my upbringing wasn't exactly conventional.

Born into an apocalypse cult to a paranoid schizophrenic with genius-level intellect, I really never had a chance at anything resembling a normal childhood. I played with barbed wire and sandbags rather than Legos, learned to read by memorizing advanced chemistry references, and got my exercise through knife fighting sessions. I'm aware that something is lost in the gap between my formative years and a normal person's.

That something, of course, is the knowledge of how to make black powder.

[The detailed bomb-making instructions genuinely featured in this chapter have been replaced on request by the publisher, who wish to avoid legal culpability for whatever it is Ian B. Urns will inevitably do in the future.]

Well, they're simple steps back on Earth, anyway. I wasn't *on* Earth, though, and I didn't have anyone to buy ninety-nine percent pure ingredients from. No e-commerce, and not even anything that wasn't created by the shadow government to brainwash the masses into complacent, consumerist cattle.

I had potassium nitrate, of course. Mother Nature, the freedom-loving bitch that she is, was kind enough to ensure that every mammal on earth naturally excretes the stuff in our shit. One must only extract it. Charcoal was a no-brainer, too. I could make that with a tree, an axe, and some dirt if I had to, and it had already been prepared in plentiful stores around the town.

The sulphur, though . . . That concerned me. As did the potassium nitrate's extraction process. It all came partially down to luck, really, and I felt that fact weighing heavily on my shoulders as I turned to the first of the idiots Shango had sent my way.

"Is there an alchemist in the village?" I asked.

My answer came from one of the women, grubby-faced and hard-eyed. I decided I liked her before the slow, plodding processes of her cognition could even vomit out an answer.

"There was, but he died early into the attacks."

I swore, and sighed. "Take me to his workspace."

Fortunately, with my Detect Element, I could be sure of identifying whatever I saw by sight. If not for that, then I'd have been stuck using trial and error. I wouldn't be able to read any labels, even if he'd used them. Damned illiteracy.

She led me there quickly, and I studied the ill-maintained little shack as I closed in on it. Realistically, we were lucky to even have this much. Redacle wasn't the sort of place where an educated man was found in every village, but I couldn't help but compare it to the far less run-down and budgeted establishment I'd gotten my ingredients from back in Jhigral.

The inside was musky, dusty, and smelled faintly of acid and ozone. A familiar smell I'd learned to pair with chemistry. It was a good sign, the sorts of chemistry I tended to dabble in would definitely have a heightened ingredient overlap with black powder. Everything was shelved and neatly tucked away, which would make things easier, so I decided to start from the door and work my way inward.

It took a lot of looking, a *lot* of fucking looking, but eventually lady luck gave me my just desserts. A nice, pale-yellow powder tucked away neatly inside a jar. The container, like everything in the place, was made from clay rather than glass— part of the reason it'd taken so long, being forced to open everything to examine them—and it didn't contain nearly as much of the stuff as I'd have liked, but it looked to be about three liters in all, and maybe four-fifths full.

I picked my brain for the relevant data pertaining to black powder creation, then worked it through the old meat calculator to quantify ratios. Two-point-four liters of sulphur, with a powder density of double water. So that gave me four-point-eight kilograms of the stuff. Luckily, sulphur was only a tenth of the final product by mass, which meant I had enough here for forty-eight kilos.

That wasn't as much as I'd have liked, but it would definitely make a boom as big as either of the larger bombs I'd crafted back in Jhigral. Bigger, even. Much bigger. Knowing it was a finite resource, though, unnerved me. Part of me started kicking myself for not pressing Shango on buying more of the stuff back in Wolney, but no. We wouldn't have been able to afford much, anyway, just enough for an extra kilo or two of explosives. Either way, that wouldn't be getting much mileage.

On its own, at least, but I'd never been banking on that anyway. First things first, though, we needed to actually make the explosive.

The potassium nitrate would be first, I decided. Mainly because I wanted to get the shit-handling over and done with. I had my happy little helpers scrape the barn floor and bring the refuse over to me, then examined it all with my Detect Element and began dumping the "purest" bits in a nice big cauldron the late alchemist had owned. It was big enough to hold probably fifty kilos or more, but I filled it only about one third of the way to make room for the other ingredient, water. Once it was all nice and wet and revolting, I started heating it up over the fireplace and waited.

If you think, in your entire life, you have smelled something bad, and that thing wasn't literal boiling shit, then I'm sorry to say you've underestimated the human nostrils' capacity for torment. It was like inhaling acid. No, worse, it was like inhaling glass. Glass dipped in acid, and heated to a hundred degrees. My eyes watered, my nose watered. God, it was bad enough to make my damned asshole water.

And the worst part? I could *see* the scent. My shitting vision, my special little power, was showing me the fecal pollutants as little flashing symbols in the air. The carbon, the hydrogen, the nitrogen. I was acutely aware of exactly how densely concentrated it was in every breath of oxygen I drew in, and my horrible, nasty computer of a brain was automatically calculating how much was left inside my lungs based on the difference in my exhalations. Whether I wanted it to or fucking not.

But I had to tolerate it because I couldn't just leave the extraction on its own. If something went wrong—God forbid a fire or damage to the cauldron—we were screwed. So I waited, tolerated, and made a lovely promise that any rotters I ran into with a still-functioning nervous system would die extra slow.

I'd leached the shit into the water already and filtered it good and proper. The evaporation was the worst stage by far, but compared to broken ribs or broken friends, I could manage the scent long enough to reach the most crucial stage. Crystallization. I gave the remnants of my newly made sludge some time to cool and settle, and when I returned, I found, as I'd suspected, that there were plenty of crystals separated and clinging to the sides of the vapor-emptied cauldron. I sieved the rest of the liquid to get all of them, then left them out to dry.

And there I had it, potassium nitrate. That was quick. Remarkably quick. I found myself blinking. I'd been expecting a lot more waiting for the processes to finish—various stages were agonizingly slow. Was there something I'd missed? Some accelerant in the cauldron? I couldn't check, so I just focused on the positive. After all, there I had it. Potassium nitrate.

Or, rather, there I had zero-point-seven kilograms of the stuff, according to the scales. I resisted the urge to pull my hair out, resisted the urge to start crying, and got back to work.

After all, I'd need about ten times as much to make all the black powder I had enough sulphur for.

CHAPTER THIRTY-NINE

Beam's POV: Day 50
Current Wealth: 1 silver, 47 copper

If I'm being totally honest, I actually panicked when Shango dumped me in front of about two dozen people with orders to teach them. My initial instruction, to go and find a suitably large open part of the village, was more to buy time than anything else. I used the walk over there to think.

Unfortunately, I was thinking slowly. Maybe it was the cold, maybe it was the imminent attack, maybe it was stage fright. You might think years in the Olympics would have prepared me for the latter, but you'd be wrong. God, I wished the rotters would hurry up.

"Alright, you lot," I called out with about as much calm as a man who'd just watched his pilot snort five grams of coke and get divorced moments before take-off, "I've been put in charge of whipping you all into shape. It's going to be hard, it's going to require focus, but—"

"We know it'll be hard," one of them interrupted. It was a wiry man who was glaring at me like I was personally responsible for the village's condition. "We've spent weeks fighting off hordes of rotters. What the hell have you done?"

Murmurs of agreement rolled out among the others, and I became acutely aware of how quickly I was losing what thin veneer of command I'd managed to scrounge up. I answered him quickly, trying to hide my desperation.

"I've killed rotters," I told him. "Lots of them. As well as trolls, and plenty of men. And I've been fighting with a sword since I was a boy."

"We don't have any swords here," another one called out, causing a second wave of agreement to bristle through the assembled people. "Who even put you in charge, anyway? Your brother? What's he done?!"

My teeth were grinding at *that* remark, but I had to admit it had a decent grounding. I was a sword fighter with no sword. I'd told Shango as much, and he'd not exactly done anything to prove himself to the locals either. Still, I was running out of ideas.

"Why are you even here, to loot us after we're all dead?" another voice called out. I frowned, tried to think of a retort, but heard more accusations flying even as I did.

"Bloody mercenaries are what you are, not heroes."

"We don't need foreigners telling us how to take care of our own town."

"Took you long enough to help, didn't it?"

It was all ridiculous. Ridiculously unfair, and ridiculously self-destructive. Were these people *trying* to get killed? Why were they so insistent on driving away the only help they'd get?

Solitaire could've probably figured it out. He could practically *smell* emotion on people, and Shango would've been able to reason everything out with brute logic. I wasn't either of my friends—brothers, now. I couldn't understand these people.

And, I realized, I didn't have to. There was one law I'd learned well since coming here, a law that even my brothers' cleverness had to kneel before. I took a step forward to employ it.

"You," I said, pointing to one of the dissenters—one who everyone else was looking to more than the rest. He froze, pointing to himself.

"Me?" he asked.

"You," I repeated. "Step out of the crowd. We're going to give everyone a little demonstration."

He did so, hesitantly. Even my authority was apparently irresistible while focused on a single target. I could see the man trembling as he approached.

"I want you to close in and try to bite me," I informed him. "Not hard, obviously, just give a demonstration for everyone. Sprint like you mean it, like I killed your child. Sprint like you're a rotter."

Again, the man was hesitant. Looking back to his friends and beginning to lurch forward only when they enthusiastically told him to go for it. I watched and waited as he came at me, studying his movements, getting the timing right in my head and remaining as still as a statue until he was only two yards away. Then I exploded into motion.

Stepping in, I placed one leg fast forward and gripped both his arms with mine, helping his momentum along by dragging his body and lowering mine. He hit my hip, then rolled fully over me as his momentum slid off my braced frame and his center was wrenched to one side. He spun about one hundred eighty degrees before finally slapping down onto the cold, hardened ground, groaning where he lay. The impact actually let out a sound, like a great table being slapped open-handed. It was a struggle for me not to wince.

I turned to the others and saw, with no small amount of satisfaction, that they were suddenly a lot quieter, staring with wide eyes and gaping mouths. I was talking before any of them could get a word out, and I sounded smug even to my own ears.

"That was a Judo throw, a technique from a style of fighting not known in your lands." I was, at least, fairly certain that martial arts weren't as advanced here as they were back on Earth. "It's one of several I know. As you can see, it's good for putting an enemy on the ground, and it works even without much strength, since it involves turning their own speed and weight against them."

From the corner of my eye, I saw the man starting to stand. I mimed out a stomp to his neck as he rose, freezing him in place.

"A downed enemy can be hurt badly, stomping is always a good choice, but you'll also have the chance to move and arm yourself if there's a weapon nearby. At worst, you can put more space between you and them to escape. Worth remembering."

More silence, stunned silence. They were impressed. I actually let myself hope, for one moment, that I might've managed to shut them all up. But there was a dissenter. Always a dissenter.

"That's not weapon fighting."

It was another of the louder ones, apparently eager to pick up where his compatriot—now rolling around and groaning at my feet—had left off. I replied with a smile.

"You're right, it isn't," I told him. "But there's a lot more overlap than you might think, you'd be amazed how many knights die from throws like the one I just showed off, when they're followed by a knife between their armor plates. Now who wants to step forward with a weapon for a different demonstration?"

Unsurprisingly, it took a bit longer to wring some volunteers out this time, and I went easier on the next few, but they still learned.

We went through everything I could think of, all the techniques and skills I'd learned for applying strength and manipulating motion. Where and how to grip, the particulars of putting that little twist in your wrist for extra power, foot placement, elbow locking. Grappling and counter-grappling and leading an enemy.

Some of it might've been useless; I wasn't sure how often rotters were likely to feint, but it all contributed to a holistic picture of combat, of melee. And it felt good.

After close to two months at the lowest rung of this world's ladder, without so much as the chance to even hold the weapons I'd actually trained with, I'd begun to forget what I was capable of. I couldn't even be sure I still *had* all the old muscle memory, but reinforcing that the knowledge was still there at least did something to abate my nerves. And seeing the people stumble their way through everything was oddly satisfying.

But it was slow progress, all the same. I'd never been a teacher, just an athlete, and practically none of the people I was dealing with now had even a tenth of the talent I'd come to expect. I suppose a friend group consisting mostly of Olympic-tier athletes would tend to do that to a guy's perspective.

We continued regardless, working away and persevering. Warming ourselves up with the exertion of it all until the sun was well past halfway across its path through the sky. That was the warning point. Better to end it all well in advance of nightfall, and give everyone a few hours to recover.

The group broke up and started going their separate ways, and I felt an uneasiness in my gut as I watched them. They hadn't learned much, really. Maybe not even enough to be noticeable. For most, it took dozens of hours to start executing moves properly, dozens of hours more to get used to using them against a resisting enemy, months of weekly and daily training to practice snapping out a decent bunch, turning on all the right joints at all the right times, not freezing up and moving past simple reaction, but truly gauging spacing enough to control it in the heat of battle.

If every one of them learned as fast as I did, maybe we'd have made halfway passable fighters of them before nightfall. If my coaches had been training them, perhaps the same result could've been achieved in half the time. But, we were stuck with what we had. It was a difference, more than nothing. But a lot less than something.

Swallowing, I turned to head back to wherever Shango had gotten to, hoping that he'd managed to get everyone else better organized than me. After all, he didn't have the option of just dropping them on their heads.

CHAPTER FORTY

Shango's POV: Day 50
Current Wealth: 1 silver, 47 copper

My brain was a giant piece of artillery, and information was the ammunition. Phrased like that, my need to walk around the shit-smelling, tattered village and take note of details and people sounded a lot cooler. I got on with it, despite my distaste for the task. Save for the fact that I'd already spent years getting used to just this sort of work at my dad's company, I was also motivated by the *uniquely* powerful desire to not be eaten alive. That was one of the few advantages of a giant zombie horde, I supposed.

Rinchester was far more categorically akin to Jhigral than Wolney, as I might've expected, but being frank, it was pretty far removed from either. Dense like the city, but altogether lacking even as much scale as the town. Only a single building in the entire place reached even as high as three stories. Apparently, it had been the mayor's office back when they'd last had one.

That was about thirty years ago.

Now it was nothing but a relic. The village had, as I discovered, more or less been ignored by the local lord who ruled over it—a bannerman of Wolney's governor. They'd become quite independent since, but not enough that they could weather the rotters, evidently. What interested me wasn't actually the story of how their culture and leadership had developed, though. Just the fact that the mayor's building was still fairly well maintained and looked like it had much thicker walls than any other. Magus made, by my guess. There had probably been one living in the village back before its fall from grace, presumably in the years when it was still watched by nobility.

Clearly they'd noticed the same little detail as me. The building was box-like, with cobbled stones and primitive mortar making up most of its composition.

Stepping inside, I could already see the hastily made barricades that proved it'd been a hideout of choice, and recently.

I called on one of the people who'd struck me as the closest thing to the rabble's leader, asking him to confirm. A tall fellow, for this world, he'd have been about average height back home. Wiry, gaunt with hunger, his hair was untidy and his eyes were sharp.

"Tucker," he said, greeting me. "Pleasure to make your acquaintance, sir."

Oddly enough, he spoke with an American accent. Texan, if I wasn't mistaken. When imagining the people in this region of the world, we had decided they'd have British accents. A foreigner? And from a long way away. I resolved to ask him about it later.

"Yes, sir, we've been hiding out here for the last few nights. As you may have seen, the rotters have gotten through several of our other walls."

I had seen. Little wooden shacks and huts with big planked walls, either torn apart or simply smashed in. There'd been dried, congealed blood inside most of them. Apparently the little piggies who built their houses out of sub-par materials didn't get to take refuge elsewhere after realizing their mistakes.

"How many fighters do you have left?" I asked, hesitantly.

Tucker only snorted. "None, we never had any real fighters. This is a lumbering village."

My jaw tightened as I stared at the blood, rephrasing my question. "How many people do you have actively fighting then?"

That gave him pause.

"Around thirty," he said after a short pause. "Last I checked we were outnumbered about ten to one, and only a few of those are even trained as guards. Most of them . . . take care of themselves first."

I swore. Not good. Very, very bad, in fact. We kept moving, and I kept tallying things. More ruined buildings, some still-standing useless ones. A barn, which already had people shoveling excrement out of it—Solitaire was hard at work then—and an old alchemist's shop. There was a bell tower, also made of stone like the town hall, and finally a storehouse which, when I checked the interior, mostly held lumber, timber, and nails.

By the time I'd finished surveying the town, the better part of an hour had passed.

I turned to Tucker as we moved out. "How are people organized?" To be honest, it should've been one of my first questions, and my only reason for putting it off had been anxiety. His answer would very possibly determine whether I even had a chance of saving this town. Whether I even had a chance of saving myself.

Going by the expression on his face as he thought of an answer, I wasn't exactly confident.

"We don't really have any official system," he admitted. "Just sort of . . . talk about things, and decide what we should do next together."

It wasn't as bad as it could've been, I decided. If nothing else, Darwinism would've taken care of the few morons that typically ruined such approaches. Still, it was another weight on my shoulders. We needed a more coherent leadership than that.

"From now on, you answer to me," I informed him and continued when I saw the protest growing on his face. "And everyone else to you. You'll see why after tonight, and you can make your decision then, but for now know that my brothers and I have a plan. We're going to make a weapon to take care of some rotters for you, we're going to add our own abilities to bolster your defenses, and we're going to fight tooth and nail to save all of you and ourselves. But the price for that is that you do as we say tonight. If we die, we die, but if we live, then you'll see that you have a chance beyond just crossing your fingers and buying time before the inevitable comes to pass."

Truth be told, it wasn't my best argument. I was tired, cold, irritated, and worried. My father probably would've smacked me for making such a dogshit point. Tucker, though, lapped it up. I guess rhetoric was a bit less advanced in this world than ours.

"Damned if we don't then," he sighed. "But only probably damned if we do. No choice, is there?"

There wasn't, and I made a note of how quick he was. Either his was a rare competence, or something about fighting an entire graveyard for weeks on end hardened people. It was probably both, and either way it was useful.

Intelligence: 6

Interesting.

We moved on for some time, until I finally came to the next of Rinchester's points of interest. Perhaps predictably, it was Beam.

I watched him training the masses, and he was doing well. Or at least I thought he was. Truth be told, I wasn't actually sure what teaching people combat skills entailed. He seemed to be doing a good job of throwing them around and beating everyone up, however, which was probably a step in the right direction.

Beside me, Tucker spoke as he watched it all himself, voice touched by a bit of awe.

"Your brother is . . . good," he said.

I eyed him, sidelong. "Very," I replied. "And there's barely a scrap of magic in him. A lot of what you're seeing is just raw physical prowess."

He swallowed. "Are you all this skilled?" the villager asked, turning eagerly to me, question infused with an almost sickening abundance of hope. It stabbed a guilty dagger into my guts to ruin it for him.

"We're not," I told him, practically watching the smile slide off his face. "But I at least can hold my own against most men, and our other brother, Solitaire, could probably fight two or more of me at once . . . And our companion, Argar, can beat any one of us if he put his mind to it. Beam included."

That at least seemed to restore *some* of the man's confidence, and his thoughtful nod actually seemed to carry a fair amount of the hope I thought he'd lost. I wasn't able to dwell on it for much longer, however. Trudging footsteps turned my focus around to the tall, furious Vittonian woman we'd been chewed out by upon first arrival.

She was even *more* furious. I braced myself for the lecture I knew was coming, watching her pull to a stop just feet from me and glare upward. She barely had to tilt her head to stare into my face.

"What do you think you're doing?" she demanded, thick, foreign accent cutting through the wind almost as easily as the wind cut through me. I weathered it regardless.

"Helping your village," I replied, flippantly. It was maybe not the best choice of words and tone, but it'd been a long day and a longer week, and we were burning daylight far faster than I'd have preferred.

She certainly didn't seem to appreciate any of those contributing factors in her reaction, however.

"Giving everyone hope," she growled. "You can't seriously think you have a chance of making any difference here, not with a performance like that." She gestured to Beam, who I thought was doing a perfectly fine job of teaching.

I couldn't begin to argue against whatever apparent flaw she'd noticed, so I simply ignored the point entirely and sought to distract her from it.

"I'm not lying to anyone," I told her. "I have hope, and so do all of you, as long as you—"

"We don't have shit," the Vittonian snarled. "And you're an imbecile if you think otherwise. Because of you these people are staying with their heels dug in. Everyone should be taking that wagon the old fool snuck off with and using it to flee, that way at least some of us would live. As far as I'm concerned, you're killing everyone you convince otherwise."

She turned on her heel and stormed off without another word, and I watched her go.

In all honesty, there was a fairly high chance she was right. But we needed money, and escaped refugees couldn't pay as well as the inheritors of a newly depopulated village. If we started evacuating, people would want to be on the carriages out, they'd turn on each other, and our chances of keeping the entire place alive would disappear. Along with it, our payout would disappear. I wasn't going to starve again.

Thinking about it all as starkly and coldly as I did made my guts squirm. But I mastered myself. What choice did we have? None. This wasn't a moral issue, it was a practical one. And, as much as I hated Solitaire for the sheer brutality he'd unleashed without even asking . . . I could hardly claim to be an idealist.

We couldn't afford to starve, couldn't afford to die, and . . . in light of our modern culture, ethics, powers . . . we couldn't afford to delay gaining the power to help this world. Was I just telling myself that as some sort of justification?

Maybe. But that didn't make it any less true. I swallowed the bitterness in my mouth and turned back to Tucker.

"Let's go and find my brother Solitaire. I think he'll have something you'd be quite interested to see."

CHAPTER FORTY-ONE

Solitaire's POV: Day 50
Current Wealth: 1 silver, 47 copper

'd asked for the town's clever clogs, and apparently the woman I'd been given was their pick. She was about as dull as might be expected of a slightly above-average human whose brain had been shriveled by malnutrition, but she was quick enough compared to most of the savage morons in this world, so I supposed she'd do.

Margaret, her name was. Prettier than she was smart, and at the very least cognizant enough to seem interested in what she was helping me do. I explained as I worked. Mostly for good reasons, but partly because I found it *incredibly* arousing to induce a look of awe on her face with every revelation.

She asked about how I was mixing things, and I explained the basic concepts of reactivity and how it could be accelerated with heat and pressure. She asked how I was turning shit into something useful, and I explained the concept of elemental composition and distillation. She asked how I knew what effect I'd get by mixing different things, and I *tried* to explain the concept of atomic nuclei, electron shells, and what both things could let you predict about two substances' interaction.

It was around that point that I saw she was completely lost, but the poor thing did her best to keep up. It was, if nothing else, nice to have the background noise while I worked, abating my monotony and distracting my senses.

I'd been making good, steady progress over the course of the day. Carving away hours of daylight and spending them frugally on the processing still required for my chemistry. Already I'd managed to make my final blend and filter it out. All that was left to do now was let the soaked powder dry out in the sun.

Luckily, all things considered, I'd had a few extra hours to spare. It would've taken a lot longer to dehydrate under moonlight. Then again, I'd have been mauled to death by zombies before I could actually use it for anything in that scenario anyway.

Shango saved me wondering what to do for the next few hours by showing up. I wasn't entirely surprised. The village wasn't big enough that I'd actually expected him to take that long cataloguing our assets. I hurried over to meet him, wanting to make use of every extra second we could before the horde of bastards showed up.

"What are we working with?" I asked, having neither the time nor patience for niceties. Shango replied in much the same way, and it unnerved me somehow. Speaking with a friend like that and being spoken to likewise. It let our situation sink in deeper than I'd noticed earlier.

I buried the observation. This was no time to wallow in it.

Shango was as efficient as ever and answered quickly, clearly.

"We have lamp oil," he explained. "Quite a lot. Farming tools, some construction hammers and such, loose timber, cobbles, more mortar that could be made and reset if needed . . ."

He went on, and I listened, nodded, and internalized. This was why the two of us had always been such a strong pair. Shango was the best researcher I knew, capable of powering through textbooks without even being touched by boredom. I'd never had the attention span for that, but I could listen to his summaries and recall practically everything if I needed to.

In this case, it took about ten minutes for me to become an expert on Rinchester defense. I paid attention, of course, even while he flitted over the list at a hundred miles per hour.

"For fortifications, we have the mayor's old building, which is already being used. There's also the bell tower, which is another stone building. Might be worth splitting some people into there—"

"Bell tower?" I asked, cutting him off. He hesitated, eying me cautiously, nodding.

I grinned.

"With a bell still in it?" I pressed.

Again, Shango nodded.

"How big?" I demanded. "How heavy? Can we get it down, or is it down already?"

Clearly, he was still confused, but he was clever enough not to waste time with pointless questions.

"It's about half a ton and maybe a foot or two wide at its mouth; it's already down."

"Take me to it," I demanded, then glanced at Argar, eying his muscles. "And get me some more idiots and a smith."

Our walk was brief, and Shango ended up pulling ahead of the others to fall in step beside me. He had that way about him, the manner of holding his arms, the slight tightness to his jaw. He smelled of hesitance and uncertainty.

I wasn't surprised when he started speaking in that hushed tone he always used for subterfuge. "What do you think of our being here?" he asked. I glared at him, and Shango sighed. "Okay, yes, fine, maybe you were right. But aside from being a smug cunt about it, what do you think of our chances? What . . . have you been preparing, Solitaire?"

I was on the verge of answering, but then I paused. He was barely even paying attention to me as I spoke. Why?

Because he wasn't asking what he'd wanted to, the pussy had stopped himself and swapped in another question at the last second. I didn't have time for that, my tolerance for such things had died sometime around my third huff of urea.

"What's really eating away at you?" I asked, too tired for any of his distractions. Shango sighed. Clearly he'd not been expecting to fool me anyway.

"Is this really worth it?" he asked. "Even if we win? We have better odds than the villagers here, but . . . but . . ."

"But you're worried we're condemning them all to death by giving them false hope and convincing them to fight."

He didn't meet my eye, and I sighed.

I could try lying to him, could manipulate him, but even I had my lines, and those were ones I wasn't willing to cross. Not to a friend, at least. Instead I shrugged.

"We're holding the fate of the world in our hands, aren't we?" I asked. "And . . . we were holding it long before now. All of this is *our* fault. We made this world regressive and medieval. We filled it with trolls and rotters. We didn't know we were, but . . . still . . ."

It was irrational, petty, stupid. And yet I couldn't quite keep the knowledge from gnawing away at me. All of these people were suffering because I'd decided to write a book.

"We can't be blamed for that," Shango began.

"Maybe you're just too bad at blaming things," I retorted, speaking over him.

He was right, of course. Whenever I wasn't, odds were he would be. And I knew I was lying to myself even as I kept doing it. But that didn't change the things I'd seen here. Nothing would.

Intent is an irrelevance next to action. Action is no more inherently unforgivable than inaction. Dead people didn't care if they were killed by a giggling villain or some dumbass writer in his teens. Dead was dead. And I'd made plenty of dead'uns in this world. A billion, perhaps, for each one I'd already personally seen.

Shango stared at me the way he often did when I said something completely reasonable, but that *society* wouldn't care for.

"Out with it," I sighed, never having been one to enjoy getting eyed like some lunatic in an asylum.

"I don't think it's on us to fix the world just because we unknowingly created it," he said, quietly, not meeting my eye. I shrugged again.

"Then how about because we have the potential to?"

That moved him, and he swore long, harsh, and loud before finally speaking again. "So we're saving the world?"

"We're saving the world," I concurred.

What I didn't tell him, though—what I could never tell him—was exactly how I realized it would be best to go about it. Because there was a particular species responsible for ruining this one, and if it remained in control, it would just keep on ruining away.

We walked a while longer, letting that settle. It occurred to me that we'd not actually discussed means before, and still hadn't. Did Shango know what I did? It would be more like him to not address something he'd figured out than not figure it out in the first place.

"The mercenaries are our first step then," he said after a while, and I nodded. It seemed only logical.

"So, we need funds for that." Shango sighed. "Which we can only get in a large quantity here, for the time being."

I didn't say anything because there was no need to. I recognized the sight of someone talking themselves into a position. All Shango needed to make his decision here was silence. So I provided it.

"Fuck it, you're right," my friend—my brother—conceded after a while. There was a new fatigue to him that I didn't like. His exhaustion and guilt weighed on me, so I did what I always did. Cracked a joke to try and take his mind off it.

"It's amazing the time we'd save if you just started every conversation like that." I grinned. Then my smile fell as I caught sight of a stone tower ahead. We'd arrived.

CHAPTER FORTY-TWO

Beam's POV: Day 51
Current Wealth: 1 silver, 47 copper

We had a few more hours of daylight to burn, but my contribution was just about done. The trainees needed rest, and I wasn't much help in tracking resources or turning them into bombs. Which left me with time to meditate.

I used it, sitting with my legs folded and my eyes closed, controlling my breathing. Forcing myself to relax against the biting tension of imminent danger. Perhaps there were more productive things to be doing, a few hours' extra practice on my own end, for example.

But I'd already worked on my movements and conditioning today, and every other day of the last week. There'd be no new advantage to find there. If I wanted an edge, it would be magical.

Half an hour, one hour, ninety minutes. It was around then that I finally put an end to it, boredom, irritation, and frustration winning over any rationale I might've clung to.

What had the stupid voice in my head said? It could only show me the ropes. I cursed. Better to have spent the time practicing.

Standing, I looked around me, surveying my surroundings for a suitably large target to test my power on. Then realizing that even that just defeated the point. I was supposed to be capable of turning anything into a weapon, right? So I'd practice just that. I forced my gaze to stop on the next thing that caught my eye and, probably through sheer probability, that thing happened to be snow.

White, blemishless, clinging to the hard ground so stiff and rigid that I might've stubbed my toe on it. The world wasn't getting colder anymore, but I guessed that was only because it'd already gotten as chilly as the air could withstand. Touching something at that temperature would be unpleasant, to say the least.

I strode over, bent down, and stuffed my hand against it all the same. I'd probably need to grab things a lot less enjoyable than snow if I was to get the most mileage out of this ability.

The cold seeped in quickly, but I ignored it. However deep and cruel, it was still just pain. I felt more every time I was on my second to last rep, and putting it aside didn't even bring me close to my mental limits.

But then I reconsidered. Ignoring pain was good, normally, but here . . . Here I was trying to connect with whatever I touched. How did one connect with an inanimate substance? Well, generally unsuccessfully. I didn't want to do it unsuccessfully. That sounded like the sort of thing that would lead to my friends being eaten by undead, so I'd have to change things up a bit.

I couldn't talk to snow, couldn't ask it questions, couldn't profess any emotions to it or read any in exchange. But I could feel what it did to me, and how it felt to my senses. If only for want of any better alternative, I started concentrating on the sensation.

My fingers were half numb and half ablaze with the pain. It felt more like grabbing something hot than cold, an ineffable burning against my skin, seeping in and making every muscle convulse in protest. I gritted my teeth against it, forced my mind back onto the site of agony, preventing my thoughts from scattering and my focus from wandering.

What was I feeling? Pain, obviously, but where from? From the lack of heat, from the very sensation of that heat being dragged out of my flesh, kicking and screaming. I wasn't feeling a substance at all; I was feeling a natural void being filled. Sure enough, the snow began bleeding into water and pooling at my feet as the temperature of my skin broke down ice crystals and left the remaining ones to drown in their corpses.

It might've just been some weird disassociation from the pain, but I started to see ice crystals breaking down. Like metal melting in a crucible, seeing their microscopic patterns collapse and crumble as the heat washed through them, picturing the resultant water swallowing others and clinging to my hands from the tension. My mind fell deeper into the vision, my concentration soon consumed by it in totality, and before long even the pain was gone.

The pain was gone, but I wasn't ignoring it. It just . . . wasn't there. How could it be?

I was beloved of the world. I could hardly expect it to hurt me.

Somehow the words felt right, felt correct. Somehow I knew them even before they occurred to me. And the moment they echoed through my mind, I felt another change.

I'd felt it before, and recognition burned so bright in my mind that I almost missed what was happening now. A coagulating rush of power, of life itself, building and diffusing from the snow as pale vapor. Like steam, like fog, like snow—and yet something else entirely. I grabbed it hard, held it tight, and felt it rest in my hand as its volume gained mass and its surface gained strength.

After a few moments, I was holding another cylindrical length, this time white where the last had been gray. Glowing all the same. I felt it in my hands, moved it around, and marveled at the lightness of it. It was like a weapon made out of . . . not even wood, something lighter. Polystyrene, cardboard. With all the strength of stone.

Its balance was so categorically removed from anything I'd trained with before that it took practice not to send it flying out of my grip with the slightest motion, and I gave myself that practice as I walked back to meet my friends. Suddenly feeling quite a lot more confident than I had earlier.

Everyone else was already gathered in the mayor's hall, more or less, and Shango had already made himself something of an executive board at the back. The man I'd seen following him around—Tucker, I think his name was—was leaning over a table talking to him. Solitaire was in one corner, fiddling with some metal. The whole place smelled of human habitation and . . . something else, too. Not gunpowder. God knew I'd inhaled enough of that to recognize it. Something more simple. Iron? Iron. It smelled like a forge.

I made myself known with a cleared throat, taking a seat by the table and throwing my gaze out through the open door. Beyond it lay the building's main hall, and it was an impressive sight, I had to say.

Solitaire had clearly been given run of the place because it now resembled one of his schizo-bunkers. Big walls of wood had been put up, embedded through the planked ground, reinforced by big logs angled upward at forty-five degrees. They had holes in them that were too small for a person but just big enough for a spear, and barbs lining the tops, which I could only imagine would shred any person who tried to climb them.

Above, I saw more logs, these ones larger, heavier. Held aloft by long lengths of rope that'd been looped around the high ceiling's rafters. I followed the rope, found it bound down on the defender's side, and realized what it was for. Untying them, we could drop hundreds of kilos of tree trunk down on anything within a few feet of the barricades. Ouch.

Someone had torn a bunch of planks out in big strips from the edge of our barricades to the main entrance, essentially creating rows of miniature trenches that'd be a nightmare to sprint through without falling, and behind the barricades themselves were more. Then more still. Row after row of defensible positions, all ready to be abandoned and re-assembled.

From the actual office that Shango was using as his meeting room, I was looking down on it all. A staircase led upward from the main killing-room down below, raising perhaps two stories into the air. Something big and covered in cloth was resting at the top of it, something I'd had to squeeze by to get in. I turned to Solitaire, question dying on my lips as he grinned.

"You'll see," the madman told me, and I suddenly found his grin leaving my curiosity a bit weakened. Somehow I imagined I *would* see, and somehow I felt a lot less eager to do so.

"How are your ribs?" I asked him, and he sighed, massaging them irritably.

"Painful, but healed. I can swing a nice big block of wood around with no issues. You alright?"

I almost screamed my answer, eager was I to share it. "I managed to tap into my magic on purpose," I told him, grinning. "I think we can count that as one extra edge during the attack."

Solitaire's grin grew even wider, in the same way a wolf's might, the same way it always was when he imagined bodies coming apart and blood staining his skin. I hid how much that disconcerted me.

"You have magic?" a voice said from behind me, low and blunt. I turned to see Argar leaning against a wall, grinning. Not like Solitaire. He was less a cat looking down on a mouse and more a kitten looking up at a playmate. A seven foot tall, four hundred pound kitten, mind you, who could lift a sumo wrestler over his head, but still a whole lot less . . . *pointy.*

"Some," I replied quickly, cursing myself for letting slip what I had. The giant didn't seem bothered one way or another, merely shrugging.

"I'll have to kill fast then," he grunted. "Can't have you stealing all the rotters before I get to them."

"Nobody's *stealing* anything," Shango cut in, glaring up at him. "We're all going to stay nice and safe behind our barricades and poke the rotters while they try to get past. If we ever actually exchange a blow with them, it'll be because we've already fucked up."

"Which we will," Solitaire added. "Just to be clear, we're not holding off hundreds of . . ."—His lip curled—"*humans*, not when they essentially have late-stage rabies and a pound of cocaine in their blood."

Argar stared at him blankly, and Solitaire sighed.

"Not when they're very angry and very strong," he amended. "So you'll be getting your fight, and we need everyone to understand that there *will* be a fight. Because otherwise they might panic when it all kicks off, and if they start screaming and crying, then *I* might not be able to resist beheading them, even apart from the obvious tactical issues it'll cause."

The giant nodded at that, seeming pleased despite the chaos being described. I just went cold.

It was one thing to know we'd be attacked, even to know that it would happen soon. Quite another, apparently, to be so precipitously near to the event that we were discussing tactics and counters. How long would we have before I was thrust into a bloodbath with everyone else? Hours?

My answer came soon enough—a shrill, panicked warning cry running through the length of the building and sending a shiver down my spine.

"ROTTERS!" a sentry called out, voice cracking with fear. "THEY'RE HERE!"

I climbed to my feet, closing my eyes and running my hand down the length of a wall, focusing on the texture of oaken paneling as it grazed my fingertips. Feeling all the magics rearing their heads again.

Time to test my new powers.

CHAPTER FORTY-THREE

Beam's POV: Day 51
Current Wealth: 1 silver, 47 copper

I hurried down the stairs, storming out into the main section of the building's interior and watching as the doors shivered beneath unseen blows from the other side. They were big things, perhaps a dozen feet high and nearly as wide, several inches thick and consisting of hardwood. We'd barred them with a big length of timber that probably would've held even if Argar had taken an axe to it.

But it was straining now, and straining badly. Flexing and bending against the pressure applied from outside, groaning as its elasticity was pushed beyond the limit, and its structure began to yield into fissures and splits.

Every new impact against it sent a shudder through the peasants assembled around us, bringing in fearful trembles as if it were their own bodies the enemy was smashing into. I found my own nerves fraying, as well, but a new sound soon took my focus. Shango's voice.

"Keep calm!" he roared, piercing through the cacophony as if his vocal cords were powering some coherent laser. "You've all faced these things before, and this time you're shielded, barricaded, and ready for them. Remember what we practiced!"

I found myself hanging onto every word, and so were the villagers. My spasming wits using Shango's voice as a lighthouse to guide themselves back from the seat of madness they'd drifted to. It was a hard sell—calmness in this storm. We'd all fought rotters before, but if Solitaire was right about hundreds coming, it'd be unlike any previous attack.

But amazingly, miraculously, Shango's booming voice actually seemed to calm the room. Halting frantic, babbling movement and boxing people in shoulder-to-shoulder in tight, readied formation.

Just a fight, I told myself, as the bar on the door began to schism further. *Just another fight. You can win. You will win. You will live.*

My thoughts were interrupted as something heavy smashed into the other side of the door, far more forceful than any other impact. The bar split fully, falling to the ground in two ruptured halves, and I had barely an instant to dwell on that fact before the door was flung wide open.

Rotters poured in from behind it. We'd been told there were hundreds, but I swore we must have been facing thousands. Revolting piles of decay and necrotic animalism, snarling and scrambling over one another, all racing to be the first with human blood in their mouths. Their flesh was covered in lesions, patchwork and tattered scalps, eyes pale yellow like congealed milk. Black drool fell from their mouths and clung to jagged teeth, and what was left of their ragged clothing flapped behind them as they all sprinted for us.

There were so many, so fast, crammed into so small a place, that they came more as a tidal wave than a formation. Actually moving in three dimensions where some were forced high over the heads of others as they smashed past each other. My heart sank at the sight of the chaos, and I forced my mind from it to touch the wood at my feet.

Wood. Unyielding, but flexible, resilient and defensive. A protection as much as a weapon, if not more so. This plank was bound by iron nails, though, and I felt their touch, too. The rigidity of them, the jagged edges. It was iron that had first made human warfare possible on a mass scale, outstripping bronze in both abundance and function, and this stretch yearned to continue that grim work.

I obliged it, standing with a new weapon in my hand. A simple weapon, one that men had been using to kill before we could even have been called men. I strode toward the barricades with my new spear in hand, magically augmented muscles quivering beneath my skin, hands tightening around its luminous grip. I was just in time for the first of the rotters to slam into the other side.

The wood held before me, if barely. Inches thick and carefully shaped to Solitaire's exact demands, I wouldn't have been entirely surprised if an elephant had bounced off it. The creatures that first impacted it died to their allies' force, rather than their own, crushed and ground to mangled mincemeat as innumerable tons of rancid muscle powered forth to pin them against the wood.

For a moment I stood, frozen. Everyone did. Then one of the fuckers—now just ten or twelve feet away—snarled at me, its eyes falling on mine through the gap in the wood. That threw me into action without another thought. My spear went high, ran clean through the barricade's opening and into the rotter's head. I felt skull surrender to ethereal iron, and twisted the weapon free to paint the wooden surfaces with sickly dark ichor. Already, though, I was turning the weapon back around in my grip, shoving it into another rotter, this time tearing an arm almost fully off at the shoulder. I adjusted my footing, moved back to give myself more room, then ran a third one through.

I perceived everything, but not with my five senses. I didn't look to see Argar taking a head clean off with one swing of a sledgehammer, didn't listen to a man's flesh tear as he got too close to a barricade and felt rotting teeth sink into his arm, didn't feel the electric energy in the air as adrenaline dissolved fear into pure, animal violence. I just knew it all. My senses bounced around the entire room, then hit my wits as ricochets with all the relevant data.

It was an incredible feeling, but it also worried me. I could experience the barricades breaking down almost as if my own nerves were threaded into them. I'd just started the process of estimating how long we had left when the logs came down.

They were like blacksmiths' hammers wielded by Zeus on bull testosterone. I actually winced as I saw the half-ton weights crunch down into the enemy mass, falling from high enough that they hit with the speed of a sprinting man. Even a sprinting *me*. The sound was gruesome, cracking bones and sliding viscera as bodies burst apart on impact. The spray of blood was violent enough that it actually flitted into visibility for a second over the barricades.

And we felt the effect immediately. A second's reprieve, then another, and finally, gloriously, a third. Just a few heartbeats spent watching the enemy mass thin and bounce harmlessly from our defense as the logs were dragged high toward the ceiling again. Then the rotters who'd been behind the ones killed finished scrambling over their bodies, and an entirely new wave hit.

The barricades were shuddering again, and everything disappeared beneath a blanket of frenzied violence. I stabbed, skewered, slashed, punched. Snarling, growling, grunting like an animal as I killed and killed and killed some more. Anything that moved before me, I skewered until it stopped. Anything that moved behind me, I screamed to back off and leave me more room to better attend my butchery. Time froze, broke, then melted to pool at my feet. A homogenous sludge, too hazy for me to gauge anything so fine as the passing of seconds.

For me, the world moved on only with each new dead rotter. Perhaps once I reached one thousand, an hour would have passed.

The logs fell, bodies burst apart, and there came another lull in the killing. Then the new wave reared up, and this time the outermost barricades were cracking, their substance beginning to yield before undead flesh.

Water could erode a mountain, and putrefaction could kill a tree. Our enemies had us cornered, I knew. They only needed the time to get at us.

"ABANDON THE OUTER BARRICADES!" I heard Shango roar, and I was turning to obey before my conscious mind even registered his order. Me, Argar, and the dozen or so others who'd been manning them scrambled back as the logs came down again, using the slight break to get behind the new set, then hauled them upward and locked them into place just in time for the rotters to break through the first layer.

Solitaire and Shango had replicated the outer barriers no more than three times, and we'd now abandoned the first row for the second. By our third retreat, we'd need the enemy weakened to a great extent. Because there wouldn't be a fourth.

They came again, and we fought them back. Impaling, bludgeoning, hacking, and smashing. The logs fell, bones broke, wood split, and the air filled with screams of fear, rage, hate, and helplessness.

One rotter actually managed to clear the barricade, falling no more than a foot before my magic spear whipped around to catch its head. With so much room, and such a clean line of sight, I could appreciate its devastating power firsthand. Watch as the bone yielded, the brains spilled out, the body slumped down, spasming and writhing. Like cutting through a tangerine, not a skull.

I didn't watch for long, though, already having my focus called back to the still-active threats gnawing at our barricade.

We killed, killed, and killed some more. Before long the barricade failed again. We fell back.

Our last barrier felt like the jaws of some giant trap, closing around us, suffocating us. Not one of us failed to sprint into the rotters, though, because death itself was coming.

The wood broke. Fuck, it broke so quickly. Crumbling, collapsing, caving. I still couldn't track the time, still had no way of gauging how fast or slow this brutality was progressing, but it was at its crescendo now. More rotters died trying to get at us—dozens maybe. I barely noticed, my eyes were affixed on the widening cracks against the wood. Heart seizing, I turned, sprinting for the stairs along with everyone else as the wood finally began to give in entirely.

We were on the second floor by the time the rotters got through, charging after us all at once, no delay at all in their barbarity, no pause in their assault. I took a moment to catch my breath, feeling my spear wet with blood and sweat as I gripped it, staring down as the enemy shrank its distance from the stairs. Twenty feet, fifteen. Closer.

Then Solitaire laughed, tearing a great cloth covering from the big thing hidden at the top of the stairs. I glanced his way to find . . . a bell.

No, not a bell. Something that had *been* a bell, clearly. But crudely reshaped. Its length heightened, its barrel thickened. I saw its base aimed upward at the sky, and three sets of hands began stuffing things down, too fast for me to identify. Then it was tipped back, held up by strength alone as it was aimed down into the mass of rotters, a torch held up at its base.

I had just enough time to see the length of string running around the metal where it was gripped by our side. Then it caught, flashing, burning. The flames ran along the length quickly, disappearing into the metal.

And then my teeth rattled, as the biggest explosion I'd yet felt rang out across the building's insides. Belching out of the bell.

Right into the enemy horde.

CHAPTER FORTY-FOUR

Solitaire's POV: Day 51
Current Wealth: 1 silver, 47 copper

Physics lesson, kids. What happens when you pack explosive material into a confined space and leave only one route for it to escape?

If you answered "you get a gun," then congratulations! You're our lucky winner.

Well, it wasn't really a gun. A gun, ideally, would've been a lot longer. The bell we'd had was a narrow one, and we'd added a few inches by heating it up and working it with the blacksmith, but there's only so much you can do to medieval brass and iron before it breaks. Fortunately, we had enough black powder to more or less compensate for efficiency with raw power.

Fifteen kilos of explosive was about the limit I'd calculated for the thing. To play it safe, we'd loaded it with ten. Ten kilos of black powder, that is, and about another ten of pebbles, nails, and even teeth and such. Anything small and hard. What was a gun without its bullets?

Well, as I said, it wasn't really a gun. And they weren't really bullets. There were a million practical concessions I'd been forced to make by circumstance and the compressive proximity of my deadline. The projectiles were angled, uneven. They would fly inconsistently and slower than was ideal. The muzzle of my weapon wasn't strangled nearly as tight as I'd have preferred, and I estimated some two thirds of its kinetic potential would be wasted in the air, compared to a more professionally made piece.

It actually hurt a bit to know that I was using a quarter of my hard-earned black powder on such a detonation. But the feeling disappeared soon enough.

It wasn't really a gun, but it didn't need to be. The proof of its success came with the sight of a tightly packed horde flying apart at the seams.

Rotters have one disadvantage against a human, other than their minds—which, in fairness, I'm yet to be fully convinced are actually below average for a Homo sapien. Their bodies are . . . well, rotting. Decayed, softened by the putrefaction of their condition.

The first row of them was nothing after the blast rang out. Spongy bodies ruined past the point of solidity as one near-sonic chunk of death after another tore through them. They must have slowed the debris slightly because the ones behind fared slightly better, and the third set better still.

Even so, I didn't count a single specimen among any of those three layers that failed to be mangled past the point of fighting. Sixty destroyed, easily, and dozens more left impeded by their wounds deeper into the horde.

We didn't have time to explain the weapon to many people, only the team now loading it, but I heard Shango screeching out to galvanize our side.

"RETREAT!" he ordered. "HURRY AND RETREAT, WE'LL ONLY BE ABLE TO STAVE THEM OFF FOR A FEW MOMENTS MORE!"

It put a very sensible haste in our ranks—if there's one thing you can trust a human to do, it's preserve itself—but that only seemed to entice the snarling rotters below, congealing their mass back into a surging wave that rushed right for us. Beam was at the top of the stairs, Argar beside him, and next to them both was a new figure. The Vitonnian woman, wearing a woolen gambeson, wielding a short spear and shield. She glared at me.

"We need to hold the stairs," she declared, "to buy time for another spell, yes?"

Burying the urge to make fun of her for the primitive mistake regarding my weapon, I nodded. She didn't hesitate even an instant before throwing herself onto the stairs and bracing her body for the enemy.

Argar rushed in after her, and Beam after him. I paused, then swore and joined them.

Four of us against hundreds wouldn't have been a fight at all usually, but the stairs were much, much narrower than the hall beyond them. Perhaps we could buy a few moments more.

Perhaps.

A mouth came for me, open, wet, filled with rotting teeth. I smashed those out first, breaking them free of the gums with a big wooden cudgel I'd found among the village's improvised armory and sending the owner back into its friends. More were behind it, though, pushing its body back to me, and I was forced a step farther up the staircase to ready my next swing. This one caved the skull in entirely, but the body hadn't even landed before a new enemy replaced it.

From the corner of my eye, I saw two things at once—Argar swinging his sledgehammer, and a rotter coming at me sidelong. I ducked, making room for the giant's strike to meet the enemy's head and smash it in half. Another backstep as they closed tighter, then my teeth rattled.

The cannon went off again.

If anything, the second shot was even more destructive than the first, and it bought us a few more moments of ease as the tide of bodies was stemmed somewhat. We fought our way back three more steps before another shot rang out. By now we were just a dozen or so feet from the cannon, which in turn was cresting a twenty-foot hall leading to the mayor's office. Thick-doored and barricaded, that had become our final retreat, and it was already packed with most of the villagers.

Forcing myself to focus, even as I fought, I surveyed the carnage. Could we buy time for one last shot? What would happen if we did? What would happen if we *didn't*?

By my estimate, we'd halved the rotters already, if not more so. But that still left the village's fighters outnumbered close to ten times over. Those weren't winning odds, even if the enemy were mindless undead sprinting into a fortified position. One more shot could shrink the gap.

But could we buy the time for it?

That was the crux of it, and my heart sank as I realized we couldn't. Already fatigue was starting to take us, we were ceding ground faster, and rapidly running out of it. It would be another minute before the bell-cannon fired again, and we'd be lucky to last so long as forty seconds without being overwhelmed.

I didn't turn to Shango, didn't need to. I just called out to him over the brutality we were spilling out around us.

"We need to break!"

No answer came at first, but I recognized the silence. Sniffed the air—ignoring the decay that was now forced fully up my nostrils by the undeads' proximity—and wondered what he was thinking.

He was thinking that he agreed, and that agreement smelled of horror, fear, panic, and regret. I recognized the concoction well enough. He felt it every time he made a major error. I'd need to have a little chat with him later about that.

Dirty nails raked my face, and I swore, headbutting their owner. Yes, we'd chat later. I was still preoccupied.

"Start backing off!" Shango roared. "Abandon the cannon, and head for the office!"

It should've been fine to give such an order. We should've had a free run back to our retreat.

We didn't.

The moment the words left Shango's mouth and echoed out across the room, the rotters redoubled their assault. Charging faster, more numinous, more forceful than before.

That wasn't *right*; it wasn't *rational*. It—*no, stop it. Shut up, Solitaire. Keep that giant brain of yours calm and use it on something useful. It's happening, which makes it both right and rational. The probability of any event is one hundred percent, after it's already occurred. Instead of bitching about it, try to figure out what caused those odds.*

For all my immediate panic, and for all the growing proximity of my enemies' snapping jaws and dragging nails, it didn't take me very long. We'd been operating on the assumption that the rotters were merely self-assembled, drawn together only by a shared interest in eating people. That was wrong. Something was controlling them, something smart enough to order them in even harder once it realized that the people responsible for blowing up a large fraction of its army might get away.

I scanned the crowd of enemies for any glimpse of something less *sticky*, but all I could see amid the thrashing limbs were more undead. Cursing under my breath, I was forced to concede the point to reality. There were more vital concerns for the time being.

We continued on our way slowly, as we backed up along the stairs. But not by choice. If any one of us had gotten what we wanted, we'd have broken and run, but the rotters had all the momentum on their side. They'd be on us before we got far, and we'd be shredded mincemeat in seconds. All we could do was stare into the face of death as it came for us, and try our best to keep poking it in the eyes while we made for safety.

The door grew closer, and so did the rotters. Black blood was staining me up to the elbows now, and the fatigue in my arms grew worse with every swing. I felt fear touch my mind, cold and crushing, like the feeling of a guillotine hanging over my neck. I was going to die; we all were. We'd failed, and this was the end of me. The great Solitaire, torn apart by mindless undead in some shitty town, never having achieved a damned thing of note. It would've been funny, if it weren't so pitifully tragic.

My thoughts scattered as I heard the sound of moving hinges and creaking wood behind me. Feet behind me. I risked a glance, saw the door was open, and called out to let the others know. We were there. We'd made it. We just needed to kill for a few more steps . . . and we did.

CHAPTER FORTY-FIVE

Shango's POV: Day 51
Current Wealth: 1 silver, 47 copper

I was first through the door, while my friends were still busy fighting on the stairs. Part of me wanted to help them, and I shut that part up with a strangling grip. There wasn't space for another person in this room, so the best I could hope for was to replace one of the existing people in here with me. If my friends were already struggling to keep the waves of undead at bay, they'd have quickly failed if it were me out there instead of one of the more competent fighters.

So, reluctantly, I waited in the mayor's office, watching, blood boiling, and heart pumping as they slowly fought their way back, while I kept the idiot villagers beside me from trapping them outside.

Solitaire, ever the self-preservation enthusiast, was first in. The Vitonnian woman followed after him. Beam and Argar seemed almost reluctant to disengage, both of them killing easily two or three more rotters than was needed before finally stepping back. The moment they did, our enemy surged on, snarling and cramming their bodies into the door, desperate to make their way into our new shelter. A spear caught one through the eye, a cudgel opened another one's skull to spray brain matter in all directions, and Solitaire jabbed his thumb so far into one of their ears that, going by the sudden spasms it started suffering, I could only deduce he'd actually managed to skewer its brain. The violence was quickly displayed and viciously delivered. It bought the rest of us a few precious seconds to force the door shut, then bar it.

The thudding came instantly, rhythmic, heavy. It ran through the now-crowded office and churned deep into every set of ears present. The panic started growing instantly.

"We're gonna die," one villager moaned, tears wetting his cheeks. He hadn't been one of the fighters. The stupid bastard had been tucked away in here the entire time, but that only meant he'd been a coward from the start. And cowardice spread like cancer.

"They're going to break through that door just like they did all the others!" another cried out.

"We're fucked! We're all going to die!"

"A window!" someone called out. "Can we—"

"There's rotters swarming around the building, waiting for us," said another. "We can't even jump!"

The panic was moving across the room like wildfire, so quick even I was having trouble keeping up with it. I tried calling out for attention, ordering faces turn to me, but the noise was so great no one present could hear me.

I was losing control.

Beam, though, kept calm, and resolved the situation in true Beam fashion. Marching across the room and drawing up to one of the babbling dissenters, then wordlessly uppercutting him so hard I swore his tiny body was actually hoisted a centimeter or two off the ground. The man fell hard, and didn't get up.

Silence rang out, all eyes turned to my friend, and his eyes turned to me.

"My brother has something to say," Beam called out, speaking calmly, despite it all, but still looking ready to knock every single living thing on the continent into unconsciousness if they gave him any more problems.

That was about as good an opportunity as I found likely to happen, and I jumped on it promptly.

"We'll be fine," I roared. "This position is far harder to break into than the last. Just look at the door. Is it suffering any damage?" It wasn't, as I'd expected. But the reason it wasn't was beyond my area of expertise. I turned to Solitaire. "Solitaire, brother, care to explain to the good people why we're safe?"

He jumped on the opportunity, and I did my best to avoid glancing at his visibly bulging crotch as he lorded his knowledge over the rest of us. "It's called the square-cube law," he explained, smugly. "Long ago, our people discovered an incredibly complex concept called basic, infant-level mathematics. The long and short of it is that as something gets larger, it gets weaker, relative to its body weight. This is why cats can fall ten feet and be fine, but horses can break their legs dropping down a five foot pit. It's also why that door is going to hold."

Solitaire got a lot of looks from that, and only some were relieved. I saw a lot of confusion and plenty of skepticism. The former was not ideal, the latter was dangerous. Fortunately, he seemed to notice it, too.

"How many rotters can get at this door?" he tried. "Three, maybe four or five at once? Compared to dozens battering the one outside. It's just as thick, and smaller things are stronger proportionally. It took the enemy two thousand, one hundred and sixteen seconds to break down the main door outside, this one will last several times longer just from how many more were able to attack the last one."

That, finally, started to spark widespread recognition, and those few villagers who still didn't understand had the concepts explained to them by their quicker-witted neighbors. The mood actually seemed to be improving before long.

Characteristically, Solitaire had to ruin it.

"Get ready to watch the windows!" he called out. "The rotters can climb over one another, and we didn't have time to board the shutters up. They'll be trying to get at us through there."

In an instant, the panic returned. But this time it was manageable. Weaker than before, sure, but we were cornered, too, so that didn't help. We'd convinced the people that there was no way the enemy could breach the door. Now we'd drawn their attention to the one actual weakness in our defenses.

And it wasn't a weakness we'd failed to cover.

Solitaire had posed the idea, and I'd agreed. We needed to kill rotters if we were to survive long-term. That's why we'd made our barricades out in the main hall, and it was why we'd left the windows accessible. The enemy would be through them soon, and blood would spill.

As if I'd conjured them just by thinking about their attack, rotters soon reared their ugly faces, smashing heads and fists through the fragile wood of the shutters, reaching out to drag their bodies inside. They didn't get far.

Hammer, spear, pitchfork, and cudgel. Rocks and bits of timber, carving knives and scythes. We went at them with everything we had on hand, actually organizing the carnage to ensure only a few of us were around the windows at once. The rotters could only come through slowly because of the awkward climb, and there were only two windows in all. That meant four people were more than enough to hold them at bay.

I watched it all with satisfaction, the tension dropping in my gut, along with everyone else's, as minutes of unending success passed. I grinned.

"I'll admit," I eventually said, turning to Solitaire and speaking quietly, "it was a good idea."

The idea of course had been his—leaving a weak point in our defense and forcing the terrified villagers to do what was best for them long-term was a stroke of brilliance even for him. And the positioning couldn't have been better.

A rotter caught a particularly nasty blow to the eye and lost its grip, plummeting out of sight.

How far would they be falling? I aimed the question at Solitaire, who replied promptly by thinking back to his view from the outside and doing a few mental calculations.

It was nothing complex, he assured me. Apparently, a similar technique to one he'd used in figuring out how tall his own house was as a kid, even before reading about the works of Euclid. Remarkable what a man can do when his brain is a compass.

"Twenty-six feet, or just under eight meters in non-caveman units. Redacle has a gravitational field more or less equal to Earth's, so that'd be yielding a velocity of twelve point five meters per second. Basically, picture getting hit by a truck going thirty miles per hour."

It wasn't as deadly as I would've hoped, but it was nothing to scoff at. If nothing else, broken bones would be occurring regularly, and death would be happening a decent number of times. They were hitting the ground faster than any human could sprint, after all, and I'd heard of death occurring in much slower impacts. Slowly but surely, we'd be whittling the enemy down.

But Solitaire had to ruin whatever surety I'd gotten from that, too. It was just what he did.

He leaned in, speaking with a hushed tone. "For what it's worth, I think there's something smarter than a rotter out there coordinating them. Probably responsible for reanimating them, and . . . possibly quite powerful." I could see him twitching slightly, but not in all the ways that usually indicated he was feeling paranoid.

Well, no points for guessing why. If he was right, and I was fairly sure he was, there was something still out there more dangerous than anything we'd spent the last hour killing. Undead, almost definitely, and smart enough to coordinate the rotters. It hadn't shown itself yet, and that made me more nervous, not less.

I was just halfway through considering what it might think to do next when the wooden frame around one of the windows ruptured apart, and the fighters keeping it from being flooded were sent flying back amid the sound of cracking timber and splintering bones.

Where they'd just been standing was now a tall man. His hair was dark, his eyes were darker, his glare was darkest of all. He wore the silks and linens of an aristocrat and carried at his side a fancy-looking rapier glittering with jewels and decorative flourishes.

At a glance, I could feel how dangerous he was—a deep, instinctual terror. The same kind a rabbit felt when stepping over a hawk's shadow. Every nerve in my body screamed at me to turn and run, even if it meant throwing myself into the rotters trying to break in through the only exits, and my mouth dried as I recognized the creature I was now facing. Maybe everyone else did, too. They were appropriately silent.

Because we were all standing before a fucking vampire.

And the vampire moved fast.

CHAPTER FORTY-SIX

Shango's POV: Day 51
Current Wealth: 1 silver, 47 copper

It was a fucking vampire. It stood like a vampire, looked at me like a vampire, and when it moved, it was all . . . vampiry. Like a panther. Like a panther on ice, with a body made of something lighter than flesh—an effortless, easy motion that seemed to demand no more from it than taking a breath. I was so caught up in the monstrous dexterity on display that I didn't even notice the speed until it was on Argar.

The giant swung well, quicker than one might expect. But his reflexes were human. They were clumsy, apish things compared to the creature attacking him, and it deftly sidestepped his hammer blow before retaliating with a neat thrust to his chest. Argar shifted to one side, but the sword still caught him anyway, sinking into his torso and dropping him in an instant.

It was then that I finally gathered the cognizance to overcome my shock and appraise the vampire.

[Appraisal]
Class: Warrior
Level: 4
Condition: Fine
Modifiers: Strength +1, Speed +1, Toughness +2
Statistics: Strength 15, Speed 15, Dexterity 4, Stamina -, Toughness 16, Alertness 14, Charisma 6, Intelligence 4

Level four, and it moved like *that?* Of course it did; it was a vampire. They were badass, in our world, ten times stronger than a human by default, and faster and tougher to boot. We'd based them on the original Dracula who, according to Solitaire, had a grip like a vice and the strength to pimp-slap familiars across a room.

As I might've deduced, by watching him crush a man's hand in his grip, then pimp-slap him across a room.

I was moving in an instant, and so was everyone else. Solitaire closing in with all his magically bolstered speed—and seeming as slow to this creature as his level one self had been to him. Beam came in from the side, glowing magical spear outstretched, and the Vittonian woman followed suit with her more mundane weapon. Their movements were so synchronized and lethally precise that I actually thought for a moment they might leave a mark on the monster before them.

Then the thing turned to Beam.

Crimson light engulfed him from head to toe, seizing his entire body and forcing it still as muscles stiffened and rigidified. The spear fell from limp fingers, and a fist crunched into his face, turning his body almost fully upside-down as it soared backward. Solitaire was on the vampire by then, swinging hard. It turned toward his blow, then blinked as he abruptly let the weapon go mid-flight.

The moment of stunned confusion bought him an instant to act, and he was efficient about it. Sinking down to a crouch, freeing a knife from his boot in one, swift move. The same knife he'd had when we were isekai'd, stainless steel and pocket-portable. It found the vampire's thigh, punching through fabric and drawing a hiss of pain from it, which turned into a knee against Solitaire's chest.

If the vampire hadn't been off balance, my friend might've died then and there. Ribs smashed in, unaugmented resilience simply walked over by the monstrous strength on display. As things were, he just went tumbling, then stopped in a convulsive heap a few feet away.

A spear came within moments of Solitaire's attack, but the vampire was just quick enough to avoid it. The Vitonnian was last to face its strength, and she folded over its fist like a pillow, dropping to her knees and vomiting. Then its eyes turned to me.

They were red; pupils elongated, ovoid slits like those of a cat. My blood ran cold as it focused on me, and my body was torn in a thousand different directions at once by my conflicting instincts. I wanted to run, to fight, to break down crying. I wanted to get it all over with and cut my own throat to spare myself a slower death, to drop down onto my knees and beg for mercy, even to pray.

But somewhere along the way, somehow, my brain just snapped, and all the wild, animalistic, idiot fear melted away beneath the glare of a towering sun of pure rationality. I spoke, and even to me my voice sounded calm.

"You didn't attack until you were attacked," I called out. "Not even after the first time, so you're here to talk. What do you want?"

The vampire's head tilted, and it eyed me in a way that was disconcerting for more than one reason. I'd seen that stare before, but never received it. It was the look my father had taught me to give something I was giving thought to buying.

"I take it you are the one who used the eastern powder here?" it asked, voice like smooth silk. Smooth silk, I reminded myself, that was currently wrapped around a jagged, rusty knife primed and ready to stick into my guts.

I blinked. Eastern powder? Did it mean what I thought it meant . . . ?

"What are you talking about?" I asked, feigning ignorance. It was tempting not to, seeing as it was apparently my knowledge that held the enemy's hand on turning all that speed against me.

"Don't play coy. I recognize the power and smell of Echoityan alchemy when I see it used upon my own forces. It is not known to these lands, and you have the skin and accent of a foreigner. Are you the one who ignited it?"

He was walking forward now, crimson eyes still on me, drawing dangerously close. And Solitaire was still sprawled out directly in his path. Barely an instant before the vampire was within reach of my friend, I answered him.

"No, that's him," I said, nodding at Solitaire. I spoke quickly to ensure his value before anything impulsive or vicious could be done to him.

The vampire paused, still scrutinous as it eyed me.

"It is," I pressed. "Ask around if you want. He spent all day working on it."

I knew the moment I saw the vampire's face that I'd said just a few words too many. It hadn't said it'd *made* it, only used it.

"It is rare, even in Echoityan, to find someone knowledgeable of the secret formulas," it noted, seeming to muse over every word even as they left its mouth. Lightning-quick, the vampire reached down to grab Solitaire, hoisting him up from the floor and shaking him for a moment. The act, or perhaps the simple proximity to an undead apex predator, proved more than enough to wake him, beating away the cloudy pain that'd been keeping him insensible and triggering a familiar, convulsive struggle in my friend's body as he found himself in the creature's grip.

The vampire threw him back to stumble away and fall against a wall. Its eyes were only on Solitaire now.

"I came to this town for its corpses," it said. "For the unseen multitudes buried beneath its soil from previous generations now gone by. What I found instead, however, was . . . progeny."

A smile crept along its face, feline and sinister.

"A man capable of mastering the Echoityan sciences of alchemy and black powder," it noted, eying Solitaire, then turned to me. "One who thinks quickly enough to stay my hand more than once." Then, it finally turned to Beam. It was a testament to the thing's deadliness that Solitaire didn't even *try* stabbing it in the back. "And . . . a warrior. A warrior of impossible bodily gifts, and a magic even I have never seen before."

Finally, the creature's eyes moved back around, coming to rest on me.

"Any of you would be a worthy addition to my kind's ranks, and so I offer you this chance to come with me and join the Ichorous Court. Live forever, as gods of the grave, or die here, tonight. The choice is yours."

I just about shat myself at that, mind racing, head coming up with nothing particularly useful despite the frenzied thought it'd thrown itself into.

"Can we . . . discuss it?" I asked at last. The vampire, to my surprise, nodded.

"Of course," it said, calmly. "You'll be making a decision about eternity. It would be remiss of me not to give you at least a few meager minutes to debate its merits amongst yourselves." It stepped back, sweeping an arm out as if to gesture us all into speech. I remained silent, Solitaire only glared, and Beam was still dribbling into the wooden floor and rolling around with his eyes crossed. Not a great ground for rational discourse, I must admit.

Still, I gave it my best go, turning to Solitaire . . . then catching the look in his eye.

Vampires were evil. Not just in a general sense. Becoming one in Redacle meant leaving all the moral cores of a person's psyche behind. Empathy, remorse, compassion. It all died as sure as your reanimated corpse. It was to be fundamentally changed. As I said, we based them on Dracula, and Dracula wasn't a story about the gray morality of undeath and monsters with bleeding hearts.

Which is why, I must say, I was quite fucking surprised to see that Solitaire was actually *considering* the offer. I wanted to hit him. I wanted to push him out the window and watch him land on the rotters. I wanted to blow him up and add him to the pile of limbs. Instead, I forced myself calm, forced myself to focus on our current predicament and concentrated on buying time.

"What do you think, brother?" I asked, hoping Solitaire had an idea I'd not thought of yet. He usually did. Usually? Almost always. If I didn't think of the smart thing, he almost definitely would have.

But he had nothing this time and told me with a fractional widening in his blue eyes. It sent a chill down my spine. I turned to the vampire, already thinking of something to try and convince him to give us the room alone.

And then I noticed Beam, silent as he lay where he was, but shifting slightly. Eyes clearing up, blinking and frowning. Body starting to move with some measure of focused dexterity.

People didn't stay knocked out for that long, generally. When they did, they probably had brain damage. How much longer until he was fully recovered? I doubted it was more than a minute.

So, could I keep the vampire occupied for that long or more? Well, I'd been taught business from an early age.

As Solitaire would say now, speaking to vampires was my special talent.

CHAPTER FORTY-SEVEN

Beam's POV: Day 52
Current Wealth: 1 silver, 47 copper

Shango was talking, Solitaire was glaring, and my mouth tasted of blood. It was comforting to realize all that when I woke up. Had I been in *unfamiliar* surroundings, it might've worried me.

"You understand, there's a lot of rumors about your, uh, kind, that we'd like to just verify with you before agreeing to anything. You die in sunlight, for example?"

I could hear something of a smile in the vampire's voice as he answered, and I waited until he started speaking to move, trusting his own words to hide the noise my clumsy, battered body made. Everything hurt, but everything tended to hurt when one wanted to be an Olympian. I ignored it. The real problem was the lethargy overtaking me, that mental weariness residing after the effects of the red light I'd been engulfed in. All in my head, but somehow more real than the tangible aches and pains of my extended fighting.

"My kind do die in sunlight, yes, but we can mitigate this weakness. The oldest of us, the purest-blooded and most powerful, can temporarily abate its glare, or use puppet bodies to operate in open daylight."

Shango swallowed. It was astonishingly good acting on his part, considering he already knew—and, in fact, had written about half of—every single factoid he'd just been told. He pressed on regardless. By now, I was halfway to my feet. If the vampire suddenly turned, he'd not fail to realize I was awake.

"And the thirst for blood? Children's blood?"

The vampire laughed openly, openly and hard. I was able to fully stand by the time it finished.

"We do not"—my hand was against the wall—"need to feed on children"—the wood was whispering to me—"to survive." A spear was tight in my grip. The vampire paused, apparently searching for words, then found them.

"For ones of my power can subsist on even animals if we choose to. It is only the elders who require human blood, and only the most ancient who must feed on their own kind."

I'd been closing in with every word, centimeters at a time, and I moved again on the last. Leaning forward, lunging, spear outstretched and muscles screaming together with the force of its propulsion.

The vampire moved faster than any creature could under the power of biology alone, but even the magic giving it velocity was just a shade too little. My weapon sank into the undead's flank, just under its ribs, and carved a jagged path through. It was a testament to its resilience, after seeing so many skulls and limbs burst apart, that I felt such resistance and cut so shallowly, but by the time my weapon escaped its victim with a streak of dark blood, I knew the wound was a severe one.

I was given further proof when the vampire spun to round on me, rapier flashing, then bounced aside as I parried it with the haft of my weapon. The force almost tore my arm out of its socket and did send me back a full step, and yet . . . it was manageable. Diminished from the monstrous intensity I'd seen before.

Our foe was weakened now. The slow trickle of dead ichor still running down its flank could attest to that. We had a chance.

"Treachery!" the vampire spat. "You would turn my offer against me? You—"

He was interrupted mid-rant when the most paranoid man currently alive body slammed him. Solitaire bounced off the vampire, finding his target anchored in place by the same magic that gave it such strength, but he forced the creature back an uneven step as he did. I didn't need prompting to move in, swinging my spear in a wide arc, then twisting it downward to change the angle moments before impact.

It was a clumsy swing, compared to what I'd have managed with a more familiar weapon, but Shango had been right. There was overlap in my abilities, more than a little, and I clipped the bastard's calf as it hastily parried me. The Vitonnian stormed past me, thrusting with her own spear, then stepping back as the vampire riposted. A villager closed in with a pitchfork, and Solitaire kicked our enemy right in his ankle just as it was raising up for another dodge.

Metal met meat, hard. Supernatural meat, probably as tough as wood, but we saw a few drops of blood run down the pale face of our enemy all the same. With a vicious hiss it turned, leaping across the room and landing just in front of the window.

"You will all die for this!" the vampire roared, voice tight with white-hot fury. "Each of you, I will drown you in the blood of your chi—"

Argar's hammer missed by mere inches as the vampire twisted from its path at the last possible moment. The iron head caught the wood paneling behind it, taking a fist-sized chunk out as it bounced off to clatter at the vampire's feet. By then, it was already lunging from the window, and within moments disappearing from sight.

I hurried to stop the thing, spear ready, nerves steeled. But the red light was back, engulfing me just as it had before. I felt sharp talons of fear sink their way into my mind, burrowing deep, whipping every synapse I had into a frenzied fear. I was too frightened to even scream. The spear dropped from my hands, my body dropped from a stand, and I fell trembling and shivering onto the ground, practically convulsive in my fear.

By the time I came to, the enemy was long gone, and I was surrounded by concerned, fearful faces.

"You alright?" Shango asked, frowning as he eyed me.

"I think he's still convulsing," Solitaire breathed, rocking me as he slapped my face, hard.

I swore. "I'm awake, you idiot."

"He's probably just hallucinating. I should slap him six or seven more times to make sure."

I pushed the psychotic asshole off me and sat up, groaning. My head was ringing, waves of pain radiating through it, and yet there wasn't a mark on me. Was this . . . a stress headache?

Made sense, I supposed. I hadn't exactly passed out from relaxation.

"Beam, are you alright?" Shango was clearly more concerned by far than Solitaire, and I felt a stab of guilt for worrying him.

"I'm fine," I snapped, more angrily, more harshly, than I intended. And much more than he deserved. Shango was wounded by my response. Even I could see that much. I sighed. "Sorry," I added. "Just . . . not nice getting disabled that easily."

He nodded, sympathetic as ever, but I saw there was a hardness to him all the same. "You had us worried there, is all."

Standing up, I surveyed our surroundings. We were still in the mayor's old office, where we'd made our last-ditch defense, and by the looks of things, we were alone in it. Solitaire answered my question before I could ask it.

"We made everyone else clear off," he explained. "Wanted a bit of privacy, you understand. It's daytime, if you couldn't tell."

The sunlight streaming in through the smashed-apart windows hadn't caught my attention before he said that, somehow. I must've been more out of it than I thought.

"Did we win?" I asked, blinking back a sudden headache. Shango nodded, Solitaire scowled.

"We did," the former replied, but even his smile was somewhat strained. "Though—"

"Bastards stole my black powder," Solitaire cut in, practically snarled, in fact. "Stupid fucking Redaclans. Can't build anything more complex than a thatch hut so they—"

"Not the time," Shango sighed, halting our friend's tirade before it could gather momentum. Solitaire scowled at him, but said nothing more. Somehow the sight was relaxing. Familiar, soothing, normal. I took it in for a moment before the inevitable wave of worry hit me.

And it did, of course. Like a steam roller landing on me from orbit. "The vampire will be back," I said, pointlessly. Both my friends nodded. I sighed. "He'll be back with more undead?"

That, at last, caused them to hesitate.

"Once you make an undead, it's made for good," Shango said, slowly. "So it probably won't be keeping any *unmade*, at least . . ."

"And the village was already resisting it before we came," Solitaire added, "which means there's a good chance it had already thrown all of its usable bodies into the assault we turned away."

Some of the tightness in my chest unraveled and faded, but not all of it. I made myself nod. "Right then," I breathed. "So we're over the worst of it?"

They hesitated, and Solitaire answered. He was the expert on siege warfare, apparently. "We don't have the cannon anymore," he explained. "But otherwise . . . yeah, numerically at least they'll probably be attacking us with half or less of what they did yesterday. The issue is that now *they* have the black powder. If the vampire knows how to use it . . ."

My blood ran cold. I wasn't sure the thin, cobbled walls of our new fortress would hold against the kinds of destruction I'd seen yesterday, and I knew we'd be killed without them. Solitaire sighed.

"It probably doesn't, though," he added. "Seemed far too impressed by us to be any sort of expert . . . probably."

It was about as much reassurance as I was likely to get, and I took it graciously.

"There's one other thing," Shango noted. "Something we were waiting for you to wake up before going over."

I eyed him, frowned, and then realized it all in an instant. My grin was so wide, the cold air hurt my teeth.

"We levelled up?" I asked.

"Let's find out," Shango replied.

CHAPTER FORTY-EIGHT

Shango's POV: Day 52
Current Wealth: 1 silver, 47 copper

[Appraisal]
Class: Emperor
Level: 10
Condition: Fine
Modifiers: +5 Toughness, +2 Strength
Statistics: Strength 7, Speed 5, Dexterity 6, Stamina 5, Toughness 10, Alertness 8, Charisma 9, Intelligence 9
Inventory: Jeans, shirt, jacket, dagger
Class Abilities: Appraisal III
Current Experience Points: 73/400
Unspent Skillpoints: 3

At any other time, I might've started laughing in triumph at the quantum leap my stats had taken. But, we were waiting for a vampire to try to kill us, bolstered by hundreds of rotters and doubtlessly out for our blood in particular. They were mean creatures, and dangerous. Even my near-enumerate self could work out that we'd be outmatched against it, however many levels we'd managed to gain since round one.

The grim despair of it all was almost a big enough distraction to keep me from noticing several details. Almost.

Firstly, of course, my eyes were drawn to my Appraisal. It was Appraisal III now, whatever that meant. I'd need to experiment over the course of the day. Any advantage we could gain from here on out would be potentially life-saving. More interestingly, though, was my experience points.

They were *insanely* high!

Reporting as much to Solitaire got me an answer quickly enough. His had grown just as explosively, as had Beam. And Solitaire was smug while explaining why.

"Looks like our XP before the next level doubled once we hit ten," he noted.

There were many things I'd have liked to hear after our ordeal the night before. That was most certainly *not* one of them. I was halfway through complaining when I noticed the final detail. The best detail.

"We leveled up twice, right?" I asked.

"Right," Solitaire replied, distractedly.

"So why do I have three unspent skillpoints?" I grinned and watched him think.

He finally answered, cautiously optimistic. That was a rare mood to catch Solitaire of all people in. "We . . . might get two per level, once we hit level ten?" he guessed.

I sighed. "We'll have to level up again to verify, which—"

"—changes exactly nothing about the next entry on our list of priorities," Solitaire said, finishing my sentence and nodding. "Yeah, it is what it is. Let's get spending in case Ball Sackula comes back and tries to jump us."

With three points to spend, my decisions felt like they had a lot less weight this time around. I had the prescience to try something before putting any points into the biggest options, though.

Nope, still nothing. Intelligence, it seemed, wasn't possible to increase even by trying to dump three skillpoints into it all at once. It was hard to be bothered by it. I wasn't entirely sure it'd even be the best choice for our immediate circumstances. It wasn't like Solitaire's big ol' ten stat was helping him think up any miracles. No new ones, at least.

I had a think about it, a long one. In many ways, this was the most important statistical decision I'd be making so far. We'd be attacked, and soon, and by something that was more than a match for us. I was tempted to choose toughness again, to keep on reinforcing myself. To look out for number one.

But I didn't. Even I wasn't a big enough bastard for that, and even still I could remember my knife blows practically bouncing off of Kratos. Reluctantly, I split my stats. One into strength, one into speed and one more into alertness.

It had been a while, I realized, since I'd felt the electrical sensation of whatever my statistics relied on infusing itself into my body. Magic, surely, because nothing else could've felt the way this did now. I closed my eyes while the sensation of taking humanity's entire anabolic steroid supply slowly threaded its way through me. Once I was done, I pulled my sheet up again to verify.

[Appraisal]
Class: Emperor
Level: 10

Condition: Fine
Modifiers: +5 Toughness, +3 Strength, +1 Speed, +1 Alertness
Statistics: Strength 8, Speed 6, Dexterity 6, Stamina 5, Toughness 10, Alertness 9, Charisma 9, Intelligence 9
Inventory: Jeans, shirt, jacket, dagger
Class Abilities: Appraisal III
Current Experience Points: 73/400
Unspent Skillpoints: 0

Seeing the impressive size of my alertness stat after only one increase left me nearly regretting my choice, but that was just the masculine urge to min-max talking. I wouldn't get very far by listening to gut instincts. Contrary to popular belief, one's gut is actually dumber, not smarter, than one's brain.

I turned to Solitaire and Beam, eagerly appraising them.

[Appraisal]
Class: Revolutionary
Level: 10
Condition: Fine
Modifiers: +4 Speed, +2 Toughness, +3 Alertness, +1 Strength
Statistics: Strength 8, Speed 11, Dexterity 8, Stamina 6, Toughness 7, Alertness 11, Charisma 3, Intelligence 10
Inventory: Jeans, T-shirt, flick knife, rocks (x3), dagger
Class Abilities: Detect Element II
Current Experience Points: 33/400
Unspent Skillpoints: 0

So, he'd decided to make himself more physically powerful across the board. Fair enough. Honestly, he already had more than enough landing power for most of our enemies. Most? Almost all of them. I thought back to the sight of his knife practically bouncing off the vampire's ankle and suddenly found myself annoyed that Solitaire hadn't focused even more on his actual killing ability. But no, most of our enemies had been human before. He had every reason to prioritize them in stat selection. Particularly when we'd be fighting hundreds of rotters as well as the vampire.

I focused on Beam next, and frowned.

[Appraisal]
Class: Dragonknight
Level: 10
Condition: Fine

Modifiers: +1 Strength, +1 Speed, +2 Toughness
Statistics: Strength 10, Speed 9, Dexterity 8, Stamina 9, Toughness 10,
Alertness 8, Charisma 6, Intelligence 5
Inventory: Jeans, flannel shirt, spear
Class Abilities: Beloved II
Current Experience Points: 10/400
Unspent Skillpoints: 4

He hadn't spent anything yet?

"Having trouble deciding, dude?" I asked, grinning even as I felt something tugging uncertainly in my gut. Beam eviscerated the smile with a single, sincere look of worry. More intense than I'd seen on him since coming to this world.

"I can't spend them," he whispered, shakily. "It's . . . not letting me. I can't . . . I just can't put them into raising any stats."

I froze, Solitaire swore, and Beam just continued staring and rapidly swallowing, keeping himself from outright panic . . . but only just. Solitaire and I both put our heads together to help him. One of us not growing stronger as we'd banked on was a first priority risk, but even after the better part of an hour, we had no luck.

Beam tried thinking, whispering, singing, snarling. At Solitaire's suggestion, he worked the desired stats into rhymes, iambic pentameter, even mathematical equations where we rearranged well-known symbols to write their names out. None of it worked. He might as well have tried to order the blood out of his body for all of our success, and by the end of it our worries had only deepened.

"It's alright," Solitaire said, eying Beam, and speaking with uncommon vigor. "Don't panic about this; we don't know what's causing it, but we have time to fix it, and we will, alright?"

Despite our friend's uncharacteristic display of not-actively-sociopathic behavior, Beam didn't seem at all comforted. His nod was crisp, swift, and forced, his face tight and paled with worry. I saw Solitaire consider something more to say, but in the end he remained silent. Probably for the best.

The three of us split up shortly after that, simply because we had too much that needed doing in the surrounding town to remain together. There was always work to be done in Redacle, and always a frosty, torturing wind ready to grab you if you failed to do it.

I got to mine first. Morale.

Somewhere between Solitaire turning the main hall into a recreation of the Somme and Beam playing drill sergeant with the improvised soldiers, we'd all become cemented as the village's leaders. That was fine by me. It was, by far, the best way for everyone to come out alive. But it did add a certain gravity to our decisions, and it meant that the moment I stepped outside, I was met with an endless list of things to do.

My first surprise came shortly after I made my way into the open air. The Vittonian woman was standing, waiting for me, glaring as she usually did and . . . with eyes that, this time, did not quite meet my own.

"I would like a word," she began, awkwardly, still not looking at me. I was more than a little taken aback, and extremely busy, but before I could tell her to fuck off my thoughts turned back to our arrival. This one had been one of the more influential voices in the village rabble, I recalled. It might be worth at least trying to get her on our side again. I doubted she'd give any of us another chance for a one-on-one, after all.

"Of course," I said, smiling, blatantly lying and pretending that I didn't have an entire encyclopedia of better things to do. "Lead the way."

Our walk was a depressing one. It took us alongside the great warehouse we'd sheltered in, giving us a nice, big look at the ruined main doors and walls that'd been scraped raw by a thousand fingernails. Just beyond it was a big pile of dead bodies. Rotter bodies. We'd had to move them from the killbox, of course. Had to. In a world like this, remaining too close to open carcasses was a guaranteed way to die. I didn't want to hack up bloody lungs because I caught something from a dead caveman. Besides, they'd been in the way of our *new* killbox anyway. Come nightfall, we'd need our defenses readied all over again, or else we'd be slaughtered, whether the enemy brought half what they did yesterday or only a quarter.

"You do care, don't you?" the Vittonian woman asked, drawing my eyes to her. I was surprised to see a more thoughtful look on her face now. Not as hostile as before, sure, but . . . not as decided either. I'd take consideration over friendliness any day.

"That's why we came," I lied. "That's why we kept fighting, even after we found out the state you were all in, and that's why we'll stay."

I saw her face shift somewhat, fractionally, and in a way even I couldn't quite read. She tightened her jaw, looking away. "Then I am . . . sorry for how I received you. I've seen one too many opportunistic swindlers in my time."

"Don't be that sorry," I replied. "You had my brother Solitaire dead to rights."

For a second she stared at me, stunned. Then she saw the flickering grin in the corner of my mouth, and it infected her. We shared a laugh that I knew both of us needed, venting it out hotly, decompressing as it left us.

Then I saw Tucker approaching, and stiffened. Play time, it seemed, was over. I had work to do.

CHAPTER FORTY-NINE

Beam's POV: Day 52
Current Wealth: 1 silver, 47 copper

T*alk to me. Talk to me, you fucking asshole of a voice. Speak!*
But it didn't.

I'd been focusing—meditating, I should start calling it—for the better part of an hour since my friends left. An hour to myself, with no distractions, no inconveniences, no danger or pressure or pain. And in that hour I'd accomplished nothing.

It had seemed to me that it was becoming *easier* to speak with whatever entity now lived in my head, that it was growing more receptive, more open. Apparently, I'd been wrong because now I didn't so much as feel a hint that there was anything even listening to me, let alone preparing an answer. It was as if . . .

. . . as if I was just a lunatic talking to himself. Well, too late for that. The time to avoid such an eventuality is *before* you start hearing voices answer back, not after. And these voices gave me provable magic powers. So back to meditation I went.

A half hour, another hour, closing in on two. Finally the reply came.

Be silent, boy-creature. You are interrupting my rest.

I nearly jumped out of my skin when I heard the voice, then stiffened.

"Why haven't you been talking to me?" I tried, hoping I'd actually get a response now. None came, and my anger boiled over. "Keep ignoring me, and I'll just keep on bugging you for a reply. You've seen me fight with a pint of blood sloshing around loose inside me; you know I'll do it."

A pause followed that, and then something that felt oddly like . . . an irritated sigh. I suppressed a grin.

I ought to ask you, failure, coward, why you are daring to inflict your conversa-tion on me. I have nothing to give a wretch like you, and you have no right to expect anything.

That did give me pause, for quite a while. I thought, considered, then sighed. "You're angry I lost?" I frowned.

I am not angry, nor sad, nor disappointed. One does not feel such things over a flea. I am merely observing your failure and punishing you thusly.

That actually did piss me off. My failure? How had I failed?

You fell to your knees, surrendering, rather than fight an enemy right in front of you, the voice replied, answering my fleeting, sub-instinctual thoughts the way it knew I hated. I didn't have time to be annoyed by the slight, though, because its actual words had hit the mark directly.

I had surrendered, hadn't I? I could remember it all vividly. A gesture from the vampire, a big wave of light, and then . . . Then every doubt I had, every fear, every insecurity was a lead weight around me. Dragging me down, pinning me, crushing me.

My mouth dried, and I heard the presence speak again.

So you do feel shame, at least. Good. Bask in it. That will add to your deserved punishment. I had hoped any creature capable of being my vessel would be a warrior with a heart cast in iron, a mighty lion upon the battlefield. At the very least, your death will free me from this mewling kitten I have been placed within.

There was a lot of information there, some given subtly, some just volunteered. I was sure Shango and Solitaire would've absorbed it all instantly, quickly mak-ing deductions and calculations, multiplying its volume through sheer weight of intellect to figure out every little thing about the presence. I wasn't them, and I was in no state to even try to replicate their genius. All I could do was lower my head, and try to ignore the voice.

Because everything it'd said was right.

I left the room trudging and bitter, making my way out of the building, hur-rying to the training grounds. There was a magic monster in my head keeping me from spending experience points and doing the one fucking thing I was good for, but if nothing else, I could help the others replace me. How many villagers were there? Thirty or so, fighting at least. I was equal to maybe ten on my own. If I could make them all ten percent more effective, I'd at least have done a fraction of what I ought to.

My walk was interrupted as the Vittonian woman pulled in beside me, eying me sympathetically, seeming rather . . . awkward. I ignored her, in no mood for conversation.

"I'm here to apologize," she said abruptly, which did draw my focus, but barely. After my failure the day before, the thought of having people fawn over me was almost worse than derision.

"Consider it accepted," I grunted, still heading for the trainees. She followed.

"I . . . had quite a speech planned," the Vit grumbled, suddenly put out. I glanced her way and saw it wasn't much more than skin deep.

"Sorry," I sighed, "but I'm really busy."

In an instant she nodded, understanding blossoming upon her face.

"Of course, then let me just cut to the important part. I intend to help you from now on, fully and totally. I . . . see now that there actually is a chance to be had in fighting, so I intend to help fight."

She already had, I recalled, put her own body on the line not twelve hours prior, fighting beside me, spearing holes in everything ahead like some hoplite plucked out of Spartan legend. The thought of having more of that was definitely a reassuring one.

"That's good," I nodded, hiding my true eagerness, "but why are you following me *now?*"

The woman blinked, as if I'd just asked why the grass looked green.

"Because you're going to train the defenders, many of which are using long pole weapons." She removed the spear affixed to her back, toying with its weight in her deft hands. I saw now that it was a properly made one—a real, actual spear. Leaf-headed blade, six feet of handle at least. The sort of thing that might get punched into a person's gut and still come out of his back with momentum to spare.

"And you're shit at spear fighting," she finished. I glared at her, thought for a moment, then grinned.

If she was good enough to notice that, she'd be good to have on our side, indeed.

Training went a lot smoother this time, for several reasons. The Vittonian was a big one. I still didn't know who she was, why she was so far from her land of birth, and in a village like this. But I was starting to have my suspicions that she was running from something. She'd definitely been in the military. Addressing the trainees like the drill sergeant in *Full Metal Jacket*, all commanding and overbearing, barking out orders so harshly that it seemed everyone was racing each other to accomplish them.

More than that, though, I was helped along by the trainees' newfound . . . *worship.*

Well, veneration might've been more accurate. All of them seemed to have gained the respect Shango had hoped they would, and more. Viewing my brothers as some heaven-sent saviors, and viewing me in particular as a guardian angel. In their eyes I could do no wrong, make no errors, and lose no fight.

Apparently, they'd forgotten the fucking fight I lost the night before.

It was a strange feeling, and the novelty took about a minute to wear off. Then it was just . . . suffocating.

I ignored it as best I could, focusing more tightly on the training and finding myself pleased to see it progressing more quickly than before. Perhaps it was because I'd made a start already, maybe it was the full-on battle they'd finally had all gathered together. Being realistic, the Vittonian definitely didn't hurt. Regardless of what the magic balance of causes was, by the time the sky was beginning to darken, and we had about an hour left of daylight, we'd made a good leap forward in cohesion, accuracy, and resilience amongst them. Or so we thought, at least. The real test would be the next fight.

And it'd be one I faced without my magic.

"You're nervous."

I smashed my face into as neutral a shape as I could manage, then turned around. It was the Vit, of course, hanging back and eying me, concerned.

"I'm fine," I lied. "Just, you know, readying for the fight—"

"My name's Helena," she cut in, interrupting me calmly, casually. "You're Beam, I know, but I'm Helena. I . . . want you to know. In case I die. In case we all die." She looked away, not meeting my eye. "In case I get everyone killed by not helping sooner, and just . . . remaining trapped inside myself."

I had no idea what to say to that, and in my awkwardness I just stared for a few moments more. Until she turned, clearing her throat and heading off.

"Well, anyway, I'm sorry, for what it's worth. Now let's go and kill some rotters."

That, at least, I could get behind. I followed after her.

CHAPTER FIFTY

Shango's POV: Day 52
Current Wealth: 1 silver, 47 copper

Beam and the Vittonian were back well before nightfall, though part of me was panicking like Solitaire at the multi-minute delay separating them from the larger mass of our new militia.

We'd all spent the day busy, even those of us who'd kept checking on Beam, and my work had been to organize the biggest workforce we could muster. With our newfound cloak of awe among the villagers, it wasn't particularly difficult. Dozens upon dozens volunteered, and quite a few more were pressured into it by Tucker and our other proponents. Most, to be fair, were far from able-bodied. The elderly, the young, the sick, and the weak. Most of the mere cowards had already joined up to start fighting, which meant most of the construction was done by those of less-than-optimal bodily strength.

But where we lacked quality, they made up for in quantity. Close to fifty working people was, still, close to fifty working people. It was amazing the things we were able to get done.

Barricades were the first priority, at Solitaire's insistence, and a close second was more of our drop-down crushing weapons. We collected the logs for them while erecting our defenses, thickening the planks used, this time, to give us those extra few minutes to poke holes in the enemy while they clawed through. There were advantages to working in a lumber village, and perhaps the biggest was all of the infrastructure. Between a river-powered saw, more ordinary sized handsaws for days, and no less than half a dozen heavy wooden axes, we had plenty to work with.

Solitaire ribbed me for my use of literal child labor, of course, but we'd already repaired and reinforced from yesterday before the sun was even halfway between noon and night. Which left us time for other precautions.

A big one was Solitaire's insistence on digging up the staircase and weakening the support for its steps, removing nails and eroding beams. Another was the reinforcements he gave one of our walls, and the big box of nails he ordered readied beside a window near its top. That confused even me, but I figured he had a plan, as usual, and had a few too many things to juggle for me to ask.

One issue we'd had last time had been the enemy closing in on barricades too quickly. Solitaire suggested we lay down nail-riddled planks pointy-side-up to slow them. Our main door was damaged beyond repair, so he proposed simply planking it over once everyone was inside. One adjustment, repair, or slight improvement after another. All implemented seamlessly.

I'd worked with him for years, you understand. We both knew how the other thought, and our skills meshed well. It was like being connected to the same nervous system.

Ideas formed in his mind, observations and points of failure, and he transmitted them quickly to me. I interpreted, considered which workers we could spare to do them, and then relayed the orders further. Like a well-oiled machine, we transformed the building around us.

Beam woke up relatively early into the process, which gave him plenty of time to do his own work on our defenders. Solitaire complained a lot about the lack of further ingredients for more explosives, but otherwise made himself useful. I just kept focused, far too close to death for any thought but self-preservation to really gain traction in my mind.

Disaster struck soon enough. Something that perhaps demonstrated our success definitely should have reassured me but only served to fray my nerves even further all the same. We ran out of things to do. Our defenses were perfect, our preparations complete, our only remaining limitation being the simple lack of space left over in our makeshift fort.

I saw Solitaire pacing from the corner of my eye once we'd retired to the mayor's office—apparently our new command center. It was just us there, alongside Beam and Argar. The Belahont Crew, we were dubbed by the villagers. Some crew—three friends and an indentured servant. Well, it could be worse. We could've been ourselves immediately upon arrival.

The skies were darkening, but I could still see pretty clearly outside. Maybe that was just all those carrots I had growing up. The villagers certainly seemed frightened enough, but either way the rotters weren't here yet. So it surprised me when Argar caught my attention with a low, hesitant question.

"Is this what you do?" I looked at him, confused. It must've shown on my face because he kept talking to clarify. "We came here, found all these people hopeless, dying, and trapped. Now they're . . . I don't know, hopeful, I suppose. Is that what you do? You just . . . help people who need it?"

It wasn't, of course. Nobody did *just* that. We'd come here because we needed money to help ourselves, to keep from starving, to make some level of positive change on this world we'd created and the people we'd inadvertently screwed over. To make it a place we could actually live our lives in, now that we'd finally realized we were stuck here.

"Yes," I lied. "Why do you ask?"

He eyed me, the way I might expect a mouse to eye cheese in a trap.

"Just . . . Most folks aren't like that," he said, sounding more than a little impressed.

That was good. Argar was excellent in a fight, but that just meant that we'd be competing with some high bidders if we wanted to keep him under us. A tie of loyalty—a tie of belief in our cause—would take time to fashion, but it would hold much better.

I barely even felt like a piece of shit as I worked on thickening it.

"I think they would be, given the chance," I told him. "I think if more people were . . . comfortable, fed, watered, warm, I think they'd have more time to concern themselves with others, and the world would be a better place."

He seemed to like that a lot, and believed it without question. Being fair, I hadn't been lying. I'd come from a world where more people were fed, watered, and warm. Things were hardly just over there. The flickering power in so many parts of Africa, the exploitation of developing nations by others, the people still sleeping in streets . . . It was all far from perfect.

But it *was* a better place than Redacle. I wasn't lying, just leaving a few truths unsaid. Maybe I should've just fed the giant some bullshit, because I felt more or less the same either way.

Argar nodded, apparently thinking quite hard now, and considering things well. That was good. The first step to persuading someone was to get them thinking. Twisting those thoughts to line up with yours was the second and last.

"How long do we have until it all kicks off?" Beam asked.

"Nineteen hundred seconds," Solitaire muttered before I could answer, still pacing, hands fidgeting and twitching. He'd never done well with imminent danger, far preferring the *present* kind.

"Half an hour," I translated for our friend, glancing outside the window again. It was darker, I thought. But still, I could see the outside well enough.

A thought occurred then. One that almost killed me. Could we have killed the rotters during the day? Chased them down, turned their slowness against them?

I considered asking Solitaire but decided against it. If it had been possible, letting any of my friends know now, when it was too late to do anything anyway, would be . . . cruel. And it probably hadn't been possible anyway. Vampires were weaker by day but still superhuman, and very good at picking hidey-holes that humans couldn't find.

The seconds ticked by, rolling into a minute, and then two. Those minutes themselves congealed like drops of water condensed against a window. Soon there were a dozen, and two dozen not long after. By then, we were all done pacing, waiting, and muttering, every single one of us on edge at once.

Whether Solitaire had counted right or not—and we were all certain he had—a few minutes from complete darkness was far too close for any sort of relaxation. Everyone was at their station, every weapon was in its wielder's hand, and every vein in the building was carrying an acidic barb of adrenaline. The fight was drawing nearer.

A few short minutes later, it reached us. Announcing itself with the sound of a dropping barrel, an igniting fuse, and an explosion as big as any Solitaire had made so far.

An explosion from outside, as the enemy detonated the black powder they'd stolen from us a day ago.

CHAPTER FIFTY-ONE

Solitaire's POV: Day 52
Current Wealth: 1, silver 47 copper

The black powder explosion was not unanticipated. Even as it rocked my teeth, I mused on how we'd all known it would come. Even as I heard the overpressure strike our outer wall, and felt the tremble run through the building, I considered how simple a person it would've taken not to foresee it. Its deflagration left a single sensation running through my core, more intense than perhaps any emotion I'd ever felt before or since.

Irritation.

What kind of moron tried to use my own weapon against me in so obvious a way? Evidently, the kind we were fighting now. And what kind of genius would fail to safeguard against such a simple tactic?

Not this one, obviously.

We'd been well prepared. A barrel of our own, stationed right beside a high window on the top floor of the building, directly above the center of its lower wall. Directly above the thinnest, most destructible part of the place. The moment the man we had assigned to it saw a fuse light, he gave the word, and we sent two more bastards over to heave the barrel up and send it careening down below.

It was filled with nails, as many as we could find. Landing just behind the enemy's hastily piled stolen gunpowder, spilling its contents out. Then the explosion came.

Black powder was a low explosive, though, not a high explosive. That meant that its shockwave didn't propagate the material's substance any faster than the actual chemical reactions themselves. It was just flames and energy jumping from one micro-scale granule to another, not a full-scale atomic event. These molecules were still small, of course—small enough that anything spreading that fast between them was still an *explosion*—but it meant that the blast power was inherently tied to pressure. To maximize it, you had to compress the explosion in a tight area with just enough space inside to let it build itself up before release. This was why there'd still been limbs left over all the times I'd used it before.

Our vampire enemy hadn't known much about black powder, though. Which was why he'd been so impressed with me, and why I'd been confident the dumbass would just have his little minions dump the barrels against our weakest wall and light them up without even taking the same measures I had to ensure they reached peak effectiveness. The resulting blast was far too weak to make a breach.

But it was more than strong enough to launch the nails we'd dropped right behind the explosion.

A minute later, the clawing was back at the front of our little fortress, sneering, snarling undead trying to hammer through wood using their own limbs and skulls as bludgeons.

It must be said, without pesky pain receptors to get in their way, their odds were looking better than fair. The material began yielding within two thousand seconds.

This time, there was an altogether different reaction. A steely, grim preparedness, and all eyes fell on the surface as it slowly continued getting whittled away. All except mine. I kept my focus on the windows, waiting for the subversion I knew was coming. In the end, I was half right. The vampire smashed himself through one of them, but not in the mayor's office. He emerged into the main area from one of the side rooms, announcing himself by flicking that jeweled rapier into a nearby villager and taking the man's head off as if his neck were tissue paper.

He'd healed from yesterday, I saw, now looking as fit as an exsanguinated fiddle. The cunt. He came flying at me without an instant's hesitation, snarling as he closed in, then pausing as Beam lunged out in front of him, jumping off a banister to land within a meter of the enemy.

A spear came around hard, and the vampire's sword met it mid-swing. Carved wood gave in to steel, splitting open with a spray of splinters and pulp, sending my friend back a step. I was already in the fight by then, though, and hacking low and wild with my hatchet. The vampire dodged, but barely.

Beam did the exact perfect thing, following me up with the bladed end of his spear and using it like a dagger to stab and whip, doubling the momentum and forcing the vampire farther back. I kept on swinging, aiming for the limbs I saw dragging behind our enemy as it stumbled away, and soon I even caught its hand.

It wasn't a deep cut, just a graze really. A tiny little tickle, a poke of the finger, a love tap. The vampire's severed thumb fell to the floor, and the creature snarled in agony like the wimpy bitch it was, clutching the wound for all of a second as its eyes practically glowed with fury.

Around that time, I sensed that continuing to fight this creature may not have been in my best interests. As always, I did some thinking, and I did it all within the span of a quarter-second.

We knew it had some game-changer, the same thing it'd used on Beam last time, and it didn't take a genius to figure out it was coming. I had about an instant to act on that knowledge, and I did so by violently shouldering my friend just as the vampire's arm blurred upward amid a flash of crimson light.

The Olympian wasn't expecting the bash, and it sent him off-kilter just as I'd hoped, leaving me alone in the path of the attack. It washed over me, red light hitting like the dying glow of a sunset, and then I felt exactly what Beam had described.

It was crushing. A knowledge—a certainty—that I was worthless, stupid, insignificant. It crawled into my mind as a thousand grasping roots, trying desperately to choke the life away from me, digging itself into my cerebrum and crushing every scrap of hope it found.

Worthless.

Stupid.

Insignificant.

Except . . . I wasn't, obviously. I was Solitaire, Bernard. I was the smartest human probably ever. I wasn't even sure my species had the cranial capacity to make something more intelligent than me. I didn't just *think* that, I knew it.

Worthless.

I was one of the only people preparing for when *They* made their move.

Stupid.

I could multiply four digit numbers in my head from age five.

Insignificant.

The entire universe was my playground, and other people weren't even provably conscious to me.

I dropped to my knees, trembling, gasping, head lowered and eyes wide in all the ways I recalled seeing on Beam. The vampire sneered, triumphant as it stepped forward. Sword raised slowly to kill me, its wielder confident he had all the time in the world.

The hardest part was not giggling as I pulled the knife out of my boot and drove it down through his.

A scream from the vampire, a taunt from me, and I was rolling out of the weapon's way. I winced at the sound of it cleaving through the wooden floor, imagining rather vividly just how much resistance my own spine would've offered. Then I leapt to my feet and closed in just as Beam did.

I was stronger, and quicker to react. The differences were small, but I'd already felt their benefits in lasting this long. For a moment, I let myself get confident. Even cocky.

The vampire picked a good move, this time, though. Taking the extra moment to lean down and rip the knife out, then throwing itself to one side. There was space between us just as there'd been last time, in the mayor's office, but we'd used our momentary advantage well. It was wounded, less mobile, possibly even mad with pain. We had a chance. I came in first to use it, retrieving my hatchet and clutching it tight.

Just in time for a new blast of red light to wash over me.

I took a single step forward before I felt its influence return, and this time it was . . . different.

You're crazy.

You're dangerous.

All your friends know it.

They hate you.

They fear you.

They're planning how to get rid of you.

A chill ran down my spine, and I felt something unfamiliar, something almost alien, that hadn't struck me since I was a little boy. Panic. Cold and cruel, like an icicle ran through my guts. My weapon dropped from limp fingers as I felt my body tremble involuntarily, legs suddenly weak, hearing suddenly muted, mouth dry and heart pounding like a war drum.

I barely even noticed the vampire step forward with its backhand, and I didn't feel the impact at all.

CHAPTER FIFTY-TWO

Beam's POV: Day 52
Current Wealth: 1 silver, 47 copper

Solitaire's feet left the ground as he caught the vampire's blow, head jerking so violently to one side that I thought his neck was broken. He flew for a few feet, half-turning in midair, body hitting a railing, then flipping over it as he plummeted down to the lower floor.

I heard him land, a distant, bone-chilling thud.

It was just me and the vampire now, but I didn't think about that. Couldn't think about that. There was no room in my head at all for anything besides the memory of seeing Solitaire fall, and the fury of knowing it was to an enemy I should've killed the day before. My legs were moving before I even told them to.

The vampire seemed surprised, but he composed himself near-instantaneously, undead nerves carrying his thoughts faster than any human's. My ruined stub of a spear was easily outranged by his sword, and I knew I'd be impaled before getting close enough to use it, so instead I just threw the thing at his face. It flew well, nice and aerodynamic with all the metal on it, and its bladed tip barely missed the vampire as it hastily sidestepped.

A single moment's reprieve came, and with that distraction, I finished my charge. Getting inside my enemy's weapon range, seizing their sword-arm and freeing a dagger from my own belt. I thrust it at the vampire's eye, hoping to run its brain through with one stab.

No such luck, of course. The bastard moved last second, and I felt my knife thud into its cheek instead. Painful for sure, going by the snarl that rang out, but not deadly. The vampire backed off and shoved me at once, forcing space between us, and I was thrown back against the railing, almost toppling over myself. Almost, but not quite, because I still held the monster's sword, and the vampire didn't seem eager to let it go.

A really stupid idea flitted across my mind, as the creature held me steady with its grip on the weapon. I threw myself back across the railing, planted my boots on its opposite side, and kicked off. The vampire sensed itself about to be dragged back to fall some twenty feet and instinctually let go, freeing me and giving up its weapon.

Though my plan was effective, it had only one minor flaw. I was now falling twenty feet myself. I winced, bracing myself for impact and slapping the ground hard to break it as best I could. Such a move worked fine when you were on the receiving end of a judo throw, not so much when you fell halfway down the height of a building. The wind was knocked completely out of my lungs, and probably my bloodstream, too, for that matter. For a moment, I just lay back gasping in forced breaths as my organs spasmed and tried to recover.

Then I caught movement above me, the vampire's. Its foot was definitely still hurt. I could see that by the way it came lurching to the railing and leapt over it. The thing's body was no more fragile than before, however.

It dropped down the full height as if it were simply stepping down two steps on a staircase, landing with a fractional bend of its knees, joints absorbing the impact with no sign of strain. I hadn't even finished fighting back the urge to hurl when it started closing in, panicked villagers standing back and staring. I couldn't blame them. Fighting rotters from behind a barricade was one thing, but this monster was something else. And it was completely unimpeded by our defenses.

Unimpeded by our defenses, but not by Argar. He came out of nowhere, charging in like a bull, thick legs powering his body ahead like pistons, broad arms swinging his hammer around like an executioner's axe. The vampire whipped its head back, hissing like an animal as the blow missed, then trying to close in and grab him. Argar was a step ahead, though, bringing a knee up into the enemy's guts, and actually managing to fold it over.

The moment of stunned gasping while it recovered from the blow was all the time he needed. His hammer came down so hard on the vampire's head that the weapon broke.

No, no, it didn't just break. The handle held. It was the iron-fucking-head that snapped apart, cast metal turning to shrapnel beneath its wielder's strength. The blow drove our enemy down, face-first into the ground hard enough to split a plank in half and bury its skull like a vegetable. Argar was a perfectionist, though, so he didn't stop there. He took the handle in both hands, broke it easily over his knee, then hefted a jagged piece up high to impale the fallen monster.

One lucky shot was about as much as could be expected, though. The vampire rolled out from under him—a stupid, telegraphed, sluggish move that would've gotten it killed in a fair fight. It worked, nonetheless. It sprang to its feet like a panther. A punch caught Argar's face, sending him reeling, and then another caught his body. Right where the sword had bitten before. That one had the giant fully folded over, coughing and groaning, right into the path of the haymaker that laid him out clean and unconscious.

It all happened fast, and while I was still forcing myself up. It all happened right before my eyes. It all happened while I was helpless, slow, weak, stupid, and simple. Without the bolstered stats that had let Solitaire last so much longer, without even the magic weapons I'd just barely learned to rely on. My mind frayed with the intensity of my fury, and the adrenaline poisoning my veins came more from the rage than the pain or fear. It was just the electric boost my muscles needed to force me up, and I surged on with the knife clutched and ready.

But the vampire turned, fast as ever, knowing now to be cautious of the handful among us whose abilities were beyond baseline human. I stopped dead in my tracks as the familiar, wretched crimson light engulfed me, starting my slow, pitiful descent to my knees.

You're dull.

I was, and I'd always known it. Solitaire and Shango would have both been smarter than three of me by themselves.

You're weak.

How could I argue? With all the potential I'd had, how could I stand next to world-class athletes and not even put in half their effort? I wasn't even a shadow of what I should've been. Wasn't even a shadow of what others would have been.

You're a coward.

And there was the final point, the crux. I was a fucking coward. Too cowardly to stave off this stupid, biting insecurity being magically thrown on me. Too cowardly to push back against Solitaire and Shango as they insisted on making everything all dark and twisted in the world I loved to build so much. Too cowardly to even get up and fight for my fallen friend. Better to die now than keep living as the wretch I was.

A coward, as I thought.

It was hard, in the heat of the moment, to separate the voice I heard whispering against my mind from my very own thoughts. I just about managed it. It wasn't me thinking that, not even under the vampire's influence. It was a presence I recognized well. *The* presence, the one I'd spent the better part of a day wrangling hints from, the one I'd had everything special about me snidely axed away as punishment for displeasing. It was speaking again, finally . . . and it was choosing to mock me rather than offer any help.

The injustice of it all made my eyes water, but with rage rather than panic. *Coward?* I wasn't the one hiding in someone else's fucking head. I wasn't the one throwing a wave of bodies at illiterate peasants just to win even more. I started standing, faster now, and the presence returned.

Are you hoping to impress me with a second wind?
I ignored it.
Are you planning to die like a man?
I ignored it.
Do you really want this to be your end?
I ignored it, and then it said something else. Differently, questioning now as I took my first step to the vampire, and the vampire took its first toward me.
Have you truly steeled yourself?
That one cut right to the center of me, and I wasn't even sure if I had. The red light returned, then it washed over me, and I felt all the old doubts.

But what was doubt? My best friends were some of the most intelligent people alive, you can't grow up next to people like that without doubt. My rivals were the strongest, fastest on earth, and I'd still won.

And whether I had doubts or not, Solitaire was still bleeding and unconscious. That was the end of it all, no matter what. My friend was hurt or dead, and it'd been my fault. I couldn't save him, but I'd make sure he didn't go to the grave without company. I lunged.

Muscles rebelled as the light tried to disable them, but I ignored them. My bones felt like jelly, and I forced them hard. My mind was slow, doubtful, hesitant. I pushed it to one side, relying on my gut instead, like I always had. And then I was taking my second step forward.

The vampire looked surprised, but I didn't feel it. I just felt tired of waiting. My body responded again, more quickly now, with a third step, then a fourth. I came up to stand just beside one of our barricades as I closed in. Then the presence returned.

One last chance. It told me, and it needn't have even bothered. Whether I was going to be given my powers back or not, I'd have lunged on this fucking monster and bitten chunks off like Solitaire if I had to.

But the magic certainly helped. I felt the tugging instantly as I moved past the barricade, and I reached out to touch it without thinking. It was all safety, all security. All defense. I felt the intent behind its craftsmanship, the skill behind its structure, the anticipation as it awaited a test against rotting flesh and snarling jaws. I took that purpose, and I drew it into myself. It congealed inside me like milk turning to butter, thickening, hardening. Gaining substance. And I shaped that substance with a thought.

My fifth step came, and I was wearing a helmet. My sixth extended it into a gorget and shoulder pads, then a breastplate and gauntlets. By the time the silvery, sleek energies covering me had finally reached my feet, I was within three paces of the vampire, and watching as the creature backed off uncertainly. I followed after it like a hungry predator, pausing only to reach down and graze the wooden floor with my fingertips.

Wood, old reliable. The first material mankind made anything at all from. Flexible, hard, sharp. It formed a spear in my hands, an oddly thick one, robust and deadly.

I saw pure panic on my enemy's face, even as the new weapon crackled and glowed a dull orange. Because there was another aspect to wood, too, that I hadn't even considered before I wrapped it into a weapon.

It was what you drove through a vampire's heart to kill him for good.

CHAPTER FIFTY-THREE

Shango's POV: Day 52
Current Wealth: 1 silver, 47 copper

'd like to say I felt hope when Beam strode toward the vampire, standing tall
and strong with magical plate armor covering every inch of him, but I
felt nothing. Nothing but concern for our fallen friend, who, by then, had
stopped convulsing and grown rather still, head gushing, eyes flitting, lips
moving in silent, mumbled curses. I knelt beside Solitaire, hands hovering
uselessly above him, throat tight. I needed to think. Always, I needed to think,
and thought was never so important as in a situation bad enough to make it
this difficult.

Reluctantly, I forced my simpler impulses back, beating them away from the
front of my mind like invading rotters, and considered the situation. I turned to
Beam, turned to the vampire, examined them both.

[Appraisal]
Class: Warrior
Level: 4
Condition: Worn
Modifiers: Strength +1, Speed +1, Toughness +2
**Statistics: Strength 15, Speed 15 (12), Dexterity 4, Stamina -, Toughness
16, Alertness 14, Charisma 6, Intelligence 4**

The creature wasn't *more* deadly than it had been, at least, but that wasn't saying much. I flitted my eyes to Beam's stats, quietly hopeful. As it turned out, I
was right to be. He'd finally managed to spend those points.

[Appraisal]
Class: Dragonknight
Level: 10
Condition: Fine
Modifiers: +2 Strength, +2 Speed, +2 Toughness, +2 Alertness
Statistics: Strength 11, Speed 10, Dexterity 8, Stamina 9, Toughness 10, Alertness 10, Charisma 6, Intelligence 5
Inventory: Jeans, flannel shirt, spear
Class Abilities: Beloved II
Current Experience Points: 10/400
Unspent Skillpoints: 0

Not close, not close at all. I wasn't sure Beam would've won with a two or one advantage. Even with most of his improvement going to speed, he was barely equal with the foot-dragging vampire after Solitaire had opened a hole in its heel. On a statistical level alone, Beam was a toddler against a pit bull.

Which meant that everything hinged on that armor of his. I forced my eyes to remain on the battle, even as instinct told me to look away.

Beam wasn't slow anymore, and his new gear didn't seem to weigh him down at all, but his enemy's reaction time was no less superhuman. The vampire danced back with all the easy grace I recalled describing myself, moving so preemptively that it seemed to be living a full second in the future from the rest of us. Beam chased it, of course, but he wasn't getting anywhere near the bastard. All the world's training couldn't make up for that difference in speed.

Further ahead I caught the main barricade—the one keeping the rotters from crawling inside—straining further. How long did we have until it broke? I glanced at Solitaire. He could've estimated, I knew, and would probably have gotten within ten percent of the answer. But, he was unconscious because I couldn't so much as contribute to a serious fight, even now. I bit the annoyance back, compartmentalized, focused.

Argar and Helena were moving, both reaching me almost at once. The Vittonian knelt down, placing her hands on Solitaire.

"I have battlefield training in medicine," she snapped. "You go, help others, leave him to me." I paused, and her eyes hardened like iron cooling in a cast. "Go!"

Swallowing, I did. Standing, raising a spear from the ground and reluctantly turning toward Beam's fight. It was going no better than before, his weapon still as far from the enemy's flitting feet as ever.

Except . . . the vampire seemed to be making fairly regular stepping motions, moving in a consistent path. I weighed my options for a moment, then sighed, cocked my arm back and threw my spear like a javelin.

It wasn't a good throw, even with my newfound magical strength. I might've hit the vampire directly, only to watch the weapon bounce off with barely a cut to even prove it had landed. But, I didn't aim for the vampire. I aimed for that magic spot between its knees, where one leg moved into and the other out of.

The shaft of the spear caught its front leg in the backstep, delaying it and staggering the vampire for an instant as its balance broke. One instant, and no more. But an instant was just enough time enough for Beam to run his new glowing-orange spear through the thing's shoulder.

A scream cut through the air, satisfying as anything I'd ever heard, and Argar was interrupting it a few moments later with the mother of all shoulder-charges. Four hundred pounds of muscle and flab crunched into the vampire with more speed than most men could manage, actually throwing it to the ground in its unbalanced state, and Beam moved in quickly to press the attack.

My eyes fell back on our front barrier, which was now sporting a large number of gaps and crevices where the wood was finally starting to give in entirely. All our defenders had already had the sense to back off, thankfully, putting themselves behind the secondary barriers, now well practiced in our brand of collapsing defense. The sight was still a fearsome one. How long had the wall held? Less than an hour, I thought. And we still had a vampire in our midst.

I couldn't help with that, not really, so instead I took to the barricades and readied myself to fight shoulder-to-shoulder with the other . . . with the other weaklings.

The door held, though, and the noise behind me only grew. I trembled, snarled, then turned and raced into the fight. This was the one that mattered, this was the one that gave us a chance. Kill the vampire, and we'd kill them all—make it bleed enough and maybe the defenders could even close in to help.

My legs trembled, even while I used them to run, but I pushed the sensation aside, along with everything else that might hinder me. I couldn't afford anything else at all in my head now.

Beam was holding his own, still, and Argar seemed to have fallen into a role of support. The vampire was keeping back, fighting from afar, wielding some giant piece of timber that looked to weigh about a quarter as much as me. Wielding it one-handed, of course, the fucking monster. I arrived just in time to see a particularly clean connection send Beam flying fully off his feet and half-flipping in the air before he crashed down hard a few meters away. Then I was in the thick of it.

My spear was in my hands, and I didn't have many better ideas than a thrust, so I tried one. It was uneven and clumsy, stabbing for the vampire's face from just out of sight. The creature still dodged it, looking more offended than worried. A hand raised, red light grew, then Argar's own weapon—a piece of timber nearly as big as the vampire's—dropped toward the enemy, forcing it to retract its limb for protection. I tried to circle our foe, to attack from a blind spot again, but it took the opportunity to circle even better, positioning me between Argar and forcing the fight into a one-on-one before I could even react.

I raised my spear and felt it snap as my block successfully caught the enemy's blow, then unsuccessfully stopped it. Over fifteen kilos of wood glanced off my thigh—not a direct hit, not even close. Most of the energy was spent as it hit the ground below, snapping floorboards.

The muscle still went dead, though, all the way to my knee, numbed into insensibility by the impact. I lurched back to avoid the follow-up swing, which came faster than I would've thought possible, and it whipped by my face so rapidly that it felt like I'd just been missed by an archer.

Argar barged me aside, actually knocking me off my feet entirely with how violently he'd shoved me. I looked up to see his club bouncing off the vampire's head. Evidently, they'd been just as surprised as me, but the creature recovered quickly enough. A shove threw Argar back, and I saw blood oozing down his side where he'd been stabbed. The wound, it seemed, was reopened.

Beam barreled into the undead thing before anything more could come of it. The two of them were a whirlwind of flying limbs, Beam's armor and weapon trailing streaks of light, the vampire's trailing nothing but an afterimage as my sluggish eyes tried and failed to follow. Two blows caught my friend, cracking, then buckling his armor. He answered with a stab that slipped past the vampire's head, then surprised it by releasing his spear and elbowing the thing across the face. Its nose bled; that was something at least, but the blow barely even fazed it. A thrusting blow to the chest sent Beam sliding backward a foot, then the creature followed up with a kick that threw him down again.

I hadn't actually noticed myself moving—certainly not drawing my knife— but I was stabbing into the vampire's exposed shoulder. Again, I seemed to surprise the monster more than anything. This time there was a fury behind the expression, which chilled my blood.

I threw a wild punch, hoping to surprise it again. Instead my fist was caught, then squeezed. I might've gotten it caught in some vice, for all the pain it caused. The agony had me on my knees in an instant, writhing and moaning, unable to even bring my blade around as my muscles spasmed. I could feel the bones creaking beneath my skin, a fascinating sensation, and a horrifying one. I found myself counting down the seconds until one of them gave. The sound of a barricade cracking open caught my ears distantly, and the terrified screams of our defenders rang out. Then boots hit the ground hard.

Helena's spear didn't hit the vampire, but it forced it back, and she turned the opening stab into a follow up faster than any amateur could manage. She kept it at bay for an entire four moves before her weapon was wrenched from her grip, and an elbow cracked against her head. She dropped instantly, and didn't move again. Without Argar's resilience, there was no wonder.

But her move had bought us enough time. Beam rose in the corner of my vision, and I turned to him as I scrambled back. I saw him standing tall, back straight, armor still glowing, and something new in his hand—the rapier our vampire friend had attacked with. Beam's fingers ran along the steel blade, dragging light across it, and the light began coalescing. First it was thick, then long, then thinning and sharpening down, its base spreading out, its tip thinning further.

By the time I realized what it was, his sword was already fully formed. A perfect Olympic saber—long, barely curved, and wicked-sharp. He squatted down in the stance I'd seen him take a hundred times before, legs springy beneath him, eyes focused ahead.

"En garde," he whispered.

The vampire came at him without another word.

CHAPTER FIFTY-FOUR

Beam's POV: Day 52
Current Wealth: 1 silver, 47 copper

There was a sword in my hand, and the entire world suddenly made sense. I had everything I needed to make sense of it. An enemy in front, friends behind, a problem to ignore, and a co-writer to help. The rotters had gotten through one barricade, they'd soon be on the others. That was fine. Shango would handle that. And I'd handle the undead that was already behind them.

It was close to being handled already, backing away from me now, nervous. Did it know what was coming? Did it sense the danger in the air?

Good. Hopefully that would make it more alert, and I hadn't had a half-decent practice bout in months. I closed in, coming in like an east wind, and the vampire tried to cut me off. It was lightning quick to react and adjusted well to its mangled foot, but the sword was light as a whisper in my hand, and I managed it as easily as I might my own fingers. The arcane blade twisted lengthwise, rolling the vampire's improvised weapon aside, then jerking down to cut across its wrist.

On a human, I'd have lanced through the tendons and veins of that arm, had its weapon dropping from limp digits, racing a spray of blood to the ground. The vampire was made of sturdier stuff, and its canvas-tough flesh got in the way of everything important. I still gave it a fright, though. My enemy backed up, and I closed in even faster than before.

My first swing was a feint, as was my second. My third never even came near the enemy, and my fourth was pivoted about a perfectly angled elbow to send it high where I'd previously gone low. The vampire was still feeling its foot wound, terrified and cautious of falling victim to another, and it bought the bait perfectly. My weapon's magical edge caught it across the face, splitting open a cheekbone and sending it against a wall. It was ducking to the side before I could impale it, but I just dragged the weapon free in such a way as to blind it with a buckshot of splinters. My shoulder caught its chest hard, giving it pause, and my next swing ate into the thigh.

My body wasn't moving, not really, it was *being* moved, being ordered around by the sword it held and carefully advised by the instincts sheltered within my gut, marching up and down, pivoting, and saluting. A good soldier, trained and tested. And more than a match, by far, for the terrified undead it now faced. The vampire took one final look at me before turning, sprinting away, and disappearing as it scaled a wall with all the grace of a frightened cat. I felt a grin sprouting, but didn't let it stay long. I wouldn't be watching an enemy flee just to come back and stab us from behind.

In the span of a thought, I was holding a javelin, rather than a sword, and my throw was aimed perfectly. Luck, more than skill, saw the glowing tip catch vampiric flesh right between the shoulders, but we took what we could get. The impact threw the enemy off balance just as it leapt to reach a window, sending it smashing hard against the wooden frame. I closed in fast, conjuring a new weapon, reaching the undead just as it climbed to its feet.

This time, I swung a machete down. Big and top-heavy, unwieldy. A cleaving weapon, made to take off limbs and hack through thick vines. The vampire was no more fragile than before, but with all my new strength and the supernatural force behind my attack, it wasn't so difficult to open up an artery and leave the oily blood squirting free.

Four more hits. That was all it took to leave the vampire down a head. It bounced as it fell, trailing blood where it rolled along the floor, body twitching slightly beside it. In moments, the entire thing had burned away to ash.

I let myself smile, then, and turned eagerly to see the undead crumbling apart with their creator's death. But none did. The barricades were shivering, not still, and manned by defenders more panicked than ever.

They were under attack now, of course. Apparently, the vampire had been a rare necromancer able to make summons that lived on past themselves. Our initial traps were expended, and all the secondary defenses had been set up with the knowledge that our primary wall would succumb eventually. It was Shango who gave me my most critical advice.

"The windows!" he roared. "Go and guard the windows; they'll be trying to scale them!"

I blanked for a second, confused, unresponsive. Then I realized what he meant. The rotters had shown us already they could close in through the higher floors yesterday. We'd barricaded them today, as well, but we didn't have nearly as much weight around them as we did the main door. How could we? Our enemy would be past soon.

They could even be past now.

Without another instant's pause I hurried up the stairs, throwing myself as fast as I could manage. Running in my armor felt strange. Its depth was present, millimeters less clearance on every side than I was used to, my effective volume increased by a fairly noticeable fraction. Such a change felt like it should be accompanied by an increase in mass. Even if it'd all been tin, I'd have felt *something*. But I didn't. I wasn't even certain whatever my weapons, and now armor, were made from even had mass at all.

I might as well have been wearing air.

It led to quite an interesting feeling of bulk and presence without substance, and tricked my body into clipping a corner or grazing a wall with every substantial turn I made. I'd need to practice to get used to it, I decided. But that was for later. Now all I had the time for was agonizing over the loss of precious milliseconds with each collision.

The first room I checked was entirely free of rotters, and its barricades were fine. Remaining where they were, as inanimate objects tended to do, boards were still nailed to the thin shutters below without a hint of strain, damage, or impact. I took it all in within half a second before moving on to the next.

A similar story played out with the next two, and it was the fourth where things went wrong. Went urgent. The barricade was being assailed, and already it was starting to yield. It took a while to build anything particularly thick, with this village's technology. Solitaire had been forced to cut corners in having our second-floor weak points sealed over. Despite the small size, I couldn't imagine this point would last for much longer.

But it would last, which meant I had to turn my focus back to others. I carried on, finding two other barricades being beaten and broken down from beyond, and made my way out into the main hall, calling down to the others from atop the railing.

"We need men up here!" I roared. "Three barricades are falling. Send me four men!"

I could manage one by myself, but I still recalled the struggle we'd had in keeping rotters back from the window during our last attempt. Two villagers per window was the minimum ratio to be sure of keeping them at bay, as I saw it. And even that felt like it may be insufficient. Better three, better five. Better we all just huddle up in the office again.

But no. We needed to bleed the enemy as much as we could manage first, like we had the other day. They were coming from multiple paths now, and the door that had kept our command center secure had already been weakened the day before. Our hackneyed repair works were far from perfect; there was every chance it would fail. If it did, and the rotters were still counted in the hundreds, we would all be killed. I saw men making their way up the stairs to join me, and I hurried to one of the windows without waiting on them.

The barriers did break. They broke high, they broke low. Some went slowly, eroded like boulders being struck by the tides, and others perished all at once in a sudden, wrenching explosion of splinters and critical strain. But all went eventually, and we were all left to kill.

We kill, too, though. We killed well.

I opened up heads with my sword, hacking and slashing away like I was making my way through a jungle thicket. Putrid blood stained the floors and walls around me, spraying against my armor and hardening into rotten crust. I took off limbs with some swings, split open skulls to expose ruined brain matter with others. And the rotters kept coming. My arms grew tired, so I adjusted my posture and favored different muscles. When those reached their limits, I switched back. There was no end to the enemy, and there felt like there was no end to my killing either. The world was made of savage corpses, and I was standing alone among them. Fine. That just meant I didn't need to worry about clipping any allies as I swung.

There was no telling how long it all took, or how many body parts I mangled to bits, before it was over. All I knew was that one moment I was splitting something nearly in half, and the next my focus was being snatched back by a sudden, frantic cry.

"We're on the last barricade, get ready to retreat!"

It was Shango, and had it not been, I might've ignored the voice entirely in my frenzy. Instead, he was just about able to pierce the fog and snatch my attention. I noted the warning, then got back to killing until the second came.

Except it didn't.

"They're retreating, they're all retreating now!"

For a moment I didn't quite register the words, and then I saw it myself. Exploding into the main section, I saw our killbox was just as clogged with bodies as last time, and our defenders just as exhausted. But they weren't pulling back this time. The rotters had their backs to us, turning and fleeing from the room, heading for the door with just as much haste as they had while battering toward us mere moments prior. I was stunned, immobile. I just stood where I was and stared.

Shango, though, was a bit quicker-witted. It was his booming voice I heard cut through the air a third time.

"After them!" he roared. "Get them while they're running, whittle their numbers away even more."

I was moving physically before I did mentally, but the realization came soon enough. This was our chance to cripple their numbers even more, and it would be stupid to give it up. I fell on them with my sword and armor both screaming at me to act.

It was a lot easier, I found, to kill the enemy when it was just trying to retreat.

CHAPTER FIFTY-FIVE

Solitaire's POV: Day 52
Current Wealth: 1 silver, 47 copper

Apparently, I'd been concussed. I didn't need telling; I'd been concussed before, but it was nice to have confirmation, at least. Had I been a normal person, who didn't have the cognizance to connect a splitting headache with hours of unremembered consciousness into a bridge leading me onto the obvious conclusion, I might've actually benefited from the knowledge. As things were, I'm afraid all it did was give the Vittonian woman an excuse to show off.

It was all I could do not to call her a cunt. Even in my addled state, I remembered hers as one of the particularly pro-suicide faces from our first arrival. Would anybody notice if I headbutted her?

A rhetorical question, of course. Randomly slamming my skull into her face was completely unthinkable. That would only worsen my headache even more. Instead, I just groaned, told her to leave me alone, and lay in my shitty, improvised hammock waiting for my vision to clear up.

Shango was with me before it did, kneeling down and eying me, concerned. I responded to that in much the same way I'd always learned to from my dear mother.

"Fuck off," I spat. He seemed relieved, not annoyed, which told me that he'd only come over to see how lucid I was. Must've been hit harder than I thought because I could smell the daylight in the air.

"How are you?" Shango's voice was cold as the grave, and as severe as something my addled brain was in no state to bring up for comparison. I resisted the temptation to answer with another groan, forcing myself into as much articulation and clarity as I could manage.

"Doing better," I replied. "Obviously. I'll be okay in a few days. Not the first hit to the head I've taken."

I did wonder, sometimes, whether I'd be less paranoid if I hadn't spent so long collecting head injuries. Perhaps I'd even be smarter. Now *that* was a disturbing thought.

I blinked. Maybe a lot smarter. My head was still ringing, and my thoughts were . . . not slow. They were scattered, bouncing everywhere so irregularly that even their usual speed was rendered pointless by the sheer chaos of it all. Spalling inside a tank.

"We won, then?" I asked, eyeing Shango, silently daring him to reply in the negative. He didn't.

"We won," my friend confirmed. "And . . . things are complicated." He winced, sighed, and continued. "The villagers are gathering up, discussing things they . . . I think they suspect we're going to leave soon, even though you're still bleeding everywhere and dying."

And Shango shouldn't have cared what they thought, particularly when he could simply assure them otherwise like he always did. Which meant . . .

"So we *are* going," I noted, not feeling any particular spasm of conscience at the thought. I saw much the opposite on Shango's face, his features churning with self-doubt and guilt.

"We have to. And we have no reason not to. The remaining rotters will just have to be their problem if they return. We stayed, we fought . . . we almost died. All of us have grown stronger now, even stronger than before, after last night, and . . . we need our money."

His tone upon saying the latter told me what this was really about. I made my way across the room to confirm, glancing out the window, eyeing the ragged buildings and splintered wood. How much of the village's timber stockpiles were now nailed against doorways and floors as barricades?

"They need the money," I observed, pointlessly. "All the money they can get. So you're feeling torn about asking for what was agreed on as our payment."

I didn't need to turn back around to see Shango's face; I could hear it in his voice. Vocal cords constricting so sharply that it made my retinas twitch.

"Aren't you?" he asked. I considered the question. Was I?

Not really, no. I'd be lying if I said I hated these people. I didn't. Perhaps I might have if I'd asked them about any of the things that modern people took for granted—bare minimum in women's rights, the immorality of randomly lynching foreigners during a drought, etc. But so far . . . none of them had actually done anything to draw my ire. They'd been pleasant, accommodating even, after the first night.

What motivated me was pragmatics, pure and simple. We needed the money, and we'd do more good with it than them. So we should have it.

I was aware that was the very sort of justification most bad people told themselves, as was the counter that the justification was fine for me, knowing I was right. That's the issue with empathy, I suppose. It makes it all too apparent that everyone else thinks they're the hero, too.

So, in the end, it came down to whose judgement I trusted most. And that was mine. It would always be mine. Leonardo da Vinci could've risen from the dead and it'd still be me. There was simply no one cleverer.

"It's not a matter of how I'm feeling," I told Shango. "My feelings, your feelings, are too small to bother considering here. We're individuals who can help lots more individuals. If your guilt stops you from doing that, then it needs to be ignored."

My friend stiffened, and I saw him considering the matter. Shango had always been excellent at reigning in his emotions. It was something he took no small amount of pride in. And it meant that there were few better ways to manipulate him than by framing a matter into the stark terms of impulse versus cognition.

Still, I wasn't sure this was a pill he'd swallow. He took his time in considering the matter.

"There's a reputation to be gained by not asking for much," Shango countered, irritatingly correct. "If we want to make a splash in this world, it won't hurt to be known as good people. Heroes even."

It was a point scored, and I acknowledged it. "We do still need more than a little, though. I want proper gear, more recruits. Argar on his own is good, but he's not a company, let alone an army."

Shango grinned at that. The annoying, bright grin of him knowing something I didn't.

"What am I missing?" I sighed, and he launched into his explanation with a relish I very much doubted he'd have managed to hide, even if he'd wanted to.

"The Vittonian woman, Helena, remember her?"

I did, cloudy as my wits still were. "The cunt, what of her?"

Shango breezed past the words chirpily. "She wants to join us."

That did surprise me, and I considered why that might be, then decided I didn't care.

"So that's two then. Still not ideal."

"Two who are both, apparently, over level ten. It's a start. No matter what kind of payout we get, we'll be leaving here with two new subordinates, both of which could give Beam a run for his money. Or at least could have, before. Don't tell me you don't see that as enough of a win."

It was hard not to, even I had to admit. But complacency got people killed, and I hadn't spent years avoiding chemical-laced tap water just to behave like government cattle anyway.

"It could be more of a win," I noted. Shango eyed me, seriously.

"These people need hope, Solitaire. They need someone to give it to them, and someone they can think will make it realistic. Tell me I'm wrong. Tell me we shouldn't be those people."

I couldn't, and didn't. Redaclans were animals, ape people, morons, savage creatures. The only way they could be expected to be moral—the only way humans, period, could be expected to be moral—was if something forced their hand. I swallowed, and nodded.

"Alright then."

Shango sighed in relief, and I guessed the exhalation was venting out about half a dozen more prepared arguments. He turned, heading for the door. "Beam is outside, training a few of the villagers one last time in case the rotters come back. I . . . think there's a good chance some of them will accompany us and join up, too. Ideally, you can go and persuade them to do so?"

"Consider it done," I agreed, heading off for just that task.

Beam wasn't so much as training them, as it happened, more playing with his new sword. Apparently, the vampire hadn't come back for his rapier. It now sat in my friend's hand, whipping around fast enough to look like a streak of sunlight, smacking clubs and spears aside. Beam's movements were patently ridiculous now, and it was only upon seeing them that I realized we'd gained a new pile of experience. I turned my mind inward, feeling for a new power in my core. It was there, just as I'd thought.

Strength, I decided, would be my best choice. I wanted my future sucker-punches to count more. And realizing I still had a scrap of power left over, I put some more into toughness. It'd been a mistake to leave my spread so concentrated, and the more actual fights we got into, the more I realized it. Treating every conflict as something to run away from was just inviting defeat. It was risky to prepare for battle, but with luck it'd be rewarding enough to compensate.

A cudgel was slapped out of a weak grip, and Beam shouldered the former wielder. It was a big man, almost as big as Shango, but weight didn't do much to keep his feet on the ground. He landed easily a yard back.

Strong, even for Beam. It was actually sort of scary how powerful he'd become. Sure, maybe tossing men around like that wasn't much compared to your average comic book character, but it hit different to see it demonstrated in person. It actually made me excited to grow stronger, not just for the security, but . . . to see what we could do next.

"Having fun?" I called out, grinning as Beam glanced my way, and left an opening for a small man with a club. The swing came fast, but he somehow evaded anyway, twisting aside at the last moment and replying with a shove. A groan came from his victim as the man landed and rolled, glaring up at Beam for an instant, then sighing.

"It's no use," he groaned. "We can't beat you, m'lord."

Every cell in my body, upon hearing the aristocratic honorific, urged me to not only correct the man, but follow through by beheading the nearest king and seizing his city's means of production. I resisted the urge, forcing myself instead to consider the term through a purely utilitarian lens.

As much as I hated to admit it, nobility might be the best way for us to actually get shit done in this land. Actually earning ourselves a title in truth, on the other hand, was a different matter altogether.

I spoke before Beam could correct the man's mistake.

"Shango sent me," I cut in. "We'll be setting off soon, so . . ." I eyed the group, making a show of pity. "I'm afraid you won't be able to train this lot for much longer."

Disappointment flashed across a dozen faces, but resignation was tightly woven within it.

"We understand," one of the men sighed. Did he? Fuck, he did. Oddly conscientious.

I forced my surprise to remain hidden, plastering a grave look across my face. "I wish we could do more, really, but . . . there are other people who need our help, other fights that need winning. I'm sorry."

Sometimes subtlety backfired, particularly with the incredibly stupid. If you dropped a hint so insubstantial and easily missed that it went entirely unnoticed, even by its intended recipient, then it wasn't much good for anything. This one found its mark, though.

I saw the gears turning behind the men's eyes, and just as I started walking away, I caught the sound of questioning on the air.

"Lord Beam, uh, forgive my asking, but . . . we've heard you recruited Helena . . ."

A smile found my features. Altruism did have its rewards, particularly when you were nice and obvious about it.

CHAPTER FIFTY-SIX

Shango's POV: Day 52
Current Wealth: 1 silver, 47 copper

Solitaire was hiding something, and it was eating him up inside. The fact that I'd even noticed the former fact was proof of the latter. Most of the time if he wanted something kept to himself, it'd stay tucked away in his head. Not when we'd spoken last. He was off, disconcerted, unbalanced. That concerned me. In the normal way, of course, I didn't like my friends being upset any more than the next guy, but also in a more . . . pragmatic way.

If Solitaire cracked, I had no doubt he'd kill a lot of people. It was a curious thing to know about one of your best friends, but I suppose I'd never really had a chance at normal relationships given who I was. Still, it was all a matter for later. I was approaching the major mass of the villagers now—Tucker, a few of the other leaders, and a dozen or so seniors were among them. All awaiting my declaration.

Perhaps I'd have been nervous, if addressing similarly sized crowds of people a million times more influential hadn't been drilled into me since puberty. No, that wasn't all. Something about Redaclans in general kept them from reaching me with their eyes. It felt almost like giving an assembly to . . . children. There was really no other way to describe it. The sheer difference in knowledge and skills, the fact that we'd *created* them . . . How did you look at people like that as equals?

Not a pleasant thought, but I stifled it.

"You've all probably guessed this already, but my brothers and I are going to depart soon," I declared, keeping my voice strong rather than loud. They'd all hear me from this distance, I knew, and the illusion of courage and confidence was more important than anything else. Now more than ever.

The revelation had numerous eyes falling with disappointment, but all the assembled people remained quiet. Good. That meant rage probably wasn't likely at all, nor many other troublesome emotions.

I continued promptly, just in case.

"I wish we could stay to help more, honestly I do. This village needs rebuilding. It needs . . . a lot. But I know that you can all do it yourselves. I've fought shoulder-to-shoulder with you, seen the quality of you all first-hand, and I'm completely certain that you don't need us anymore. The vampire's forces are in tatters, the vampire itself is dead. You're all . . . perhaps not safe, but under your own power now."

That seemed to strike a positive chord with them all, and I caught a few approving glances flit between the men and women watching me. I figured flattery was the best way to go here. People always took what their superiors said to heart. Show them faith and confidence, and they considered it more reflective of you than them. People remembered kindness.

"We remember what you showed us," one of the people called out, full of confidence, in the way men got when it was only half-forced.

The agreement he received from those around him bolstered my nerves a bit. I hadn't been lying, per se, about much of anything I'd told them. I really did want to stay and help, just not enough to actually do it. It was a comfort to know they at least thought they had things handled.

"Thank you for everything, my Lord," another cut in before I could think of any suitably heroic deflection. While I was still staring, surprised, another spoke up.

"You saved my daughter."

"You tell your brother Beam that he took the 'ead off a rotter t'was about to have my throat out."

One after another, they all spoke up, heaping praise and thanks upon me, all with looks in their eyes that I'd seen before. In religious zealots trying to convince me the apocalypse was nigh.

Good God, I hadn't expected this. We'd come here to be heroes, not bloody . . . whatever this was. I was forming a damned personality cult!

It was . . . not . . . a problem, I realized, and not least because we'd be leaving soon. I supposed it should've been expected, too. Save a bunch of people who've been taught that they're worth less than the dirt growing up, and you'll tend to get quite a lot of disproportional gratitude. Still, I was glad to be moving on from it.

With a suitable stoic grimace and a suitably dashing nod, I quieted them all down and said my piece. "Yes, well, most of what happened here was because of all of you. Remember that. All of *you* saved yourselves. My family just gave you the tools you needed to do so. We'd have all died together if your village hadn't had so much steel in its spine."

More beaming smiles, which made this the perfect moment to break the news. "However, we do require our payment. As I said, my family is moving on, and if we're to help more people . . . well, we'll need to finance our future work."

It didn't go over nearly as badly as I might've feared, which was to say I didn't prove all of Solitaire's paranoid worries right and have my head jabbed onto a dirty spike. Still, it definitely knocked the wind out of the villagers' sails. Their fault, really. I'd never pretended to be some heaven-sent savior. I just . . . wasn't going to starve again. We all negotiated with the uneasy manner of people that had grown fond of one another and weren't all too eager to jeopardize that by discussing money. Fortunately, none of us really pushed too hard for an advantage, least of all me.

I knew that the village would mostly be holding back out of necessity, which meant there would only be so much insistence could even do anyway. We'd come here all too aware that the rewards wouldn't be anything to crow home about. That was fine. Money was still money. In the end, I moved away with pockets that were heavier by two gold and thirty silver. It could've been better, could've been worse, but if nothing else, we'd be able to survive on this for an appreciable fraction of a year, and even stay in a city. I headed off to bring my friends—brothers—the news.

Solitaire met me halfway to Beam, and it was damned good to see him up and moving again, even after knowing he'd recovered. His eyes were clear of the foggy concussion he'd woken up with, and his face and mouth moved as deftly as ever.

"How powerful am I?" he asked, abruptly. I suppressed a smile, despite all the horror, fear, pain, and guilt this world had introduced us to. I was looking at a form of progression more satisfying than perhaps any we'd ever encountered before. Watching stats go up was a lot more gratifying when they directly infused your own body.

[Appraisal]
Class: Revolutionary
Level: 12
Condition: Fine
Modifiers: +4 Speed, +4 Toughness, +3 Alertness, +3 Strength
Statistics: Strength 10, Speed 11, Dexterity 8, Stamina 6, Toughness 9, Alertness 11, Charisma 3, Intelligence 10
Inventory: Jeans, T-shirt, flick knife, rocks (x3), dagger
Class Abilities: Detect Element II
Current Experience Points: 178/440
Unspent Skillpoints: 0

I read it out for him, and he grinned.

"Nine toughness, ten strength," Solitaire echoed, flexing his arms absently as if doing so might show him his new advancements. "So we're definitely getting two skillpoints per level now, and if my hypothesis is true that we double in strength every three points, this might make me as physically powerful as some of the strongest humans back on earth."

"Yeah, well, we'll have to wait until another time to test that out," I noted.

[Appraisal]
Class: Emperor
Level: 12
Condition: Fine
Modifiers: +5 Toughness, +3 Strength, +3 Speed, +1 Alertness
Statistics: Strength 9, Speed 9, Dexterity 6, Stamina 5, Toughness 10, Alertness 9, Charisma 9, Intelligence 9
Inventory: Jeans, shirt, jacket, dagger
Class Abilities: Appraisal II
Current Experience Points: 223/440
Unspent Skillpoints: 0

My own expenditure had been in speed, of course. Three points there and one in strength, more to round my stats off than anything, and I'd noticed a difference in the brief tests since. I'd had four skillpoints to spend, too, not just one. It seemed that that was the benefit of our higher levels. Could we expect to get three per level once we hit twenty?

That was a thought for later. For now I just enjoyed the progress, and frowned.

"People might notice how rapidly we're growing in power soon," I warned Solitaire, and he nodded as instantaneously as he always did when I brought up a thought he'd already been playing with.

"Here's why we have a bit of wiggle room," he replied. "Most people haven't seen much actual fighting from us. Those that did were typically fighting as well, and so far none have even been credible sources anyway. Not actively—criminal villagers is about the strongest testament someone can find in regards to our previous strength."

He was right, but that didn't make me wrong.

"It'll become a problem over time no matter what," I noted. "Even if people are just hearing stories, those stories will be getting more impressive over time. Eventually it'll come out that we can . . . you know, strengthen this fast."

My friend sighed and nodded. "It will, which is why we need to keep from being our company's main fighters soon. We have money, we have two recruits. I say we get more mercenaries, and magic. Magic above all else. We can afford tuition now."

That lit a bonfire of excitement in my gut. Magic. Actual, genuine magic. The idea of using it myself was like seeing Corvan perform his own the first time, multiplied by a hundred. Would I be any good at it? I could only hope so, but even if I wasn't, a few years of training would make me the closest thing this world was likely to get to proper artillery.

"And I want a lab," Solitaire finished, clearly picking his moment quite carefully and speaking only as my excitement began to reach a critical mass.

I eyed him. "A lab?"

He looked rather embarrassed, suddenly, feet shifting while he answered. "Yes, lots of people have labs. I want one, to mix chemicals and stuff."

"It'd be good to have more gunpowder . . ." I thought aloud, and Solitaire grinned.

"Oh, that's just the start. Give me a bit, and plenty of funding, and we'll have the raw ingredients for nitroglycerin, maybe even set up a forge to make some proper . . ." He trailed off, and laughed.

"What is it?" I pressed, but Solitaire only laughed harder, taking his sweet time answering. "Oh, nothing, I had an idea for a steel-making process. What do you think about us getting into the metal industry? It'll take a bit of start-up cash, but if the mercenary outfit makes us enough . . . I think we might just be selling steel to entire kingdoms."

I joined him in his grin, gold suddenly feeling heavier in my pocket, heart suddenly lighter in my chest.

Maybe we could fix this world, after all. And maybe, if we couldn't, we could at the very least make ourselves comfortable in it.

INTERLUDE TWO

The little boy grinned as he saw water spill over from the class sink, carefully taking the large container it dripped into and hoisting it up. He was careful while pouring it out to be measured and moved through the simple arithmetic of calculating its new volume in almost no time at all. Mathematics had never been something to learn for him. It was simply a thing he'd done, requiring no more focus than breathing.

He showed every stage of the process, of course, eager to ensure that his discovery was well understood and observed. It was exciting enough to simply share with his classmates, but the boy cared far more about teaching them how to replicate it, letting them awe themselves by using the very same method. He'd expected grins, giggles, the bright eyes of dawning understanding. What he got instead were bored frowns, skeptical glares, and sneering laughter.

They asked him, with no excess of friendliness, what he was even doing. The boy paused, attempting to explain how one could work out the amount of space an object occupied by the volume of water it forced out of the sink. How it was a form of three-dimensional measurement more precise than would otherwise be possible.

"What's the point of knowing that?"

The boy blinked, eyeing the girl who'd asked. It was Lois. She was among the biggest in their class, a head taller than most of the girls and any of the boys, with a mean streak to match her size. She'd never liked him, and he'd never quite understood why. He found himself confused at her response, frowning as he answered.

"It lets you . . . build things. You know, you can work out how heavy something will be before you even make it. Work out what things are made of, too, by—"

"You can just ask an adult for that, idiot." She laughed. Several of the others joined in, and the boy felt his temper flashing.

"Adults don't know this," he snapped.

That only brought on a new chorus of laughter, and a new volley of derision.

"Of course they do."

"They don't know, but you worked it out?"

"Just making things up to try and impress people."

"You're a weirdo."

He'd heard it all before, heard it all often, but something about the taunting irked the boy more today. Irked him past his ability for self-control. He started crying, tears coming against his will, body trembling as its tiny frame was racked by emotions too big for it to support.

The teachers were soon called, of course, and he spent much of the remaining day alone, sitting isolated outside of class and far from the taunts of his classmates. That was fine by him. The boy had never much enjoyed being around others to begin with, and each time he made an attempt it only ended . . . well, ended in much the same way his most recent attempt had.

But such things gnaw at a child, and he soon found himself wondering whether the problem was him. He was left to his concerns right up until the day ended, and he was given leave to return home.

The boy lived in a small house, but it had always been comfortable to him. Interior cramped by the thick spread of engine parts, tools, and raw materials. On one table, a screwdriver shared precipitously finite space with a homemade, impro-vised welding torch. Another housed a large cutting tool made from scratch with the power of a car battery and tungsten thread. It was all familiar to him, all comfort-ing, even. The boy had never liked open spaces. He headed promptly for his mother.

As was often the case, she was working in her own space, a little desk tucked away in the living room lit by directional lamplight and packed with material. Her art had always been good, exceptional even, near-photorealism since she'd hit puberty, though her career in the craft had been short lived. People had not been interested in the work of a woman who spoke like her and came from where she had, not when she'd pursued it. She didn't look up as her son entered, keeping her sharp features aimed at the page before her. Only when a tiny, slight sniffle escaped the boy did she eye him, recognizing instantly the feelings he'd spent the better part of a day burying. She was kneeling beside him in an instant.

"What's the matter?" she demanded, not touching him as she spoke. Never that. The boy had never enjoyed contact with others, and he'd inherited the trait maternally. Her hands hovered around him, orbiting without grazing, conveying without contacting. It didn't leave him feeling any less comfort than might an embrace.

As sobs threatened to reemerge, he told her. It was a small incident, without doubt, and yet he was only nine years old. Such things are enlarged to the mind of a child, and more so to this one. His had always been a brain to exaggerate the tiniest of trivialities and make fleas into dragons. That was maternal, too.

"It's alright," the boy's mother soothed. "It's alright, you're home now. Cheer up, eh? How about we go out for something to eat later. Would you like that?"

Sniffing and nodding, he muttered a barely audible confirmation that he would, glancing up at his mother to find her face creased with worry and . . . something else.

"But you know . . . this isn't going to stop happening."

He froze, tears almost dragged free once more at the very idea.

"This is what people do. The nail that sticks out gets hammered down. You're different from them, different in a way they don't understand, and don't want to. Maybe different in a way they couldn't understand even if they tried. You're . . . You're not one of them. They know it, and you need to know it, too. Trying to please them, impress them, amuse them— You're just painting a target on your back."

Despite the gentleness of her tone, the boy was not comforted. Despite the harshness of her claims, he was not hurt. He only nodded. Even at his young age, his mind was advanced enough to see the truth in what she said.

Among adults, he'd found himself comfortable in conversation, but they always treated him like a simpleton, like they might a normal child. Among children, his body and age matched, but the boy could never understand how they enjoyed what they did, or how he knew what they didn't. It seemed to him that nowhere in all the world was a match for him, and that fewer places still wanted him.

Lip trembling, he nodded, and his mother finally touched him. Not much, just a fleeting thing, a graze of fingertips against hair. It was the exact amount of contact she'd calculated would put the both of them most at ease. She had calculated correctly, of course, for the boy's mind was not so far beyond what hers had been at his age. It was this that gave her the most sympathy.

"Listen, you need to learn not to care. Understand? You need to just . . . accept that you're not like them . . . Do you remember what I told you about playing cards?"

The boy nodded, his memory as flawless then as it would be for the rest of his life, retrieving the relevant information with all the photographic accuracy of his mother's art.

"The only way to avoid people trying to cheat you is by playing on your own."

She smiled, and nodded.

"Good boy. Now let's go and get something to eat, my little Solitaire."

A ring, wide and well-defined, occupied by two children sparring with blunted foils and sweat-sodden faces. Their eyes were narrowed with concentration, jaws tight with exertion, minds occupied entirely by the fight.

Neither had reached puberty quite yet, the older boy eleven, the younger merely ten. Their ages were close enough that talent was the bigger separator between them than development, and it was the smaller boy who pushed back his elder. Thin metal rang against thin metal, rattling haphazardly out into the air once or twice per second. Each time the sound rang, the older boy was forced back another step. An untrained eye might mistake their bout for some practiced choreography, but such an illusion came only from their preternatural skill.

Were either of these boys to die, the one who remained living would have indisputable claim to the title of Earth's foremost fencing genius.

An unexpected twist sent one sword an inch farther left than was anticipated by its opponent, and the resulting block came milliseconds too late to keep it from slipping past. Metal flexed, a blunt tip struck a shoulder, and the touch was called. Both boys stepped back, taking their helmets off to reveal grinning, gap-toothed faces.

"You were close this time," the younger of them said and laughed, shaking his brother's hand as they'd both been taught to do after a win. His brother shook back, mirroring his smile.

"Closer every time, I think." It was a lie, and they both knew it, but the younger of them was far too kind to correct such things. "Fancy another go?" he asked, eagerly.

His brother was not free to spar often, which only ever left him with their instructor, Derek. Derek had been an Olympian once, though never countable among the best, and despite his years having long since advanced past fifty, he was still spry enough that it was a rare day for either boy to even graze him. The youngest of them was certain he'd surpass their mentor eventually, but there was little satisfaction to be found in handily losing to an opponent twice one's size.

"I think I'm up for it," the elder grinned, then glared as Derek stepped forward.

"No, you're done for the day," the old man cut in, coolly, rigidly. There was never any arguing with him when his voice got like that. The boys had learned that long ago.

"I feel fine," the elder snapped, trying anyway. Nothing came of it, of course, and a muscle jumped in his jaw as he glared up at their instructor. "Let me show you."

Some time passed before the boy finally agreed to take a rest, and he moved to the side of the ring. He'd grown energetic in his arguing, moving around, pacing, and hopping—developing a body not quite able to master the adrenal energy infusing it in the wake of his fight. In most children, such a thing wouldn't have been any real concern. The elder was not most children.

His heart seized, a sudden, choking pain that squeezed his chest into agonized spasms and had him strangled by the very air in his throat. He dropped down to his knees, trembling and gasping, and in an instant his brother and tutor were by his side.

He lived, of course. His family was well aware of his condition, and well prepared to keep him safe in spite of it. When the boy's eyes next opened, they came to rest on his bed, his stabilizing medical equipment, and his little brother asleep by his side. It must have taken him some time to awaken, for the smaller child's slumber was deeply set and unshaking.

A weak heart was what his parents had described. Poor at pumping his blood, and getting poorer still as his body aged and his circulatory pathways lengthened. Some days he could be the athlete, dancing and fighting and wrestling. Others . . . Others he'd risk death in the attempt.

Days passed, then weeks, then years. The boys continued their training, just as they always had, but it became far scarcer. The elder's growing frame demanded ever more of his withering heart, and the tortured organ proved a match for the challenge less and less often. Eventually, it was a rare day in which he could spar for even so much as minutes.

"It's fine," he'd tell his younger brother, lying each time. "We all have our good luck and bad. At the very least, this is happening to me instead of you. You'll actually go places!"

Repeat a lie often enough and you might even convince yourself. The boy managed to lull himself into a near-acceptance of the bare, cruel facts of his life. Almost. He was thirteen now, and it still stung seeing his younger brother spar. The child was barely into the changes of puberty, but already he could beat Derek more often than not.

He never lost to his elder any more, not since the cruelties of life had kept him from his training. As one brother had grown enfeebled and sickly, however, the other seemed only to rise. Training like a maniac, driven on inexorably by the knowledge of his brother's illness. The younger tortured himself with his work, tearing the flesh from his palms, ripping muscles to pieces and reforging them into bands of wrought iron. More time passed.

Life is an unpredictable thing. Cruel and callous. Ironic. A brother died. The younger. He was walking home one morning when a car struck him, speeding dozens of miles per hour over the limit, impacting the child with such velocity and force as to leave no hope of survival. His hardened bones and musculature gave no real resistance against the ton of steel battering them.

His family and friends wept, snarling their regret and bitterness, and none more so than his elder. Even after years of chronic agony and invalidity, nothing could have prepared him for such a loss.

But, life is an unpredictable thing. Cruel and callous. And, above all, ironic. The younger brother's heart survived his accident, paramedics arriving soon enough to save his organs, if not his life. And it was put to good use.

In later years, the elder would come to consider the legality of his transplant. He was sure there were waiting lists for such things. He'd been skeptical, even, that his brother had been a valid donor—the child was, after all, a child. But, at the time he only accepted it. The surgery was a success, the recovery no harder than the condition he'd lived with for years, and at its end, he had a new chance.

But health and stability were of little comfort to him. He heard his little brother's voice on every breeze, saw his frame in every shadow. And, simply holding a sword again was a reminder that they would never again spar, no matter how long he lived. The elder had lived on where the younger had died, and the world had been robbed of its foremost genius.

He resolved to do whatever he could to make the most of his chance, and turn himself into whatever approximation of his more gifted sibling he could. If only to honor the sweet little boy he'd grown up with, whose smile had been as bright as a sunbeam.

The heir had made his father angry, and not for the first time. It was always something with the man, and usually something petty. This time, it was pettier than usual. He'd brought friends home.

It hadn't been in any intrusive way. Their house was big enough that the heir could keep his associates tucked away at one side and have no risk at all of them ever even encountering his father. By chance, however, the older man had come to speak with him, and in doing so seen the strangers present. Etiquette had kept him from protesting before them, but the moment they were gone, the heir received his father's displeasure.

"How could you be so stupid?"

He steeled himself against it, as usual. An accusation of stupidity was tame compared to the sorts he'd usually expect. His father didn't relent.

"Well, boy? How? What were you thinking?"

The heir knew, from many years of hard learning, that there was rarely a correct answer when replying to his father, and lots of wrong ones. He kept his silence most of the time for that reason. Being demanded an answer . . . That was a problem, because it meant he couldn't afford to safely avoid committing to any singular answer without having it interpreted as further insolence.

So, he thought. What was the most likely thing to diffuse this rage? He'd need to know what its cause was, first, but that wasn't hard to deduce. His father was endlessly fearful of others working against him.

"I wanted to see how they'd try to approach me, to learn how they might try to get close to me."

His father's eyes defrosted, just a shade, and he weighed his son with a new consideration. Thoughtful, perhaps a fraction impressed.

"And you didn't tell me first?"

"I didn't want to bother you with it."

That was perhaps a word too many, for his father's face tightened again.

"Always tell me before inviting snakes into my home, understand? You can experiment all you want with yourself, but not with me. You knew they were only here to slither close to you, to curry favor and gain wealth, and still you let them under my roof?"

The heir said nothing, simply awaiting his father's tirade to reach its end. It didn't take long. Fortunately, the old man had never been particularly skilled at sustaining any complex thought, and the anger he was venting out seemed enough of a contrivance to challenge him plenty. He was gone soon enough.

The heir didn't know what to do at that, already rather missing his friends. He didn't get to see them often. They went to school, he didn't. They were permitted to go outside at all hours, he wasn't. The heir of his father's "empire" was too important for such things, his mind demanding tutorship like a sword demanded sharpening. On some days, he might have spent the hours with his brother, Taiwo, but the boy was far less restrained by their patriarch than the heir, and was nowhere around. And so he simply wandered, idle and thoughtless, until his lessons next began.

The next day, his father took him to some insubstantial meeting or another among the executives of his company. It was the first time the heir had ever attended one, but his father insisted that fifteen was more than old enough. He was seated in one corner to watch in silence—always in silence—while it all unfolded.

The heir watched, accustomed to doing so, and learned. And when at last the event was over, his father took him to one side and asked him what he'd seen. He answered him, impressed him, and listened to him as the man tried to offer fleeting insights into his own genius. It was infuriating.

His father was not an unintelligent person, but his mind was semi-remarkable at best. His ascension in class had been luck and dedication more than native genius. Like so many powerful men, however, he'd convinced himself he was one of the world's greats, and became desperate to model his cleverest son in his image.

Well, the heir would let him have what he wanted, for a while at least. It would lubricate the churning gears of his life more effectively than anything else. That was one thing he'd learned from his father, intentional or not.

Working people was often about surrender and a deft-handed touch. Perhaps he would gain something from their lessons one day.

The years went by, the days bled together. He found his life growing lethargic and stagnant, sluggish and still. There were very few things in need of doing, for one born to even half as much wealth as him. Motivation came through necessity, and necessity was never assassinated as completely as by excess. He moved around, flitting from place to place, ever absorbing the languages and cultures of all the areas his father's tendrils of capital touched.

After a while, the world became a small thing. It was rare for the heir to remain in the same place as long as a fortnight before being whisked off to some meeting or deal occurring elsewhere on the globe, and he continued in this state for some time. He did not have the opportunity to make friends, and was increasingly kept from uniting with those he already had.

The one constant, though, was bigotry. It was the great shadow lurking over any black man born in Africa, omnipresent across the earth and omnipotent in its ability to move others. It is one thing to have melanin in the skin and curls in the hair, but quite another to be African. The heir learned just this fact through a thousand miserable lessons.

One day, though, things changed. The heir had started to reach the end of his growing, and at last he was given a permanent assignment by his father. Or a long-term one, at the very least. He was to settle in one of several properties within America, ever the seat of all their family's most profitable jewels, and manage it himself. He would be counted, immediately, among the most powerful men within the company, and granted a level of autonomy touched by few others.

Pure nepotism, of course. The heir was gifted, ingenious even, and vastly experienced through the unique diligence and exertive lessons granted during his childhood. Nonetheless, he would have received no such offer were he not of his father's blood, and he knew it. He accepted regardless, settling in a city of his choice, and then something strange happened.

With an address finally cemented, he found his friends speaking to him more frequently. Then, eventually, visiting. Within a month he was meeting with two of his oldest friends, and within the next they all lived together. Free time stretched out for all of them, with the heir's own wealth and excess now extended past the scope of necessity by his father. They interacted, they joked, they felt all the grating rust of long estrangement falling away.

And one day, they began to speak with one another about writing a book.

CHAPTER FIFTY-SEVEN

Shango's POV: Day 55
Current Wealth: 2 gold, 31 silver, 47 copper

The villagers had given us a bit of food for the road, and we were grateful for it. Not as grateful as we were for the carriage, though.

It wasn't to keep, of course. They didn't have so many that they could afford to let us do that—they didn't have more than one, in fact—but we were allowed to ride along as they sent out their first venture to try to buy some of the resources needed to help them rebuild. Henri was the one driving it, the old man who'd first called on us to defend Rinchester. Somehow that felt appropriate. Appropriate, and . . . satisfying.

He still had that bottomless sadness to him, maybe always would, but there was a certain hope to the old man now that uplifted me. He was seated, steering, in the front, happily chatting away with us all as we made our way out of town.

Unexpectedly, the Vittonian woman seemed to have gotten rather comfortable alongside us already. I imagined that had something to do with the impression we'd made, but part of it was surely just her general . . . hardiness. I'd met soft people before. One tended to do a lot of that when one *was* a soft person, and she was on the opposite end of that spectrum, reminding me of Solitaire or Beam. Adaptable, practical, malleable. It was a good trait to find in someone I'd be entrusting to fight alongside me, and it didn't go unappreciated.

The cold was still an ever-present thing of course, but even that felt like it'd abated. Perhaps our ever-strengthening bodies were just more resilient, or perhaps it was the magical, emotional glow of knowing we'd made the world a better place. Perhaps it was the extra blankets. Either way, things were looking up.

Oh, who was I kidding. It was definitely the blankets, and it was definitely the magical toughness. A bout of heroics was one thing, but I'd sooner die than catch myself being *poetic* about it. And I didn't exactly need to be for that moral satisfaction to keep filling me up.

But our journey was days long, and the woods were far less densely packed by rotters after we'd thinned the horde by some few hundred. It seemed likely the vampire's death had dispersed them for good, and if not, we weren't entirely worried at the prospect of fighting those that were left after strengthening ourselves so much and weakening their little army. This gave us plenty of time to think.

Think and worry.

Well, being fair, we actually didn't have *that much* to worry about. We were well funded-ish, and had about two hundred fifty extra kilos of muscle to back us up on the off chance that our flawless ethics and persuasive arguments failed to move any more natives. But there were a lot of factors to consider before we started expanding more.

Namely, the simple split between brute force and chemistry.

"We have the money for sulphur, for anything now. I can make us shit you wouldn't even believe," Solitaire insisted, more eager than I'd have liked. Even as a kid he'd spoken the same way about explosives and incendiaries, and it was more than I could take now that the topic had moved onto using them on living breathing *people*.

Quite apart from that, I wasn't certain about the rationality of it.

"Being known as people who can do that might bring unwanted trouble, and I'm not sure it's the most cost-effective way of producing weapons anyway," I countered. "You did say you'd only be able to make a few kilos of gunpowder with all the money we had, right? How often are we going to be getting into big enough fights to justify the price?"

It felt quite simple, framed as a business decision, and I was still awaiting Solitaire's answer when Helena cut in.

"Wait, you're not actual wizards?"

I eyed her, and Solitaire laughed.

"You heard the vampire talking about us using foreign alchemy," he noted. She didn't seem amused.

"Foreign alchemy is magic, no?"

"No," he replied, with alarming patience. "No more than cooking is. When you mix certain things in certain conditions, they can change their very substance, combining or separating. Some of these combinations have effects that neither of the smaller parts do. Think of it like mixing fire and ice, if you want. Neither one is a liquid, but combining them lets you produce something that is."

That got a thoughtful look from her, and I allowed myself a moment to admire Solitaire's explanation. For all his talk of being the poor, tortured genius surrounded by plebeian ape men, he could certainly simplify things when he needed to.

"Can we get back to the argument?" I prodded, and Solitaire jumped into speech again like a spring being released.

"Right, yes. You're wrong and stupid. Let me explain why." He cleared his throat. "I'm going to make a gun."

I paused, eyed him, and felt my excitement growing.

"Before you ask, it's not going to be an automatic weapon, but it's also not going to just be a dumbass muzzle-loader either. Should manage a fire rate of thirty to sixty rounds per minute if it works out. Though, I'll probably need a blacksmith to actually make the components."

I wasn't much good at thinking through numbers, but even I could picture how rapid that sort of fire rate was compared to the bows we'd been getting used to. More to the point, Solitaire had made it abundantly clear over the years how deadly a supersonic chunk of lead was compared to virtually any man-powered weapon.

"Alright then," I conceded and sighed. "We'll start working on a gun."

Solitaire grinned, Beam eyed him uncertainly, and Argar and Helena just looked confused. I was actually looking forward to seeing their reactions to the weapon once it was finally made.

The last leg of our journey breezed by quickly enough, with more casual conversation as we familiarized ourselves with our new member and went over some of the highlights from our most recent fight. Beam was perhaps the loudest, repeatedly ensuring that we were vividly aware he had, in fact, beaten up and killed a vampire. I almost wished he'd lost just so the smug bastard would keep quiet about it.

One early morning, we were back at the city of Wolney. Carriage rattling up to its front gate, awkward and shaky as any we'd ridden. This time, though, the guards halted us.

"Names?" one of them asked. I answered, and the man paused. "I don't believe you have clearance to be inside the city today."

"Clearance?" I asked, genuinely confused. There'd been no need for clearance the last time we came here. The man only nodded, distractedly.

"Clearance, sir," he replied. "New gate watch I'm afraid."

That left a sour taste in my mouth, but I pushed it back. "Well . . . can I speak with your boss, or . . . Perhaps we can work another arrangement out?"

I didn't want to part with any of our newly claimed money, but if it meant getting inside, it didn't seem I had much choice.

The man hesitated, then nodded. "Yes, one moment sir." He disappeared into the walls, and wasn't gone even a second before Solitaire spoke.

"He's going to try to kill us." I rolled my eyes, and Solitaire slammed a fist down into the carriage. "No, fuck you! He's going to. Listen to me for once, please."

Solitaire was speaking fast, tongue tripping over itself, eyes wide. I recognized all the signs of an encroaching paranoia attack and knew in an instant that there wasn't much anyone could do to talk him down from it. I forced myself calm, meeting his eye to let him focus on me.

"Alright, sorry. I'm willing to listen at least. Why do you think that?"

"He recognized us," Solitaire said, instantly, "and he's afraid. He knows who we are, knows what we can do, and knows that we'll be inclined to kill him. He's gone off to tell someone—probably the person who told him to watch out for us— that we've finally turned up. Mark my words, he'll be back with a . . . an army, or a gang, or something."

I did my best to pick out each word from the syllabic soup he was spewing out, and considered them. When Solitaire said he saw something in a person— emotion or deception—he wasn't *usually* wrong. Whatever you could say about the conclusions he'd draw, his actual observed information was generally good, which made this worth looking into, at least. I didn't know about some ambush, but I could believe the guard had recognized us. His behavior had felt stilted to me, too.

"I could scale the wall," Beam offered. "Peer over the top, see what he comes back with."

"Yes," Solitaire pressed. "The barracks is hundreds of meters from the gate. You'll see them coming from miles off."

I considered it, but not for long. There weren't that many reasons not to.

"Just don't slip and die," I advised my friend. Beam smiled, hurrying to the wall and scaling it.

Just a precaution, just a safeguard, just a way of helping Solitaire ground himself for however long his newest spike of neurosis took to run its course. Nothing was going to come of it.

It came as quite a surprise when Beam dropped down thirty feet, landed in the snow with a grunting thud that I can only guess would've broken something when he'd first arrived here, and hurried to the carriage.

"It's fucking Corvan," he snapped. "The guard is coming with Corvan. We need to go! We need to fucking go right now!"

Well, that put some wind under our heels.

Solitaire babbled about how right he was, how stupid we all were, and how it was our fault a big, evil wizard was going to vaporize us. To his credit, he was quick in working even while he did, ordering the carriage around. The old man seemed to trust us enough not to hesitate, and we were lurching along quickly, mules lashed and dragging us along almost as fast as a man could sprint.

"How far was he?" Solitaire snapped at Beam. Our friend thought for an agonizingly long moment before replying.

"A few hundred meters, maybe—maybe three?"

Solitaire cursed. "Three minutes, then, we'll be half a mile away if we're lucky. He might catch us if he has his own mount tethered nearby."

A silence fell, all of us realizing that only luck would keep him from catching up to us. How had the bastard survived? Stupid question. Obviously he was more jumpy and quicker than we'd expected. How had he found us?

Again, stupid. We'd headed straight to the nearest city.

I cursed my own stupidity, my own laxness, even as I felt the wind picking up as we accelerated, tearing along into the snow. Where could we go? Where to?

"Elswick," Solitaire growled. "Random city plucked from my mind. Do you know where it is?" His question was for the old man, who looked back at him, fearful, and nodded.

"What's happening?" he asked.

"Something very dangerous," I replied. "But not something that we don't have a chance of getting away from. Hurry on."

Without another word, he did.

CHAPTER FIFTY-EIGHT

Solitaire's POV: Day 61
Current Wealth: 2 gold, 23 silver, 41 copper

We'd ditched the old man the first chance we got, and it'd been for his own good. We'd made our exit at some no-name town we passed and rented ourselves some new transport. A nicer carriage, this time, or rather a faster one, pulled by proper horses. Including the food we'd bought, it hadn't set us back that much either.

Man, it really did feel nice to actually have money.

Even still, money didn't do everything, not in the volumes we had at least. It took us more than a few days to actually reach our newest destination, and the shivering, miserable travel experience was just perfect for worsening our already jagged moods.

So much so, in fact, that I didn't even notice we'd been here for over two months already. Two months. Was that really it? It felt so . . . short, so inconsequential, so fleeting. If two months had changed us all as much as this, what might another two years do? I buried the thought. Unless it turned me into a magus-proof dragon, I really couldn't afford to consider the possibilities.

Elswick reared up on the horizon, and within a half day we were there. The place was odd, its walls taller than Wolney's, its gates more thickly built. Despite that, we didn't actually have much issue getting through them.

"We're safe," Shango breathed, as we passed beneath an absurdly big portcullis. I hesitated, shrugging.

"We're safer," I decided. Truth be told, I wasn't certain the magus wouldn't just *guess* which city we'd headed to next, but at the very least he'd be working on random chance now. And if he tried to move in on the other city nearest

Wolney—Ghinddra—then he'd be costing himself an extra few days. We'd be safe for a week, at worst, and probably longer.

Probably. Always something, always that niggling little uncertainty. I could already feel the well-oiled gears of logical leaps and deductive aggression preparing to start grinding away again inside my head, a master-crafted clockwork of paranoia and violence.

No, not paranoia, fuck them. I'd been right, which made it cleverness. Perhaps I ought to remind everybody again.

Perhaps not. I'd spent enough of our journey smugly going on about that fact already.

Past the walls, Elswick wasn't actually that much different from Wolney. Its streets were more uniform, maybe, but they were still overwhelmingly shit-sodden and packed with human traffic. The scent of life was pungent on the air, watering our eyes while it told a similar tale of inequality in the architecture and infrastructure. This time we didn't bother with the higher class areas. We just made our way straight for the poorer ones. We had a very particular goal in mind, after all.

Beam and Shango split off to find me a suitable workspace, and I made my way into the city in search of a suitable magic instructor. Honestly, I was annoyed by the job, even knowing I was by far the best for it given my previous attempt, but that irritation didn't last long at all. Because the second magus I approached was the very same woman I'd finally agreed to learn from in Wolney.

"It's you," she said, blinking rapidly, just as I resisted the urge to knife her in the eye. It was a coincidence, I guessed, and that guess turned into certainty as I read the genuine surprise on her face. If Corvan had brought her over, or told her to watch out for us, she'd not have been shocked to see me.

"Hello again," I managed, hiding how close she'd come to being turned into a new coat of red paint for the ground. In my experience, that tended to bother people.

"What are you doing here?" The magus frowned. "You're . . . You followed me for lessons?"

"I came here to set up a few things," I replied. "Lessons being among them, but I didn't follow you. It's just a strange coincidence that we're both here."

She nodded, not seeming particularly concerned with the matter, in any case, and moved back to the work she'd been doing. Some weird alignment of glowing crystals, the sort of thing I might've once described just to give a magus something to idly do to remind the reader of a given scene that they were magic.

"So you are here for lessons then?" she guessed. I nodded.

"How much are they going to set me back?" The woman raised her eyebrows, chewing a lip thoughtfully.

"I'll be frank with you. I don't think you can afford them. Five silver a day at a minimum, more likely closer to ten."

It was a gut punch, but not unanticipated. We'd always made magic prohibitively exclusive in Redacle. It'd been one of the ways we'd explained warfare not devolving into a "having the most magi" contest.

"And what is that dependent upon?" I tried. She didn't even glance at me.

"How gifted you are," she replied. "Whether you're gifted enough to learn at an appreciable rate. Most aren't."

I knew that already, of course, being the magic system's writer. I considered the facts, then sighed.

"I'll take a lesson today then, if you're available. So long as you don't retroactively decide it costs more than ten silver."

She eyed me, thought about it, then sighed and nodded. "Alright, fine. Wait there for a few minutes while I finish this."

I did, and fortunately, she was quick about it. We began our lesson.

Oddly enough, a lot of it was *new* to me. We'd always preferred powerful, established characters in our stories, my friends and me, which meant that we'd not directed much time to writing about the early learning process. I got to see it all, essentially, for the first time.

She had me focus on recreating the feeling from my initial test, at first. Apparently, the early practices were best done immediately following it for this reason, to ensure that as little was lost from the expensive testing before the actual training began. Fortunately, my memory meant that she might as well have waited mere seconds. I stretched my mind back to those old feelings—the buzzing, the energy, the sensation of being swarmed by hornets. It all came easily enough, probably in no small part thanks to the striking discomfort of it all, and I used it well.

Within a few hours I was consistently making little beads of light between my hands, and the magus was gaping at me as if I'd just benched a mountain range. Too late, I realized, the gifts we'd been given on transit to this world might just have leaned into other areas as impressively as they did our own personal powers.

"How well did I do?" I asked, feigning uncertainty. She didn't answer for a second, just kept staring.

"I've . . . never even heard of someone who picked magic up this fast, not even half as fast. Even Zekitan the Great wasn't conjuring light until his tenth hour of study."

I was hasty in replying. "Well, you know, some people are better at different stages than others—"

"No," she cut in. "Not the basics, not the actual act of learning. That's designed by hand to test your general aptitude. You . . . Fuck."

I eyed the woman in silence, waiting to see what she'd do with the information. If she decided it needed to be shared, that would be a problem. We needed to avoid the kind of attention this would bring until we were strong enough to at least take care of ourselves, but . . .

No, she wasn't. I could see a lot of things on her face, a lot of ideas in her eyes, but not that. This one seemed more concerned than anything.

"Who else has seen you try magic?" she asked.

I resisted the urge to grin. "Nobody, yet."

It was that "yet" that had her practically flinching, and I pressed on to seize my momentum.

"I'm guessing you're smart enough to realize what sort of advantage this might bring to you," I noted. "Training me, I mean. The most gifted magus . . . ever, perhaps? An absurdly talented one, at least. So how about we arrange a new deal. Train me now, for free, and in a decade or two, when I'm one of the strongest magi alive, I guarantee I'll keep you comfortable. You can leech off me whether I become some king's court magus, a general's secret weapon, or just decide to make my own home somewhere remote . . . I have always *wanted* a floating tower."

She was considering it, and that was good. I decided to press her before her thoughts could harden.

"I mean we both know I'll be going somewhere. It's essentially a guarantee, and even if you don't agree to this, there's plenty of other magi who might, right?"

That sealed the deal, the knowledge that she'd accidentally given up her own exclusivity. The moment I found out how gifted I actually was, every magus in the city became a potential source of free training, and she knew it.

By the speed with which she spoke next, I could tell she wasn't confident in out-bidding them in that regard. "I want one thousand gold a year in twenty years," she replied, hastily.

I pretended to think about it, then sighed. "Nine hundred."

Her eyes narrowed. "You're pretending to bargain so I'll think I managed to talk you back up to a thousand and feel like I won, aren't you?"

God, I did like this one. Shango was still quicker, for sure, but I'd only met a few geniuses of her speed in my life. And they'd all been back home, with brain matter that hadn't adapted to deal with a scarcity of protein and energy.

"You got me," I shrugged. "People are usually less likely to chafe at something if they think it's their idea or doing."

She glared at me, but only for a second, her look melting into an irritated sigh. "Very well then," she acquiesced. "I agree. To a thousand."

"Brilliant." I grinned. "Then let's get started."

CHAPTER FIFTY-NINE

Beam's POV: Day 61
Current Wealth: 2 gold, 23 silver, 41 copper

We had a budget of about one gold, according to Shango. That ought to have been enough to rent a long-term place suitable for us. In fact, he assured me that he didn't intend to spend anywhere near that much on it. That was a relief because I really didn't want to see nearly half our money disappear all over again.

The two of us made our way through the city with Argar and Helena at our backs, figuring that the pair of muscle-bound giants might make any arguments we saw fit to throw a bit more *persuasive*. We'd begun to get a knack for navigating the nauseating city design that was so common for this world. Even so, it took us a while before we actually made it to our first potential property. We had needed to ask around until we found one that was for rent. I really did miss the internet.

It was a warehouse, sort of. Small and squat, feeling like it'd been cross-bred with a storage closet. Its owner was some old guy, who didn't look exactly pleased to see us, but whose attitude brightened up immediately once we held out our coin. His eyes expanded to almost the size of his head as he eyed the gold piece flitting between Shango's fingers.

"I'll give it to you for a month," the man said quickly, "for that gold."

Shango smiled. "You're not getting this gold off me, first of all," he replied. "I'm only showing it to you so you know we're not going to short you on whatever money we end up owing. I assume you'd have just asked us to anyway if I hadn't?"

The man glared and gave a fraction of a nod.

"Good. Then what's your *actual* offer?" Shango asked. "And before you say anything, let me just point out that I've already figured out you don't even use this dwarf warehouse of yours. I'm guessing you bought it last minute a while ago to meet a sudden influx of required space, right? It's far enough from your other properties that it'd just lose you money to have it alongside them, and the fact that you've not managed to sell it tells me that I'm not exactly looking at premium land here. So, what would you like for a month of its use?"

If his jaw had tightened any more, the man's teeth might've cracked. He took a few seconds to think before replying to Shango's observations, which gave me plenty of time to be nice and impressed by my friend.

"Twenty silver," he said at last.

Shango snorted. "That's absurd, you're asking for more than . . ." He hesitated, thinking, not as good as Solitaire when it came to math. ". . . thirty copper a day?"

"I don't get thirty copper a day for smashing open heads," Argar cut in, volunteering the information as if it were merely some interesting little piece of trivia. He crossed his arms as he said it, sleeve tugging back slightly to reveal a bicep that looked more categorically akin to the component of some giant engine than a piece of anatomy.

The man paled.

"Six silver," he said at last. "Final offer."

Shango looked for just a second like he might argue, or simply walk away, but in the end he sighed. "It's not your final offer, is it?" he asked. "Your final offer would be next to nothing, given that you're earning no coin at all from the place."

The man opened his mouth to argue, then Shango spoke over him.

"Deal anyway. Consider it a show of goodwill."

His surprise was matched only by my own, but I knew better than to say anything about it. The man, likewise, only paused, blinked, then nodded before managing a strained, gruff "Thank you," as if eager to regain some kind of control. His eyes hardened as he followed up with a demand. "I'll be having my rent up front, first of every month."

"Of course." Shango smiled, placidly. "Here you are." He handed a few coins over, which seemed to have the man about as disoriented as if Argar had just leaned over and punched him in the head.

That had always been how Shango did things, though. When someone tried to square their feet and push against him, he'd simply step back. Offer no resistance, let them fall over themselves in the attempt. People couldn't take control of what was just handed to them; he'd explained it all once before.

I'd known his methods, but I'd not really seen them that often. Every time I did, it was a sharp reminder that Solitaire wasn't the only genius in my friend group. Scary.

Our new landlord was gone soon, and I followed Shango into the building. The atmosphere inside hit us like a wall of frozen shit, its stench so strong and concentrated that it was almost a physical thing. My eyes watered instantly as I strained them to examine the interior with the aid of a few beams of light pouring in from its open door.

Shango was the first of us to regain his bearings, surveying the place with about as much neutrality as could've been expected. I joined him.

It was perhaps three hundred square feet, with a ceiling just barely tall enough that the giga-troll we'd fought could've stood up straight. Rats scurried around as the light hit them, dirty and, well, rat-like, and the air was so clotted by debris that I could actually see it as ant-sized particulates in the sun.

"Glad to see you'll be getting your money's worth," Argar said with a chuckle. "Looks like a right perfect place to be saving the world from."

Shango glared at him, an evil look seeping into his eyes. "I know," he sighed. "It's far from perfect. Fortunately, we have our loyal warriors to clean it up a bit in preparation for Solitaire to work his magic."

Argar swore, and Helena only eyed Shango, suddenly looking . . . jagged.

"You are not going to make me clean rat shit out of a building," she told him, as if it were a bare statement of fact.

My friend tilted his head, weighing her. "You wanted to help us, didn't you?"

"Help you," Helena snapped, "fight for you, protect you, and make some change in this world. *Not* shovel literal shit."

Shango's face flashed with the ghost of a smile, just for an instant, then it was buried.

"So you think it's beneath you?"

She glared, and he continued.

"Solitaire shoveled shit, you know, to make his explosives. He spent the better part of a day—"

"Fine," the Vittonian snapped, glaring harder. "Fine, you made your fucking point. Happy? I'll help clear it up."

Shango smiled. "Beam, you're still working on your magic, right?" he asked. I answered with a nod, and he looked thoughtful. "Right. Well, keep doing that. I think I'm going to give my own a bit of a go."

He'd spent much of our journeys doing just that, but hadn't quite discovered anything new yet. I found myself suspecting that maybe there *wasn't* anything new for him. I kept it to myself, regardless, not wanting to ruin his apparent good mood.

For the last few days, I'd been testing my own powers, too. Learning the ins and outs. The major limit I'd uncovered was that, apparently, I could not give my weapons nor my armor to other people. Not in any practical sense. Once I let go of one, it didn't take long for it to disperse entirely, which meant that at best I could arm an ally for seconds. That might find its use anyway. Argar with a big axe or such made with the same magic as my sword might well take trees down with a few swings, but it wouldn't let us outfit an entire company with magic gear or anything.

That sparked a thought.

"When do you think we'll be able to get our hands on some proper armor?" I asked Shango, glancing at Helena and Argar. She had something, at least, albeit nothing more than some thick woolen gear I'd been told was called a gambeson. Argar was practically walking around in normal clothes, and I didn't trust his skin to stave off a blade as well as it had Solitaire's teeth.

My friend seemed equally convinced, sighing.

"Twenty gold or so will get us a full suit of plate armor. Maybe . . . Uh, maybe twenty-five for us, given our sizes."

My heart fell, but Shango pat my shoulder and said, "It's not as hard as it sounds. I mean, Solitaire's building us a fucking gun, right?"

That did lift my spirits a bit, given that it was, in fact, a fucking gun he was talking about. I nodded and almost left it at that.

"I just want you all to be safe," I managed, not meeting my friend's eye, suddenly awkward at the admission. "Putting a bit of steel around you would help with that, not that I intend on anything or anyone laying a finger on you under my watch anyway."

Shango nodded.

"We've got our feet under us now," he promised me. "Things will get better soon, but for now . . . Well, first off, we need work." He sighed, turning to Helena. "You're literate, right?" She nodded, seeming surprised to be asked, and Shango was quick to continue. "Then come with me. We're going to go and look for some work."

CHAPTER SIXTY

I was pleasantly surprised to find Argar and Helena had done most of the shit-shoveling when I arrived at my new laboratory. Really, the entire conversation I'd had when Beam approached me to explain the situation before I went inside was an emotional rollercoaster. Rage first, upon hearing about the state of the interior, then relief upon finding out that it was being taken care of already. Finally, a certain pragmatic satisfaction. I'd be needing shit, after all, and having some gathered already was convenient if nothing else.

The sight of Helena, the rather attractive woman that she was, disgusting herself with the work of moving it around was just icing on the cake. But I moved past that quickly, sadly far too busy to indulge my lust.

By the time I'd gotten back, the job was mostly done already, and Shango had set off on a shopping trip. I found that much out from Helena, who'd accompanied him on his other outing to find us some work. Obviously having my interest piqued by that fact, I asked her for more details.

There was work in Elswick, as we'd hoped, and there was more of it than anywhere we'd been yet. The city had been having some issues with locals. Nothing major, really, nothing awful. Just a few thousand tribal orcs causing trouble for the humans with raiding parties. I grinned.

Where there was conflict, there was money to be made for resolving it, and orcs were tough. Bigger than humans, taller and stronger by far. Helena told me how they had been growing more intense, not less, over the months since it really started, and I believed her. This was a problem that could continue pricking the city's nobility for some time, which meant it was an excellent source of revenue for us.

But I was getting ahead of myself; we needed actual killing ability first. Magic was nice and all, but it was a slow process to actually learn it. Biggest prodigy in history and, so far, I was just about capable of simulating the effects of a flickering lightbulb. That wouldn't be the most effective weapon against a giant, gray-skinned barbarian, so we'd need to look into other means. Fortunately, Shango was back soon after we finished shoveling the mess out of the warehouse, carrying with him all my heart could desire.

Big vials and mixing glasses, an alembic, mortar and pestles, mixing buckets, and other things. We'd discussed the equipment I might need on our way to the city, of course. Although a lot of medieval alchemy was complete bullshit, a good portion of the things devised to help mix materials for it were pretty on point.

I wouldn't be trying to turn my piss into gold, though. That would be absurd. Why do that when I could turn shit into gunpowder? That was where the money was at.

Well, the black powder was just step one, in any case. It wouldn't do us too much good on its own, but there were plenty of ways to mitigate its natural disadvantages.

Shrapnel was one of them, sort of. The use of ball bearings or other solid projectile fillings in hand-usable explosive devices goes back centuries, but there's a major fundamental issue with it when using black powder. Namely, black powder is weak as shit. If you want enough for a decent sized explosive, it gets heavy fast, and I wasn't entirely certain about where the magic balance between ineffectual weakness and enough weight that I couldn't throw it far enough to not be in the kill radius lay. It would be an interesting thing to experiment with, but later. There were productive things of more immediate value.

We set off while the shit was boiling—not actually a sentence that has *ever* been stranger to my vocabulary, mind you—and headed for a smith. It wasn't particularly hard to find one nearby. Our warehouse, like most, was in the city's "industrial sector," or it would've been if the city weren't owned by mud people who hadn't even discovered industry yet. Either way, finding an ape man who was good at folding metal didn't take us long.

The shop was a small thing, as were most in Redacle, and we were assailed by a blast of hot air and iron-scented winds as we entered. It was cramped inside, metal tools and fittings hanging from every surface, save for a single space near the center. About twenty square meters had been cleared out and were occupied by only three things—smithing equipment that was affixed to the ground and walls, a screaming-hot lump of metal, and a big, broad-shouldered man using both.

We watched for a few moments, seeing how he bullied the metal into shape with remarkable speed. I glanced at Shango and wasn't surprised when he nodded, silently mouthing the words *level eight* to me.

That made sense. Redacle, in the books, had had such things as legendarily forged weapons capable of cutting through chainmail. There'd always been smiths and craftsmen of supernatural skill, just as there'd always been warriors of superhuman strength. It seemed the mysterious system we were gaming reflected that with greater-than-one levels.

I cleared my throat to get the man's attention, and he replied without so much as glancing up.

"Not now," he answered. "Need to finish this piece before it cools again. First heating is best for flexibility."

Slightly put out, I nonetheless kept quiet while I waited for him to finish. It didn't take more than a minute or two, thankfully, and by the time the man was done, I just felt even more hopeful that he'd actually comprehend my design.

"Now, what do you want?" the man asked.

I took a step forward, taking the lead. Shango was good at fucking people over like a politician, sure, but when it came to matters of molecules and math, I didn't trust anyone alive more than myself.

"We need you to make something for us." I replied. "Obviously. Thing is, it's advanced. The reward you'll get for doing so is a design you can use yourself however you'd like, to sell or show off or shove up your ass if you want. But the first is just for us."

He didn't look impressed. Doubtless, plenty of people tried to sway one another with impossible offers all the time here. God knew they did enough of that back on earth.

"What's the request?" he asked. "And what design would I be paid with?"

"The design is for a sort of shifting mechanism designed to move an object and substance from one cylinder to another," I explained. "If you accept, I can draw it out for you on some paper. Your payment will be the designs for a repeating crossbow capable of firing thirty times in a minute."

I could see I had him enticed, and the man was careful in swallowing before replying. Obviously, he was sharp enough to at least *attempt* to hide his eagerness, which probably made him sharp enough not to be convinced yet.

"How can something like that work?" he challenged.

I shrugged. "It's obvious, really. Mostly it uses gravity. Would you like to see?"

The man hesitated, thought, came close to saying something before pausing, then sighed and nodded. "Show me."

He gave me parchment, a quill, and one chance to draw it all out. Fortunately, I used it well enough.

Now, being clear, I actually had no idea how to build a repeating crossbow. I knew they'd been used largely in China, and I knew what their approximate rate of fire was, but that was about it. Fortunately, it's not actually that difficult to work out how something would've worked, provided you know a few key details about its shape and function.

I knew, for example, that the Chinese version I was thinking of had a big box on top of it, which was my clue that it was probably packing a top-mounted magazine and that gravity was used to load it. From there, I just thought about the most logical and efficient ways to have the bowstring draw itself, to keep jams from occurring, to make it easy and smooth to detach one magazine for another. I thought as I drew, and continued drawing, even as my hand started to throb from the pressure of carving lines across tough animal hide.

By the time I was done, the blacksmith looked quite impressed, which impressed me in turn. He must've been piecing together the design as it came to me, reading over my shoulder. That was a sign that he was good at his job.

"I could just take this knowledge and make the design myself," he noted, "now that you've shown it to me. Even try to recreate my own. What's stopping me from doing that?"

I was ready for the question, of course. Ready, too, for him not to ask, which would've been a sure sign of his planning to do just that in secret.

"If you do that, I'll just sell it to every other smith I meet in the city, and then every other city. You'll lose the advantage of being first to produce it, and the only one to have hard schematics. I won't have near-exclusivity, but I'll have a lot of gold."

He weighed me, then sighed. "Alright, show me the second design."

This one was a bit harder, but not too difficult. Lots of axes and shifting piston mechanisms. I essentially needed to keep two separate cylinders for containing munitions—one for the actual solid projectiles, another for the powder. I ended up deciding on a design that worked—a sort of shifting chamber that would press open latches to let the contents of each spill into the main barrel—and drew it all out as clearly as I could manage.

Mr. Blacksmith wasn't as impressed this time, but I hadn't expected him to be. Even if he'd known what black powder was, which was doubtful, I'd be surprised if he was familiar with the idea of using it as a propellant. I might as well have shown him a smart phone for all his ability to comprehend.

"I can certainly make this," he noted with a frown. Clearly the poor bastard had been hoping for a simpler job. "Should take me . . . a week, perhaps."

A week was a lot quicker than I'd been expecting, but I hid my surprise. Evidently there were advantages to levelled craftsmen.

"Excellent," I said, grinning. "My brother can work out the specifics of pay and delivery." I gestured for Shango to do his thing, and he did.

We were moving back to our warehouse soon enough, finding Argar waiting outside—we had, of course, left the most advanced weapons' manufactory in the country at least *guarded* while we were out. His face was a mask of worry as we neared, however, and I immediately hurried to him.

"The thing," he gasped. "The thing you said would be happening in a few hours, it's already happening now."

I barged inside and found that, sure enough, crystals were lining the boiling cauldron we'd left.

But that was wrong. It hadn't been nearly long enough for potassium nitrate to crystalize, not long enough at all. And then I remembered that something had happened faster than anticipated last time, too.

My nasty, terrible, no-good, very bad computer of a brain started churning away like always.

CHAPTER SIXTY-ONE

Shango's POV: Day 61
Current Wealth: 2 gold, 11 silver, 41 copper

For a moment, Solitaire had on one of his freak-out faces, and I was about ready to try and hold him down with Beam before he could turn any nearby appliances into an improvised explosive. Old habits, of course. Given the technological disadvantage, it took him quite a lot more work to commit acts of terrorism in Redacle than it had back home, but even if it hadn't, he didn't go the direction I'd been expecting.

A calm broke over him, thoughtful and considering. I was so relieved to see my friend *not* attempt to re-enact the Vietnam War that I almost didn't think to ask what was on his mind. Almost.

"Solitaire—"

"My power," he interrupted not even looking at me. "I must have been right. This reacted far, far too quickly. Happened before, too. Must be something about me. Revolutionary. I'm not just going to spread Marxism to everyone." Solitaire turned, affixing me with a stare of solar intensity. "My powers let me see elements, predict reactions. I think they can speed them up, too."

The look I gave him must've been a particularly blank one, because he actually got annoyed upon seeing it.

"If you can *speed up* a reaction, then there's no reason you can't make reactions happen that wouldn't normally," he snapped. "Like a catalyst, sort of, except not really because— Ugh, just . . . This means a lot, it means we might be able to skip a few steps in our chemistry, might even be able to combine things . . . more easily." He trailed off, words clearly turning incoherent as his mind detached from the conversation, and Solitaire eyed the equipment and resources set up across the room. He was quick in plucking crystals out of the cauldron, dropping them into a vat of water he'd started boiling almost as soon as he entered, then eying it.

Even I saw what happened next, crystals breaking down near-instantly, dissolving within moments. A grin tilted his mouth.

"Mix that yellow powder with the charcoal dust," he ordered. I realized the instructions were for me, and I quickly got to performing them, handing him the mixture just in time for him to continue his work with it. Once again, it all reacted near-instantly, dissolving, mixing, synthesizing. Solitaire's excitement was growing, and mine was rising right alongside it.

Within ten minutes, his frenzied work was done, and he turned to the room at large with one of the biggest smirks I'd ever seen him wear.

"Two things to note," he declared, much to the relief of a now thoroughly perplexed Helena and Argar. "First, we have our explosive powder a lot sooner than expected. The second . . . is that I actually am a wizard, after all."

Neither of them looked particularly impressed, but his words reminded me of something.

"Your magical instruction," I cut in. "How did that go?"

Solitaire glanced at me, almost distractedly. "Oh, right, turns out I'm the most gifted magus in history or something." I stared at him, and he grinned. "You probably are, too, by the way. Beam as well. I mentioned you both to the woman who taught me, and she agreed to test and train you both, though she seemed skeptical as hell. She's playing a long-term game by basically investing in people who she believes have the magical talent of the Emperor of Mankind."

We'd been getting a lot of good news lately, and at the risk of sounding like Solitaire, it was making me start to worry about what was in store for us. One couldn't have this much positivity without some karmic balance.

Still, that was nothing to let actually affect my decisions. A gut feeling was nothing near as accurate as a brain feeling.

"I'll head over as soon as I can," I agreed, then glanced at the chemistry set up. "What are we doing with this?"

Solitaire hesitated. "I know we wanted to keep this all a secret, but . . . I think we might be able to sell it for money."

I chewed my lip thoughtfully, waiting for him to continue.

"Just think about how much people would pay for this sort of thing. Think about what it could do to tip the tables for basically any military who had them. Yes, that'd make us extremely noticeable and attract a lot of unwanted attention, but we'd be enriching ourselves so quickly it'd barely matter. What are they going to do when we're standing behind two hundred hired men with pointy sticks and chainmail? How about two thousand? How about a quarter million?"

He had a point, as he always did. But Solitaire's issue had never been point-lessness; what concerned me was that when he *did* have a point, he tended to try and forcibly insert it into other people's urethras.

"What sort of money do you suppose we could be getting from this?" I'd directed my question to the room at large.

"For a weapon like the one you used against the rotters, you could easily ask—" Helena quickly tried.

"Not that," Solitaire cut in. "Never that. I don't want these simpletons to get their hands on guns. How much for a big explosion in all directions? Probably enough to kill a few dozen rotters, maybe more."

She looked slightly confused but moved past it quickly enough to reply, "Dozens of gold, easily."

Solitaire glanced at me, and I sighed.

"Okay, yes. We know it'll be a lot, but the risk is insane."

"We'll be quick about spending it then." Solitaire suggested. "First thing's first, armor for everyone. Proper armor—steel plate, chainmail beneath, the works. We'll have that smith work on more Solis guns—"

"Solis guns? Really—"

"And within a few weeks, we'll be blowing off heads from hundreds of meters away," he continued, ignoring me.

"If someone tries to copy our work?" I asked. "Just barges in and insists on seeing it?"

"I'll keep an explosive charge here ready to blow everything up." He shrugged, smirk playing at the corner of his mouth. That earned a sidelong glance from a few of us. Solitaire's pyromania was getting a bit difficult to ignore.

We went back and forth a while longer, then eventually reached an agreement. We'd sell the gunpowder.

Something in my gut twisted at the thought of handing people weapons. I didn't like the idea of being responsible for what was done with them. Certainly not by these people. I'd spent plenty of time criticizing Western countries for selling arms to dictatorships back on Earth. In fact, so had Solitaire. And yet he hadn't even blinked at the mention of this.

I eyed my friend, trying to gauge what I could of his feelings, but as usual he was a locked box. Whatever cracks had appeared after the vampire fight, they were closed up now. Either that, or he was just turned to keep them from my sight.

"So, tomorrow is probably the best time for you to head off and see the magus woman," he cut in, snapping me from my thoughtful stupor.

"Right, yeah, tomorrow, makes sense." I nodded, forcing a smile. It wasn't hard to make the excitement wrapped around it seem sincere. Despite every-thing, the idea that I might be some wizard demigod was one hell of a mood lifter.

Solitaire, though, seemed to catch my apprehension anyway, face flashing with something for just a half-instant, then falling back to normal.

"I'll finish our first batch then. You won't be able to do much practicing until tomorrow, so this seems like a convenient time for you to head out and find a suitable buyer for the gunpowder."

It seemed that a lot of what I'd been doing lately was negotiating prices and purchasing or buying. Then again, that had been a lot of what I'd done during my teenage years. I supposed I couldn't complain. If nothing else, I wasn't boiling shit for hours every day. I trudged out of Solitaire's workshop, money in my pocket—just a few silvers for safety—and Argar at my back, eager to find the source of our next success.

Something told me it wouldn't exactly be difficult.

CHAPTER SIXTY-TWO

Shango's POV: Day 61
Current Wealth: 2 gold, 11 silver, 41 copper

'd expected to have quite an easy time selling our new explosive powder. I'd been wrong. It was a *ridiculously* easy one.

As it turns out, in a pre-industrial society, there's quite a strong demand for a magic powder that can blow a troll's legs off at close range. A quick demonstration with the meager amount I brought with me left the very first person I asked about it eager to purchase. He was a mercenary, of course, and one of the wealthier ones. A level twenty-two man in his mid-forties, clearly experienced and hardened by decades of practice. He'd probably have beaten the vampire we'd fought back in Rinchester, even without the set of solid steel plate armor I'd seen him with.

Fortunately, he wasn't so powerful that a three hundred-year anachronism would fail to benefit him. We did our business quickly, and I left with a deal secured.

We'd trekked quite a ways across the city, and it took us some time to get back to the warehouse. Almost an hour. By the time we did, though, things had changed.

Solitaire was seated in one corner, looking smugly at Argar and me as we walked in, gesturing to his workspace with a big grin splitting his face from one ear to the other.

"Black powder," he declared. "About thirty kilos' worth—enough for two genuine, certified war crimes. Hope you found a buyer."

I told him what happened, giving the details as quickly as I could, hard as it was to speak clearly. This was big—very, very big. We'd been planning on the assumption that every reasonable portion of explosives would be hours of effort for us. Solitaire had moved our schemes along very far and fast with this new revelation.

"He wants them in grenade form, like the sample I showed him," I finished, having demonstrated about a quarter-kilogram's worth of the stuff. "Offered to pay two silver for each portion."

Solitaire did the math faster than I could even notice. "It costs us about one silver for two kilos," he explained, "and this would let us sell those two kilos for sixteen silver, making a profit of fifteen. So we have enough right now for four gold and twenty-four silver."

Four gold and twenty-four silver, for a single day of shopping and work. I almost started jumping up and down on the spot. I turned around and saw broad grins plastered across everyone's faces.

"I'll take the powder to him right now then," I announced. "After that, we'll start looking into equipment. We're still on plate armor, right?"

"We are," Beam nodded. "But I thought you were learning magic?"

"Right . . ."

"I'll sell it," Solitaire assured me. "You go and become Gandalf. God knows we have enough time to do whatever now. We're never gonna starve again."

Despite the instinctual urge for us all to just stay and celebrate, we ended up going our separate ways. I was soon at the magus' shop. I entered to see the woman Solitaire had described, already eyeing me expectantly. She was healthier than I'd imagined, and taller, too. I supposed magi tended to be better fed here, not as withered and shrunken.

"I'm Shango Belahont," I told her with a smile, and she just nodded.

"Right, Solitaire's brother, my new student. Apparently. He seemed confident you'd be as gifted as he is."

I wasn't so sure, in truth, but Solitaire tended to have a way of intuiting things like that. I just shrugged.

"Only one way to find out, right?"

"Right, sit down."

I did, and she administered the test quickly. Neither of us was particularly surprised to find that I passed. What we were really waiting for—me more than her—was to see how *much* of the gift I'd been fortunate enough to enter this world with.

As it happened, quite a lot.

I knew something odd was happening when the woman remained visibly surprised within a short span into our lessons, but it wasn't until I'd already finished the few hours of practice that I got the chance to ask her about it.

"You've made more progress than your brother," she choked out, seemingly in disbelief as the words left her mouth. I enjoyed a smile to myself before replying.

"You're sure?"

"Of course," she snapped, seeming affronted. Odd. I suppose it mustn't have been pleasant to meet someone so innately good at a craft you'd spent years honing.

"Alright," I said in a soothing tone. "Sorry, I just wanted to check."

"You just wanted to hear me say it again," she accused, glaring daggers at me, "to stroke your ego."

I hesitated, then nodded. She was right about that, and more than a little clever to have noticed it.

"Well, congratulations," the magus continued with a resigned sigh. "You've supplanted your brother for the position of most gifted user of magic in recorded history. Do break the news to him lightly, will you?"

"I'm sorry if I seemed smug," I cut in, forcing myself to be serious. "I just . . . got some very good news. I'm sure you can understand why it might have left me in a good mood."

"Yes, I can," the woman sighed. "Please forgive my attitude. I've just had quite a lot of foundational magical theory shaken right in front of me. Twice. You'll want lessons alongside your brother then?"

"I will," I concurred. "And for our other brother, Beam, if his gift is comparable."

She shrugged. "Three of you. Of course there are. Very well. I'll do what I can, but I expect a castle all to myself once you're all ruling the country."

By her tone, I couldn't tell if she was joking or not. There'd certainly be less predictable shifts throughout Redacle's history. The ability to use magic in the highest orders was something that could do a lot of military heavy lifting for a nation. Could, and had. And if one threw an army behind that much power . . . Well, there wasn't much that would stop it.

Even an army that didn't have guns as standard-issue.

I was getting ahead of myself, though. I gave the magus my thanks and left her shop, moving quickly back to the warehouse. Solitaire and Beam were awaiting me as I returned.

"We've been talking . . ." Solitaire began, unnecessarily. I knew they'd been talking. They had been far too anticipatory to have just been waiting around doing nothing while I was gone. ". . . about our next base of operations."

Weird way to phrase it, but I caught his meaning and said, "You're about to suggest that we splurge on a higher class inn?" I grinned. He didn't smile back.

"No," Solitaire replied, paused, and gave Beam a chance to cut in.

"He's about to suggest we let him build his dream schizo bunker and set up shop."

I blinked, eying my friends while Solitaire glared at the swordsman.

"In less assholish terms than that," the Revolutionary sighed. "Yes, I was. I don't want to just live in some random inn now that we know there's a mad magus after us—particularly when we're about to basically broadcast our current location to him."

"So you want to build a house instead?" No, of course he didn't. I corrected my question before he could. "You want to build a *fortress*?"

Solitaire smiled. "Finally, someone who understands my genius—"

"We can't, though," I snapped. "Can we? No, we can't. What are you . . ." Oh, but we were learning magic. And magi could do lots of things.

It's about time I explained how their powers work. Basically, in Redacle, the world is made from . . . passages, you might say. The written-word kind. Yes, I know, I know. Anyway, magi could tweak these a bit, reshape and rethread. The less obvious the change, the more reliably they could make it, and the more powerful the magus, the more overt they could afford to be.

That was why it was a lot easier and safer for Corvan to knit Beam's ribs back together than, say, growing him a new set entirely. They also tended to specialize. Healing was relatively rare, but not that much.

Stone and earth, though, that was fairly commonplace. It was the reason that even the shitty medieval towns we'd been encountering had walls stretching dozens of feet up. Hell, it was the reason people had full-plate armor centuries before gunpowder. Now, magi charged enough for their powers, given the inherent risks and difficulties, that actually commissioning one to build something for you would just about empty your coffers. But if you got powers of your own . . .

For us, the writers, magic had been a cheap convenience to explain all the anachronisms that came with a pop-cultural depiction of medieval times.

For us, the survivors and the magical geniuses, it might be much, much more.

"It depends on how quickly we can learn to master our powers," I replied at last, not even bothering to hide the considering note from my voice. I'd barely spent half a second thinking about matters, but for Solitaire that would've felt like an agonizingly long stretch. He didn't let whatever neurotic irritation was currently tormenting him show, though. He only grinned.

"We shouldn't take that long, right? Zhariak took . . . what, half a month to become a novice? And he was less talented than the best in history."

Zhariak, the main character from our book. A budding magus and overall arrogant bastard. An odd thought occurred to me then, as I realized that he was very possibly wandering around somewhere out there, sharing a planet with me, breathing in the same atmosphere. Somehow that smashed the gap between my reality and Redacle's fantasy more than any of the undeniably concrete pain or pleasure I'd felt here.

Not enough to distract me from Solitaire's words, though.

"Half a month is still probably longer than we'll have. It'll take Corvan less than half that time to reach us, and we'll still have to actually build."

"I can take Corvan," Beam cut in, confidently.

We both stared at him.

"The fuck you can," Solitaire said, gaping.

"And you're not trying to either," I added, feeling a migraine suddenly growing. "He'd destroy you."

Before the swordsman could quote a certain white-haired *Jujutsu Kaisen* character, and thus force my hand into strangling him, Helena piped up.

"You're scared of a magus chasing you down, but won't you be wealthy enough to hire your own soon? If only for a day."

That gave all of us something to consider for a moment.

"Not necessarily," Solitaire said. "We're still limited in our production by the actual ingredients to gunpowder. We'll be racking up more than a share of wealth, no doubt, but I don't want to bet on having enough to hire multiple magi. And I don't like the idea of trusting in only one to get the better of Corvan. Even if they're his superior, they might have a stroke of poor luck."

"So what do we do then?" Beam frowned. "Mercenary work?"

Solitaire and I shared a look, and nodded. We'd been putting it off for long enough, I supposed. We were always going to have gotten into another fight eventually. Might as well hurry it along.

"Mercenary work," I agreed. "Let's gear up."

Ian B. Urns is the coauthor of the Author's Nightmare series, originally released on Royal Road. He writes dark fantasy stories with all the action, humor, and horror he can cram in. Having penned six novels thus far and developing his skills with each new book, he hopes to continue expanding into other genres. Urns lives in the United Kingdom, where he avoids natural light and eye contact with other living things.

A. C. Erinle is the coauthor of the Author's Nightmare series, originally released on Royal Road. A Nigerian novelist who favors character-driven fantasy and world-building, he has penned several books now, sharpening his writing skills with each one. He spends his free time frolicking in nature and otherwise enjoying life, before marching back into his Writing Hole. His stories are dark, but they never fail to be optimistic. Erinle currently resides in Lagos.

RESPAWN YOUR YOUR CURIOSITY

follow us on our socials

podiumentertainment.com

@podiumentertainment

/podiumentertainment

@podium_ent

@podiumentertainment

www.ingramcontent.com/pod-product-compliance
Lightning Source LLC
Chambersburg PA
CBHW032344310726

48973CB00007B/1851